Walter Bradford Woodgate

Boating

Walter Bradford Woodgate

Boating

ISBN/EAN: 9783337397630

Printed in Europe, USA, Canada, Australia, Japan

Cover: Foto ©Andreas Hilbeck / pixelio.de

More available books at **www.hansebooks.com**

BOATING

BY

W. B. WOODGATE

WITH AN INTRODUCTION BY THE REV. EDMOND WARRE, D.D.

AND

A CHAPTER ON ROWING AT ETON

BY R. HARVEY MASON

WITH NUMEROUS ENGRAVINGS AFTER FRANK DADD
AND FROM PHOTOGRAPHS

LONDON

LONGMANS, GREEN, AND CO.

1888

DEDICATION

TO

H.R.H. THE PRINCE OF WALES.

———◦✦◦———

BADMINTON : *March*, 1887.

HAVING received permission to dedicate these volumes, the BADMINTON LIBRARY of SPORTS and PASTIMES, to HIS ROYAL HIGHNESS THE PRINCE OF WALES, I do so feeling that I am dedicating them to one of the best and keenest sportsmen of our time. I can say, from personal observation, that there is no man who can extricate himself from a bustling and pushing crowd of horsemen, when a fox breaks covert, more dexterously and quickly than His Royal Highness; and that when hounds run hard over a big country, no man can take a line of his own and live with them better. Also, when the wind has been blowing hard, often have I seen His Royal Highness knocking over driven grouse and partridges and high-rocketing pheasants in first-rate workmanlike style. He is held to be a good yachtsman, and as Commodore of the Royal Yacht Squadron is looked up to by those who love that pleasant and exhilarating pastime. His encouragement of racing is well known, and his attendance at the University, Public School, and other important Matches testifies to his being, like most English gentlemen, fond of all manly sports. I consider it a great privilege to be allowed to dedicate these volumes to so eminent a sportsman as His Royal Highness the Prince of Wales, and I do so with sincere feelings of respect and esteem and loyal devotion.

BEAUFORT.

PREFACE.

A FEW LINES only are necessary to explain the object with which these volumes are put forth. There is no modern encyclopædia to which the inexperienced man, who seeks guidance in the practice of the various British Sports and Pastimes, can turn for information. Some books there are on Hunting, some on Racing, some on Lawn Tennis, some on Fishing, and so on ; but one Library, or succession of volumes, which treats of the Sports and Pastimes indulged in by Englishmen—and women—is wanting. The Badminton Library is offered to supply the want. Of the imperfections which must be found in the execution of such a design we are conscious. Experts often differ. But this we may say, that those who are seeking for knowledge on any of the subjects dealt with will find the results of many years' experience written by men who are in every case adepts at the Sport or Pastime of which they write. It is to point the way to success to those who are ignorant of the sciences they aspire to master, and who have no friend to help or coach them, that these volumes are written.

To those who have worked hard to place simply and clearly before the reader that which he will find within, the best thanks of the Editor are due. That it has been no slight labour to supervise all that has been written he must acknowledge; but it has been a labour of love, and very much lightened by the courtesy of the Publisher, by the unflinching, indefatigable assistance of the Sub-Editor, and by the intelligent and able arrangement of each subject by the various writers, who are so thoroughly masters of the subjects of which they treat. The reward we all hope to reap is that our work may prove useful to this and future generations.

THE EDITOR.

The author desires to record his thanks and indebtedness to the following gentlemen, for much kind co-operation and assistance, and for leave to reproduce passages from their valuable works upon aquatics :—Geo. G. T. TREHERNE, Esq., author of 'Record of the University Boat Race'; E. D. BRICKWOOD, Esq. ('Argonaut'), author of 'Boat Racing'; L. P. BRICKWOOD, Esq., Editor of the 'Racing Almanack'; the Proprietors of the 'Field'; the Proprietors of 'Land and Water,' and Mr. R. G. Gridley for kindly assisting with the Map of the Cambridge Course.

ILLUSTRATIONS.

(ENGRAVED BY W. J. PALMER, J. D. COOPER, AND G. PEARSON,
AFTER DRAWINGS BY F. DADD AND PHOTOGRAPHS BY G.
MITCHELL, HILLS & SAUNDERS, AND MARSH BROS.)

FULL-PAGE ILLUSTRATIONS.

	ARTIST	
GENERAL VIEW OF THE HENLEY REGATTA	From a photograph	Frontispiece
METHOD OF STARTING THE COLLEGE EIGHTS PRIOR TO 1825, OXFORD	Frank Dadd	To face p. 28
STARTING THE EIGHTS, OLD COURSE, HENLEY	Frank Dadd	,, 40
COACHING UNIVERSITY CREW	Frank Dadd	,, 68
EMBARKING	Frank Dadd	,, 84
PAIR OARS—IMMINENT FOUL	Frank Dadd	,, 124
BUMPING RACE—WAITING FOR THE GUN	From a photograph	,, 170
OFF THE BROCAS	Frank Dadd	,, 202
THAMES WATERMEN AND WHERRIES	Frank Dadd	,, 218
CLIEFDEN (RIVER SCENE)	From a photograph	,, 242

WOODCUTS IN TEXT.

	ARTIST	PAGE
VIGNETTE ON TITLE-PAGE	Frank Dadd	
FLEET OF EGYPTIAN QUEEN	From a photograph	11
ANCIENT BOAT DEPICTED ON VASE	Frank Dadd	15
BAS-RELIEF OF ANCIENT GREEK ROWING BOAT	Frank Dadd	19
ANCIENT GALLEY FIGHT, FROM POMPEII	Frank Dadd	21
HENLEY COURSE (BETWEEN RACES)	From a photograph	26
OXFORD BOAT IN 1829	From 'Record of the University Boatrace'	31
BUMPING RACES (OLD STYLE)	From 'Record of the University Boatrace'	33

x ILLUSTRATIONS.

	ARTIST	PAGE
A COLLEGE PAIR	From a photograph	37
TOWING GUARD BOATS UP HENLEY REACH	From a photograph	39
PAIR-OAR	From a photograph	41
GONDOLA	From a photograph	43
BISHAM COURT	From a photograph	53
MARLOW	From a photograph	66
A SCRATCH EIGHT ('PEAL OF BELLS')	From a photograph	75
MEDMENHAM ABBEY	From a photograph	79
'PROSE'	Frank Dadd	83
BISHAM COURT REACH	From a photograph	92
FEATHER 'UNDER' THE WATER	From a photograph	102
PRACTISING STROKE (1)	From a photograph	110
PRACTISING STROKE (2)	From a photograph	110
PRACTISING STROKE (3)	From a photograph	111
PRACTISING STROKE (4)	From a photograph	111
A COLLEGE FOUR	From a photograph	118
FOUR-OAR	From a photograph	121
NEAR MEDMENHAM	From a photograph	123
CLOSE QUARTERS	Frank Dadd	127
A SPILL	Frank Dadd	133
SCULLING RACE, WITH PILOTS IN EIGHT-OARS	Frank Dadd	139
PUMPED OUT	Frank Dadd	141
THE LAST OF THE THAMES WHERRIES	From a photograph	142
'POETRY'	Frank Dadd	153
GOING TO SCALE	Frank Dadd	157
SMOKING IS FORBIDDEN	Frank Dadd	165
'RUN A MILE OR TWO'	Frank Dadd	167
FOUR-OAR	From a photograph	178
EARLY AMATEURS	Frank Dadd	192
WINDSOR	From a photograph	200
A FOUL	Frank Dadd	238

MAPS

SHOWING

THE OXFORD COURSE	To face p.	288
„ CAMBRIDGE „	„	296
„ HENLEY „	„	318
„ PUTNEY „	„	322

CONTENTS.

CHAPTER | | PAGE

I. INTRODUCTION 1

II. THE RISE OF MODERN OARSMANSHIP 26

III. SCIENTIFIC OARSMANSHIP 53

IV. COACHING 66

V. THE CAPTAIN 79

VI. THE COXSWAIN AND STEERING . . 92

VII. SLIDING SEATS . 102

VIII. FOUR-OARS . . . 118

IX. PAIR-OARS . 123

X. SCULLING 127

XI. BOAT-BUILDING AND DIMENSIONS . 142

XII. TRAINING 153

XIII. ROWING CLUBS 178

XIV. THE AMATEUR, HIS HISTORY AND DESCRIPTION 192

XV. ROWING AT ETON COLLEGE 200

XVI. WATERMEN AND PROFESSIONALS . . . 217

XVII. LAWS OF BOAT-RACING (THEIR HISTORY, AND RULES OF THE ROAD) 238

'THE TEMPLE OF FAME' . . . 243

APPENDIX 313

INDEX 331

a

Erratum.

Page 119, line 19, *for* Bodleian *read* Radleian.

INTRODUCTION.

As parts of human life and practice the out-of-door games and amusements with which Englishmen are familiar have had a long course of development, and each has its own history. To trace this development and history in any particular case is not always an easy task. Most of the writers who deal with these subjects treat the 'Origines' in a summary fashion. Not a few ignore them altogether. The Topsy theory, ''spects it growed,' is sufficient.

And yet if it be possible to deal more philosophically with a subject of the kind, the attempt ought not necessarily to be devoid of interest. It involves a retrospect of human life and human ingenuity. It will trace development in man's ways and means, marking points which in some regions and with some races have determined the limit of their progress, and in others have served as stepping-stones to further invention. It will present facts which will not only not be disdained by the true

B

student of men and manners, but will serve to broider the fringes of serious history, and will give additional light and colour to the record of the character and the habits of men. For indeed the sports and pastimes of a people are no insignificant product of its national spirit, and react to no small degree upon national character. They have not unfrequently had their share in grave events, and the famous and oft-quoted saying of the Duke of Wellington respecting the playing fields at Eton (*se non è vero, è ben trovato*) contains a truth, applicable in a wider sense to national struggles and to victories other than Waterloo.

Pastimes and amusements generally may be divided into two main classes: (1) those that have been invented simply as a means of recreation, such as cricket, tennis, racquets, etc. ; and (2) those that have their origin in the primary needs of mankind. The latter have in many cases, as civilisation has advanced, and the particular needs have been supplied in other ways, survived as pastimes by reason of the natural pleasure and the excitement and the emulation which accompanied them. Of this latter class, those that have appropriated the name of 'sport' *par excellence*, such as hunting, shooting, fishing, etc., hold the field, so to speak, in antiquity, as compared with other pastimes, having their origin in the initial necessities and natural instincts of man, which compelled him to fight with and to destroy some wild beasts, that he might not himself be eaten, and to catch or kill others that he might have them to eat.

The spirit of emulation and the pride of skill, and the desire of obtaining healthy exercise for its own sake, have been among the principal causes which have converted into sports and pastimes man's means and methods of locomotion. Almost every class of movement which can be pressed into that form of competition which is called a race, or in which a definite comparison of skill is possible, has been enlisted in the host of amusements with which civilisation consoles its children for the loss of the wild delights of the untutored savage.

Among these perhaps the most important and the most conspicuous is Rowing, which as a serious business has played no inconsiderable part in great events of human history, and as a pastime is inferior to none of the class to which it belongs. Its votaries will not hesitate to claim for it even the chief place, by reason of the pleasure and emulation to which it so readily ministers, as a healthful exercise, and as a means of competitive effort requiring both skill and endurance.

But the oar, before it ministered to recreation, had a long history of labour in the service of man, which is not yet ended, and itself was not shaped but by evolution from earlier types, of which the paddle and ultimately the human hand and arm are the original beginnings.

Will it be wearisome to speculate on these beginnings, and to try to cast back in thought and research for the first origins of the noble pastime which forms the subject of the present volume? Fortunately, in savage life still extant on the habitable globe we have the survival of many, if not of all, the earliest types of locomotion. Man in his natural condition has to follow nature, and by following to subdue her in his struggle for existence. Climate and race differentiate his action in this respect, and results, under parallel circumstances, similar, though different in detail, attend his efforts in different parts of the world.

A land animal, he is from the first brought face to face with water, deep water of lakes, and of rivers, and of the sea, and in all these he finds bounds to his desires, as well as things to be desired ; opposite shores to which he wishes to cross, fish and vegetable growth which he wants for food. Horace tells us that ' oak and triple brass he had around his breast who first to the fierce sea committed his frail raft,' but the first man who committed *himself* to deep water, and essayed the oarage of his arms and legs, must have been free from such incumbrances, and yet have had a stout heart within him. And simultaneously with, or even prior to such adventure, must have been others of a similar character aided by a piece of wood, or a bundle of rushes, or an inflated skin, the elementary boat, the very embryo of navigation. Such beginnings are still in evidence on the western coast of Australia, where savages may be seen sitting astride on a piece of light wood and so venturing forth upon the waters of the sea. Homer, who in the Odyssey delights in making the man of many counsels and many devices, with all his wealth of what was then modern experience, find himself reduced to the shifts and expedients of a man thrown, like the savage, upon his own solitary resources, pictures to us Ulysses seated astride upon the mast of his shipwrecked vessel and paddling with both hands, thus reverting in his distress, as no doubt others have done since, to the very earliest method of navigation, now only practised for choice by savages, whose progress in navigation, as in other things, has been checked at this early stage, and who remain the nearest visible types of primitive man.

But some savages, other than they, did make progress in the matter of locomotion by water, and the next step was the raft, of which the earliest type known is the sanpan, three pieces of buoyant wood tied together. On this construction, which supplied the earliest generic names both in the east and in the west (sanpan, σχεδίη, *ratis*), a man would stand and paddle and move along upon the water, and assert his power of hand and eye with the weapons with which native ingenuity had already supplied him.

In warm climates, where swimming had become a necessity, and the very children from their earliest years had been habituated to the water, the familiarity that breeds contempt of the very danger which at a previous stage acted as a deterrent, would soon encourage attempts to improve, and enlarge, and increase the speed of the rude vessel in common use. These attempts would naturally follow the line of providing the means for conveying in safety other things besides the living freight of the human person. There would also arise the very natural desire to keep things dry, which would spoil if wetted. Hence the enlargement of the raft, and then the protection afforded by platforms raised upon its central surface, or by planks laid edgewise so as to make a defence, a breastwork against the wave.

And no doubt by this time the use of the sail for propulsion had become familiar, and man had already prayed his god for 'the breeze that cometh aft, sail-filler, good companion.' But interesting as it would be to trace the effect of the sail upon the construction of vessels and their development, we must leave that pleasant task to those who, in the present series, will treat of the yacht and its prototypes (ἄκατοι).

The earliest method of propulsion was with the human hands. In the picture of Ulysses seated on the mast and keel of his shipwrecked vessel, which he had lashed together with the broken backstay made of bullhide, paddling with his hands on either side, Homer, as we have seen, has presented us with the hero of the highest civilisation known to him reduced to the straits of the merest savage ; and he has again enforced this idea in his picture of the same hero of many wiles and many counsels devising for himself the means of escape from the island of Calypso, and, not without divine suggestions, constructing for himself, like an ancient Robinson Crusoe, a primitive raft, with certain improvements and additions ; a broad raft be it remembered, and not a boat. A boat would mar the conception which presents to us the civilised man driven back to the straits of barbarism by the unique circumstances in which he is placed.

This is the point which ingenious commentators, who have given elaborate designs and figures of Ulysses' *boat* and written pages upon its construction, seem to have missed. The poet has added colour to his picture by bringing the new and the old together. And of a truth new and old exist together and continue throughout the ages of man in marvellous juxtaposition. The fast screw liner off the Australian coast may pass the naked savage oaring himself with swarthy palms upon his buoyant log, and almost every stage of modern invention in ship-building and ship propulsion has had alongside it the three-timbered sanpan, and the original types of raft that float in the Malay Archipelago.

But we must follow the development of our special pastime through its embryonic stage to a moment when, all unknown and unseen in the womb of time, like the sudden changes which differentiate the gradual ascents from a lower to a higher being, unseen, unknown, and unwritten in history, that great event occurred, the birth of the first 'dug-out' canoe. Unnoticed perhaps at the time, the importance of the event was recognised by the poet in after ages as a real forward step in the onward progress of the arts.[1] 'Rivers then first the hollowed alders felt.'

To some primitive man or men in advance of their fellow men, the idea of flotation, as apart from the mere buoyancy of the material, had occurred, and suggested the hollowing out of the log. Wherever and whenever this was first effected, it was a great event in the world's progress. A simple thought had wedded fact destined to be fruitful to all future ages. O prototype of the longboat—of the frail eights which freighted with contending crews speed yearly over Father Thames amidst the cheers and applause of thousands ! Where wast thou launched ? What dusky arms propelled thee ? What wild songs of exultation heralded thy first successful venture ? Once achieved, what present benefits, what future triumphs didst thou not ensure to man ? In the power of carrying something, or anything beside the living freight, dry and secure, and in the increased facility of movement and of turning, must have been manifest from the first the advantage of the canoe over the raft, where the lapping of the water and the wash of the wave, in spite of all contrivances, could scarce be kept out. How soon must efforts have been made to increase this advantage to obtain greater carrying power and greater speed ! The application of the sail was made possible by the ingenious adaptation of the outrigger, a trunk of light wood laid parallel to the side of the dug-out at some feet distance, and attached to it by transverse bars. The oldest type and the type with this

[1] Virg. *Georg.* i. 136 : ' Tunc alnos primum fluvii sensere cavatas.'

improvement still survive, and the ingenious models of such craft which were exhibited at the Fisheries Exhibition in London a few years ago will have been noticed by many of our readers. Twin vessels like the ' Castalia,' and, if we are to believe the learned Graser, the great Tesseraconteres of Ptolemy, had their primitive germ, so to speak, in this early stroke of genius. It may appear strange to some boating men who are accustomed to hear a good deal about outriggers, that this outrigger of which we have been speaking has nothing to do with the outrigger with which they are familiar. It never apparently passed into the Western Seas. The Mediterranean knows it not. The Andaman Islands and the Seychelles are its western-most limits.

But if the invention of the dug-out canoe was a step onward in the general progress of the arts, being the appreciation and application of a principle in nature, a still greater triumph was achieved, and the particular art still more decidedly advanced, by him who first constructed the canoe properly so called. Herein was the real prototype of the *species* boat. A skin of bark, duly cut and shaped so as to taper towards the ends and be wide amidships, was attached to a longitudinal framework or gunwale all along its upper edges, and this itself was kept apart and in shape by three or more transverse pieces stretching from side to side, while a series of curved laths of soft wood, the extreme ends of which also fastened to the gunwale, served to keep the vessel itself in shape and to protect the bark skin from the tread of men and from the immediate incidence of any weight to be carried. ' Ce n'est que le premier pas qui coûte.' The idea once conceived, whether in one place or in many, and at whatever time or times, could not be lost and must soon have been fruitful in development. Of this class by far the most common is the birch-bark canoe, which, though found also in Australia, is properly regarded as having its home upon the American continent. If not the original of the type, yet it deserves particular attention owing to the peculiarity of the material of the skin, which combines lightness and toughness and pliability. A truly ingenious and original idea to flay a birch tree and make a boat of its skin ! In the framework of the canoe we have the embryo *ribs* and *inwale* of the future boat, and the three cross-ties may be regarded as the ancestors of *thwarts* to be born in time to come. As yet no keel. But that was soon to be. Go north, and trees become scarcer and dwindle in size. The birch is no longer of sufficient girth to serve the ingenious savage in the construction of a canoe. But the inventive genius of man was not to be denied. Skins of beasts, or woven material made waterproof, stretched upon a frame would serve for the same purpose as bark. But a stronger framework was necessary for a material thinner and more pliable than bark. And accordingly in all this class (except the coracle) we find stronger and more numerous timbers, including a longitudinal piece from stem to stern, and uprights at each end acting as stempost and sternpost respectively. The rude canvas-covered vessels of Tory Island, off the west coast of Ireland, still preserve one development of this type, close at home to us ; while the cayaks of the Esquimaux and the larger fishing canoes of the Alaskans and the Greenlanders exhibit the skin-clad variety in many forms. In one of the models exhibited at the Fisheries Exhibition the framework showed in great perfection the ingenuity of the savage, to whom wood was a very scarce and precious article, short pieces being made to serve fitted together and fastened with thongs of hide, the whole being covered with a stout walrus skin. Even outriggers (as understood by the English oarsman) made of double loops of hide just long enough to cross each other and enclose the loom of the oar, were attached to the inner side of the gunwale.

Not only bark and skin and canvas-covered canoes exist and seem to have existed from an unknown antiquity, but a similar cause to that of which we were just speaking, viz. a scarcity of wood or of suitable wood, led to the construction of canoes of wood made of short pieces stitched together, and approaching more nearly to the type of vessel which may be called a boat. To these belong the canoes of Easter Island made of drift

wood, and of many other islands in the Pacific, which are truly
canoes and propelled by paddles, and the same peculiarity of
build extends to the Madras surf boats, which are more truly
boats. Many of these are tied together through holes drilled
or burnt through a ledge left on the inner side of the plank or
log, a peculiarity noticeable as appearing even in the early vessels of the Northern Seas. The stitched boat has not a nail
or a peg in her whole composition, but the structure, though
liable to leak, is admirably suited for heavy seas and surf-beaten
coasts, and owing to its pliability will stand shocks which would
shatter a stiffer and tighter build. This being so, it is not sur-
prising that vessels larger than canoes or boats were constructed
(some authorities say even as large as 200 tons burden) upon
this principle, which is certainly one of very great antiquity.

There is also a curious analogy in the progress of construction
of these sea-going craft with the natural order in the construction
of fishes, that is to say, if the ganoids are to be considered antecedent to the vertebrates among the latter. For in the case of the
stitched vessels the hull is the first thing in time and construction,
the ribs and framework being, so to speak, an afterthought, and
attached to the interior when the hull has been completed,
whereas the later and modern practice is to set up the ribs and
framework of the vessel first and to attach the exterior planking
afterwards. But the invention of trenails and dowels must have
preceded the later practice, and have led the way to the building of such boats as those described by Herodotus (ii. 96), the
ancestors of the Nile ' nuggur ' of modern times. Ulysses, as a
shipwright well skilled in his craft, uses axe and adze and
auger, and with the latter makes holes in the timbers he has
squared and planed, and with trenails and dowels ties them together. The wooden fastenings, be it remarked, are in size and
diameter severally adapted, the first to resist the horizontal,
the second to resist the vertical strain to which the raft would be
exposed upon the waves. All this, we may observe, points to
a stage anterior to that in which the use of metal nails and ties
in ship- and boat-building had been introduced. Trenails and

dowels are however still in use, and have a natural advantage over iron in the construction of wooden vessels, owing to the absence of corrosion, which in early times must have caused difficulties as to its employment for boat-building. Copper, on the other hand, though free from this objection, would be less available by reason of expense and the great demand for it for other purposes.

And now we have reached a point where we enter upon the borders of history. No doubt, if we knew more about the venerable antiquity of China, we might be able to add interesting facts, showing the development from the earliest sanpan to the great river boats, and the growth of that curious art which produced the Chinese junk, a vessel undoubtedly of a very antique type. But this knowledge is not ours at present, and so we must turn to the equally venerable civilisation of Egypt for information upon the subject. In Egypt fortunately the tomb paintings have preserved to us a wealth of illustration of boats and ships, some of which, if we may trust the learned, take us back to dates as early as 3000 B.C. In turning over the interesting plates of such works as Lepsius's 'Denkmäler,' or Duemichen's 'Fleet of an Egyptian Queen,' we are struck by the reflection that, if at that early date boats, and ships, and oars, and steering paddles, and masts, and sailing gear had all been brought to such a stage of perfection, we must allow many centuries antecedent for the elaboration of such designs, and for the evolution of the savage man's primary conception of canoe and paddle.

However this may be, the lovers of our pastime, if they will consult the pages of the works above mentioned, will find rowing already well established as an employment, if not as an amusement, in the hoar antiquity of Egypt. Not only the Nile water, whether the sacred stream was within his banks or spread by inundation over the plain within his reach, was alive with boats, busy with the transport of produce of all sorts, or serving the purposes of the fowler and the fisherman, but the Red Sea and the Mediterranean coasts were witnesses of the might and power of Pharaoh, as shown by his fleets of great vessels

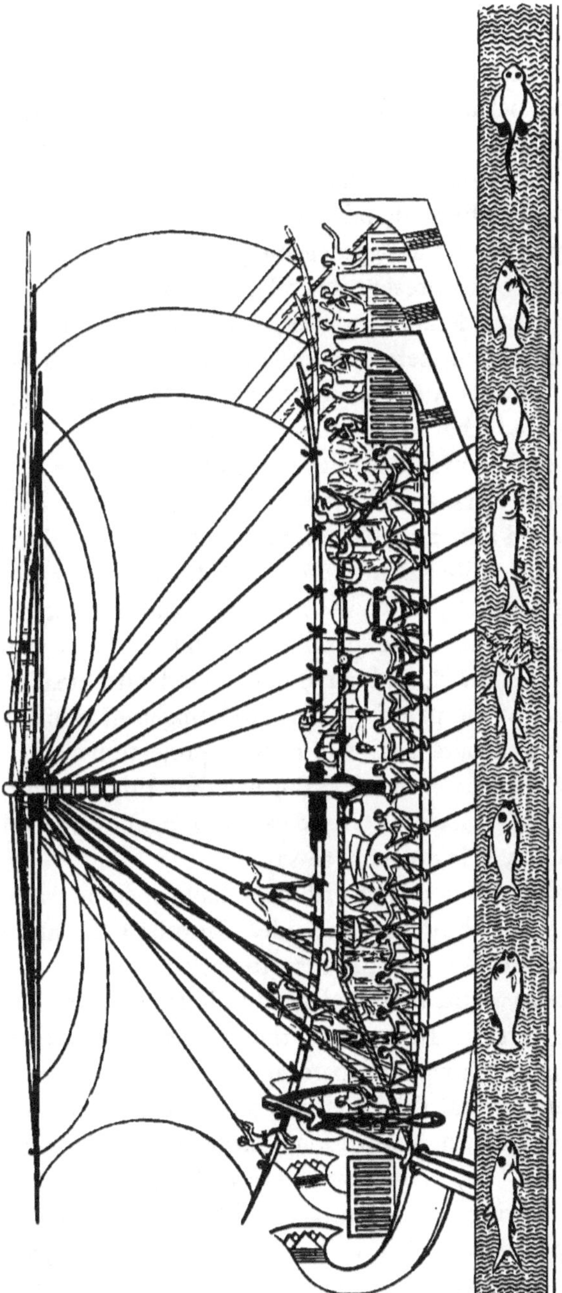

FLEET OF EGYPTIAN QUEEN.

fully manned, ready with oar and sail to perform his behests, ready to visit the land of Orient, and bring back thence the spices and perfumes that the Egyptians loved, together with apes and sandal wood, or else to do battle with the fierce Pelesta and Teucrians and Daunians who swarmed in their piratical craft upon the midland sea, entering the Nile mouths, and raiding upon the fat and peaceable plains of the Delta.

The Egyptian boats present several noticeable features. Built evidently with considerable camber, they rise high from the water both at stem and stern, the ends finished off into a point or else curved upwards and ornamented with mystic figure-heads representing one or other of the numerous gods. The steering is conducted by two or more paddles fastened to the sides of the boat in the larger class, and sometimes having the loom of the paddle lengthened and attached to an upright post to which it is loosely bound. A tiller is inserted in the handle, and to this a steering cord fastened, by which the helmsman can turn the blade of the paddle at will. The paddles vary but little in shape. They are mostly pointed, and have but a moderate breadth of blade. In some of the paintings they are being used as paddles proper, in others as oars against a curved projection from the vessel's side serving as a thowl. But whether this is solid or whether it is a thong, like the Greek τρυπωτήρ, against which the oarsman is rowing, it is not easy to say.

The larger vessels depicted with oars have in some cases as many as twenty-five shown on one side. In others the number is less. But it is quite possible that the artist did not care to portray more than would be sufficient to indicate conventionally the size of the vessel. In some of the vessels there are apertures like oar-ports, though no oars are shown in them, which raise a presumption that the invention of the bireme, the origin of which is uncertain, may with some probability be attributed to the Egyptians. The larger vessels are all fitted with sailing gear, and the rowing is evidently subsidiary to the sail as a means of locomotion. The wall paintings of Egypt give us ample details of Egyptian ships and boats extending over a period, as we are told, of twenty centuries and more. In them we have a glimpse of the maritime enterprise, in which the oar must have taken a principal part, of the races which inhabited the seaboard of the Mediterranean in which piracy had its home from very early times. Teucrians, Dardanians, Pelesta (? Pelasgians), Daunians, Tyrrhenians, Oscans, all seem to have been sea-going peoples, and at intervals to have provoked by their marauding the wrath of Pharaoh and to have felt his avenging hand.

But of all the seafaring races that made their homes and highways upon the waters of the great inland sea, the most famous of early times were the Phœnicians. According to some accounts connected with Capthor (Copts), and according to others emigrants from the coast of the Persian Gulf, their genius for maritime enterprise asserted itself very early, so that already before Homer's time they were masters of the commerce of the Mediterranean, and had rowed their dark keels beyond the mystic pillars that guarded the opening of the ocean stream.

And yet, though the facts are certain, we know but little of these famous mariners, of their vessels and their gear. The only representation of their vessels is from the walls of the palaces of their Assyrian conquerors, an inland people, not likely to detect or appreciate any technical want of fidelity in the likeness presented. And, accordingly, the pictures are conventional, telling us but little of that which we should like to know about their build, and oars, and oar ports, &c. The date, moreover, is not in all probability earlier than 900 B.C.

Such being the case, we are driven for information to the more ample store of Greek literature, and to Greek vases for the earliest representations of the Greek vessel.

Homer abounds in sea pictures. He has a wealth of descriptive words, touches of light and colour which bring the sea and its waves and the vessel and its details with vivid and picturesque effect before us. His ships are black and have their bows painted with vermilion, or red of some other tone ; they are sharp and swift, and bows and stern curve upwards like the horns of oxen. And withal they are rounded on both sides, and well timbered and hollowed out, and roomy, having by the gift of the poet a facile combination of all the opposite qualities, so desirable and so difficult in practice to unite. As yet there is no spur or ram, but round the solid stempost shrieks the wave, as the vessel is urged onward either by the mighty hands of heroes, or the god-sent breeze that follows aft. Nor is the vessel decked, except for a short space at bow and stern, where it had raised platforms. On the quarter-deck, so to speak, of the stern sat the great chiefs, whose warriors plied the oar, and there they laid their spears ready for use. There also was the standing place of the steersman who wielded the long paddle which served to guide the vessel. The thwarts which tied the vessel's sides together (yokes or keys as they are called) served as benches for the oarsmen ; those amidships had the heaviest and longest oars, so that they were places of honour reserved for the heaviest and strongest men, e.g. for Hercules and Ancæus in the Argo. Whether the 'sevenfoot,' to which Ajax retreats from the stern deck, when defending the Greek ships against the Trojans and hard pressed by them, be bench or stretcher, it gives us an idea of the breadth of the Homeric vessel at or near the place of the stroke oar. Long low galleys they must have been, with a middle plank running fore and aft, interrupted by the 'tabernacle,' in which the mast when hoisted was secured, having fore and back stays. The warriors were oarsmen, the oarsmen warriors. The smallest complement, as Thucydides observes, was fifty, the largest one hundred and twenty.

It is doubtful how far the Alexandrine poets can be relied upon as giving accurate information respecting details of ancient use. Yet we have many lifelike pictures and a great profusion of details, drawn no doubt from the ample stores of antiquarian knowledge which these laborious men of letters had at their service in the great Alexandrine library, and these go to fill up that which is lacking in the Homeric picture. And so when Apollonius the Rhodian paints for us such scenes as those of the building of the Argo, the launching, the detail of the crew, and the starting of the vessel, we cannot help feeling that they are described *con amore*, not of the sea, or of ships, or of rowing, but of the literary beauty of similar descriptions by earlier poets. In a word, they are at second hand. But better this than none at all.

The 'bireme,' or two-banked vessel, does not appear in Homer. But, as we have seen, it was probably in existence before Homer's time. If of Egyptian parentage, it was adapted for use on the Mediterranean waters by the shipwrights of Sidon or Tyre. It is a curious reflection that this remarkable evolution of banked vessels should, so far as we can judge, have

ANCIENT BOAT DEPICTED ON VASE.

occupied about two thousand years ; the curve, if we may use the expression, of development rising to the highest point in the useless Tesseraconteres of Ptolemy, and after Actium declining to the dromons and biremes of the Byzantine Emperor Leo, and finally subsiding into the monocrota or one-banked vessels, the galleys of mediæval times.

The problem which taxed the ingenuity of those early ship-wrights was briefly this, how to get greater means of propulsion by increasing the number of oars, without such increase in the length of the ship as would, by increased weight, neutralise the advantage and still further diminish that facility in turning

which was of the greatest moment to the ancient war-vessel.
Galleys with fifty oars on either side had already been constructed,[1] and all the speed that a hundred pairs of hands could
give had been obtained, when the invention of the bireme exhibited the means of nearly doubling the power without much
increasing the weight to be moved, since but little additional
height or breadth was required.

The normal adjustment of the horizontal space between
the oarsmen was then, as it is now, regulated by that canon of
the ancient philosopher, ' Man is the measure of all things.'
Twice the man's cubit gives room for his legs when in a sitting
posture.   Hence the two-cubit standard ($\sigma\chi\tilde{\eta}\mu\alpha$ $\delta\iota\pi\eta\chi\alpha\ddot{\imath}\kappa\acute{o}\nu$)
which is referred to by Vitruvius as the basis of proportion in
other constructions besides ships and boats.   Given this as the
interscalmium (space between the thowls) or distance between
points at which the oars in the same tier were rowed, it is clear
that the rowing space of a vessel's side would be, for a penteconter, or twenty-five a side, seventy-five feet, and for a heca-
tonter, if there ever was such a thing, 150 feet.   To this must
be added the parts outside the oarage space ($\pi\alpha\rho\epsilon\xi\epsilon\iota\rho\epsilon\sigma\acute{\iota}\alpha$), for
the bows ten feet, and something more, say twelve feet, for the
stern.   So that a penteconter would be a long low galley of
about ninety-seven feet in length.   The new invention nearly
doubled the number of oars without increasing the length of
the oarage space.

It was found that by making apertures in the vessel's sides at
about three feet from the water and dividing the space between
the (zyga) thwarts, room could be made for a second row of
men with shorter oars, but still handy and able to add to the
propulsion of the vessel.   For these seats were found in the
hold (thalamus), and hence while the upper tier of the bireme
took their name from the zyga, benches or thwarts, and were
called ' Zygites,' the men of the lower tier were called 'Thalamites.'   These names were continued when the invention of
the ' thranos,' or upper seat, had added a third or upper tier

---

[1] Perhaps even with a hundred, if $\dot{\epsilon}\kappa\alpha\tau\acute{o}\zeta\upsilon\gamma\epsilon\varsigma$ is to be taken literally.

with longer oars to the system, and so introduced the trireme.
If the number of the zygites in the penteconter was twenty-five
a side, and the first bireme was a converted vessel of that class,
the number of thalamites, owing to the contraction of the
bow and the stern, would necessarily be two or three a side
less. Thus we may consider a converted penteconter to have
been capable of carrying a rowing crew of between 90 and 100
men. Similarly a triaconter would have been capable of adding
nearly twenty pairs of arms to her propelling power. When, in
consequence of the new invention, vessels were expressly built as
triremes, we may imagine that for convenience' sake the benches
or zyga would be a little raised, so as to give more room for
the raised seat of the thalamites that was fastened on to the
floor of the vessel.

The narrowness of the vessels affected the disposition of
the rowers in the Greek galleys in a peculiar way. It is
evident from the testimony of the ancients that they adhered
strictly to the principle of ' one man to each oar.' The arrangement seen in mediæval galleys was absolutely unknown to them,
and would not have suited them. It belongs to a different
epoch and a different order of things, when the invention of
the ' apostis ' had made the use of large sweeps rowed by two
or three men possible, and a vessel with sets of three rowing
upon the same horizontal plane might be called a trireme,
though utterly unlike the ancient vessel of that name.

In the ancient vessel the tiers of oarsmen must have sat in
nearly the same vertical plane, obliquely arranged, one behind
and below the other. Thus in the bireme the zygite, as he sat
on his bench, had behind him and below him his thalamite
whose head was about 18 inches behind the zygite thwart and
a little above it. Moreover, as his seat was now a little raised,
the zygite required an *appui* for his feet, which was formed for
him on the bench on which the thalamite next below and in
front of him was sitting ; on either side of him his feet found a
resting-place. As the zygite fell back during the stroke and
straightened his knees, there was plenty of room for the thala-

C

mite below to throw his weight also on to his oar. There
seems to have been but little forward motion of the body. The
arms were stretched out smartly for the recovery, as we learn
from Charon's instructions to Dionysus in the 'Frogs' of
Aristophanes, and then a *driving smiting* stroke was given (cf.
the words ἐλαύνειν, παίειν, ἀναρρίπτειν ἅλα πηδῷ) and the brine
tossed up by the blade.

When once the principle had been established, by which
additional power could be gained without increasing the length
of the vessel, and had been tested by practical experience, its
development was sure to follow. What century witnessed the
birth of the trireme is not certain, but probably by 800 B.C.
the earliest vessels of this description had been launched. The
quick-witted sharp-eyed Greek was not slow to copy, and by
the beginning of the next century the busy shipwrights of
Corinth were building the new craft for Samians as well as for
themselves.

It is, however, in the Attic trireme such as composed the
fleets of Phormio and Conon that historical interest has centred,
and though quinqueremes were commonly in use in the second
and third centuries, B.C., and even still larger rates of war vessels constructed till they were *inhabilis prope magnitudinis*,
unwieldy leviathans, such as the sixteen-banked flagship of
Demetrius Poliorcetes, yet the interest in the trireme has never
failed, and the splendour of its achievements has insured to
it an attention on the part of the learned which no other class
of vessel has been able to attract to itself. The problem of
construction of the trireme, and of the method of its propulsion,
has exercised the ingenuity of scholars ever since the revival
of letters. It has a literature of its own, and it may fairly be
said that if the enigma has not been solved, it is not for want
of industry or acumen.

One point we may as well make clear at once, viz., that
whatever was the vessel the ancients invariably went upon
the principle, *One man, one oar.* Volumes have been wasted
in attempts to prove that the arrangement of the ancient galleys

with respect to propulsion were identical with, or very similar to, those of the mediæval galleys of Genoa or Venice. But the mediæval galleys were essentially *monocrota*, or one-banked vessels, though they may have been double-banked or treble-banked in the sense that two or three men were employed upon one oar.

Another distinction that it is necessary to note with reference to the ancient galleys is that they were called *Aphract* or

BAS-RELIEF OF ANCIENT GREEK ROWING BOAT.

Kataphract according as the upper tier of rowers was unprotected and exposed to view, or fenced in by a bulwark stout enough to protect them from the enemy's missiles. The system of side planking is observable as already adopted in some of the Egyptian vessels, though of the Greeks the Thasians are credited with the invention.

In the year 1834, during the process of excavating some

ground for new public buildings in the Piræus near Athens, some engraved stone slabs were found built up in a low wall which had been uncovered. These were happily preserved and deciphered, and were found to be records of the dockyard authorities of the Athenian admiralty in the second and third centuries before Christ. Many interesting details were thus brought to light which were set in order by the illustrious scholar Boeckh in his volume entitled 'Urkunden über das Seewesen des attischen Staates.' His pupil Dr. Graser has carried on his researches by the examination of innumerable coins, vases, etc., and has rescued the subject from much of the obscurity which enveloped it. The following description of the trireme, based upon his labours, is quoted, by permission, from the new edition of the 'Encyclopædia Britannica,' vol. xxi. pp. 806, 807.

In describing the trireme it will be convenient to deal first with the disposition of the rowers and subsequently with the construction of the vessel itself. The object of arranging the oars in banks was to economise horizontal space and to obtain an increase in the number of oars without having to lengthen the vessel. We know from Vitruvius that the 'interscalmium,' or space horizontally measured from oar to oar, was two cubits. This is exactly borne out by the proportions of an Attic aphract trireme, as shown on a fragment of a bas-relief found in the Acropolis. The rowers in all classes of banked vessels sat in the same vertical plane, the seats ascending in a line obliquely towards the stern of the vessel. Thus in a trireme the thranite, or oarsman of the highest bank, was nearest the stern of the set of three to which he belonged. Next behind him and somewhat below him sat his zygite, or oarsman of the second bank ; and next below and behind the zygite sat the thalamite, or oarsman of the lowest bank. The vertical distance between these seats was 2 feet, the horizontal distance about 1 foot. The horizontal distance, it is well to repeat, between each seat in the same bank was 3 feet (the seat itself about 9 inches broad). Each man had a resting-place for his feet, somewhat wide apart, fixed to the bench of the man on the row next below and in front of him. In rowing, the upper hand, as is shown in most of the representations which remain, was held with the palm turned inwards towards the body. This is accounted for by the angle at which the oar was worked. The lowest rank used the shortest oars, and the difference of the length of the oars on board was caused by the curvature of the ship's side. Thus, looked at from within, the rowers amidship seemed to be using the longest oars, but outside the vessel, as we are expressly told, all the oar-blades of the same bank took the water in the same longitudinal line. The lowest or thalamite oar-ports were 3 feet, the zygite 4¼ feet, the thranite 5½ feet above the water. Each oar-port was protected by an *ascoma* or leather bag, which fitted over the oar, closing the aperture against the wash of the sea without impeding the action of the oar. The oar was tied by a thong, against which it was probably rowed, which itself was attached to a thowl (σκαλμός). The port-hole was probably oval in shape (the Egyptian and Assyrian pictures show an oblong). We know that it was large enough for a man's head to be thrust through it.

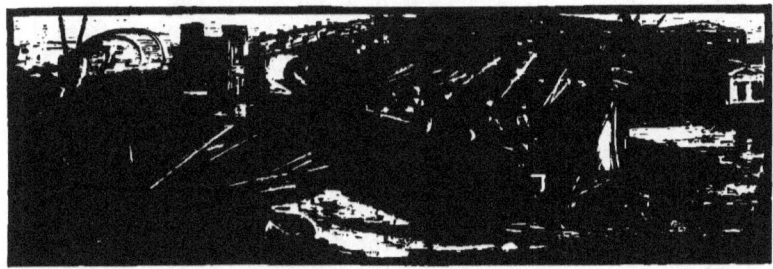

ANCIENT GALLEY FIGHT, FROM POMPEII.

The benches on which the rowers sat ran from the vessel's side to timbers which, inclined at an angle of about 64° towards the ship's stern, reached from the lower to the upper deck. These timbers were, according to Graser, called the diaphragmata. In the trireme each diaphragma supported three, in the quinquereme five, in the octireme eight, and in the famous tesseraconteres forty seats of rowers, who all belonged to the same 'complexus,' though each to a different bank. In effect, when once the principle of construction had been established in the trireme, the increase to larger rates was effected, so far as the motive power was concerned, by lengthening the diaphragmata upwards, while the increase in the length of the vessel gave a greater number of rowers to each bank. The upper tiers of oarsmen exceeded in number those below, as the contraction of the sides of the vessel left less available space towards the bows.

Of the length of the oars in the trireme we have an indication in
the fact that the length of supernumerary oars (περινέῳ) rowed from
the gangway above the thranites, and therefore probably slightly
exceeding the thranitic oars in length, is given in the Attic tables
as 14 feet 3 inches.   The thranites were probably about 14 feet.
The zygite, in proportion to the measurement, must have been 10½,
the thalamite 7½ feet long.   Comparing modern oars with these,
we find that the longest oars used in the British navy are 18 feet.
The University race is rowed with oars 12 feet 9 inches.   The proportion of the loom inboard was about one third, but the oars of
the rowers amidship must have been somewhat longer inboard.
The size of the loom inboard preserved the necessary equilibrium.
The long oars of the larger rates were weighted inboard with lead.
Thus the topmost oars of the tesseraconteres, of which the length
was 53 feet, were exactly balanced at the rowlock.

The Attic trireme was built light for speed and for ramming
purposes.   Her dimensions, so far as we can gather them from the
scattered notices of antiquity, were probably approximately as follows :—length of rowing space (ἔγκωπον), 93 feet ; bows, 11 feet ;
stern, 14 feet ; total, 118 feet ; add 10 feet for the beak.   The
breadth at the water-line is calculated at 14 feet, and above at the
broadest part 18 feet, exclusive of the gangways ; the space between
the diaphragmata mentioned above was 7 feet.   The deck was
11 feet above the water-line, and the draught about 8 to 9 feet.   All
the Attic triremes appear to have been built upon the same model,
and their gear was interchangeable.   The Athenians had a peculiar
system of girding the ships with long cables (ὑποζώματα), each
trireme having two or more, which, passing through eyeholes in
front of the stem-post, ran all round the vessel lengthwise immediately under the waling-pieces.   They were fastened at the stern
and tightened up with levers.   These cables, by shrinking as soon
as they were wet, tightened the whole fabric of the vessel, and in
action, in all probability, relieved the hull from part of the shock
of ramming, the strain of which would be sustained by the waling-
pieces convergent in the beaks.   These rope-girdles are not to be
confused with the process of undergirding or frapping, such as is
narrated of the vessel in which St. Paul was being carried to Italy.
The trireme appears to have had three masts.   The mainmast
carried square sails, probably two in number.   The foremast and
the mizen carried lateen sails.   In action the Greeks did not use
sails, and everything that could be lowered was stowed below.

The mainmasts and larger sails were often left ashore if a conflict was expected.

The crew of the Attic trireme consisted of from 200 to 225 men in all. Of these 174 were rowers—54 on the lower bank (thalamites), 58 on the middle bank (zygites), and 62 on the upper bank (thranites),—the upper oars being more numerous because of the contraction of the space available for the lower tiers near the bow and stern. Besides the rowers were about 10 marines (ἐπιβάται) and 20 seamen. The officers were the trierarch and next to him the helmsman (κυβερνήτης), who was the navigating officer of the trireme. Each tier of rowers had its captain (στοιχαρχός). There were also the captain of the forecastle (πρωρεύς), the 'keleustes' who gave the time to the rowers, and the ship's piper (τριηραυλής). The rowers descended into the seven-foot space between the diaphragmata and took their places in regular order, beginning with the thalamites. The economy of space was such that, as Cicero remarks, there was not room for one man more.

Such, we may believe, was the trireme of the palmy days of Athens. Built for speed, it was necessarily light and handy, and easily turned, so that the formidable beak could be plunged into the enemy's side, the moment a chance was given. But it required sea room for its manœuvres, and in a narrow strait or land-locked harbour, such as that of Syracuse, was no match for the solid balks of timber with which Corinthian and Syracusan shipwrights strengthened the bows of their vessels. Against these the pride of Athens was hurled in vain, only to find itself broken up and rendered unseaworthy by the crash of its own ram.

With the defeat of Athens comes in the fashion of larger vessels with more banks of oars, quadriremes, quinqueremes, and so on up to sixteen banks, when the increase of the motive power had been more than overtaken by the increase in bulk and weight. The principles of construction in these larger vessels seem to have been the same as in the trireme. The space for each man was probably somewhat less, and the handles of the upper tiers of oars were weighted with lead, so as to give a balance at the thowl between the parts outboard and inboard.

A question difficult to solve has often been raised respecting the pace at which these ancient galleys could be propelled. If five-man power could be taken as equivalent to one-horse power, then for the propulsion of the trireme there would have been available about thirty-five horse power, but that would hardly give a very high rate of speed.

There is a passage in Xenophon[1] in which he speaks of a distance of about 150 nautical miles, from Byzantium to Heraclea, as possible for a trireme in a day, but a long day's work. Assuming eighteen hours' work out of the twenty-four, a speed of something over eight knots per hour would be required for this, which may perhaps seem excessive. Still we may believe that by a crew when fresh a pace not less than this could be achieved.

The Romans, though it may be inferred from treaties with Carthage and with Tarentum that they had some kind of fleet in the time even of the kings, yet did not apply themselves readily to maritime pursuits, and made no serious effort to become masters of the Mediterranean till the first Punic War. We hear then of their copying a quinquereme which had fallen into their hands by accident. A fleet was constructed in sixty days from the time that the trees were first cut down, and meantime crews were practised diligently in rowing on dry land in a framework of timber which represented the interior of the vessels that were building. This first essay at extemporising a fleet does not seem to have been very successful. But nothing daunted they persevered, and the second venture under the Admiral Duillius took with it to sea a new invention called the 'corvus,' a sort of boarding bridge by which, when it once fell on the enemy's vessel, the Roman infantry soon found its way on to his deck, and made short work with the swarthy African crew. This revolutionised the maritime struggle, and gave unexpectedly the naval superiority to Rome. The large vessels of war (*alta navium propugnacula*) continued to be built until the time of Actium, when the light Liburnian galleys, which were

---

[1] *Anab.* vi. 42.

biremes, were found to be more than a match for the leviathans, whose doom from that moment was sealed.

From that time, with the exception of the accounts of *naumachiæ*, there is very little of interest about galleys to be gathered. The coins and the paintings of Pompeii show us craft degenerating in type. The column of Trajan exhibits biremes as still in vogue. Later on there is a light thrown upon the subject by the *Tactica* of the Byzantine Emperor Leo about 800 A.D., who gives directions as to the building and composition of his fleet, which is to consist of biremes, or dromones as he calls them, and light galleys with one bank of oars.

From these latter eventually sprang the mediæval galley, which however differed from the ancient galley in the arrangement of its oars by the use of the 'apostis,' a projecting framework which took the place of the ancient 'parodus,' and upon which the thowls were placed, against which the long sweeps could be plied by two or three men attached to each. For full and accurate descriptions of these mediæval vessels the reader who has any curiosity on the subject should consult the ample works of M. Jal. His *Archéologie Navale* and *Glossaire Nautique* contain the fullest information as regards the build, and fittings, and crews of the mediæval galley. The sorrows and sufferings of 'la Chiourme' were enough to give rowing a bad name, as an employment too cruel even for slaves and fit to be reserved for criminals of the worst description.

It is in England, and in the hands of English free men and boys, that the oar has maintained an honourable name, as the instrument of a pastime healthy and vigorous, with a record not inglorious of struggles in which the strength and skill of the nation's youth have contended for the pride of place and the joy of victory.

CHAPTER II.

THE RISE OF MODERN OARSMANSHIP.

HENLEY COURSE (BETWEEN RACES).

GENERAL.

WRITTEN records of rowing performances in the last century are but scarce. In 1715 Mr. Doggett, comedian, founded a race which has survived to the present day—to wit, 'Doggett's coat and badge' (of freedom of the river). 'Watermen' have to serve as 'apprentices' for seven years, during which time they may not ply for hire on their own account, but only on behalf of their masters. When they have served their time they can become 'free' of the river, on payment of certain fees to the Corporation.

In order to encourage good oarsmanship, prizes which paid the fees for freedom, and bestowed a 'coat and badge' of merit, have often been given by patrons of aquatics. Doggett's prize is the oldest of its class, and of all established races. The contest used to be from London Bridge to Chelsea against the ebb

—a severe test of stamina ; and formerly six only of the many
applicants for competition were allowed to row, being selected
by lot.   The race is now reformed.   It is managed by the
Fishmongers' Company.   The course is changed, so far that it
is now rowed on the flood.   This makes it fairer ; on the ebb,
it is hard to pass a leader who hugs the shore in the slack tide.
Trial heats' are now rowed, to weed off competitors till the
old standard number of six only are left in.   Authentic records
of the race exist since 1791.

Mr. Brickwood, who has taken much pains to look up old
accounts, informs us in his 'Boat Racing' that the Westminster
'water ledger,' dating June 1813, is the earliest authentic record
of Thames aquatics of this century.   We venture to give the
result of Mr. Brickwood's researches in his own words :—

This book commences in the year 1813 with a single list of
the six-oared boat 'Fly,' viz., Messrs. H. Parry, E. O. Cleaver,
E. Parry, W. Markham, W. F. de Ros, G. Randolph.   The
'Fly' continued to be the only boat of this school down to 1816
inclusive, in which latter year it 'beat the Temple six-oared boat
(Mr. Church stroke), in a race from Johnson's dock to Westminster
Bridge, by half a boat ; the latter men having been beat before ;' to
which is added a note that the Temple boat 'requested the K. S.
to row this short distance, having been completely beat by them
in a longer row the same evening.'   In 1817 there was a six-oar
built for Westminster, called the ' Defiance,' and 'sheepskin seats
were introduced.'   In 1818, the ' Westminster were challenged by
the Etonians,' and a six-oared crew was in course of preparation
for the race, but the contest was prohibited.   In 1819 an eight-oar
called the ' Victory' was launched, but the six-oar ' Defiance'
appears to have been the representative crew of the school, for
there is a note that in the spring of 1821 'the boat improved
considerably and beat the " Eagle " in a short pull from Battersea to
Putney Bridge.'   In 1823 a new six-oared cutter was built, and the
name of ' Queen Bess' given in honour of the illustrious foundress.
In 1823 this boat was started from the Horseferry at half past five
in the morning, and reached Chertsey bridge by three o'clock.
On their way back they dined at Walton, and again reached the
Horseferry by a quarter before nine.   The crew of the eight-oar
' Victory' in the same year 'distinguished themselves in the

Temple race and several others.' A new eight called the ' Challenge '
was launched in 1824, and the record says this boat did beat every
boat that it came alongside of, as also did the ' Victory.' And
again in April 13, 1825, this boat (' Challenge ') started from the
Horseferry at four minutes past three in the morning, reached
Sunbury to breakfast at half past seven, and having taken luncheon
at the London Stairs, just above Staines, went through Windsor
bridge by two o'clock in the afternoon. After having seen Eton,
the crew returned to Staines to dinner, and ultimately arrived at
the Horseferry, having performed this distance in twenty-one
hours. The locks detained them full three hours, and, including
all stoppages, they were detained seven hours. A waterman of
the name of Ellis steered the boat in this excursion, and both
steered and conducted himself remarkably well.

Such are some of the early Westminster School annals, as
collated by Mr. Brickwood. One cannot help feeling that if
these long journeys were samples of the school aquatics, it is not
to be wondered that parents and guardians of old days imbibed
prejudices against rowing, and considered it injurious both to
health and to study.

In the following decade there seem to have been plenty of
aquatics current. The ' Bell's Life ' files of those days teem
with aquatic notes. One day we read (dated May 26, 1834)
a self-exculpatory letter from Dr. Williamson, head-master of
Westminster School, explaining why he did not approve of his
scholars rowing a match against Eton, and complaining of the
' intemperance and excesses which such matches lead to.'

On July 3, says ' Bell ' of July 6 in that year, a match was
rowed between a randan (Campbell, Moulton, and Godfrey)
and a four-oar (Harris, Eld, Butcher, and Dodd, Cole cox.)—
from Putney to Westminster. The randan were favourites, and
led ; but Moulton fainted, and the four won. The race was
for a purse of 70*l.*—50*l.* for winners and 20*l.* for losers. In
the same paper, Williams challenges Campbell to a match—
apparently for the incipient title of Champion of the Thames.
Williams wishes Campbell to stake 40*l.* to 30*l.*, because he is
six years the younger. Compare the modesty of these stakes

METHOD OF STARTING THE COLLEGE EIGHTS PRIOR TO 1825—OXFORD

with those for which modern champion, and some less important matches, are rowed !

'Lyons House' seems to have been a sort of resort for amateurs. Cole, who steered the waterman's four (*supra*) *v.* the randan, is described as the waterman of those rooms.

On July 8, same year, a Mr. Kemp, of the 3rd Dragoon Guards, matches himself for a large stake to 'row his own boat' from Hampton Court to Westminster and back in nine hours. Time is favourite, but Mr. Kemp wins by 27 minutes, having met the tide for several miles of his voyage. Such are a few samples of the current style of aquatic sports between 1830 and 1840.

The 'Wingfield Sculls' were founded in 1830, given by the donor, whose name they bear, to be held as a challenge prize by the best sculler of the day from Westminster to Putney, against all comers, on the '4th of August for ever'—so a silver plate in the lid of the old box which holds the silver sculls bears testimony. Since its foundation the prize has been more than once placed on a different footing. Parliaments of old champions and competitors for the prize have been summoned, and the original donor gave assent to the changes of course and *régime*. Lists of winners and competitors from year to year, with notes as to the course rowed, will be found in 'Tables' later on. The race has from its earliest years been described by amateurs as equivalent of 'amateur championship.' A panoply of silver plates has grown up in and around the box which holds the trophy, and on these plates is recorded the name of each winner from year to year. About a quarter of a century ago a 'champion badge' was instituted. It consists of a small edition of the Diamond Sculls (Henley) challenge prize ; as to shape, it is a pair of silver sculls crossed with an enamel wreath and mounted on a ribbon like a 'decoration' or 'order.' There is a 'clasp' for the year of winning. A second win only adds a fresh clasp with date, but no second badge. The secretary of the 'order' is Mr. E. D. Brickwood, himself winner of the title in 1861

UNIVERSITY TRAINING.

Eight-oars had been manned at Eton before they found their way to Oxford. At Cambridge they appeared still later. At both Universities a plurality of eight-oars clubs had existed for some seasons before the first University match— 1829.

In 1881, at the time when the 'Jubilee' dinner of University boat-racing was held, the writer took the opportunity of the presence in London of the Rev. T. Staniforth, the stroke of the first winning University eight, to inquire from him his recollections of college boat-racing in his undergraduate days.

Fortunately for posterity, Mr. Staniforth had kept a diary during his Oxford career, and it had noted many a fact connected with aquatics. He kindly undertook to bring to London at his next visit his diaries of Oxford days. He met the writer, searched his diaries, and out of them recorded history which was taken down from his lips, and reduced to the following article, which appeared in 'Land and Water' of December 17, 1881.[1] It is now reproduced verbatim, by leave. The writer regrets to say that, from various causes, he has been unable to pursue his researches beyond the dates when Mr. Staniforth's diaries cease to record Oxford aquatics.

There must be many an old oarsman still alive who can recall historical facts between 1830 and 1836, and it is hoped that such memories may be reduced to writing for the benefit of posterity, and for the honour of the oarsmen of those years, before *tempus edax rerum* makes it too late.

The writer considers that he will do better thus to reproduce verbatim his own former contribution to 'Land and Water' than to paraphrase it. The more so because much of the text of it is actually the ἔπεα πτερόεντα of the old Oxford stroke, taken down as uttered from his lips to the writer, and read over again

---

[1] See Appendix.

to him for emendation or other alteration, before the interview
in question was concluded. It may be added that Mr. Staniforth kindly showed to the writer the actual text of the
diaries referred to,.from which he refreshed his memory and
recorded the appended history.

As to the intermediate history between 1830 and 1837, in
which year the Brasenose boating record opens (two seasons
before an O.U.B.C. was founded), Christ Church started head
in 1837 ; therefore, apparently, they finished head in 1836.

Mr. Brickwood, in his book on 'Boat Racing,' has collected

OXFORD BOAT IN 1829.

some history of these years, but unfortunately he does not
record the source, so that what might be a tree of knowledge
for inquirers to pluck more from seems to be sealed against
our curiosity. We have, however, to thank him for the following
information, which we reproduce (page 157 of 'Boat Racing'):—

1833.—Queen's College is chronicled as head of the river at
Oxford, this being the only record between 1825 and 1834. Christ
Church, it is true, was said to have kept that position for many
years, but the precise number is not given. However, there seems
no doubt that Christ Church was head in 1834, 1835, and 1836,
after which the official record commences.

Mr. Brickwood, moreover, seems to have gleaned from some independent source sundry valuable details of early Oxford races. He tells us that 'the first known races were those of the college eights in 1815, when Brasenose was the head boat, and their chief and perhaps their only opponent was Jesus.' He speaks of four-oared races in the next ensuing years, and of a match between Mr. de Ros' four and a pair manned by a B.N.C. man and a waterman—won by the pair. Then comes some information as to the years 1822, 1824, and 1825, which exactly tallies with Mr. Staniforth's journals, save that Mr. Brickwood ascribes the discontinuance of the races in 1823 directly to the recorded quarrel between B.N.C. and Jesus ; whereas Mr. Staniforth attributes it to the untimely death of Musgrave (*supra*).

The first University race took place in 1829, over the course from Hambledon Lock to Henley. Mr. Staniforth states that till the Oxford went to practise over the course, no one thought of steering an eight through the Berks channel, past 'regatta' island. However, the Oxonians 'timed' the two straits, and decided to select the Berks one, if they got the chance. They took that channel in the race and won easily. A foul occurred in the first essay at starting, and the boats were restarted. This pair of pioneer University crews produced men of more than usual celebrity in after life : two embryo bishops, three deans, one prebendary, and divers others hereafter

> In hamlet and hall
> As well known to all
> As the vane of the old church spire.

The full list of the crews engaged in this and in all other contests in which Universities were represented, will be found in 'Tables' towards the end of this volume. At this time there was no O.U.B.C., nor did such an organisation exist until 1839, when a 'meeting of strokes' of the various colleges was convened, and a generally representative club was founded. At Cambridge a U.B.C. had existed since 1827. In that year the system of college eights seems to have been instituted, according to the testimony of Dr. Merivale, still Dean of Ely, and a member of the C.U.B.C. crew of 1829. Trinity were head of the river on that occasion, and there seems to have been also a Westminster club, of an independent nature in Trinity. The records of college racing at Cambridge seem to be unbroken since their institution ; whereas those of Oxford were for many years unofficial and without central organisation, and consequently without official record, until 1839. The Brasenose Club record dates from 1837.

BUMPING RACES (OLD STYLE).

The next occasion in which a University eight figured was in a match which somehow seems to have slipped out of public memory, though it occurred several years later than the first match between the Universities. The writer was talking to old George West, the well-known Oxford waterman, in 1882, at the L.R.C. boat-house, while waiting for the practice of the U.B.C. crews of that year. Casually old George remarked, ' I steered a University eight once, sir.' The writer looked incredulous. ' Yes, against Leander—Leander won,' quoth George. The writer had known West since his school days, and had heard him recapitulate his aquatic memories times out of mind, but

D

never till that hour had he heard any allusion to this Leander match. Only the year before, the 'Jubilee' dinner of old Blues had taken place, and all who had ever been known to have represented their University in a match or regatta were asked to join in the celebration. At that date not one of the executive had any inkling of this match, although one of the Oxford crew, the present Bishop of Norwich, could certainly have been found at an hour's notice. Letters from old oarsmen, who had not actually rowed for the flag (often because there was no match during their career), used to pour in while the jubilee feast was in preparation, asking for admittance to it. None of this Oxford crew seem to have put in any claim. A slight, though an unintentional one, was thus perpetrated upon all of them, whether alive or dead, by the omission to record them as old Blues on that occasion. When the writer compiled the history of 'Old Blues and their Battles,' which Mr. G. T. Treherne incorporated in his book of 'Record of the University Boat Race,' and which was published soon after the jubilee, neither of these gentlemen was aware of this race. No speaker at the banquet seemed to remember or allude to it. Yet, on referring to old files of 'Bell's Life,' record of this match is to be found. Since it was recorded in that journal, it seems to have been unnoticed in any print till now. Better late than never ; the performers in it are now officially brought to light, and their names will be found in the tables of University oarsmen and their opponents, later on.

This match was for 200*l*. a side. Leander would row on no other terms, and insisted on having their own waterman to steer them, as they did in their later matches against Cambridge. This was the only Oxford University eight ever steered by a professional. Only one of the 1829 crew seems to have remained to do duty in this race. The Pelham referred to is now Bishop of Norwich. He used, before this, to row in the Christ Church eight behind Staniforth. The Waterford is the former marquis of that ilk, who lost his life later on through a fall when hunting. *En passant*, it may be mentioned that

Bishop Selwyn (of C.U.B.C. crew 1829) and Pelham of Oxford 1834, each begat sons who rowed for their respective Universities : Selwyn, junr. 1864 and 1866 ; Pelham, junr. 1877 and 1878. The latter oarsman unfortunately lost his life in the Alps very shortly afterwards. J. R. Selwyn has succeeded his late father as a colonial bishop. Inasmuch as we here record, for the first time for two generations, a lost chapter of University Boat Racing, we think it will be of interest to append the account given, in ' Bell's Life ' of that day, of this forgotten match.

EIGHT-OARED MATCH—LONDON AND THE OXFORD AMATEURS FOR £ 200.[1]

This interesting match was decided on Saturday week at Henley Reach. The Trinity boat, built by Archer of Lambeth, proved successful on a former occasion when opposed to the Oxonians, was, we understand, again selected by them in the first instance, but they ultimately decided on rowing in a boat built by Searle, which they considered had been unjustly denounced ' a rank bad un,' simply on the score of the Cambridge gentlemen and the Westminster Scholars having lost their matches in her— the former against Oxford, and the latter against the Etonians.

The gentlemen of Oxford selected a large but peculiarly light eight belonging to Mr. Davis of Oxford. On Friday the London gentlemen left town for Henley, and took up their quarters at the Red Lion. Noulton of Lambeth was selected to steer them. Although Oxford were favourites on the match being first concocted, it was with difficulty that a bet could be made on the Londoners on the last two days, and then only at 6 to 4 against Oxford.

At about 6.30 the contending parties arrived in their cutters near the lock, to row from thence against the stream to Henley Bridge, which is reckoned two and a quarter miles.

The names of the respective parties and their stations in the cutters were as follows :

London—Bishop (stroke), Captain Shaw, J. Bayford, Lewis, Cannon, Weedon, Revell, Hornemann.

Oxford—Copplestone (stroke), Lloyd, Barnes, Pelham, Peard, Marsh, Marquis of Waterford, Carter. The latter was steered, we believe, by a boy belonging to the lock.

[1] *Bell's Life*, Sunday, June 26, 1831.

Mr. Hume and Mr. Bayford were appointed umpires on part of the London gentlemen, and Mr. Lloyd and another gentleman on the side of Oxford.

The Oxford gentlemen won the toss and took the inside station. The umpires having a second time asked if all was ready, receiving an answer in the affirmative, gave the signal. In less than a dozen seconds the London gentlemen almost astounded their opponents by going about a boat's length in advance, so rapid were their strokes when compared with those of Oxford. The Oxford gentlemen soon recovered. Before half the distance had been rowed London were two lengths in advance. The Oxonians, finding they were losing ground, made a desperate effort and succeeded in coming within a painter's length. On nearing the goal the exertions of each party were increasing. One London gentleman (Captain Shaw) seemed so much exhausted, that it was feared he would not hold out the remaining distance. Noulton, seeing this and fearing the consequence, observing the Oxford gentlemen fast approaching them, said that 'if the Londoners did not give it her it would be all up with them.' They did give it her, and the consequence was they became victorious by about two boats' lengths. The distance was rowed in 11¼ minutes.

The exertions at the conclusion of the contest became lamentably apparent. Captain Shaw nearly fainted and had to be carried ashore ; Mr. Bayford was obliged to retire to bed instantly ; so was also one of the Oxford gentlemen. The others were more or less exhausted.

The London gentlemen rowed to town on Tuesday, and were greeted on their way with cheering and cannon. On arriving at Searle's a *feu-de-joie* was fired.

Note.—Of the various performers in this Oxford crew, the following notices of the after career of some may be of interest. Messrs. Copplestone and Pelham rose to adorn the episcopate. Mr. Peard became known to fame as ' Garibaldi's Englishman,' and played an important part in the cause of the liberation of Italy.

There had been a second University match in 1836, this time from Westminster to Putney (see Tables). No official record exists of this. It is said that 'light blue' was on this occasion first adopted by Cambridge. Certainly in 1829 the

Cantab crew wore *pink*, while Oxford sported blue. The late Mr. R. M. Phillips, of Christ's, used to tell the writer that he it was who fortuitously founded light blue on this occasion. He was on the raft at Searle's when the Cantab crew were preparing to start (either for the race or for a day's practice) the race so far as recollection of Mr. Phillips' narrative serves the writer. One of the crew said, 'We have no colours.' Mr. Phillips ran off to buy some ribbon in Stangate. An old Etonian accompanied him, and suggested 'Eton ribbon for luck.' It

A COLLEGE PAIR.

was bought, it came in first, and was adhered to in later years by Cambridge.

In 1837 the head college crews of the two Universities rowed a match at Henley. The Brasenose book says, Christ Church were head, but took off because their Dean objected to their rowing at Henley ; the effect of their 'taking off' was to leave Queen's College, on whom the representation of the college crews would devolve, with the titular headship.

The B.N.C. book says, the Queen's crew went, 'as was

usual,' to row the head boat of Cambridge, and beat them
easily. The latter statement is correct. Mr. Brickwood in his
treatise demurs to the accuracy of the B.N.C. allegation that
such matches were 'usual,' and research qualifies his scepticism.
The B.N.C. hon. sec. of that day seems to have been drawing somewhat upon his imagination. He had probably heard
of these various Leander and other matches at Henley in
other years ; hence his inference.

1837.

Henley. College match.

QUEEN'S.	LADY MARGARET (St. John's).
1. Lee, Stanlake.	1. Shadwell, Alfred H.
2. Glazbrook, Robert.	2. Colquhoun, Patrick.
3. Welsh, Jos.	3. Wood, H. O.
4. Robinson, John.	4. Antrobus, Edmund.
5. Meyrick, Jos.	5. Budd, R. H.
6. Todd, Jos.	6. Fane, W. D.
7. Eversley, John.	7. Fletcher, Ralph.
Penny, Chas. J. (stroke).	Hurt, Robert (stroke).
Berkeley, Geo. T. (cox.).	Jackson, Curtis (cox.).

The names of the Queen's and St. John's crews are here
given, instead of recording them in the lists of University oars,
for this was not strictly a University race, though in those days
it had almost as much prestige as one.

In 1839 the third University match was rowed, and Henley
Regatta was founded. At the Universities, about this date,
various prizes were established, all of which gave a stimulus to
oarsmanship.

Pair-oar races were established at Oxford in 1839. They
were rowed with coxswains until 1847. At Cambridge similar
pairs were founded in 1844, and were rowed from the first without coxswains. The obsolete rudder of the Oxford pairs is
now held by the coxswain of the head eight. The Colquhoun
Sculls had been founded at Cambridge in 1837. 'University
Sculls' were instituted at Oxford in 1841. Four-oar races, each

crew to be from one college, were founded at Oxford in 1840, and at Cambridge in 1849. Thus, by the latter year, each U.B.C. had its set of contests for all classes of craft—eights, fours, pairs, and sculls. Lists of the winners of these various honours from year to year will be found elsewhere in this volume.

Aquatics may be said to have reached full swing with the completion of these institutions at the Universities. Matches between the Universities were propounded annually by one or other club from 1839, but time and place could not always be

TOWING GUARD BOATS UP HENLEY REACH.

agreed upon, nor could 'dons' be always persuaded to allow men to row in such races. There was many a hitch in old days, from one cause or another. Since 1850 the U.B.C.'s have annually met each other in some shape or other at Henley, or in a match ; since, and including, 1856 matches over the Putney course have been annual. Since 1859 neither University has put on at any regatta.

Various causes tended to stimulate rowing, e.g. regattas and also professional racing, which is dealt with separately under the head of 'Professionals.' A perusal of the tables of records of

Henley and other regattas will also show how competitions gradually increased in number, and also in the fields which they produced.

REGATTAS.

The institution of Henley Regatta in 1839 was the outcome of the various eight-oared matches which have been rowed on that part of the river during the ten years preceding. The regatta began with one prize only, the Grand Challenge Cup, a trophy which is unique for classical design, and which is to this day the 'blue ribbon' for amateur clubs. The gradual growth of Henley may be traced by perusal of a leading article contributed by the writer of this chapter to the 'Field,' in the July of 1886, on the eve of the greatest change which the regatta has undergone, that of alteration of the course. The article is now reproduced,[1] through the courtesy of the proprietors of that journal.

The new course, as compared with the old one, will best be understood by reference to the map of the reach, which appears elsewhere. The change has had only two trials, those of 1886 and 1887, but it may be said that so far rowing clubs which frequent Henley are unanimous in approving of the alteration ; and so are all retired oarsmen, whose personal experience of the regatta was under the old *régime.*

The old course was very one-sided. In the middle third of a mile—on a stormy day—with a stiff wind from W. or S.W., the shelter of the Bucks bushes—especially before house-boats and steam launches multiplied and monopolised the frontage of the Bucks and Oxon shores—used to reverse entirely the advantage otherwise pertaining to the Berks stations. On such a day the Berks station placed most boats hopelessly out of the race, unless they could keep within a length of the Bucks boat till the 'point' was reached—in which case the poplar corner made a pretty counterpoise to the advantage of Bucks shelter, and caused some interesting finishes. Under the new *régime* not more than two boats can row in one heat ; and as the course is

---

[1] See Appendix.

STARTING THE EIGHTS—OLD COURSE, HENLEY

now staked out, and neither competitor can hug the bank, the
difference between windward and leeward stations, even when
hereafter a gale shall blow, will no longer be so glaring as of
old.

The Universities no longer compete at Henley. In these
days of keelless boats more practice is needed, in order to do justice to the craft, than when heavier and steadier craft were used.
It is found to be impossible to collect all the eight best men of
either U.B.C. twice in one year. Examination and other causes

PAIR-OAR.

reduce the ranks more or less ; and, as the annual Putney match
between the Universities is considered by them to be of more
importance than any other contest, they devote their best energies
to that, and leave minor sections of either U.B.C. to fight Henley
battles. It is found that a good college eight, or a club crew of
which some one college forms a nucleus, can be got together
better, in the limited time available for practice for the regatta,
than eight better men who probably cannot find time to practise
all together for more than a week, and who will further, for the
same reason, be short of condition.

Till 1856, it was the custom for the U.B.C.'s, if they could not agree as to time and place for a match, to assent to meet each other in the Grand Challenge ; and such meetings ranked practically as University matches. Records of these *rencontres* of the U.B.C.'s will be found in tables at the end of this volume, together with a history of Henley past and future.

The 'Seven-oar episode' of 1843 was not a University match or meeting. The O.U.B.C. were entered at Henley ; Cambridge were represented by the 'Cambridge Rooms ;' but the C.U.B.C. was not officially represented by that crew. Just before the final heat, the Oxford stroke fainted, and the Cambridge reasonably objected to the introduction of a substitute. The Oxonians then decided to row with seven oars. They had a wind abeam, favouring the side which was manned by only three oars. They eventually won by a length, or thereabouts.

In 1843 the Thames Regatta was started, and greatly supplemented the attractions of Henley. The mistake of this regatta was the rule which made challenge prizes the permanent property of any crew which could win them thrice in succession. By this means the Gold Cup for eights, the *pièce de résistance* of the regatta, passed in 1848 to the possession of the 'Thames' Club. The regatta lingered on one year longer, shorn of its chief glory, and then died out.

Records of the winners of the chief prizes at it, amateurs as well as professionals, will be found in 'Tables.'

In 1854 a new Thames regatta, called the 'National,' was founded. It was supported by the 'Thames Subscription Club,' and died with that club in 1866. In the last year of its existence it introduced amateur prizes as well as the usual bonuses for professionals. In 1866 a very important regatta was founded—the Metropolitan. Its founders expected it to eclipse Henley, by dint of offers of more valuable prizes, but it never took the fancy of the University element, and for want of the wider-spread competition which strong entries from the U.B.C.'s would have produced, it never attained the prestige of

Henley. Still the honours of winning eights, fours, pairs, or
sculls at it rank, in amateur estimation, second only to Henley.
Barnes Regatta is of very old standing. The tideway is always
a drawback to scenery, but Barnes always used to produce
good audiences and good competitors. Its chief patrons were
tideway clubs and the Kingston Rowing Club.

Walton-on-Thames flourished in the ' sixties.' It has now

GONDOLA.

died out. It was as a picnic second only to Henley. The
course was rather one-sided, and hardly long enough to test
stamina.

Molesey Regatta, of less than ten years' growth, now holds
much the same station in aquatics that Walton-on-Thames
once claimed. It draws its sinews of war from much the same
up-river locality that used to feed Walton.

Kingston-on-Thames has a longer history than any regatta

except Henley. Its fortunes hang on the Kingston Rowing Club, but it is well patronised by tideway clubs.

Regattas have for a season or two been known at Staines and Chertsey, but they depended on some one or two local men of energy, and, when this support failed, they died out.

Reading has a good reach, and has of late come to the fore with a good meeting and a handsome challenge cup.

To return to watermen's regattas. The late Mr. J. G. Chambers, and a strong gathering of amateur allies of his, revived a second series of Thames regattas in 1868 ; these meetings were confined to watermen and other professionals, whose doings are scheduled in 'Tables' hereafter. How the second series of Thames National regattas followed the fate of series No. 1, and of the 'Royal Thames Regatta' before that, will be found in the chapter on professional rowing. The so-called 'International' Regatta lived but two years, and fell through so soon as its mercenary promoters came to the conclusion that they could not see their way to harvest filthy lucre out of it.

There used to be a well-attended regatta at Talkintarn, in the Lake district. It died out from causes similar to those which led to the collapse of the 'Royal' Thames regattas, i.e. the dedication of its prizes to those who could win them a certain number of times consecutively. The Messrs. Brickwood thus became the absolute owners of the chief prize for pairs, and a Tyne crew became the proprietors of the four-oar prize.

The Tyne, the Wear, Chester, Bedford, Tewkesbury, Worcester, Bridgenorth, Bath, and other provincial towns produce regattas, but none of them succeed in drawing many of the leading Thames clubs, and without these no regatta ever establishes even second-class prestige.

The rules of Henley Regatta are here appended. They serve to inform intending competitors of the code under which they will have to enter and to row, and they may also offer valuable hints to other regatta executives, present and future.

HENLEY ROYAL REGATTA.

Established 1839.

President.

THE RIGHT HONOURABLE LORD CAMOYS.

Stewards.

THE MAYOR OF HENLEY.

The Rt. Hon. the EARL OF MACCLESFIELD.
W. H. VANDERSTEGEN, Esq.
ALEXANDER C. FORBES, Esq.
J. F. HODGES, Esq.
HENRY KNOX, Esq.
J. W. RHODES, Esq.
W. D. MACKENZIE, Esq.
HENRY HODGES, Esq.
The Rev. E. WARRE, D.D.
F. WILLAN, Esq.
CHARLES STEPHENS, Esq.
JOHN NOBLE, Esq.
The Rt. Hon. W. H. SMITH, M.P.

FREDK. FENNER, Esq.
H. T. STEWARD, Esq.
Colonel BASKERVILLE.
HUGH MAIR, Esq.
Sir F. G. STAPYLTON, Bart.
W. H. GRENFELL, Esq., M.P.
J. H. D. GOLDIE, Esq.
The Rt. Hon. LORD LONDESBOROUGH.
T. C. EDWARDES-MOSS, Esq., M.P.
J. COOPER, Esq.
J. PAGE, Esq.
A. BRAKSPEAR, Esq.
The Rt. Hon. the EARL OF ANTRIM.

A. BRAKSPEAR, *Hon. Treasurer.*
J. F. COOPER, *Secretary.*

CONSTITUTION.

On May 16, 1885, at a meeting of the stewards, the following resolutions were agreed to :—

1. That the stewards of Henley Regatta shall constitute a council for the general control of the affairs of the regatta.

2. That the stewards shall elect a president, who shall, if present, take the chair at the general meetings.

3. That the chairman shall have a casting vote.

4. That not less than *five* shall form a quorum at the general meetings.

5. That two ordinary general meetings shall be held in each year, one in the month of May and another in the month of November.

6. That other general meetings shall be summoned by the secretary, when ordered by the president, or at the request of any two stewards, in writing, provided that not less than fourteen days' notice shall be given of any such meeting.

7. That the stewards shall elect annually, at the meeting in November, from their own body, a committee of management.

8. That the number of the committee shall not exceed twelve, of whom not less than *three* shall form a quorum.

9. That the committee shall elect one of their own body to act as chairman.

10. That the committee be empowered to manage and exercise control over all matters connected with the regatta, excepting such as shall involve the alteration of any of the published rules of the regatta.

11. That the committee shall present a report, together with a statement of accounts, to the stewards, annually, at the November meeting in each year.

12. That meetings of the committee shall be summoned by the secretary when ordered by the chairman, or at the request of any two members of the committee, in writing, providing that not less than one week's notice be given of any such meeting.

13. That the committee shall have power to make and publish by-laws respecting any matter connected with the management of the regatta, not already determined in the published rules.

14. That no alteration shall be made in any of the foregoing resolutions, or in any of the published rules of the regatta, except at a general meeting specially convened for that purpose, of which fourteen days' notice shall be given, such notice to state the alterations proposed, and unless the alteration be carried by a majority of two-thirds at a meeting of not less than nine stewards.

QUALIFICATION RULES.

The Grand Challenge Cup,
FOR EIGHT-OARS.

Any crew of amateurs who are members of any University or Public School, or who are officers of her Majesty's army or navy, or any amateur club established at least one year previous to the day of entry, shall be qualified to contend for this prize.

The Stewards' Challenge Cup,
FOR FOUR-OARS.

The same as for the Grand Challenge Cup.

The Ladies' Challenge Plate,
FOR EIGHT-OARS.

Any crew of amateurs who are members of any of the boat clubs of colleges, or non-collegiate boat clubs of the Universities, or boat clubs of any of the Public Schools, in the United Kingdom only, shall be qualified to contend for this prize ; but no member of any college or non-collegiate crew shall be allowed to row for it who has exceeded four years from the date of his first commencing residence at the University ; and each member of a Public School crew shall, at the time of entering, be *bonâ fide* a member '*in statu pupillari*' of such school.

The Visitors' Challenge Cup,
FOR FOUR-OARS.

The same as for the Ladies' Challenge Plate.

The Thames Challenge Cup,
FOR EIGHT-OARS.

The qualification for this cup shall be the same as for the Grand Challenge Cup ; but no one (coxswains excepted) may enter for this cup who has ever rowed in a winning crew for the Grand Challenge Cup or Stewards' Challenge Cup ; and no one (substitutes as per Rule 7 excepted) may enter, and no one shall row, for this cup and for the Grand Challenge Cup or Stewards' Challenge Cup at the same regatta.

The Wyfold Challenge Cup,
for four-oars.

The qualification for this cup shall be the same as for the Stewards' Challenge Cup; but no one shall enter for this cup who has ever rowed in a winning crew for the Stewards' Challenge Cup; and no one (substitutes as per Rule 11 excepted) may enter, and no one shall row, for this cup and for the Stewards' Challenge Cup at the same regatta.

The Silver Goblets,
for pair-oars.

Open to all amateurs duly entered for the same according to the rules following.

The Diamond Challenge Sculls,
for sculls.

Open to all amateurs duly entered for the same according to the rules following.

GENERAL RULES.

Definition.—1. No person shall be considered an amateur oarsman, sculler, or coxswain—

(*a*) Who has ever taken part in any open competition for a stake, money, or entrance fee;

(*b*) Who has ever knowingly competed with or against a professional for any prize;

(*c*) Who has ever taught, pursued, or assisted in the practice of athletic exercises of any kind for profit;

(*d*) Who has ever been employed in or about boats, or in manual labour for money or wages;

(*e*) Who is or has been by trade or employment, for wages, a mechanic, artisan, or labourer, or engaged in any menial duty.

Eligibility.—2. No one shall be eligible to row or steer for a club unless he has been a member of that club for at least two months preceding the regatta, but this rule shall not apply to colleges, schools, or crews composed of officers of her Majesty's army or navy.

Entries.—3. The entry of any amateur club, crew, or sculler, in the United Kingdom, must be made ten clear days before the regatta, and the names of the captain or secretary of each club or crew must accompany the entry. A copy of the list of entries shall be forwarded by the secretary of the regatta to the captain or secretary of each club or crew duly entered.

4. The entry of any crew or sculler, out of the United Kingdom, must be made on or before March 31, and any such entry must be accompanied by a declaration, made before a notary public, with regard to the profession of each person so entering, to the effect that he has never taken part in any open competition for a stake, money, or entrance fee; has never knowingly competed with nor against a professional for any prize; has never taught, pursued, or assisted in the practice of athletic exercises of any kind for profit; has never been employed in or about boats, or in manual labour for money or wages; is not, and never has been, by trade or employment, for wages, a mechanic, artisan, or labourer, or engaged in any menial duty; and in cases of the entry of a crew, that each member thereof is a member of a club duly established at least one year previous to the day of entry; and such declaration must be certified by the British Consul, or the Mayor, or the chief authority of the locality.

5. No assumed name shall be given to the secretary, unless accompanied by the real name of the competitor.

6. No one shall enter twice for the same race.

7. The secretary of the regatta shall not divulge any entry, nor report the state of the entrance list, until such list be closed.

8. Entrance money for each boat shall be paid to the secretary at the time of entering, as follows :—

	£	s.	d.
For the Grand Challenge Cup . .	6	6	0
„ Ladies' Challenge Plate . .	5	5	0
„ Thames Challenge Cup . .	5	5	0
„ Stewards' „ „ . .	4	4	0
„ Visitors' „ „ . .	3	3	0
„ Wyfold „ „ . .	3	3	0
„ Silver Goblets . . .	2	2	0
„ Diamond Challenge Sculls .	1	1	0

E

9. The committee shall investigate any questionable entry, irrespective of protest.

10. The committee shall have power to refuse or return any entry up to the time of starting, without being bound to assign a reason.

11. The captain or secretary of each club or crew entered shall, seven clear days before the regatta, deliver to the secretary of the regatta a list containing the names of the actual crew appointed to compete, to which list the names of not more than four other members for an eight-oar and two for a four-oar may be added as substitutes.

12. No person may be substituted for another who has already rowed or steered in a heat.

13. The secretary of the regatta, after receiving the list of the crews entered, and of the substitutes, shall, if required, furnish a copy of the same, with the names, real and assumed, to the captain or secretary of each club or crew entered, and in the case of pairs or scullers to each competitor entered.

Objections.—14. Objections to the entry of any club or crew must be made in writing to the secretary at least four clear days before the regatta, when the committee shall investigate the grounds of objection, and decide thereon without delay.

15. Objections to the qualification of a competitor must be made in writing to the secretary at the earliest moment practicable. No protest shall be entertained unless lodged before the prizes are distributed.

Course.—16. The races shall commence below the Island, and terminate at the upper end of Phyllis Court. Length of course, about 1 mile and 550 yards.

17. Boats shall be held to have completed the course when their bows reach the winning-post.

18. The whole course must be completed by a competitor before he can be held to have won a trial or final heat.

Stations.—19. Stations shall be drawn by the committee.

Row over.—20. In the event of there being but one boat entered for any prize, or if more than one enter, and all withdraw but one, the crew of the remaining boat must row over the course to be entitled to such prize.

Heats.—21. If there shall be more than two competitors, they shall row a trial heat or heats ; but no more than two boats shall contend in any heat for any of the prizes above mentioned.

22. In the event of a dead heat taking place, the same crews shall contend again, after such interval as the committee may appoint, or the crew refusing shall be adjudged to have lost the heat.

Clothing.—23. Every competitor must wear complete clothing from the shoulders to the knees—including a sleeved jersey.

Coxswains.—24. Every eight-oared boat shall carry a coxswain ; such coxswain must be an amateur, and shall not steer for more than one club for the same prize.

The minimum weight for coxswains shall be 7 stone.

Crews averaging 10½ stone and under 11 stone to carry not less than 7½ stone.

Crews averaging 11 stone or more, to carry not less than 8 stone.

Deficiencies must be made up by dead weight carried on the coxswain's thwart.

The dead weight shall be provided by the committee, and shall be placed in the boat and removed from it by a person appointed for that purpose.

Each competitor (including the coxswain) in eight- and four-oared races shall attend to be weighed (in rowing costume) at the time and place appointed by the committee ; and his weight then registered by the secretary shall be considered his racing weight during the regatta.

Any member of a crew omitting to register his weight shall be disqualified.

Flag.—25. Every boat shall, at starting, carry a flag showing its colour at the bow. Boats not conforming to this rule are liable to be disqualified at the discretion of the umpire.

Umpire.—26. The committee shall appoint one or more umpires to act under the Laws of Boat-racing.

Judge.—27. The committee shall appoint one or more judges, whose decision as to the order in which the boats pass the post shall be final.

Prizes.—28. The prizes shall be delivered at the conclusion of the regatta to their respective winners, who on receipt of a challenge prize shall subscribe a document of the following effect :—

' We, A, B, C, D, &c., the captain and crew of the and members of the   Club, having been this day declared to be the winners of the Henley Royal Regatta   Challenge Cup, and the same having been delivered to us by E F, G H, I K, &c., Stewards of the Regatta, do hereby, individually and collectively, engage to return the same to the Stewards on or before June 1, in accordance with the conditions of the annexed rules, to which also we have subscribed our respective names.'

Committee.—29. All questions of eligibility, qualification, interpretation of the rules, or other matters not specially provided for, shall be referred to the committee, whose decision shall be final.

30. The Laws of Boat-racing to be observed at the regatta are as follows (*see chapter on this subject*).

A good deal of the history of old regattas at which watermen contended is necessarily mixed with the history of the rise of professional racing, and will be found to be dealt with under that heading in another chapter.

BISHAM COURT.

CHAPTER III.

SCIENTIFIC OARSMANSHIP.

IF a thing is worth doing at all it is worth doing well, whether it be undertaken in sport or as a means of livelihood.

The first principles of oarsmanship may be explained to a beginner in a few minutes, and he might roughly put them into force, in a casual and faulty manner, on the first day of his education.

In all pastimes and professions there is, as even a child knows, a very wide difference between the knowing how a thing is done and the rendering of the operation in the most approved and scientific manner.

In all operations which entail the use of implements there are three essentials to the attainment of real merit in the operation. These are, firstly, physical capacity ; secondly, good tools to work with ; thirdly, practice and painstaking on the part of the student.

For the purposes of the current chapter we shall postulate the two former, and confine the theme to details of such study and practice of oarsmanship as are requisite in order to attain scientific use of oars or sculls.

When commencing to learn an operation which entails a new and unwonted exercise, distinct volition is necessary on the part of the brain, in order to dictate to the various muscles the parts which they are to play in the operation.

The oftener that a muscular movement is repeated the less intense becomes the mental volition which is required to dictate that movement ; until at last the movement becomes almost mechanical, and can be reproduced without a strain of the will (so long as the muscular power is not exhausted).

One object of studied practice at any given muscular movement is to accustom the muscles to this particular function, until they become capable of carrying it out without requiring specific and laborious instructions from the headquarters of the brain on the occasion of each such motion. Another object and result of exercise of one or more sets of muscles is to develop their powers. The anatomical reasons why muscles increase in vigour and activity under exercise need not be here discussed ; the fact may be accepted that they do so.

Hence, by practice of any kind of muscular movement, the student increases both the vigour and the independence of action of the muscles concerned.

In any operation with implements there is some one method of performing the same which experience has proved to be the most effectual for the purpose required. There will be other methods, or variations of method, which will attain a somewhat similar but less effectual and less satisfactory result.

It requires distinct volition in the first instance to perform the operation in an inferior manner, just as it does to perform it in the most approved manner, to perform ' clumsily ' or to perform ' cleverly.'

Naturally, if the volition to act clumsily be repeated a sufficient number of times, the muscles learn independent clumsy action with as much facility as they would have otherwise acquired independent clever and scientific action. Hence the importance of knowing which is the most approved and effectual method of setting to work, and of being informed of the result, good or bad, of each attempt, while the volition is still in active force, and before the 'habit' of muscular action, perfect or imperfect, is fully formed.

We all know that, whether we are dealing with morals or with muscles, it is a matter of much difficulty to overcome a bad habit, and to form a different and a better one relating to the same course of action.

When the pupil begins to learn to row the brain has many things to think of ; it has several orders to distribute simultaneously to its different employés—the various muscles required for the work—and these employés are, moreover, 'new to the business.' They have not yet, from want of practice, developed the vigour and strength which they will require hereafter ; and also they know so little of what they have to do that they require incessant instruction from brain headquarters, or else they make blunders. But in time both master and servants, brain and muscles, begin to settle down to their business. The master becomes less confused, and gives his orders with more accuracy and less oblivion of details ; the servants acquire more vigour, and pick up the instructions with more facility. At last the time comes when the servants know pretty well what their master would have them do, and act spontaneously, while the master barely whispers his orders, and has leisure to attend to other matters, or at all events saves himself the exertion of having momentarily to shout his orders through a speaking-trumpet. Meantime, as said before, the servants can only obey orders ; and, if their original instructions have been blunders on the part of the master, they settle down to the reproduction of these blunders.

Now it often happens that an oarsman, who is himself a

good judge of rowing, and is capable of giving very good instructions to others, is guilty of many faults in his own oarsmanship. And yet it cannot be said of him that he 'knows
no better' as regards those faults which he personally commits.
On the contrary, if he were to see one of his own pupils rowing
with any one of these same faults, he would promptly detect it,
and would be able to explain to the pupil the why and the
wherefore of the error, and of its cure. Nevertheless, he per-
petrates in his own person the very fault which he discerns
and corrects when he notes it in another ! And the reason is
this. His own oarsmanship has become mechanical, and is
reproduced stroke after stroke without a distinct volition. It
became faulty at the time when it was becoming mechanical,
because the brain was not sufficiently conscious of the orders
which it was dictating, or was not duly informed, from some
external source, what orders it should issue. So the brain gave
wrong orders, through carelessness or ignorance, or both, and
continued to repeat them, until the muscles learnt to repeat
their faulty functions spontaneously, and without the immediate
cognisance of the brain.

This illustration, of which many a practical instance will be
recalled by any rowing man of experience, serves to show the
importance of keeping the mind attentive, as far as possible, at
all times when rowing, and still more so while elementary rowing is being learnt, and also of having, if possible, a mentor to
watch the endeavours of the student, and to inform him of any
error of movement which he may perpetrate, before his mind
and muscles become confirmed in an erroneous line of action.

The reader will therefore see from the above that it is
important for any one who seeks to acquire really scientific
oarsmanship, not only to pay all the mental attention that he
can to the movements which he is executing, but also to secure
the presence of some experienced adviser who will watch the
execution of each stroke, and will point out at the time what
movements have been correctly and what have been incorrectly
performed.

Having shown the importance of careful study and tuition in the details of scientific oarsmanship, we now enter into those details themselves, but still confine ourselves to what is known as 'fixed' seat rowing, taking them separately, and dealing first with the stroke itself, as distinct from the 'recovery' between the strokes.

While carrying out the stroke upon general principles, the oarsman, in order to produce a maximum effect with a relatively minimum expenditure of strength, has to study the following details :

1. To keep the back rigid, and to swing from the hips.

2. To maintain his shoulders braced when the oar grasps the water.

3. To use the legs and feet in the best manner and at the exact instant required.

4. To hold his oar properly.

5. To govern the depth of the blade with accuracy, including the first dip of the blade into the water to the moment when the blade quits it.

6. To row the stroke home to his chest, bending his arms neither too soon nor too late.

7. To do so with the correct muscles.

8. To drop the hands and elevate the oar from the water in the right manner and at the right moment.

Then again, when the stroke is completed and the recovery commences, the details to be further observed are :

9. To avoid 'hang' or delay of action either with hands or body.

10. To manipulate the feather with accuracy and at the proper instant.

11. To govern the height of the blade during the recovery.

12. To use the legs and feet correctly and at the right moments of recovery.

13. To keep the button of the oar home to the thowl.

14. To regulate the proportionate speeds of recovery of arms and of body, relatively to each other.

15. To return the feathered oar to the square position at the right time and in the correct manner.

16. To raise the hands at the right moment, and so to lower the blade into the water at the correct instant.

17. To recommence the action of the new stroke at the right instant.

These several details present an apparently formidable list of detailed studies to be followed in order to execute a series of strokes and recoveries in the most approved fashion. In performance the operation is far more homogeneous than would appear from the above disjointed analysis of the several movements to be performed. The division of movements is made for the purpose of observation and appreciation of possibly several faults, which may occur in any one of the movements detailed. As a fact, the correct rendering of one movement—of one detail of the stroke—facilitates correctness in succeeding or contemporaneous details ; while, on the other hand, a faulty rendering of one movement tends to hamper the action of the body in other details, and to make it more liable to do its work incorrectly in some or all of them. Experience shows that one fault, in one distinct detail, is constantly the primary cause of a concatenation of other faults. To set the machine in incorrect motion in one branch of it tends to put the whole, or the greater part of it, more or less out of gear, and to cripple its action from beginning to end of the chapter.

Taking these various details *seriatim*.

1. The back should be set stiff, and preserved stiff throughout the stroke. Obviously, if the back yields to the strain, the stroke is not so effectual. Besides, if the back is badly humped the expansion of the chest is impeded ; and with this the action of the pectoral muscles and of the shoulders (of both of which more anon) is also fettered. Further, the lungs have less freedom of play when the back is bent and the chest cramped ; and the value of free respiration requires no explanation.

We have said that the back must be stiff. If the back can be straight, from first to last, stiffness is ensured, *ipso facto*. If the back is bent, care must be taken that the bend does not increase or decrease during the stroke; whether straight or bent, the back should be rigid.

The conformation and development of the muscles of the back are not quite the same in all subjects. With some persons absolute straightness of back comes almost naturally; with others the attainment of straightness is not a matter of much difficulty. With others, again, a slight amount of curve in the back is more natural under the strain of the oar, even with all attention and endeavour to keep the back flat. With such as these any artificial straightening of the back, that places it in a position in which the muscles, as they are adapted to the frame, have not the fullest and freest play, detracts from rather than adds to the power of the oarsman.

But in all cases it is important that the back, whether straight or slightly arched, should be rigid, and should swing from the hips. If the swing takes place from one or more of the vertebræ of the spine, the force which the oarsman can by such actions produce is far less than would be the case if he kept his spine rigid and had swung to and fro from his hips.

In order to facilitate the entire body in swinging from the hips, and not from one of the vertebræ, the legs should be opened, and the knees induced outward, as the body swings forward. The body can then lower itself to a greater reach forward, and directly from the hips; whereas if the knees are placed together the thighs check the forward motion of the body, and compel it, if it remains rigid, to curtail its forward reach. (If the vertebræ bend when the swing from the hips is checked by the bent knees, the extra reach thus attained is weak, and of comparatively minor effect.)

Next (2) the shoulders have to be rigid. If they give way, and if the sockets stretch when the strain of the oar is felt, the effect of the stroke is evidently weakened. Now if the shoulders are stretched forward at the beginning of the stroke, the muscles which govern and support them have not the same power of rigidity that they possess when the shoulders are well drawn back at the outset. The oarsman gains a little in reach by extending his shoulders, but he loses in rigidity of muscle, and consequently in the force which he applies to the oar.

3. The legs and feet should combine to exercise pressure against the stretcher at the same moment, and contemporaneously with the application of the oar to the water. If they press too soon, the body is forced back while the oar is in air ; if too late, the hold of the water is weak, for want of legwork to support the body.

4. The oar should be held in the fingers, not in the fist ; the lower joints of the fingers should be nearly straight when the oar is held. The hold which a gymnast would take of a bar of the same thickness, if he were hanging from it, is, as regards the four fingers of the hand, the same which an oarsman should take of his oar. His thumb should come underneath, not over the handle.

5 and 10. Government of the depression or elevation of the blade, respectively, during stroke and recovery, is a matter of application of joints and of muscles. This much may be borne in mind, that the freer the wrist is, the better is the oar governed; and if an oar is clutched in the fist the flexibility of the wrist is thereby much crippled.

6. The arms should begin to bend when the body has just found the perpendicular. The upper arm should swing close to the ribs, worked by the shoulders, which should be thrown well back.

7. The ' biceps ' should not do the work; for, if it does, either the hands are elevated or the level of the blade altered—if the elbows keep close to the side; or else, if the level of the hands is preserved, then the elbows dog's-ear outwards. In either case the action is less free and less powerful than if the stroke is rowed home by the shoulder muscles.

8. The part of the hand which should touch the chest when the oar comes home is the root of the thumb, not the knuckles of the fingers. If the knuckles touch the chest *before* the oar

comes out of water, the blade is 'feathered under water'—a common fault, and a very insidious one. If, on the other hand, the oar comes out clean, but the first thing which touches the chest is the knuckle, then the last part of the stroke will have been rowed in *air*, and not in *the water*.

9. Dealing now with recovery. The hands should rebound from the chest like a billiard-ball from a cushion. If the hands delay at the chest they hamper the recovery of the body—e.g. let any man try to push a weight away from him with his hands and body combined. He will find that, if he pushes with straight arms, he is better able to apply the weight of his body to the forward push than if he keeps his arms bent.

Having shot his hands away, and having straightened his arms as quickly as he reasonably can, his body should follow; but his body should not meantime have been stationary. It should, like a pendulum, begin to swing for the return so soon as the stroke is over.

If hands 'hang,' the body tends to hang, as above shown; and if the body hangs, valuable time is lost, which can never be regained. As an illustration: suppose a man is rowing forty strokes in a minute, and that his body hangs the tenth of a second when it is back after each stroke, then at the end of a minute's rowing he will have sat still for four whole seconds! An oarsman who has no hang in his recovery can thus row a fast stroke with less exertion to himself than one who hangs. The latter, having wasted time between stroke and recovery, has to swing forward all the faster, when once he begins to recover, in order to perform the same number of strokes in the same time as he who does not hang. Now, although there is a greater effort required to row the blade square through the water than to recover it edgewise through the air, yet the latter has to be performed with muscles so much weaker for the task set to them that relatively they tire sooner under their lighter work than do the muscles which are in use for rowing the blade through the water. When an oarsman becomes 'pumped,' he feels the task of recovery even more severe than that of

rowing the stroke. Hence we see the importance of econo-
mising as far as possible the labour of those muscles which are
employed on the recovery, and of not adding to their toil by
waste of time which entails a subsequent extra exertion in
order to regain lost ground and lost time.

10. The manipulation of the blade through the water is
of great importance, otherwise the blade will not keep square,
and regular pressure against the water will not be attained.
Now, since the angle of the blade to the water has to be a
constant one, and since the plane on which the blade works
also is required to be uniform, till the moment for the feather
has arrived, it stands to reason that the wrists and arms, which
are changing their position relatively with the body while the
stroke progresses, must accommodate themselves to the pro-
gressive variations of force of body and arms, so as to maintain
the uniform angle and plane of the oar. Herein much atten·
tion must be paid to maxim 4 (*supra*). If an oar is held in the
fist instead of in the fingers, the play of the muscles of the
wrist is thereby crippled, and it becomes less easy to govern
the blade.

11. On a somewhat similar principle as the foregoing, the
arms, on the recovery, are changing their position and angle
with the body throughout the recovery ; but the blade has to
be kept at a normal level above the water all the time. It is
a common fault for the oarsman to fail to regulate the height
of the feather, and either to ' toss ' it at some point of the recovery
or else to lower it till the blade almost, if not quite, touches
the water. Nothing but practice, coupled with careful obser-
vations of the correct manner of holding an oar, can attain that
mechanical give-and-take play of muscles which produces an
even and clean feather from first to last of recovery.

12. We are still, for the sake of argument, dealing with
fixed-seat oarsmanship. Slides will be discussed subsequently.

In using the legs, on a fixed seat, for recovery, the toes
should feel the strap, which should cross them on or below the
knuckle-joint of the great toe. Each foot should feel and pull

up the strap easily and simultaneously, so as to preserve even position of body. The legs should open well, and allow the body to trick between them as it swings forward.

13. If the body swings true, the oar will keep home to the rowlock ; there should be just sufficient fraction of weight pressed against the button to keep it home ; if it is suffered to leave the rowlock, the oarsman tends to screw outwards over the gunwale, and also, when he recommences the stroke, he loses power by reason of his oar not meeting with its due support until the abstracted button has slipped back against the thowl.

14. The pace of recovery should be proportionate to the speed of stroke. If recovery is too slow, the oarsman becomes late in getting into the water for the next stroke ; if he is too quick, he has to wait when forward in order not to hurry the stroke.

15. Too many even high-class oars are prone to omit to keep the oar feathered for the full distance of the recovery. They have a tendency to turn it square too soon. By so doing they incur extra resistance of air and extra labour on the recovery, and they are more liable to foul a wave in rough water. The oar should be carried forwards edgewise, and only turned square just as full reach is attained. It should then be turned sharply, and not gradually.

16. The instant the body is full forward, and the oar set square, the hands should be raised sharply to the exact amount required in order to drop the blade into the water to the required depth, so as to cover it for the succeeding stroke.

17. The new stroke should be recommenced without delay, by throwing the body sharply back, with arms stiff and shoulders braced, the legs pressing firmly and evenly against the stretcher, so as to take the weight of the body off the seat, and to transfer its support to the handle of the oar and the stretcher, thus making the very most of weight and of extensor muscles in order to give force to the oar against the water.

N.B. Before closing these remarks, it should be added that,

with reference to detail 12, it is assumed that the oarsman, having progressed to the scientific stage, has so far mastered the use of the loins as to be able to combine their action with that of the toe against the strap in aiding the recovery of the body. If he tries to rely solely on the motor power for recovery from the strap, and the toes against it, he will not swing forward with a stiff back, and will be in a slouched position when he attains his reach forward.

The Rev. E. Warre, D.D., published in 1875 some brief remarks upon the stroke, in a treatise upon physical exercises and recreations. They are here reproduced by leave, the writer feeling that they can hardly be surpassed for brevity and lucidity of instruction upon the details of the stroke.

Notes on the Stroke.

The moment the oar touches the body, drop the hands smartly straight down, then turn the wrists sharply and at once shoot out the hands in a straight line to the front, inclining the body forward from the thigh-joints, and simultaneously bring up the slider, regulating the time by the swing forward of the body according to the stroke. Let the chest and stomach come well forward, the shoulders be kept back ; the inside arm be straightened, the inside wrist a little raised, the oar grasped in the hands, but not pressed upon more than is necessary to maintain the blade in its proper straight line as it goes back ; the head kept up, the eyes fixed on the outside shoulder of the man before you. As the body and arms come forward to their full extent, the wrists having been quickly turned, the hands must be raised sharply, and the blade of the oar brought to its full depth at once. At that moment, without the loss of a thousandth part of a second, the whole weight of the body must be thrown on to the oar and the stretcher, by the body springing back, so that the oar may catch hold of the water sharply, and be driven through it by a force unwavering and uniform. As soon as the oar has got hold of the water, and the beginning of the stroke has been effected as described, flatten the knees, and so, using the muscles of the legs, keep up the pressure of the beginning uniform through the backward motion of the body. Let the arms be rigid at the beginning of the stroke. When the body reaches the perpendicular, let the elbows be bent and dropped close past the sides to the rear

—the shoulders dropping and disclosing the chest to the front ; the back, if anything, curved inwards rather than outwards, but not strained in any way. The body, in fact, should assume a natural upright sitting posture, with the shoulders well thrown back. In this position the oar should come to it and the feather commence.

N.B.—It is important to remember that the body should never stop still. In its motion backwards and forwards it should imitate the pendulum of a clock. When it has ceased to go forward it has begun to go back.

There are, it will appear, from consideration of the directions, about twenty-seven distinct points, *articuli* as it were, of the stroke. No one should attempt to coach a crew without striving to obtain a practical insight into their nature and order of succession. Let a coxswain also remember that, in teaching men to row, his object should be to teach them to economise their *strength* by using properly their *weight*. Their weight is always in the boat along with them ; their strength, if misapplied, very soon evaporates

MARLOW.

CHAPTER IV.

COACHING.

FOR reasons which were set forth at the commencement of the chapter on scientific oarsmanship, the very best oar may fail to see his own faults. For this reason, in dealing with the methods for detecting and curing faults, it seems more to the point to write as addressing the tutor rather than the pupil. The latter will improve faster under any adequate verbal instruction than by perusing pages of bookwork upon the science of oarsmanship.

A coach may often know much more than he can himself perform ; he may be with his own muscles but a mediocre exponent of his art, and yet be towards the top of the tree as regards know-ledge and power of instruction.

A coach, like his pupils, often becomes too ' mechanical ' ; he sees some salient fault in his crew, he sets himself to eradicate it, and meanwhile it is possible that he may overlook some other great fault which is gradually developing itself among one or more of the men. And yet if he were asked to coach some other crew for the day, in which crew this same fault existed, he would be almost certain to note it, and to set to work to cure it.

For this reason, although it does not do to have too many mentors at work from day to day upon one crew, nevertheless the best of coaches may often gain a hint by taking some one else into his counsels for an hour or two, and by comparing notes.

We have said that it is not absolutely necessary that a good coach should always be in his own person a finished oarsman ; but if he is all the better, and for one very important reason. More than half the faults which oarsmen contract are to be traced in the first instance to some irregularity in the machinery with which they are working. That irregularity may be of two sorts, direct or indirect—direct when the boat, oar, rowlock, or stretcher is improperly constructed, so that an oarsman cannot work fairly and squarely ; indirect when some other oarsman is perpetrating some fault which puts others out of gear.

If a coach is a good oarsman on his own account (by 'good' we mean scientific rather than merely powerful), he can and should test and try or inspect the seat and oar of each man whom he coaches, especially if he finds a man painstaking and yet unable to cure some special fault. Boatbuilders are very careless in laying out work. A rowlock may be too high or too low ; it may rake one way or other, and so spoil the plane of the oar in the water. An oar may be hog-backed (or sprung), or too long in loom, or too short ; the straps of a stretcher may be fixed too high, so as to grip only the tip of a great-toe, and the place for the feet may not be straight to the seat, or a rowlock may be too narrow, and so may jam the oar when forward.

These are samples of mechanical discomfort which may spoil

F 2

any man's rowing, and against which it may be difficult for the most painstaking pupil to contend successfully. If the coach is good in practice as well as in theory of oarsmanship, he can materially simplify his own labours and those of his pupils by inspecting and trying the 'work' of each man in turn.

He should bear in mind that if a young oar is thrown out of shape in his early career by bad mechanical appliances, the faults of shape often cling to him unconsciously later on, even when he is at last furnished with proper tools. If a child were taught to walk with one boot an inch thicker in the sole than the other, the uneven gait thereby produced might cling to him long after he had been properly shod.

Young oarsmen in a club are too often relegated to practise in cast-off boats with cast-off oars, none of which are really fit for use. Nothing does more to spoil the standard of junior oarsmanship in a club than neglect of this nature.

Having ascertained that all his pupils are properly equipped and are properly seated, fair and square to stretchers suitable for the length of leg of each, the next care of a coach should be to endeavour to trace the *cause* of each fault which he may detect. This is more difficult than to see that a fault exists. At the same time, if the coach cannot trace the cause, it is hardly reasonable to expect the pupil to do so. So many varied causes may produce some one generic fault that it may drive a pupil from one error to another to tell him nothing more than that he is doing something wrong without at the same time explaining to him how and why he is at fault.

For instance, suppose a man gets late into the water. This lateness may arise from a variety of causes, for example :

1. He may be hanging with arms or body, or both, when he has finished the stroke, and so he may be late in starting to go forward ; or

2. He may be correct until he has attained his forward reach, and then, may be, he hangs before dropping his oar into the water ; or

3. He may begin to drop his oar at the right time, but to do

COACHING UNIVERSITY CREW

so in a ' clipping ' manner, not dropping the oar perpendicularly, but bringing it for some distance back in the air before it touches the water.

Now to tell a batch of men—all late, and all late from different causes as above—simply that each one is ' late ' does little good. The cure which will set the one right will only vary, or even exaggerate, the mischief with the others.

Hence a coach should, before he animadverts upon a fault, of which he observes the effect, watch carefully until he detects the exact cause, and then seek to eradicate it.

Another sample of cause and effect in faults may be cited for illustration. Suppose a man holds his oar in his fist instead of his fingers. The effect of this probably will be a want of accuracy in 'governing' the blade. He may thereby row too deep ; also only half feather ; also find a difficulty in bending his wrists laterally, and therefore fail to bring his elbows neatly past his sides. The consequent further effect may well be that he dog's-ears his elbows and gets a cramped finish. This will tend to make his hands come slow off the chest for the recovery ; and this again may tend to make his body heavy on the return swing.

Here is a pretty, and quite possible, concatenation of faults all bearing on each other in sequence, more or less. To be scolded for each such fault in turn may well bewilder a pupil. He will be taken aback at the plurality of defects which he is told to cure. But if the coach should spot the faulty grip, and cure that by some careful coaching in a tub-gig, he may in a few days find the other faults gradually melt away when the one primary awkwardness has been eradicated.

These two illustrations of faults and their origins by no means exhaust the category of errors which a coach has to detect and to cure.

Sundry other common faults may be specified, and the best mode of dealing with them by coaches supplied.

Over-reach of shoulders.—This weakens the catch of the water, and also tends to cripple the finish when the time comes to row the oar home. The shoulders should be braced well back. The extra inch or less of forward reach which the over-reach obtains is not worth having at the cost of weakening the catch and cramping the finish. The fault is best cured by gig-coaching and by demonstrating in person the correct and the wrong poses of the shoulders.

Meeting the oar.—This may come from more than one cause. If the legs leave off supporting the body before the oar-handle comes to the chest, the body droops to the strain from want of due support ; or if the oarsman tries to row the stroke home with arms only, ceasing the swing back ; and still more, if he tries to finish with biceps instead of by shoulder muscles, he is not unlikely to row deep, because he feels the strain of rowing the oar home in time, with less power behind it than that employed by others in the boat. He finds the oar come home easier if it is slightly deflected, and so unconsciously he begins to row rather deep (or light) at the finish, in order to get his oar home at the right instant.

Swing—faults of may be various. There may be a hang, or conversely a hurry, in the swing ; and, as shown above, the causes of these errors in swing may often be beneath the sur-face, and be connected with faulty hold of an oar, or a loose or badly placed strap, or a stretcher of wrong length, or from faulty finish of the preceding stroke. Lateness in swing may arise *per se*, and so may a ' bucket,' but as often as not they are linked with other faults, which have to be corrected at least simultaneously, and often antecedently.

Screwing either arises from mechanical fault at the moment or from former habits of rowing under difficulties occasionally with bad appliances. If a man sits square, with correct oar, rowlock, and stretcher, he does not naturally screw. If the habit seems to have grown upon him, a change of side will often do more than anything else to cure him. He is screwing because he is working his limbs and loins unevenly ; hence the obvious policy of making him change the side on which he puts the greater pressure.

Feather under water.—The fault is one of the most common, the remedy simple. The pupil should be shown the difference between turning the oar-handle before he drops it (as he is doing) and of dropping it before he turns it as he ought to do ; and it should be impressed upon him that the root of the thumb, and not his knuckles, should touch his chest when the oar comes home, and should be done *before*, and not after, he has dropped his handle to elevate the blade from the water.

If a crew feather much under water, it is a good plan to seat them in a row on a bench, and give each man a stick to handle as an oar. Then make them very slowly follow the actions of the coach, or a fugleman. 1. Hands up to the chest, root of thumb touching chest. 2. Drop the hands. 3. Turn them (as for feather) sharply. 4. Shoot them out, &c.

Having got them to perform each motion slowly and distinctly, then gradually accelerate the actions, until they are done as an entirety, with rapidity and *in proper consecution.* The desideratum is to ensure motion, No. 3 being performed in its due order, and *not before* No. 2.

Five minutes' drill of this sort daily before the rowing, for a week or two, will do much to cure feather under water even with hardened sinners.

Swing across the boat.—This is an insidious fault. The oarsman sits square, while his oar-handle moves in an arc of a circle. He has an instinctive tendency to endeavour to keep his chest square to his oar during the revolution of the latter. A No. 7 who has to take time from the stroke by the side of him is more prone than others to fall into this fault. The answer is, let the arms follow the action of the oar, and give way to it, and endeavour to keep the body straight and square. Keep the head well away from the oar, and its bias will tend to balance the swing.

Bending the arms prematurely is a common fault. Sometimes even high-class oars fall into it after a time. Tiros are prone to it, because they at first instinctively endeavour to work with arms rather than with body. Older oars adopt the trick in the endeavour to catch the water sharply at the beginning. Of course they lose power by doing so ; but they do not realise their loss, because, feeling a greater strain on their arms, they imagine that they must therefore be doing more work.

Lessons in a tub-gig are the best remedies for this fault.

' Paddling ' is an art which is of much importance in order to bring a crew to perfection, and at the same time it is too often done in a slovenly manner compared with hard rowing.

The writer admits that his own views as to how paddling should be performed differ somewhat from those of sundry good judges and successful coaches. Some of these are of opinion that paddling should consist of rowing gently, comparatively speaking, with less force and catch at the beginning of the stroke and with less reach than when rowing hard, but with blade always covered to regulation depth. When the order is given to ' Row,' then the full length should be attained and the full ' catch ' administered.

The writer's own version of paddling differs as follows. He is of opinion that the difference between paddling and rowing should be produced by working with a ' light '—only partially covered—blade when paddling. The effect of this is to ease the whole work of the stroke ; but at the same time the swing, reach, and catch should be just the same as if the blade were covered. Then, when the order comes to ' Row,' all the oarsman has to do is so to govern his blade that he now immerses the whole of it, and at the same time to increase his force to the amount necessary to row the stroke of the full blade throughout the required time.

Those good judges who differ from him as aforesaid base their objections to his method chiefly on the ground that it requires rather a higher standard of watermanship to enable an oarsman so to govern his blade that he can immerse it more or less at will, and yet maintain the same outward action of body, only with more or less force employed, according to amount of blade immersed.

The writer admits that his process does entail the acquisition of a somewhat higher standard of watermanship than the other system. But he is none the less of opinion that this admission should not be accepted as a ground for teaching the other style.

In the first place, it would seem to him better to try to raise the standard of watermanship to the system than to lower the system to meet the requirements of inferior skill. In the second, there seems to be even greater drawbacks to the system preferred by his friends who differ from him. For instance, under the alternative system the oarsman is taught to *alter* his style of body when paddling, but to maintain a uniform depth of blade. He is taught to apply less sharpness of catch, and less reach forward. To do so may tend to take the edge off catch, and to shorten reach, when hard rowing has to be recommenced.

It is plain that paddling cannot be all round the same as rowing ; there must be an alternative prescribed. The writer says, in effect : ' Alter only the blade (and so the amount of force required), and maintain outward action of body as before.'

Those who take the other view say, in effect : ' Maintain the same blade, and alter the action of the body.'

It must be admitted that those who differ from the writer are entitled, from their own performances as oarsmen and coaches, to every possible respect ; and the writer, while failing to agree with them, hesitates to assert that for that reason he must be right and they wrong.

One further reason in favour of paddling with a light blade may be added. When an oarsman is exhausted in a race, it is of supreme importance that, though unable to do his full share of work, he should not mar the swing and style of the rest. Now if such an oarsman, when nature fails him, can row lighter and so ease his toil, he can maintain swing and style with the rest. But if, on the other hand, he keeps his blade covered to the full, and seeks relief by rowing shorter and with less dash, he alters his style and tends to spoil the uniformity of the crew.

Watermanship is a quality which can hardly be coached ;

it may, therefore, seem out of place to deal with it under the head of coaching. Yet in one sense it pertains to coaching, because a mentor takes into calculation the capacity of an oarsman for exercising watermanship when making a selection of a crew.

Watermanship, as a technical term, may be said to consist in adapting oneself to circumstances and exigencies during the progress of a boat. A good waterman keeps time with facility, a bad one only after much painstaking—if at all. A good waterman adapts himself to every roll of the boat, sits tight to his seat, anticipates an incipient roll, and rights the craft so far as he can by altering his centre of gravity while yet plying his oar. A bad waterman is more or less helpless when a boat is off its keel, or when he encounters rough water. So long as the boat is level, he may be able to do even more work than the good waterman, but when the boat rolls he cannot help himself, still less can he right the ship and so help others to work, as can the good waterman.

Good watermen can jump into a racing boat and sit her offhand ; bad watermen will be unsteady in a keelless boat even after days of practice.

One or two good watermen are the making of a crew, especially when time is short for practice. They will raise the standard of rowing of all their colleagues, simply by keeping the balance of the boat. Sculling and pair-oar practice tend to teach watermanship. They induce a man to make use of his own back and beam in order to keep the boat on an even keel. We do not for this reason say that every tiro should be put to take lessons of watermanship in sculling-boats and light pairs : far from it. He will be likely in such craft to contract feather under water, and possibly screwing, in the efforts to obtain work on an even keel, after his own uneven action has conduced to rolling.

University men produce far fewer good watermen than the tideway clubs, and with good reason. The career on the river at Oxford or Cambridge is brief, and many a man goes out of residence while he is only on the threshold of aquatic science, both in practice and theory ; although, on account of his big frame, he may have been taught artificially to ply an oar, and with good effect, in a practised eight. Watermanship, like skating, cannot be acquired in a day, and the younger a man takes to aquatics the more likely is he to acquire it. There is hardly a bad waterman to be seen as a rule in a grand challenge crew of London R.C. or Thames R.C. men. Among University oars, watermanship is oftenest found in those who have rowed as schoolboys.

To coaches generally of the present and of future generations we may say that there is nothing like having a tenacity of purpose, and declining to listen to the shoals of excuses which pupils are inclined to propound in order to explain their shortcomings.

A SCRATCH EIGHT ('PEAL OF BELLS').

There should be no such thing as 'I can't' from a pupil. On the other hand, the coach should do his best to render the excuse untenable by ensuring proper 'work' at each thwart. A coach should not be carried away by every whisper of criticism by outsiders ; and yet at the same time he should realise as said at the beginning of this chapter, that, however able he may be, he has a natural tendency to become blind to faults which are being daily perpetrated under his nose—the more so if he has been specially of late devoting his attention to some different class of fault in his men. For this reason he should not decline to listen to suggestions from mentors who otherwise may be his inferiors in the art, and to give them all attention before he decides how to deal with them.

In dealing with the selection of men for a crew he has to consider various points. He has to calculate for what seats such and such an oarsman will be available, as regards weight and capacity generally for the seat. He has to bear in mind the date of the race for which he is preparing his men ; many an oarsman may be admittedly unfit for a seat if the race were rowed to-morrow, and yet he may show promise of being fit for it six months hence. A may be better than B to-day ; but A may be an old stager hardened in certain faults, and of whom no hope can now be entertained that he will suddenly reform. B may be as green as a gooseberry, and yet the recollection of what he was two or three weeks ago, compared to what he is now, may warrant the assumption that by the day of the race, some time hence, B will have become the better man of the two.

A coach who takes a crew in hand halfway through their preparation should be prepared to hear evidence as to what was the standard of merit of certain men some time back, compared with their present form ; otherwise he may delude himself as to the relative merits and prospects of the material which he has to mould into shape.

Just as orators are said to learn at the expense of their audience, so coaches do undoubtedly learn much at the expense of the crews which they manage. Many a coach will agree that he has often felt in later years that, if he had his time over again with this or that oarsman or crew, he would now form a different judgment from what he formerly did.

In concluding this chapter we cannot do better than extract from Dr. Warre's treatise on Athletics certain aphorisms for the benefit of coaches, which he has tersely compiled under the head of 'Notes on Coaching' :

NOTES ON COACHING.

In teaching a crew you have to deal with—

> A. Crew collectively.
> B. Crew individually.

A. *Collective.*

1. *Time.* —*a.* Oars in and out together. *b.* Feather, same height ; keep it down. *c.* Stroke, same depth ; cover the blades, but not above the blue.

2. *Swing.*—*a.* Bodies forward and back together. *b.* Sliders together. *c.* Eyes in the boat.

3. *Work.*—*a.* Beginning—together, sharp, hard. *b.* Turns of the wrist—on and off of the feather, sharp, but not too soon. *c.* Rise of the hands—sharp, just before stroke begins. *d.* Drop of the hands—sharp, just after it ends.

General Exhortations.—' Time !' ' Beginning !' 'Smite !' 'Keep it long !' and the like—to be given at the right moment, not used as mere parrot cries.

B. *Individual.*

1. Faults of position.
2 Faults of movement.

N.B.—These concern body, hands, arms, legs, and sometimes head and neck.

1. Point out when you easy, or when you come in, or best of all, in a gig. Show as well as say what is wrong and what is right.

N.B.—Mind you are right. *Decipit exemplar vitiis imitabile.*

2. To be pointed out during the row and corrected. Apply the principles taught in ' E. W.'s ' paper on the stroke, beginning with bow and working to stroke, interposing exhortations (A) at the proper time.

N.B.—Never hammer at any one individual. If one or two

admonitions don't bring him right, wait a bit and then try again. For coaching purposes, not too fast a stroke and not too slow. About thirty per minute is right. Before you start, see that your men have got their stretchers right and are sitting straight to their work.

He teaches best who, while he is teaching, remembers that he has much to learn.

MEDMENHAM ABBEY.

CHAPTER V.

THE CAPTAIN.

THE captain of a boat club is the most important member of it, from a practical point of view. In some clubs, as with the Universities, he is nominally as well as practically supreme—is president as well as captain. In clubs on the Thames tideway, such as Leander, London, Thames, and as in the Kingston club higher up river, there is a president elected as the titular head of the club, but that functionary is chiefly ornamental, to add dignity to the society, and to instil sobriety into its councils. Such a president is usually some old oarsman of renown, long ago retired from active service, one whose name carries weight and influence, but who has neither time nor inclination to interfere with the oarsmanship of the members.

It is the captain who can make or mar a club. He is the general officer in command of the forces, while the president (when such an extra official exists) is more of a field-marshal-enjoying *otium cum dignitate* at home. The qualifications upon which a captain is, or should be, selected by his club are, in the first place, personal merit as an oarsman and knowledge of his craft ; in the second, a due seniority, so that he may have proper influence, both socially and in an aquatic sense, over those whom he is appointed to command ; thirdly, tact and common sense.

Deficiency in either one of these desiderata is often fatal to a captain's chances of success in his office. If he is a bad oar, and lacking in practical knowledge compared with those under him, it will little avail him to be a person of senior standing in the crews and of social position. He will fail to carry with him that prestige and confidence which should be the attribute of all commanders who expect to lead men to victory. If, on the other hand, he is a good oar, even the best of his club, and yet is a fledgling in age, he will find it difficult to maintain his command over sundry jealous seniors, and will, more than all, require the third requisite of tact, which is less liable to be found in a mere lad than in a man of the world who has well passed his majority.

A captain should be self-reliant without being obstinate ; he should be good-tempered but not facile ; he should be firm but not tyrannical, energetic but not a busybody. A captain has usually a host of counsellors, and he too well realises the fallacy of the adage that in a multitude of counsels there is wisdom. If he were to pay attention to all the advice offered to him he would never be able to have a mind of his own. And yet he will do well not to run to the opposite extreme, nor to decline to listen to anyone who ventures to offer him a suggestion. If he is captain of a University crew he will find his bed anything but one of roses. The eyes of the sporting world are upon him from the commencement of Lent term. Daily he will receive letters from individuals of whom he has never before heard, offering him advice and criticising his line of action. Many of his correspondents will be anonymous, and too many of them splenetic. He must not be surprised to see himself anonymously attacked in print for the selections which he is making for a crew to represent his club. He will be accused of partiality if he selects some man of his own college in preference to an out-college man. He will find himself abused if he decides to take an important oar in his own hands, such as stroke or No. 7. He will be inundated with speculative appeals from vendors of commodities who hope for gratuitous advertisement of their wares. One of them will send him a nondescript garment, and will assure him that if he will allow his crew to row in dress of that build he and they shall be robed gratis in it, and be assured of victory. Quack medicines will be proffered him, and photographers will pester him and his crew daily with requests to stand for an hour in a nor'-easter for their portraits.

Within the circle of his own club matters will not always run smoothly. Sometimes he finds himself in the unpleasant position of having, after due consideration and counsel, to dispense with the services of some old brother blue who has fallen off from his quondam form, or who, though good enough among an inferior crew of a preceding year, is not up to par compared with new oarsmen of merit who have come to the fore since the last spring.

Nevertheless, with all these drawbacks to office, a University president or captain of a college has perhaps an easier task in managing his crew than a captain of an elective club on the Thames that is preparing for Henley or some similar contest. In college life the brevity of career gives a special standing and prestige to seniority, and the president of a U.B.C. is not likely to be a very junior man. *Esprit de corps* does much to keep College and University crews together, and there is less likelihood of mutiny in such clubs than in those which are purely elective, and which compete with each other for securing the best oarsmen of the day. A malcontent college oar cannot

G

throw himself, even if he will, into the arms of another college ; still less can a dissatisfied candidate for one shade of blue ' rat ' and desert to the enemy. But in tideway and other clubs on the Thames there is such a brisk competition for good oarsmen that a man who finds he is likely to lose his chance of selection in one club has opportunities for obtaining distinction under some rival flag, and very possibly he already belongs to more than one such club, and can put his services up to auction as it were. If he finds that he will be relegated to some comparatively unimportant seat in the club which has claims of longest standing upon him, he may, if he is unpatriotic and cantankerous, look out in some other club for a berth of greater distinction. Such men are not uncommon, and are thorns in the side of any captain. They tax his sixth sense of tact more than anything : if he gives way to them, he risks spoiling the arrangement of his crew ; if he stands firm, he may send a valuable man over to the enemy. On the other hand, it must be said that many rival captains would decline to accept the services of a deserter of this sort, and would feel that if such an one would not be true to one flag, he could not be safely trusted for long to row under another.

Beside this sort of malcontent, whose ambition is to be *aut Cæsar aut nullus,* the captain has to contend with obstructives of other classes. There is the habitual grumbler, who is never happy unless he has a grievance. To-day he cannot row properly because the boat is always down on his oar. Yesterday he was complaining that his rowlock was too high, and he had leave to lower it accordingly. He may not be really bad-tempered, nor mutinous ; even his growls have a *triste bonhomie* about them ; in one sense he is a sort of acquisition to the social element of the crew, for his grumblings make him a butt for jokes and rallies. But when this system of grumbling goes beyond a certain point it sorely tries a captain's patience.

Another sort of incubus is the old hand, who has never risen beyond mediocrity, who has plenty of faults, but who can be relied upon for a certain amount of honest work, and who fills a place better than some very backward oarsman. The old stager is case-hardened in his crimes; they are second nature to him, and, in spite of coaching, still he maunders on in the same old style, with the same set faults. He has a time-honoured screw, a dog's-eared elbow, and yet he possesses what many of the better-finished oarsmen do not—watermanship—

' PROSE.

and can keep on at work in a rolling boat when many neater oarsmen are all abroad if the ship gets off her even keel. Not to coach his too obvious faults may make visitors fancy that the old screw is a pattern fugleman to be copied for style; and yet to spend objurgation on one so stiff-necked is disheartening waste of wind.

Discipline is all-important in a crew, and it usually requires
tact to maintain it. If the captain is a triton among minnows,
he can better afford to hector ; but, as a rule, he runs the risk
of mutiny, or at least of producing sulkiness, if he treats his
crew as if they were galley-slaves. If he is in the boat, working
with them, sharing their toils and privations, his task becomes
easier on this score ; for the crew realise that, however irksome
the orders for the day may be, they are felt just as much by the
commander as by the rank and file. If a member of the crew
openly defies a captain, the bad example is too dangerous to be
tolerated. To expel a mutineer may ruin the chance of victory
for an impending race, but it will be best for the club in the
long run, and will be likely to save many a defeat.

The writer has in mind two such incidents which occurred
to himself at different times while officiating as captain of a
club. In each case the mutineer was the stroke, and the *spes
gregis.* He resented being told to row slower, or faster, as
the case might be, and presently flatly declined to be dictated
to. In each case the boat was instantly ordered ashore, and
the grumbler was asked to step out. His place was filled by
some emergency man, he was left ashore, and was told at the
end of the day that the captain regretted to be obliged to
dispense with his services. In each case the rest of the crew
buttonholed their late stroke, and put the screw upon him to
beg pardon, and with success. The one stroke was reinstated
at his old post ; the other was also put back to the boat, but
at No. 6. In both cases mutiny was stamped out once and for
all. Of these two men it may be said that one eventually rose
to be stroke of a winning University eight, and the other of a
winning Grand Challenge crew. In each case they were great
personal friends of the captain, and there was no interruption
of social relations through the peremptory line of conduct
pursued. Many old fellow-oarsmen of the writer will doubtless
recognise these incidents, in which names are naturally omitted.

Punctuality is an important detail of discipline in a crew.
It is a good system to order a fine to be levied by the secretary

EMBARKING

upon anyone who exceeds a certain limit of grace from the hour fixed for practice. It is better that the secretary or treasurer should levy it than the captain, because thereby the captain in this detail places himself under the subordinate officer's jurisdiction, and is himself fined if he is late. He can do this without loss of dignity, and in fact adds to his influence by submitting as a matter of course to the general regulation. It spoils the discipline of a crew if a captain takes French leave for himself, and keeps his men dancing attendance upon him, and yet rates them when one of them similarly delays the practice.

In making up a crew a captain is often in an invidious position. It is said by cricketers that the danger of having a leading bowler for captain of an eleven is that he is often judicially blind as to the right moment for taking himself off. Similarly, for a stroke to be captain, or rather for a likely candidate for strokeship to be captain, may be productive of misunderstandings and mischief to the crew. In old days stroke and captain were synonyms. The 'stroke' was elected by the club. He was supposed to be the best all-round oar, and as such to be capable of setting the best stroke to the crew. His office attached itself to his seat. In sundry old college records of rowing we find the expression 'a meeting of strokes,' where. in modern times we should speak of a 'captains' meeting.' The U.B.C.'s departed from this tradition more than forty years ago. Since then captains have been found at all thwarts, even including that of the coxswain. Most college clubs followed the U.B.C. principle forthwith, but not all so. We can recall an incident to the contrary. At Queen's College, Oxon, there remained a written rule that stroke should be captain as late as about 1862. In or about that year a Mr. Godfrey was rowing stroke of the Queen's eight in the bumping races, and was *ex-officio* captain. He had previously stroked the Queen's torpid, and with good success. One night during the summer races Queen's got bumped (or failed to effect a bump). Some of the crew laid the blame of their failure upon their stroke, for having rowed, as they alleged, too rapid a stroke. A college meeting had to be called, and a new stroke to be 'elected,' before a change could be made in the order of the boat for the next night's race ! Mr. Godfrey was asked to resign his seat as stroke, which of course he did, and took the seat of No. 6. His successor was thus elected captain. Much sympathy for Mr. Godfrey's unfortunate statutory deposition from command was openly ex-' pressed by out-college oarsmen, and the result was before long that a change was made in the code of the Queen's College Boat Club, and its adaptation to that of the more advanced rules which found favour with the majority of the U.B.C.

However, just as a bowler at cricket is prone to be blind to his own weaknesses, and to be imbued with ambition to do too much with his own hands at moments when they have lost their cunning, so when a captain has claims, not superlative, to the after-thwart, there is always some danger lest his eager- ness to do all he can may blind him as to the best choice for that seat. In some cases, as with (of late) Messrs. West and Pitman, respectively strokes and presidents of their U.B.C'.s, or in the cases of such oarsmen as Messrs. W. Hoare, W. R. Griffiths, M. Brown, J. H. D. Goldie, R. Lesley, H. Rhodes, &c., all of whom had won their spurs as first-class strokes before they were elected to the presidency, the coincidence of stroke and captain has done no harm and has found the best man in the right place. Nevertheless, it is advisable to caution all captains on this score, and to suggest to them that, when they find themselves sharing a candidature for an important seat, they will do well to ask the advice of some impartial mentor, and abide by it.

At Eton the traditional law of identity of stroke and cap- tain held good, with natural Etonian conservatism, until a date even later than that of the previously related anecdote of Queen's College. So far as we can recollect, the first instance in which an Eton eight was not stroked by its captain was in 1864. In that year Mr. (now Colonel) Seymour Corkran was captain of Eton. He was a sort of pocket Hercules, of great breadth and weight, scaling close upon 13 st. Eton crews were, not then so heavy as in these days, and the wondrous old Eton 'Mat-Taylor' boat, which then was still in her prime, would not satisfactorily carry so heavy a weight in the stern.. Mr. Corkran placed himself at No. 7, and installed a light-weight, Mr. Mossop, at stroke. In this year Eton won the Ladies' Plate for the first time, University College leaving them to walk over for it, after University had had a severe losing race earlier in the day against the Kingston Rowing Club for the final heat of the Grand Challenge.

The duties of a captain are not confined to the mere selection of his racing crew for the moment, nor to the preservation of order and *régime* in the matter of training. If he is to do his duty by the club, he should be on duty pretty well all through the season. He should keep his eyes open to note any raw oarsman who shows signs of talent, and mark him to be tried and coached into form hereafter. A captain of an elective club can do much to maintain the credit of his flag by looking up suitable recruits who have not yet joined a leading club, and by inducing them to put themselves under his care, and to submit themselves for election. One of the best oars that ever rowed at Henley, who became an amateur champion (Mr. W. Long), was secured for the L.R.C. by the prompt energy of the then captain of that club, on the occasion of Mr. Long's *début* at Henley Regatta. On that occasion he came from Ipswich, to row for the pairs, with a partner much inferior to himself. They did not win, but Mr. Long's hitherto unknown merits were at once seen, and his enlistment in the L.R.C. ranks had very much to do with the long series of victories, especially in Stewards' Cup and other four-oar races, which for some seasons afterwards attended the fortunes of the L.R.C.

Per contra, to show how a good oarsman may be going begging, in 1867 Mr. F. Gulston was not asked to row either by London or Kingston; he went to Paris to row in a pair-oar, and still the L.R.C. overlooked him, though he was a member

of their club, and though the L.R.C. were entered for the
international regatta on the Seine. Mr. Gulston was nearly,
probably quite, as good an oarsman then as in his very best
days ; but his light, though not hid under a bushel, was openly
disregarded by his club. Through the minor regattas of the
summer he took refuge with an ' Oscillators ' crew, and shoved
three inferior men behind along at such a pace that next season
it was impossible to ignore him. He became stroke of the
L.R.C. Grand Challenge crew in 1868, and won the prize easily.

A president of a U.B.C. has not the responsibility of
looking after recruits for his club. He has only to see
that he does not overlook the merits of those who are in it,
among the hundreds of young oarsmen who come out each
season in the torpids, lower divisions, and college eights. The
' trial eights ' of the winter term have to be made up by him.
Each captain of a college crew is requested to send in the
names of ten or more candidates for these trials ; but it is not
safe for a president to rely entirely upon the lists so furnished
to him. He is morally bound to give a fair trial to all the
candidates who are thus officially submitted to his notice ; but
he ought also on his own account to have taken stock during
the summer races of the promising men of each college crew.
The opinions of college captains as to who are likely to make
the best candidates for University rowing must not always be
relied upon. It has often happened that better men have been
omitted than those whose names have been sent in to be tried.

We have known a watchful president ask of a college captain
to this effect :

' What has become of the man who rowed No. 6 in your
torpid ? '

' He played cricket all the summer, and did not row in the
summer eights.'

' You have not sent in his name ? '.

' No, I thought him too backward ; he has never been in a
light boat in his life, and he only began to row last October
when he came up as a freshman.'

'Can I see him to-morrow and try him?' says the president; and eventually this cricketer of the torpids is hammered into shape, and subsequently wears a double blue.

The above is no exaggerated picture of what has been known to result from careful supervision by a president of the college rowing which comes under his notice. In 1862 Messrs. Jacobson and Wynne rowed in the Oxford crew; the writer believes, from the best of his recollection, that neither of these gentlemen was named in the two primary picked choices which had been sent in to represent Christ Church in the trial eights. But the then president, Mr. George Morrison, had observed them when they were rowing for their college earlier in the season, and took note of them as two strong men, who might be converted by coaching into University oars; and he proved to be correct.

A captain of a large club usually has his hands so full of duties connected with representative or picked crews that he can hardly be expected to find much time for systematically coaching juniors. This preliminary work he is obliged to depute to subordinates. In a London club there is usually a sort of subaltern, or sometimes an ex-captain, who undertakes to instruct junior crews or those who are competing for the Thames Cup at Henley. In a college club it is a common practice to elect a 'captain of torpid,' who is usually some one who has rowed in the college eight, but who has not the physique to compete for a seat in the University crew. At Cambridge a large college club puts on so many crews for the bumping races that it is necessary to find separate coaches for nearly each boat. Even when this occurs, a really energetic captain will endeavour to spare a day now and then to supervise the efforts of his subalterns. At Oxford it is, or used to be, customary for the five committee men of the O.U.B.C. to make a point of coaching in turn, when asked, those college eights which had no 'blue,' nor old oarsmen of experience, to instruct them. All these arrangements tend to raise the standard of rowing in various colleges, and so in the U.B.C. generally.

The time comes when a captain retires from office, but it is quite possible that he may find time to row again for his flag after he has laid down his bâton. In his new *rôle* he can do, in another line, quite as much to preserve discipline as when he held the office in his own person. He should be the foremost to set an example of subordination and of strict observance of regulations and of training. Nothing does more to strengthen the hands of a new captain than the spectacle of his late chief serving loyally under him; and, on the other hand, nothing does more to weaken the new ruler's authority than the example of an ex-captain self-sufficient and too proud to acknowledge the sway of his successor. The ex-captain does not lose caste by strict subordination ; unless his successor is a man devoid of tact, he will freely take his predecessor into his counsels ; and, on the other hand, the predecessor should be careful not to support anarchy by interfering until he is asked to advise. We have known the entire *morale* of a college crew upset because the ex-captain, a University oar, has taken French leave and ordered an extra half-glass of beer for himself (beyond the statutory allowance), without observing the formal etiquette of first asking the leave of his successor, whose standing was only that of college-eight oarsmanship. Such a proceeding at once made it more difficult than ever for the new captain to preserve discipline and strict attention to training orders among the thirsty souls with whom he had to deal. In some college boat clubs there is a rule that the captain must be resident in college. The object of this is to prevent the archives and trophies of the boat club, which are in custody of the captain, from passing outside the college gates, and so possibly getting astray in lodgings. Such a rule as this naturally prevents many a senior oarsman from holding the office (for after a certain standing undergraduates migrate from college walls to lodgings). In such cases those members of the college club who belong to the University eight constantly find themselves under the formal authority of one who does not pretend to equal their skill or knowledge of aquatics. As a rule these retired generals work harmoniously with their inferior but commanding in-college oarsman ; but cases do occur where want of tact on the part of one or both parties has a very mischievous effect, and causes the club to take a lower place on the race-charts than it might have attained had all parties co-operated loyally for the support of the flag.

The position of captain of a club, whether rowing, cricket, or athletics, is a very useful school for any young man, if he uses his opportunity aright. It teaches him to be self-reliant ; to avoid vacillation on the one hand and obstinacy on the other ; to exercise tact and forbearance, and to set a good example on his own part of observance of standing orders. All these lessons serve him well in after-life. No man is the worse, when fighting the battle of the world, for having learnt both how to obey orders implicitly and also how to govern others with firmness and tact. He will look back to many a decision which he came to, and will perhaps be able to console himself by reflecting that at the time he acted according to the best of his lights ; but none the less he will perceive that he was then in error, and that as he sees more of aquatics, or of any other branch of sport, he finds that he is only beginning to learn the best of it when the time comes for him to take his departure from the scene of actual conflict. If he will apply the analogy to his career in life, whatever that may be, he will prosper therein all the more by reason of the practical lessons which he gained when his arena was purely athletic.

BISHAM COURT REACH.

CHAPTER VI.

THE COXSWAIN AND STEERING.

THE 'cock-swain' wins his place chiefly on account of his weight, provided that he can show a reasonable amount of nerve and skill of hand. A coxswain is seldom a very practical oarsman, although there have been special exceptions to this rule, e.g. in the case of T. H. Marshall, of Exeter, Arthur Shadwell, of Oriel, and a few others. But if he has been any length of time at his trade he very soon picks up a very considerable theoretical knowledge of what rowing should be, and is able to do very signal service in the matter of instructing the men whom he pilots. When a youth begins to handle the rudder-lines there is often some considerable difficulty in inducing him to open his mouth to give orders of any sort. Even such biddings as to tell one side of oars to hold her, or another to row or to back-water, come at first falteringly from his lips. It is but natural that he should feel his own physical inferiority to the men whom he is for the moment required to order about so peremptorily, and diffidence at first tends to make him dumb. But he soon picks up his *rôle* when he listens to the audacious orders and objurgations of rival pilots, and he is pleased to find that the qualities of what he might modestly consider to be impudence and arrogance are the very things which are most required of him, and for the display of which he earns commendation.

Having once found his tongue, he soon learns to use it. When there is a coach in attendance upon the crew, the pilot is not called upon to animadvert on any failings of oarsmen ; but when the coach is absent the coxswain is bound to say something, and, if he has his wits about him, he soon picks up enough to make his remarks more or less to the purpose. The easiest detail on which he offers an opinion is that of time of oars. At first he feels guilty of ' check ' in singing out to some oarsmen of good standing that he is out of time. He feels as if he should hardly be surprised at a retort not to attempt to teach his grandmother ; but, on the contrary, the admonition is meekly accepted, and the pilot begins at once to gain confidence in himself. Daily he picks up more and more theoretical knowledge ; he notes what a coach may say of this or that man's faults, and he soon begins to see when certain admonitions are required. ·At least he can play the parrot, and can echo the coach's remarks when the mentor is absent, and before long he will have picked up enough to be able to discern when such a reproof is relevant and when it is not. In his spare time he often paddles a boat about on his own account, and this practice materially assists him in understanding the doctrines which he has to preach. As a rule, coxswains row in very good form, when they row at all ; and before their career closes many of them, though they have never rowed in a race, can teach much more of the science of oarsmanship than many a winning oar of a University race or of a Grand Challenge Cup contest.

A coxswain is the lightest item in the crew, but unless he sits properly he can do much harm in disturbing the balance of a light boat. He should sit with a straight back; if he slouches, he has not the necessary play of the loins to adapt himself to a roll of the boat. He should incline just a trifle forward; the spring of the boat at each stroke will swing him forward slightly, and he will recoil to an equal extent on the recovery. His legs should be crossed under him, like a tailor on a shop-board, with the outside of each instep resting on the floor of the boat. He should hold his rudder-lines just tight enough to feel the rudder. If he hangs too much weight upon them, he may jam the tiller upon the pin on which it revolves, so that, when the rudder has been put on and then taken off, the helm does not instantly swing back to the exact *status quo ante*; and in that case the calculation as to course may be disturbed, and a counter pull from the other line become necessary, in order to rectify the course.

A coxswain will do best to rest his hand lightly on either gunwale, just opposite to his hips. He should give the lines a turn round his palms, to steady the hold on them. Many coxswains tie a loop at the required distance, and slip the thumb through it; but such a loop should not be knotted too tight, for when rudder-lines get wet they shrink; so that a loop which was properly adjusted when the line was dry will be too far behind in event of the strings becoming soaked.

When a coxswain desires to set a crew in motion, the usual formula is to tell the men to 'get forward,' then to ask if they are 'ready,' and then to say 'go,' 'row,' or 'paddle,' as the case may be. When he wishes to stop the rowing, without otherwise to check the pace of the boat, the freshwater formula is 'easy all,' at which command the oars are laid flat on the water. In the navy the equivalent term is 'way enough.' 'Easy all' should be commanded at the beginning, or at latest at the middle, of a stroke, otherwise it is difficult for the men to stop all together and to avoid a half-commencement of the next stroke.

If a boat has to be suddenly checked and her way stopped, the order is 'Hold her all.' The blades are then slightly inclined towards the bow of the boat, causing them to bury in the water, and at the same time not to present a square surface to back-water. The handle of the oar should then be elevated, and more and more so as the decreasing way enables each oarsman to offer more surface resistance to the water. So soon as the way of the boat has been sufficiently checked, she can be backed or turned, according to what may be necessary in the situation.

In turning a long racing-boat care should be taken to do so gently, otherwise she may be strained. If there is plenty of room, she can be turned by one side of oars 'holding' her, while bow, and afterwards No. 3 also, paddle her gently round. If there is not room for a wide turn, then stroke and No. 6 should back water gently, against bow, &c. paddling.

A coxswain, when he first begins his trade, is pleased to find how obedient his craft is to the touch of his hand; he pulls one string and her head turns that way; he takes a tug at the other line, and she reverses her direction. The ease with which he can by main force bring her, somehow or other, to the side of the river on which he desires to be tends at first to make him overlook how much extra distance he unnecessarily covers by rough-and-ready hauling at the lines. 'Argonaut'[1] very lucidly uses the expression 'a boat should be *coaxed* by its rudder,' a maxim which all pilots will do well to make a cardinal point in their creed.

When a boat is once pointing in a required direction, and her true course is for the moment a straight one, the pilot should note some landmark, and endeavour to regulate his bows by aid of it, keeping the mark dead ahead, or so much to the right or to the left as occasion may require. In so doing he should feel his lines, and, so to speak, 'balance' his bows on his *point d'appui*. His action should be somewhat analogous to what the play of his hand would be if he were attempting to

[1] Mr. E. D. Brickwood.

carry a stick end upwards on the tip of his finger. He would quickly but gently anticipate the declination denoted by each wavering motion of the stick, checking each such deviation the moment it is felt. In like manner when steering he should, as it were, 'hold' his bows on to his steering point, regulating his boat by gentle and timely touches; if he allows a wide deviation to occur, before he begins to correct his course, he has then a wide *détour* to make before he can regain his lost position. All this means waste of distance and of rowing energy on the part of the crew.

In steering by a distant landmark the coxswain must bear in mind that the parallax of the distant mark increases as he nears it ; so that what may point a true course to him, for all intents and purposes, when it is half a mile away, may lead him too much to one side or other if he clings to it too long without observing its altered bearing upon his desired direction.

When a coxswain has steered a course more than once he begins to know his landmarks and their bearing upon each part of the course. There is less strain upon his mind, and he becomes able to observe greater accuracy. There is nothing like having the 'eye well in' for any scene of action. A man plays relatively better upon a billiard-table or lawn-tennis ground to which he is well accustomed than on one to which he is a stranger ; and a jockey rides a horse all the better for having crossed him before the day of a race. However good a coxswain may be, he will steer a course more accurately, on the average, in proportion as he knows it more or less mechanically.

There is also a good deal in knowing the boat which has to be steered. No two ships steer exactly alike. Some come round more easily than others ; some fetch up into the wind more freely than others. In modern times it has been a common practice for builders to affix a movable 'fin' of metal to the bottom of a racing eight or four, under the after canvas, which fin can be taken out or fixed in at option. In a cross wind this helps to steady the track of a boat ; but, unless wind is strong and is abeam for a good moiety of the distance, the draw of the water all the way occasioned by the fin costs more than the extra drag of rudder which it obviates for just one part of the course.

In steering round a corner a coxswain should bear in mind that he must not expect to see his boat pointing in the direction to which he desires to make. His boat is a tangent to a curve, the curve being the shore. His bows will be pointing to the shore which he is avoiding. It is the position of his midship to the shore which he is rounding that he should especially note. The boat should be brought round as gradually as the severity of the wave will allow. If the curve is very sharp, like the corners of the 'Gut' at Oxford, or 'Grassy' or Ditton corners at Cambridge, the inside oars should be told to row light for a stroke or two. It will ease their labour, and also that of the oars on the other side.

When there is a stiff beam wind the bows of a racing craft tend to bear up into the wind's eye. The vessel is making leeway all the time ; therefore if the coxswain on such an occasion steers by a landmark which would guide him were the water calm, he will before long find himself much to leeward of where he should be. In order to maintain his desired course he should humour his boat, and allow her bow to hold up somewhat into the wind (to windward of the landmark which otherwise would be guiding him). To what extent he should do so he must judge for himself, according to circumstances and to his own knowledge of the leeward propensities of his boat. To lay down a hard-and-fast rule on this point would be as much out of place as to attempt to frame a scale of allowance which a Wimbledon rifleman ought to make for mirage or cross-wind, when taking aim at a distant bull's-eye.

Generally speaking a coxswain should hug the shore when going against tide or stream, and should keep in mid-stream when going with it. (Mid-stream does not necessarily imply mid-river.) Over the Henley course, until 1886, a coxwain on the Berks side used to make for the shelter of the bank below Poplar Point, where the stream ran with less force. The altera-

H

tion (for good) of the Henley course which was inaugurated in 1886 has put an end to this, and both racing crews now take a mid-stream course. The course is to all intents and purposes straight, and yet it will not do to keep the bows fixed on one point from start to finish. There is just a fraction of curve to the left in it, but so slight that one finger's touch of a line will deflect a boat to the full extent required. The church tower offers a landmark by which all pilots can steer, keeping it more or less to the right hand of the bows, and allowing for the increase of its parallax as the boat nears her goal.

Over the Putney water the best course has changed considerably during the writer's personal recollections. Twenty years ago the point entering to Horse Reach, and opposite to Chiswick Church, could be taken close. The Conservancy dredged the bed of the river, and also filled up a bight on the Surrey shore. This transferred the channel and the strongest current to the Middlesex side. In 1866 a head wind (against flood tide) off Chiswick raised the higher surf near to the tow-path, showing that the main stream flowed there. It now runs much nearer to the Eyot.

Also the removal of the centre arch of old Putney Bridge drew the main flood tide more into mid-river than of old ; and since then the new bridge has been built and the old one altogether removed, still further affecting the current in the same direction. There is a noticeable tendency in the present day, on the part of all pilots, whether in sculling matches or in eight-oar races, to take Craven Point too wide and to bear off into the bay opposite, on the Surrey shore. The course should be kept rather more mid-stream than of old, up to Craven steps, but the point should be taken reasonably close when rounding ; there should not be, as has often been seen during the last six years, room for a couple more boats to race between the one on the Fulham side and the Craven bank.

In old days, when Craven Point used to be taken close, and when the set of the tide lay nearer to it than now, there ensued an important piece of pilotage called 'making the shoot.' It consisted in gradually sloping across the river, so as to take the Soapworks Point at a tangent, and thence to make for the Surrey arch of Hammersmith Bridge. This 'shoot' is now out of place : firstly, because the tide up the first reach from the start of itself now tends to bring the boat more into mid-river off the Grass Wharf and Walden's Wharf; secondly, because the Soapworks Point should now be taken *wide*, and not close. The reason for this latter injunction is that the races of to-day, by agreement, go through the centre arch of Hammersmith Bridge. Now the flood tide does not run through the bridge at right angles to the span. It is working hard across to the Surrey shore. Therefore, if a boat hugs Soapworks Point as of old, and as if the course lay through the shore arch, that boat will have to come out, *across* tide, at an angle of about 25° to the set of the tide, in order to fetch the outer arch and to clear the buttress and the steamboat pier. Year after year the same blunder is seen. Pilots, of sculling boats and of eight-oars alike, wander away to the Surrey bay off Craven ; then they hug the shore till they reach the Soapworks foot-bridge, and then they have to cross half the tide on their right before they can safely point for the outer arch of the Suspension Bridge. A pilot should endeavour to keep in mid-river off Rosebank and the Crab Tree, and after passing the latter point he will, while pointing his bows well to the right of the arch which he intends to pass under, find the river move to the left under him, until, with little or no use of rudder, he finds himself in front of his required arch just as he reaches the bridge.

After passing the bridge a boat should keep straight on for another two hundred yards, else it will get into dead water caused by the eddy of the Surrey pier. At Chiswick the course may be taken wide (save and except, as in all cases, where force of wind alters circumstances). The main tide runs nearest to Chiswick Eyot. Horse Reach should be entered in mid-river ; there is little or no tide on the Surrey point below it.

Making for Barnes Bridge, the boat should keep fairly near to the Middlesex shore—how near depends upon whether the race is ordained to pass through the centre or the Middlesex arch of Barnes Bridge. Once through Barnes Bridge, the course should sheer in (if the centre arch has been taken) until the boat lies as if it had taken the shore arch. It should attain this position by the time it breasts the 'White Hart.' The river is here a horseshoe to the finish. In linear measure a boat on the Middlesex side has nearly two lengths less to travel than the one outside it between Barnes Bridge and the 'Ship.' The tide runs nearly as well within sixty feet of the shore as in mid-river at this point, hence it pays to keep about that distance from the Middlesex bank.

The old Thames watermen who instruct young pilots over the Putney course are often inclined to run too much in the grooves which were good in their younger days, when they themselves were racing on the river. Their instruction would be sound enough if the features of the river had not undergone change, as aforesaid, in sundry details. The repeated blunders of navigation lately seen perpetrated by watermen as well as amateurs between Craven Steps and Hammersmith make us lose much faith in watermen's tuition for steering the metropolitan course. We would rather entrust a young pilot to some active member of the London or Thames Rowing Clubs. These gentlemen know the river well enough as it now is, and are not biassed by old memories of what it once was but is no longer.

University coxswains have easier tasks in these days than their predecessors before 1868. Until the Thames Conservancy obtained statutory powers in 1868 to clear the course for boat-racing, it used to be a ticklish matter to pick a safe course on a flood tide. There would be strings of barges towed, and many more sailing, others 'sweeping,' up river. Traffic did not stop for sport. Coxswains often found themselves in awkward predicaments to avoid such itinerant craft, more so when barges were under sail against a head wind, and were tacking from shore to shore. In 1866 a barge of this sort most seriously interfered with the Cambridge crew in Horse Reach, just when Oxford had, after a stern race, given them the go-by off the

Bathing-place. It extinguished any chance which might have been left for Cambridge.

In the preceding year C. R. W. Tottenham immortalised himself by a great *coup* with a barge. She was tacking right across his course (Oxford had just gone ahead after having been led by a clear length through Hammersmith Bridge). This was just below Barnes Bridge. Many a pilot would have tried to go round the bows of that barge. At the moment when she shaped her course to tack across tide there seemed to be ample room to pass in front of her. Tottenham never altered his course, and trusted to his own calculations. Presently the barge was broadside on to Oxford's bows, and only a few lengths ahead. Every one in the steamers astern stood aghast at what seemed to be an inevitable smash. The barge held on, and so did Oxford, and the barge passed clear away just before Oxford came up. Even if she had hung a little, in a lull of wind, it would have been easy for Oxford to deflect a trifle and pass under her stern. Anything was better than attempting to go round her bows, which at first seemed to be the simplest course to spectators not experts at pilotage. It must be admitted that so much nerve and judgment at a pinch have never before or since been displayed by any coxswain in a University match. Tottenham had his opportunity and made the most of it. He steered thrice afterwards, but even if he had never steered again he had made his reputation by this one *coup*. In justice to other crack coxswains, such as Shadwell and Egan of old, and, *par excellence*, G. L. Davis in the present day, we must assume that if they had been similarly tried they would have been equally triumphant.

FEATHER 'UNDER' THE WATER.

CHAPTER VII.

SLIDING SEATS.

I. THEIR ORIGIN.

WHEN sliding seats were first used they completely revolutionised oarsmanship, and caused old coaches whose names were
household words to stand aghast at the invention.

The best use of them was but imperfectly realised by those
who first adopted them ; and many of the earliest examples of
sliding-seat oarsmanship were sufficiently unorthodox, according
to our improved use of them in the present day, to justify the
declaration of more than one veteran whose opinion was always
respected that—'if that is sliding, it is not rowing.'

The mechanical power gained by a sliding seat is so great
that even if he who uses it sets at defiance all recognised principles of fixed-seat rowing, he can still command more pace than

if he adhered to fixed-seat work. It was the spectacle, in earlier days of the slide, of this unorthodox sliding style beating good specimens of fixed-seat oarsmanship which so horrified many of the retired good oarsmen of the fixed-seat school. Before long the true use of the slide became better understood, and thus oarsmen—at all events scientific amateurs—began to realise that, while bad sliding could manage to command more pace than good fixed rowing, yet at the same time good sliding (which will be explained hereafter) will beat bad sliding by even more than the latter can distance good fixed-seat work.

Just a similar sort of prejudice was displayed against the earlier style of rowing in keelless boats. When these craft first came in, oarsmen had little or no idea of 'sitting' them; they rolled helplessly, and lost all form, but nevertheless they travelled faster in the new craft than when rowing in good style in old-fashioned iron-shod keeled boats. In a season or two style reasserted itself, and it was found that it was by no means impossible to row in as neat a shape in a keelless boat as in a keeled one.

Sliding on the seat had been practised long before the sliding seat was invented, but only to a modified extent. Robert Chambers of St. Antony's, the quondam champion, tried it now and then, and when preparing for his 1865 match with Kelley he used to slide a trifle, especially for a spurt, and to grease his seat to facilitate his operations. Jack Clasper, according to Mr. E. D. Brickwood's well-known treatise on Boat-racing, used to slide to a small extent on a fixed seat when he rowed in a Newcastle four which won on the Thames in 1857. Of this detail the writer has himself no recollection. Also, in 1867, a Tyne sculler, Percy, tried sliding on a fixed seat in a sculling match against J. Sadler on the Thames (so Mr. Brickwood relates). But none of these earlier sliders made much good out of their novelty. The strain on the legs caused by the friction on the seat prevented the oarsman from maintaining the action for long, and meantime it took so much out of him that it prematurely exhausted his whole frame.

In 1870 Renforth's champion four used to slide on the seat
for a spurt, but not for a whole course.   They beat the St. John's
Canadian crew very easily while so rowing in a match at Lachine,
but we believe that they would have won with about as much
ease had they rowed on fixed seats.   In the same year a 'John
o' Gaunt' four from Lancaster came to Henley Regatta and
rowed in this fashion, sliding on fixed seats.   They had very
little body swing, and their style showed all the worst features
of the subsequent style which became too common when sliding
seats were first established.   They did almost all their work by
the piston action of the legs, and their limbs tired under the
strain at the end of three or four minutes.   They led a light
crew of Oxford 'Old Radleians' by three lengths past Fawley
Court, and then began to come back to them.   The Oxonians
steadily gained on them, but had to come round outside them
at the Point, and could never get past them, losing the race by
less than a yard.   Enough was seen on this occasion to convince
oarsmen that the Lancastrian style was only good for half-mile
racing.   In the final heat for the Stewards' fours a good L.R.C.
crew beat the Lancastrians with ease after going half a mile.
The Radleians would doubtless have also gone well by the Lancastrians had the course been a hundred yards longer.

So far the old fixed seat had vindicated itself for staying
purposes.   But in the following year a problem was practically
solved.   It seems that (so Mr. Brickwood tells us) an oarsman
comparatively unknown to fame, one Mr. R. O. Birch, had used
an actual sliding seat at King's Lynn Regatta in 1870.   Mr.
Brickwood seems to have been the only writer who took cognisance of this interesting fact.   University men and tideway
amateurs, also professionals so far as we can gather, seem not
to have heard of, or at least not to have heeded, the experiment.   Had Mr. Birch been a leading sculler of the day,
possibly the innovation might have been adopted earlier than
it was.

Meantime in America the sliding seat had been better
known, but had not been appreciated.   Mr. Brickwood tells us

that a Mr. J. C. Babcock, of the Nassau Boat Club, constructed a sliding seat as long ago as 1857. Also that W. Brown, the American sculler, tried one in 1861, but abandoned it. In 1869 Mr. Babcock once more devoted himself to the study and construction of sliding seats, and brought out a six-oared crew rowing on slides. But the invention did not obtain much recognition, although Mr. Babcock was of opinion that his crew gained in power of stroke through the new apparatus.

How the seat came to be at length adopted arose thus. In 1871 two Tyne crews went to America to compete in regattas. One of these was Renforth's crew, and, as detailed elsewhere, Renforth died during a race against the St. John crew. Robert Chambers (not the ex-champion) took his place later on for sundry regattas. The Tyne crews rowed with a good average of success in America. Taylor, who commanded the other Tyne four, raced a States four, called the Biglin-Coulter crew, rowing with sliding seats. These Biglin-Coulter men did not prove themselves, as a whole, any better than, if so fast as, the British crew ; consequently there was nothing to draw especial attention to their apparatus. Of the two British crews, that stroked by Chambers proved itself on the whole, through various regattas, faster than Taylor's four.

Taylor bided his time. He proposed a match on the Tyne between the two British fours, and the offer was accepted. The match came off in the fall of the same year. Taylor's men had their boat fitted with sliding seats, and kept their apparatus 'dark' from the world and from their opponents. They used to cease sliding when watched, and kept their apparatus covered up. When the race came off, Taylor's crew decisively reversed the American regatta form, and beat Chambers's crew easily. This was ascribed to the slide, information as to which leaked out after the race. The next University race was not rowed with slides, but a couple of minor sculling races in the spring were rowed with them. In June of that year a very fine L.R.C. four (Messrs. J. B. Close, F. S. Gulston, A. de L. Long, and W. Stout) rowed a four-oared match on the Thames against

the Atalanta Club of New York.   The L.R.C. men used slides.
That did not affect their victory; they were stronger and better
oarsmen than the Americans, and could have won easily on
fixed seats ; but what gave a fillip to slides was the clear testimony of these four oarsmen of undoubted skill to the advantage which they felt themselves gain by their use.   Instantly
there was a run upon slides.   Henley Regatta was impending.
The L.R.C. crews were all fitted with them for that meeting.
Several other crews took to them after reaching Henley,
and after seeing the superiority which London obtained by
them.   Kingston and Pembroke (Oxon) had their boats fitted
with slides less than a week before the race.   Pembroke was a
moderate crew, and only entered because they held the Ladies'
Plate.   At first, in practice, Pembroke did about equal time
over the course with Lady Margaret, both crews being on fixed
seats.   But the day after Pembroke got their slides they improved some 15 secs. upon the time of Lady Margaret, who
kept to their old seats.   It must, however, be recorded that
the Ladies' Plate was won by a fixed-seat crew—Jesus, Camb.
This crew was by far the best in material of all the entries at
the regatta.   Their individual superiority enabled them to give
away the slide to Pembroke, and had they taken to slides even
for the last few days they would probably have also won the
Grand Challenge.   As it was, that prize fell to the L.R.C., a
crew which had four good men, and then a weak tail.   The
sliding seat had now fairly established its claims.   It should
be added that Pembroke, with two good and two moderate
men, won the Visitors' Plate from a very good Dublin four,
about the best four that Dublin ever sent to Henley.   Pembroke used slides, and the Dublin men had fixed seats.   (Slides
alone won this race for Pembroke.)   The Pembroke slides
were on wheels—a mechanism which was soon afterwards discarded by builders in favour of greased glass or steel grooves or
tubes, but which seems to be returning to favour in 1886 and
1887.

II. THEIR USE.

In order to understand the true action in a slide, it will be well to recall the action of fixed-seat rowing. On the fixed seat the swing of the body does the main work, being supported by the legs, which are rigid and bent.

On a slide the legs extend gradually, while at the same time they support the body. On a fixed seat the body moves as the radius of a circle that is stationary ; on a slide the body moves as the radius of a circle which is itself in motion. Suppose a threepenny-piece and a half-crown placed alongside of each other, concentrically, with a common pivot. Let the three-penny-piece roll for a certain distance on the edge of a card. Then any point in the circumference of the half-crown will move through a curve called a 'trochoid.' This is practically the sort of curve described by the head or shoulders of an oars-man who rows upon a sliding seat.

The actual gain of rowing power by means of this mechanism is considerable. The exact extent of it is not easy to arrive at, there being various factors to be taken into consideration.

In the first place, the length of reach, or of the 'stroke,' is considerably increased. Mr. Brickwood in 1873 conducted some scientific experiments on dry land upon this subject, in con-junction with the editor of the 'Field' and Mr. F. Gulston. The result of these measurements was to demonstrate (in the person of Mr. F. Gulston) a gain of about 18 inches in length of stroke upon a 9-inch slide.

In 1881 some casual experiments of a similar sort were con-ducted on a lawn at Marlow by the Oxford crew then training there. The writer was present, and, so far as he remembers, the results practically confirmed the estimate of Mr. Brickwood above recorded, allowance being made for the fact that the gentleman by means of whose body the ideal stroke was measured at Marlow was longer-bodied and longer in the leg than Mr. Gulston.

As a second advantage, the sliding seat decidedly relieves the abdominal muscles and respiratory organs during the recovery. In dealing with scientific racing we have previously remarked that the point wherein a tiring oarsman first gives way is in his recovery, because of the relative weakness of the muscles which conduct that portion of the action of the stroke. It therefore is obvious that any contrivance which can enable a man to recover with less exertion to himself will enable him to do more work in the stroke over the whole course, and still more so if the very contrivance which aids recovery also gives extra power to the stroke.

On the other hand, there are two drawbacks to the slide. One of these is, that when sliding full forward the legs are more bent than would be the case on a fixed seat. The body cannot reach quite so far forward over the toes on a full slide as it can on a properly regulated fixed seat. This slightly detracts from the work of the *body* at the beginning of the stroke.

Again, when a slide is used to best advantage, the greatest mechanical benefit occurs just when the body arrives at the perpendicular, and when the legs are beginning to do the greater portion of their extension. This causes the greater force of the stroke to be applied behind the rowlock, in contradiction of all old theories of fixed-seat oarsmanship.

Taking all *pros* and *cons* together, it has been practically proved beyond doubt to every rowing man for more than a decade that the slide gains much more than it sacrifices. Even bad sliding secures sufficient advantage to beat fixed-seat row-ing (*ceteris paribus*), and good sliding completely distances fixed-seat performances. It is often remarked that the 'times' performed by sliding-seat crews are not glaringly superior to those of• fixed-seat annals. This is correct. Nevertheless the balance is clearly in favour of sliding performances. The actual difference is much greater than times happen to disclose ; it is somewhat fallacious to draw deductions from averages of recorded times, unless the individual condition of wind and weather, and of close or hollow races, be also chronicled for each year. On

p. 106 record is given of the actual gain attained by Pembroke College crew within ten days of their essaying the use of slides. It may be added that Kingston, who adopted slides about the same day, displayed much about the same increase of speed, as shown by clocking and by comparing their times with those of other crews before and after their adoption of slides.

Another matter throws light on the question, and that is the records of practice times—which are, on the whole, more trustworthy to prove an average than race times. Races have to start at fixed hours, irrespective of weather, whereas practice can select smooth days for trials. The records of sliding trials—over Henley courses and tideway—when wind and water have been favourable, show a much greater advance over similar practice trials of fixed-seat crews than is disclosed by the racing times of sliders. The writer believes that he is not far wrong in estimating the difference between sliding and fixed seats, in an eight or four, over the Henley course at 15 secs. (rough), and at something well over half a minute over the Putney course. Scullers gain more by slides than oarsmen, because they can work square throughout to the stretcher, whereas the oarsman's handle tends to place the strain at different angles to his body as the stroke progresses.

Not much importance need be attached to the fact that the first University race rowed on slides eclipsed all its predecessors (and successors) for time.[1] It is well known that a gig eight with fixed seats on a good flood could do much faster time than a racing and sliding ship on a neap. The 1873 race hit off a one-o'clock tide and fair weather ; and it would equally have surpassed all or most predecessors if the crews had not used slides. But still it was fortuitous that the first race of this class in the U.B.C.'s series should thus indicate the novelty by time record.

What is more striking is the ease with which times of about twenty minutes or under are now repeatedly accomplished, and by moderate crews, on moderate tides, and often with breezes

[1] See Tables.

unfavourable. Till slides came in twenty minutes had only once been beaten, and that was by the Oxford crew of 1857 in prac-

PRACTISING STROKE (1).

tice (19 min. 53 sec.); and as Mr. T. Egan, at that date editor of aquatics in 'Bell's Life,' then recorded in that journal, the oldest

PRACTISING STROKE (2).

waterman could hardly recall such springs as foamed through Putney arches that week, and especially upon that day of trial.

In 1871 Goldie's (third) crew were supposed to do wonderful time (20 min. 11 sec.), on a good spring and smooth

PRACTISING STROKE (3).

day. It sufficed to make them hot favourites. In these days a sliding crew that could not beat 19 min. 40 sec. on a

PRACTISING STROKE (4).

smooth spring tide would be reckoned to have a bad chance of success.

The value of slides is therefore beyond dispute, but the oarsman should realise that good sliding distances bad sliding quite as far as bad sliding can beat fixed seats.

Hence the importance of using the slide to the best advantage. To realise what he has to do, let a man test separately his two forces which he has presently to combine. Let him row an ordinary fixed-seat stroke : this shows him the power of his swing ; then let him sit upright, holding his oar, and, having slid up forward, kick back with rigid back and arms. He will feel that he grips the water even more forcibly for the instant ˜by the second than by the former process. The fallacy of bad sliders is to be content with this gain of power in the action last named, and to substitute slide for swing (the arms eventually rowing the stroke home in either case). The problem which an oarsman has to solve is to *combine* the two actions.

In order to do this, he should realise an important fact, viz. that the body cannot work effectually unless it receives support from the extensor muscles of the legs. Therefore, if he slides before he swings, or if he completes his slide before he completes his swing, any swing which he attempts after the slide is played out is practically powerless. Also, if the swing is thus rendered helpless, so also is the finish of the stroke with the arms, for these depend upon the body for support, and the body cannot supply them with this support unless the legs in their turn are doing their duty to the body.

Bearing this amount of theory in mind, the oarsman should put it into practice thus. He should get forward (and immerse his blade, as on a fixed seat). Then, at the moment he touches the water, he should bring his body to bear upon the handle, just as if he were for the instant rowing on a fixed seat ; his legs should be rigid, though bent, at the instant of catch. (See No. 1, p. 110.) So soon as the catch has been applied, the oar-handle begins to come in to the operator. Now comes a bit of watermanship and management of the limbs which require special attention, and which few oarsmen, even in these days of improved sliding, carry out to exact perfection. The knees have been elevated by the slide (if it is anything over 4 inches) to a height over which the oar-handle cannot pass without being elevated in its turn. Therefore, having once made his catch with rigid knees, the pupil should then begin to slide, contemporaneously with his swing, for a small distance, until he has brought his knees to such a level that the oar-loom can pass over them (No. 2, p. 110). He should during this period of the stroke slide only just so much as is required in order to bring his knees to the necessary height before the oar reaches them. By the time that the oar comes over them he will be about the perpendicular (No. 3, p. 111). Now comes that part of the stroke which, on a slide, is the most effective. The body should from this point swing well back, much further so than would be orthodox upon a fixed seat ; all the time that the body is thus swinging back the legs should be extending, and the pace of extension should be regulated according to the length of slide. In any case the slide and swing should terminate contemporaneously (No. 4, p. 111). The arms, as in fixed-seat rowing, should contract and row the stroke home while the body is still swinging back. They should not begin to bend until the trunk has well passed the perpendicular.

The oarsman must bear in mind that the moment for finishing his slide should be regulated, not by the length of the *slide*, but by *the length of his swing*, and the latter should go well back until his body is at an angle of about thirty degrees beyond the perpendicular. Suppose he has a long slide, say of 10 inches or more, and he decides, either from fatigue or because he need not fully extend himself, to use only part of his slide ; or suppose he is changed from a boat fitted with 11-inch slides to one with 9-inch ditto, he must not, when using the shorter slide, allow his legs to extend as rapidly as they did when they had a longer distance to cover. If he fails to observe this he will 'hurry' his slide, and will bring it to an end before the swing is completed, thus rendering the latter part of the swing helpless for want of due leg-support. If slide and swing are not arranged contemporaneously, it is far better

I

that a balance of slide should remain to be run out after the swing has finished than *vice versâ*. The legs can always push, and so continue the stroke, even if the body is rigid ; but the body cannot conversely do anything effective for the stroke when once the legs have run their course.

The recovery on a sliding seat is not quite the counterpart of that on a fixed seat. On the fixed seat the recovery should be the converse of the stroke : i.e. the arms, which came in latest, while the body was still swinging back, should shoot out first, while the body is beginning its return swing ; and just as the first part of the stroke was performed with straight arms and swinging body, so the last part of the recovery should disclose a similar pose of arms and body. But upon a slide there is not exactly such a transposition on the recovery of the motions which are correct for the stroke. The hands play the same part as before ; they cannot well be too lively off the chest and in extension, because the knees require more clearing on slides, and the sooner the hands are on the safe side of them the less chance is there of fouling the water on the return of the blade. But, as regards· the relations between slide and swing, these should *not* bear the same relation conversely which they did to each other during the stroke. The pupil was enjoined not to let his slide run ahead of his swing while rowing the stroke through ; but on the recovery he may, and should, let his slide get well ahead, and be completed before the body has attained its full reach forward. The body should not *wait* for the swing to do its duty first, but it should begin at once to recover, though more leisurely than the legs. The reasons for this are :—

1. The pace of the slide lends impetus to the trunk, and eases the labour of the forward swing ; it transfers some of the exertion of recovering the trunk from the abdominal muscles, which are weak, to the flexors of legs and loins, which are much more powerful, and are better able to stand the strain.

2. The body needs some purchase upon which to depend for its recovery, and the legs can aid it in this respect much

more effectually when bent than when rigid. Therefore, since staying power is greatly affected by the amount of exertion involved in recovery (as explained in previous pages), the oarsman will last longer in proportion as he thus omits the recovery of his trunk, by accelerating his slide on the return.

Many good oarsmen slide until the knees are quite straight. In the writer's opinion, this is waste of power : the knees should never *quite* straighten ; the recovery is, for anatomical reasons, much stronger if the joint is slightly bent when the reversal of the machinery commences (No. 4, p. 111). The extra half-inch of kick gained by quite straightening the knees hardly compensates for the extra strain of recovery ; also-leg work to the last fraction of a second of swing is better preserved by this retention of a slight bend, and an open chest and clean finish are thereby better attained. Engineers, who know what is meant by a 'dead point' in machinery, will at once grasp the reason for not allowing the legs to shoot quite straight.

When a crew are being coached upon slides, it is of great importance to get the slide simultaneous, and as nearly as possible equal. A long-legged man, sculling, may use a much longer slide than a short man. But in an eight, if the long man fits his stretcher as if for sculling, he will be doing more than his share, and may be unable to shoot so long a slide through in the required time, except by dint of 'hurrying' it ; and, if he does this latter, the result is to cripple his swing, as shown *supra*. There must be a certain amount of give-and-take in arranging slides in an eight or four oar. That length of slide is best which all the crew can work simultaneously and effectively, preserving uniformity of swing and slide.

When tiros are being taught their first lesson in sliding, they should be placed on very short slides, say 3 inches at most. The centre of the slide only should be used. The runners should be blocked fore and aft, so that when the slide stands half way ($1\frac{1}{2}$ inch from foremost block), the distance from the seat to the stretcher should be just as much as the man would require if he were on a fixed seat.

I 2

Young hands are less likely to make their stroke all slide and no swing if they have at first only such length of slide as above indicated. When the slide of 3 inches has been mastered, it may be lengthened, inch by inch. In thus lengthening the slide, it is best to add, at first, more to the forward part of the slide than to the back part, i.e. say, for a 4-inch slide, $2\frac{1}{2}$ inches before and $1\frac{1}{2}$ inch behind, the point of seat for fixed-seat work, to the same stretcher. This arrangement prevents the pupil from lacking leg-support at the end of his swing, and teaches him to feel his legs well against the stretcher till the hands have come home to the chest. When 4 inches have been mastered, add another inch forward and about half an inch back, and so on. In time the beginner will reach the full range of his slide forward, while yet he is 'blocked' from using the full distance back. When he becomes proficient in this pose, his slide back can be increased by degrees until he attains a full slide. The great thing is to induce him from the first to combine his slide with his swing, and not to substitute the former for the latter.

When slides first came in shocking form was seen upon them, as previously stated. This was a venial result of oarsmen being driven—by emulation to win prizes in races immediately impending—to attempt to run before they had learnt to walk, so to speak. The year 1873 saw worse form among amateurs than the writer can recall in any season. In 1874 matters began to mend. The two University strokes of that year, Messrs. Rhodes and Way, had each been at pains to improve his style since he had last been seen in public at Henley. Each seemed to realise that he had been on a wrong tack, and set to work to alter his style radically. These same gentlemen were strokes of their respective U.B.C.'s in 1875, and the improvement was still more palpable. The Oxonian had an exceptionally fine lot of men behind him ; the Cantab had two or three weak men in the bows who did not do justice to him. But none the less, when these crews performed at Putney, old-fashioned critics, who had been till then prejudiced against the new machinery, as being destructive to form, were fain to admit that after all, when properly managed, slides could produce as good form of body and shoulders as in the best of the old days. The Leander crew which won the G.C.C. at Henley in that year showed admirable sliding form. It was stroked by Mr. Goldie, who had rowed all his University races on a fixed seat. When he first took to a slide (for sculling) he fell into the same error as many other amateurs, almost entirely substituting slide for swing. But for this oversight he might have won both Diamond and Wingfield sculls. He soon saw his error, like Messrs. Rhodes and Way, and when he stroked Leander in 1875 no one could have recognised him as the same man who had been contesting the Diamonds in 1872. These three fuglemen strokes did much to elevate the standard of sliding among amateurs ; it was chiefly through their examples, crowned with success, that the earlier samples of sliding oarsmanship became better realised. Professionals remained blind in their own conceit, as is shown in another chapter, but from this date amateur oarsmanship completely gave the go-by to professional exhibitions of skill and science in aquatics.

A COLLEGE FOUR.

CHAPTER VIII.

FOUR-OARS.

THE fewer the number of performers in a boat the longer does it take (with material of uniform quality) to acquire absolute evenness of action. This may seem paradoxical, but none the less all practical oarsmen will, from their own personal experiences, endorse the statement. It has been said that it takes twice as long to perfect a four as an eight, twice as long to perfect a pair as a four, and twice as long to perfect a sculler as a pair. This scale may be fanciful, but it is approximately truthful; it refers, of course, to the education of oarsmen for work in the respective craft, from their earliest days of instruction. It means that a higher standard of watermanship has to be attained, in order to do justice to the style of craft rowed in, according as the ship carries more or fewer performers. Many an oarsman who by honest tugging can improve the go of an eight-oar will do more harm than good in a light four, and will be simply helpless in a racing pair.

Four-oar races, with the exception of some junior contests, are now rowed in coxswainless craft. The first of these seen in Europe was that of the St. John's Canadian crew (professional, but admitted for the nonce as amateurs) at the Paris International Regatta 1867. All the other crews carried steerers. The Canadians had the windward station in a stiff wind, and won easily. Next year the B.N.C. Oxon Club produced a four thus constructed at Henley. The rules did not forbid this; but the novelty scared other competitors and threatened to spoil the racing in that class. The stewards accordingly passed a resolution forbidding any of the entries to dispense with a coxswain, and under cover of this disqualified the B.N.C. four when it came in ahead.

Next year the resolution referred to remained in force (as regards the Challenge Cups), but a presentation prize for fours without coxswains was given, and was won by the Oxford Bodleian Club. In 1871 the chief professional matches were rowed without coxswains; but no more prizes were given for this class of rowing at Henley until 1873, when the Stewards' Cup was classed for 'no coxswains.' At Oxford college fours were similarly altered, but the steering was so bad that it was seriously proposed to revert to the old system. A similar proposal was made with regard to Henley. Fortunately, wiser counsels prevailed, and oarsmen realised that it was better to attempt to raise their own talents to the standard required for the improved build than to detract from the build to suit the failings of mediocrity. In 1875 the Visitors and Wyfold Cups were emancipated from coxswains, and since then the standard of amateur four-oar rowing has gradually risen to the requirements of the improved class of build.

Steerage is of course the main difficulty in these pairs. Three different sorts of apparatus have been used in them. Two of these are much of the same sort. One, generally in use to this day, consists of two bars projecting from the stretcher, and working horizontally in slits cut in the board. The foot presses against one bar or other to direct the rudder. Another process is to fix a shoe to the stretcher, in which the oarsman places his foot. This shoe works laterally. The third is one tried by the writer in 1868. Every inventor thinks his goose a swan, and possibly the writer is over-sanguine as to the merits of his own hobby. It consists of two bars laid on the stretcher, like a very widely opened letter V, the arms of the V pointing in the direction of the sitter. Each arm is hinged at the apex of the V. The stretcher is grooved, so that either arm can be pressed into the groove, flush with the surface of the stretcher. Behind each bar is a spring. The bars cross the stretcher just about the ball of the foot. The hinge is sunk deep in the wood, so that the arms of the levers do not begin to project above the wood till some 5 inches on either side of the centre of the stretcher. The feet are placed in ordinary rowing pose, in the middle of the V, where the levers lie below the flush surface of the stretcher. The strap, though tight, has a *wide* loop, to admit of slight lateral movement of the feet. To put on rudder either foot is slipped half an inch or so outward. This brings it on to the lever of that side, and the pressure of the foot drives the lever flush. This pressure and movement of the lever, by means of another small lever and swivel outside the gunwale, in connection with it, works the rudder line. When steerage enough has been obtained, a half-inch return of the foot to its normal pose releases the lever, and the spring behind it at once brings it to *status quo ante.*

Now in the other two mechanisms above cited, the same foot has to steer *both* ways. Hence, for one of the two directions, the toe must turn in like a pigeon's. This must, for the moment, cripple leg-work, especially on slides. Again, with lateral movement in first and second machines, it is difficult for the steerer to know to exactness when his rudder is 'off.' He may, in returning it after steerage, leave it a trifle on, or carry it the other way too far. If so, he has to counter-steer a stroke or two later, till he feels that his rudder is free and trailing.

The writer claims for his own invention that it never removes the feet from the proper outward-turned pose against the stretcher, and that the springs under the lever ensure the rudder swinging back and 'trailing' so soon as a lever is released.

Whatever apparatus is used, *wires*, not strings, should lead the rudder, and should not be too tight ; they will pull enough, though slightly loose.

Anyone may steer ; the best waterman, if not too short-sighted, should do so, but stroke should not take the task if anyone else is at all fit for it.

FOUR-OAR.

The steerer should not be repeatedly looking round, as regards his course. If he is sure of no obstacles lying in his path, he can, when once he has laid his boat straight for a reach, watch her stern-post, and keep touch on it, to hold it to some landmark.

A coxswainless four really facilitates oarsmanship. It re-covers from a roll more freely than the old-fashioned build with a pilot. It is uneven rowing which causes a roll, but when once equilibrium has been disturbed the coxswain has more difficulty than the crew in regaining balance. The oarsmen aid themselves with their oars, as with balancing poles. The removal of the coxswain therefore tends to reduce the rolling, and facilitates the speedy return of the ship to her keel when momentarily thrown off it. Coxswainless fours at Henley travel now much more steadily than did those with coxswains fifteen years ago. A runner on the bank, to look out for obstructive craft, is useful in practice. It enables the steerer to keep his eyes on his stern-post, and to guide his course thereby in confidence, without repeated twists round to see if any loafing duffer is going to smash his timbers. The pace of a first-class coxswainless four, in smooth water, for half a mile is quite as great as that of a second-class eight-oar with a coxswain. The abolition of coxswain has improved the speed of fours some forty seconds over the Henley course.

One good resulted from the attempt of B.N.C. in 1868 to row without a coxswain. It opened the eyes of the regatta executive to the unfairness of tolerating boy coxswains. The University clubs used to carry boys of four or five stone. In that very year the 'Oscillators' had a four-stone lad, while University College carried an eight-stone man. There was just as much difference between these two fours in dead weight carried as between B.N.C. (with no coxswain) and the Oscillators. University clubs are *ex officio* debarred from obtaining boys to steer. This inequality had been complained of by college crews time after time. Old Mr. Lane, the usual vice-chairman, used to sneer at the complaint, and say, 'If a boy can do in one boat what it takes a man to do in another, it is not fair to prohibit the boy.' If this were logical, then, *pari passu*, there could be no unfairness for one man to do single-handed what in other boats it took a man and a boy (or two men) to do, viz. both row and steer. Mr. Lane's fallacy was exploded by this *reductio ad absurdum* of his tenets, and regulation weights for coxswains were initiated for following years.

NEAR MEDMENHAM.

CHAPTER IX.

PAIR-OARS.

MORE than one master of oarsmanship has declared that good pair-oar rowing is the acme of oarsmanship. Just as there are fewer oarsmen who can do justice to a four-oar than to an eight, so when we come to pair-oars we find still fewer performers who can really show first-class style in this line of rowing. Much as watermanship is needed in a four, it is still more important to possess it when rowing in a pair. One, or even two men, out of a four-oared crew may be what would be considered bad watermen, i.e. not *au fait* at sitting a rolling boat, and not instinctively time-keepers. Yet, if the other two men have the quality of watermanship, the four may speedily fall together, provided the two outsiders show sound general principles of style. In a pair-oar, if either of the hands is a bad waterman, the combination will never rise above mediocrity. In pair-oar rowing there is needed a *je-ne-sais-quoi* sort of mutual concession of style. One man is stroke and the other bow, but there is in good pair-oarsmen an indefinite and almost unconscious give-and-take action on the part of both men. The style of the two is a sort of blend.

Old Harry Clasper, when asked which steered, of himself and his son Jack, in a pair, said that 'both steered.' To do this is the acme of homogeneous rowing. Of two partners one may, and should, act as chief ; but his colleague should be co-operating with him, and almost anticipating his motions and orders.

When two strange partners commence work, they should make up their minds not to row 'jealous.' If each begins by trying to row the other round, they will disagree like Richard Penlake and his wife. They had better each try to see who can do least work : sit the boat, paddle gently, studying to drop into the water together, to catch the water together, to finish together, to feather together (and cleanly), and to recover together. The less work they try to do, while thus seeking to assimilate their motions to each other, the quicker will they settle down.

As to rowing each other round, such emulation should never enter their heads. To row a partner round is no proof of having done more work than he towards propelling the boat. One man may catch sharply and row cleanly, and in a style calculated to make a boat travel ; his colleague may slither the beginning and tug at the end, staying a fraction of a second later in the water than the other, but rowing no longer in reach. The latter will probably row the boat round ! A tug at the end of a stroke turns a boat much more than a catch at the beginning ; yet the latter propels the racing boat far more. Of course, if two men row alike in style and reach from end to end, and one puts on all through the stroke a trifle more pressure, the ship will turn from the greater pressure. But, unless it can be guaranteed that the style of each partner is identical all through the stroke, 'rowing round' does not prove a superiority of work.

PAIR OARS—AN IMMINENT FOUL

We have said that good watermen will sit a pair where bad ones will roll. So far so good. But good watermen, first beginning practice with each other, must not assume that because they do not roll their uniformity is therefore proved. Their power of balance can keep the boat upright, even though there may be at first some inaccuracies of work. Thus to balance a boat requires a certain amount of exertion ; in a race, at this stage, this labour of balancing would take something off the power of the stroke. Besides, until the two oars work with similar pressure through the whole stroke, the keel cannot be travelling dead straight. Steady though good men may be at scratch, they will gain in pace as they continue to practise, and insensibly assimilate their action. With bad watermen cessation of rolling is a sign that the styles have at last assimilated ; with good watermen the deduction is not necessarily sound.

In old days pair-oars rowed without rudders. The two oars guided the ship. It was best to let the stronger man steer. He could thus set his partner to do his best all the way in a race, could ease an over or two, or lay on that much extra, from stroke to stroke, according as the stern-post required balancing on the landmark which had been selected as its *point d'appui*. To learn each other's strength and to know the course, to know by heart when to lay on for this corner, or to row off for that, was the study of practice and tested watermanship. In modern times a thin metal rudder is usually used, steered as in coxswainless fours. In a beam wind this materially aids pace, it enables the leeward oar to do his full share, instead of paddling while his partner is toiling. Even in still water it is some gain, provided the helm can be easily 'trailed' when not wanted. The facility with which such a pair can be steered tempts men to omit to study that delicate balance of a boat's stern on its point which was the acme of art before rudders came in. We have seen a (rudderless) pair leave a wake up Henley reach, from island to point, on a glassy evening, as straight as if a surveyor's line had been stretched there. In fact, to steer such a pair, with a practical partner, was, if anything, easier to some men than to steer an eight. The stern-post lay in view of the oarsman, and could be adjusted on its point like a gun barrel, whereas the actual bows of an eight are unseen by a coxswain.

Except a sculling boat, a pair-oar is the fastest starting of all craft ; but if it is thus easy to set in motion at the outset of a race, it is plain that it can be spurted later on as suddenly. Bearing this in mind, there is no object in starting a pair in a race at a speed which cannot go all the way. There is as much scope for staying in a pair as in an eight ; more in fact, for the pair takes the longer to do the same distance as the eight. The start should be quick, but it is best to keep a stroke or two per minute in hand for a rush hereafter, if needed, when the pulse of the enemy has been felt, and when partners have warmed to their work.

Pairs are best rowed with oars somewhat smaller all round than those which are used for eights or fours. The pair, more than any other craft, requires to be caught sharp and light ; an oar that is not too long in the shank nor too big in the blade best accomplishes this. 'Dimensions' recommended for 'work' in various craft will be found scheduled elsewhere in this volume.

To conclude the subject of pairs, it may be added, if partners wish to assimilate, they must make up their minds to avoid recrimination. If the boat goes amiss say, or assume, 'it is I,' not 'you,' who is to. blame. Keep cool and keep your head in a race. If the steersman bids 'easy' half a stroke, be prompt in so doing. To delay to right the course at the correct instant may take the ship lengths out of her course. A stroke eased in time, like a stitch, often saves nine, and perhaps obviates sticking in the bank.

CLOSE QUARTERS.

CHAPTER X.

SCULLING.

SCULLING needs more precision and more watermanship than rowing. The strongest man only wastes his strength in sculling if he fails to obtain even work for each hand. A pair-oar requires more practice to bring it to perfection than any other boat manned by oars, but a sculler requires considerably more practice than any pair of oarsmen. Strength he must have in proportion to his weight, if he is to soar above mediocrity, but strength alone will not avail him unless he gets his hands well together.

His sculls will overlap more or less. It is practically immaterial which hand he rows uppermost ; the upper hand has a trifle of advantage, and for this reason Oxonians, whose course is a left-hand one, usually scull left hand over. The first difficulty which an embryo sculler has to contend with is that of attaining uniform pressure with square body and square legs upon a pair of arms which are not uniformly placed. One arm has to give way to another to enable the hands to clear each other when they cross ; and yet while they do this the blades which they control should be buried to a uniform depth. How to attain this give-and-take action of the arms is better shown by even a moderate performer in five minutes of practical illustration than by reams of book instruction.

The aspirant to sculling honours had better, when commencing to learn, take his first lesson in a gig. A wager boat will be too unsteady, and will retard his practice ; 'skiffs' are usually to be obtained only as teach boats with work at sixes and sevens. A dingey buries too much on the stroke, and spoils style. The beginner should find a stiff pair of sculls, true made, and overlapping about the width of his hands. He should ask some proficient to examine and to try his sculls, and to tell him by the feel whether they are really a pair. The best makers of oars and sculls too often turn out sculls which are not 'pairs,' and when this is the case the action of him who uses them cannot be expected to be even on both sides of his frame. Having got suitable sculls, let the sculler arrange his stretcher just a shade shorter than he would have it for rowing. He can clear his knees with a shorter stretcher when sculling than when rowing, as he can easily see for himself. A stretcher should always be as short as is compatible with clearing the knees.

Whether or not the pupil is proficient in sliding, he had better keep a fixed seat while learning the rudiments of sculling ; it will give him less to think about ; he might unconsciously contract faults in sliding while fixing his mind elsewhere—in the direction of his new implements.

He should see that his rowlocks are roomy. In most gigs there is a want of room between thowl and stopper. A sculler requires a wider rowlock than an oarsman, because his scull goes forward to an acuter angle than an oar, with the same reach of body. Nothing puts out a sculler's hands more than a recoil of the scull from the stopper, for want of room to reach out. The sculler should examine whether his rowlocks are true ; the sills of them should be horizontal, not inclined, and most of all not inclined from stern to bow ; the latter defect will at once make him scull deep. Next, let him examine his thowl. This should be clean faced, not 'grooved' by the upper edge of the loom of oars which have been handled by operators who feather under water, and who thus force at the finish with the upper edge and not with the flat back of the loom. Half the hack gigs that are on hire will be found to have rowlocks so worn, grooved, and disfigured, that not the best sculler in the world can lay his strength out on them until he has filed them into shape. The thowl should show a flush surface, and rake just the smallest trifle aft, so as to hold the blade just a fraction of an angle less than a rectangle to the water, but this 'rake' should be very slight.

Having now got his tools correct, the workman will have no excuse for grumbling at them if he fails to do well. Let him begin by paddling gently and slowly. He had better not attempt to work hard. If he sees some other sculler shooting past him in a similar boat, he must sink all jealousy. Every motion which he makes in a stroke is now laying the foundation of habit and of mechanical action hereafter ; hence he must give his whole mind to each stroke, and be content to go to work steadily and carefully. He must feel his feet against his stretcher, both legs pressing evenly. He must hold his sculls in his fingers (not his fists), and let the top joint of each thumb cap the scull. This is better than bringing the thumb under the scull ; it gives the wrists more play, and tends to avoid cramp of the forearm. He must endeavour to do his main work with his body and legs, when he has laid hold of the water. He should keep his arms rigid, and lean well back. Just as he passes the perpendicular his hands will begin to cross each other. Whichever hand he prefers to row over, he should

K

stick to. When the hands begin to cross, he should still try to keep the arms stiff, and to clear the way by slightly lowering one hand and raising the other. Not until his hands have opened out again after having crossed should he begin to bend his arms and to bring the stroke home to the chest. He should try to bend each arm simultaneously and to the same extent, and to bring each hand up to his breast almost at his ribs, at equal elevations. He must try to feather both sculls sharply and simultaneously.

If he finds any difficulty in this, he will do well to give himself a private lesson on this point before he proceeds further. He can sit still and lay his sculls in the rowlocks, and thus practise turning the wrists sharply, on and off the feather, till he begins to feel more handy in this motion.

On the recovery he should shoot his hands out briskly, the body following but not waiting for the hands to extend—just as in a 'rowing' recovery. When the recovering hands begin to cross each other the lower and upper must respectively give way, and so soon as they open out after the cross, they should once more resume the same plane, and extend equally, so as to be ready to grip the water simultaneously for the succeeding stroke.

Very few scullers realise the great importance of even action of wrists. If one scull hangs in the water a fraction of a second more than another, or buries deeper, or skims lighter, the two hands at that moment are not working evenly. Therefore the boat is not travelling in a straight line ; therefore she will sooner or later, may be in the latter half of the very same stroke; have to be brought back to her course. In order to bring her back, the hand which, earlier, was doing the greater work, must now do less. Therefore the boat has not only performed a zigzag during the stroke, but also she has been, while so meandering, propelled by less than her full available forces, first one hand falling off through clumsiness, and afterwards the other hand shutting off some work, in order to equalise matters.

As the sculler becomes more used to his action, he will find his boat keep more even. At first he will be repeatedly putting more force on one hand than on another, and will have to rectify his course by counterwork with the neglected hand. Some scullers, though otherwise good, never steer well. They do not watch their stern-post, to see if they go evenly at each stroke ; still less, if they see a slight deflection to one hand after one stroke, do they at once rectify the deviation by extra pressure on the other hand during the ensuing stroke. A good steerer in sculling will correct his course even to half a stroke ; if through a bend, or a wave, or other cause, he sees one hand has taken the other a little round by the time that the sculls are crossing, he will row the other hand home a trifle sharper, and so bring the keel straight by the time he feathers. When a sculler gets more settled to his work, and has got over the first difficulty of clearing his hands at the crossing, he will begin to acquire the knack of bringing the boat round to one hand, without any distinct extra tug of that scull. He will press a trifle more with the one foot, and will throw a little more of his weight on to the one scull, and so produce the desired effect on his boat.

When a sculler promotes himself to a light boat, he must be very careful not to lose the knack of even turns of wrists which he has been so assiduously studying in his tub. In the wager boat, far more than in the tub, is the action of the sculler's body affected and his labour crippled by any uneven action of either hand. The gig did not roll if one hand went into the water an infinitesimal fraction of a second sooner, or came out that much later than the other hand. But the fragile sculling boat, with no keel, and about thirteen inches of beam, resents these liberties, and requires ' sitting ' in addition, when-ever any inequality of work takes her off her balance. The sculler must especially guard against feathering under water. He is more tempted to do so now, while he is in an unsteady boat, than when he was in his sober-going gig. He feels instinctively that if he lets his blades rest flat on the water for

K 2

the instant, when his stroke concludes, he obtains for the
moment a rectification of balance ; the flat blades stop rolling
to either side ; when he has thus steadied his craft, then he
can essay to lift his blades and to get forward.   If he once
yields to this insidious temptation, he runs the risk of spoiling
himself as a sculler, and of ensuring that he will never rise
beyond mediocrity.   The hang back, and the sloppy feather,
which are to be seen in so many second-class scullers, may
almost invariably, if the history of the sculler be known, be
traced to want of nerve and of confidence in early days to
feather boldly, and to lift the sculls sharp from the water,
regardless of rolling.   Of course, for the nonce, the sculler can
sit steadier, and therefore make more progress, if he thus
steadies his craft with his blades momentarily flat ; and it is
because of this fact that so many beginners are seduced into
the trick.   But let the sculler pluck up courage, and endeavour
to imagine himself still afloat in his gig.   Let him turn his
wrists as sharply as when he was in her, and lift his blades
boldly out, not even caring if he rolls clean over.   There really
is little chance of his so capsizing.   If he rolls, his one blade
or other floats in the water, and being strung over at the rowlock, cannot well let his boat turn over, so long as he holds on
to the handle.   Meantime, he must sit tight to his boat, and
use his feet to balance her with his body.   He must not try to
row too fast a stroke ; a quick stroke hides faults, and speed
tends to keep a light craft on an even keel so long as her crew
are fresh ; but style is not learned while oarsmen or scullers
are straining their utmost.   If the sculler finds that he really
cannot make progress in his wager boat, he must assume that he
wants another spell of practice in his tub, and must revert again
to her for a week or two, or more.   If he will only persevere in
studying even and simultaneous action of hands, he will get his
reward in time.

He should not be ambitious to race too soon.   Many a
young sculler spoils himself by aspiring to junior scullers' races
before he is ripe for racing.   It is a temptation to have a ' flutter,'

just to see how one gets on, but it is of no use to race unless the competitor has had some gallops beforehand ; and it is in trying to row a fast stroke before they can thoroughly sit a boat that so many scullers sow seeds of bad style, which stick to them long afterwards, and perhaps always. When at last the sculler has learned to sit his boat, to drop his hands in simultaneously, to feel an even pressure with both blades, to see his stern-post hold on true, and not waver from side to side ; when he is able to drop and turn both wrists at the same instant, to lift both blades clean away from the water, and to shoot out his hands without fouling either his knees or the water, then he has mastered more than half the scullers of the

A SPILL.

day—even though he can only perform thus for half-a-dozen strokes at a time without encountering a roll. He can now lay his weight well on his sculls, and can make his boat travel. He will have done well if all this time he has abstained from indulging in a slide ; he does not need one as yet, he is not racing, and the fewer things he has to think about the better chance he has of being able to devote his attention to acquiring even hands and a tight seat. Once let him gain these accomplishments, and he can then take to his slide, and in his first race go by many an opponent who started sculling long before him, but who began at once in a wager boat and on a slide.

A very good amateur sculler—J. E. Parker, winner of the Wingfield Sculls in 1863—used to say that he always went back until his sculls came out of the water of their own accord. As a piece of chaff, it used to be said of him, by his friends, that there was a greasy patch on his fore canvas, where his head came in contact with it at the end of his stroke. Of course this was only a jest, but undoubtedly Parker swung farther back than most scullers, perhaps more than any amateur. The secret of his pace, which was indisputable, as also his staying power, probably lay to a great extent in this long back swing of his. He also sculled exceedingly cleanly, his hands worked in perfect unison, and his blades came out clean and sharp. The writer cannot recall any sculler whose blades were so clean, save Hanlan and also W. S. Unwin in 1886. Much of the secret of each of these scullers lay in the evenness of their hands ; they wasted no power. F. Playford, junior, was a more powerful sculler, and apparently faster than either of the above-named amateurs (*ceteris paribus* as to slides, *quâ* Parker) ; but taking his reach and weight into consideration, it is not to be wondered if Playford was in his day the best of all Wingfield winners. The late Mr. Casamajor was a great sculler. He also had a very long back swing, and clean blades. He never had such tough opponents to beat as had Playford, but at least it could be said of him that he was unbeaten in public in any race.

Steerage apparatus is in these days fitted to many a sculling boat. The writer, as an old stager, is bound to admit that he had retired from active work before such mechanism was used, he therefore cannot speak practically as to its value for racing. So far as he has watched its use by scullers, he is induced to look upon the contrivance with suspicion. On a stormy day, with beam wind for a considerable part of the course, such an appendage will undoubtedly assist a sculler. It will save him from having an arm almost idle in his lap during heavy squalls. But on fairly smooth days, or when wind is simply ahead, a rudder must surely detract more from pace (by reason of the water which it catches, even when simply on the trail) than it ever will save by obviating the operation of rowing a boat round by the hand to direct her course. Again, the fittings which carry the rudder must, when the rudder is unshipped, hold a certain amount of water to the detriment of speed. Also, if a boat is pressed for a spurt, there must be some risk of the tiller of the rudder (however delicately made), and the wires which control it, pulling and drawing the water. When the canvas ducks under water on recovery, it is important that the water should run off freely when the boat springs to the stroke. If a post stands up at the stern, however thin and metallic, this must to some degree check the flow off of the water. Again, the feet must be moved to guide this rudder ; while they are thus shifting, the fullest power of the legs can hardly be applied. A sculler who is in good practice, and who is at home with his boat and sculls, should be able to feel his boat's course through each stroke, and to adjust her at any one stroke if she has deviated during the preceding one. On the whole, barring circumstances such as a stiff westerly wind at Henley, or a gale on the tideway course, scullers will do best without rudders ; and if a competitor desires to provide against the contingency of weather which will make a rudder advantageous, he had better, if he can, have a spare boat fitted for that purpose, so that if the water after all is smooth he will not be carrying any projecting metal at his stern to draw the water and to check his pace.

There is another objection to the use of rudders, especially for young scullers. It tempts them to rely on the rudder to rectify their course, instead of studying even play of hands so that the boat may have no excuse for deviating at all in smooth water.

All that has been said of the use of slides applies equally to sculling as to rowing. The leg action, as compared to swing, should be just the same when sculling as in rowing. That is, the slide should last as long as the swing. Now, in sculling, a man should go back much further than he does when rowing an oar. When he has an oar in his hand there is a limit to the distance to which he can spring back with good effect. His oar describes an arc ; when he has gone back beyond a certain distance the butt of his oar-handle will come at the middle of his breast or even more inside the boat. In such a position he cannot finish squarely and with good effect. Therefore he cannot go back *ad lib.* But the sculler is always placed evenly to his work, it is not on one side of him more than another. He should, when laying himself out for pace, swing back so far that his sculls come out just as his hands touch his ribs. In a wager boat, when well practised, he can afford to let his sculls overlap as much as six or even seven inches. But, after all, the extent of overlap is a matter of taste with so many scullers, that it would be unwise to lay down any hard and fast rule, beyond saying that at least the handles should overlap four inches, or, what is much the same, one hand should at least cover the other when the sculls lie in the rowlocks at right angles to the keel.

To return to the slide in sculling. Since the back swing should be longer in sculling than in rowing, and as there is a limit to the length which any pair of legs can slide, and since also it has been laid down as a rule that both when sculling and when rowing the slide should be economised so that it may last as long as the swing lasts, the reader will gather that the legs will have to extend more gradually when sliding to sculls than when sliding to oars. Therefore a man accustomed to row on slides, and whose legs are more or less habituated to a certain extension coupled with swing when rowing, must keep a watch upon himself when sculling lest his rowing habits should make him finish his slide prematurely, when he needs to prolong his swing for sculling. Unless his slide lasts out his swing, his finish, after legs have been extended, will only press the boat without propelling her.

In rowing an oarsman is guilty of fault if he meets or even pulls up to his oar. In sculling, with a very long swing back it is not a fault to commence the recovery of the body while the hands are still completing their journey home to the ribs. The body should not drop, nor slouch over the sculls while thus meeting them. It should recover with open chest and head well up, simply pulling itself up slightly, to start the back swing, by the handles of the sculls as they come home for the last three or four inches of their journey. Casamajor always recovered then, so did Hanlan, so did Parker, and any sculler who does likewise will sin (if he does sin in the opinion of some hypercritics of style) in first-class company. The fact is, this very long swing back (with straight arms) entails much recovery, and yet materially adds to pace. The sculler can afford to ease his recovery in return for the strain of his long stroke. Also lest his long swing should press the boat's bows, he can ease her recovery as well as his own, so soon as the main force of the long drag comes to an end. In the writer's opinion, unless a sculler really does go back *à la* Casamajor & Co. with straight arms and stiff back, and until his sculls come out of the water almost of their own accord as he brings his hands in, it is not an advantage for him to pull himself up to his handles to this trifling extent at the finish. A sculler who does not swing back further than when he is rowing, will do best to row his sculls home just as he would an oar.

In racing all men like a lead. If a sculler can take a lead with his longest stroke, swinging back as far as he can, and can feel that he is not doing a stroke too fast for his stamina, by all means let him do so ; but let him be careful not to hurry his stroke and thereby to shorten his back swing simply for the sake of a lead. Many a long-swing sculler spoils his style, at all events for the moment, by sprinting and trying to cut his opponent down. It is almost best for him if he finds that his opponent has the pace of him, and if he therefore relapses to his proper style, and bides his time. If he does so, he will go all the faster over the course for sticking to his style regardless of momentary lead. Some scullers lay out their work for pace, regardless of lasting power. When Chambers rowed Green in 1863, he tried to head the Australian, flurried himself, shortened his giant reach, lost pace, and, after all, lost the lead. When he realised that, force pace as much as he could, Green was too speedy, the Tyne man settled to his long sweep, and at once went all the faster, though now sculling a slower stroke.

It was not long before Green began to come back to him, and the result of that match is history.

Similarly, the writer recollects seeing the celebrated Casamajor win the Diamonds for the last time, in 1861. He was opposed by Messrs. G. R. Cox and E. D. Brickwood. Cox was a sculler who laid himself out for fast starting : he used very small blades, he did not swing further back than when rowing, and he sculled a very rapid stroke. He had led both Casamajor and H. Kelley in a friendly spin earlier in the year, and it was said that it was to vindicate his reputation as being still the best sculler of the day that the old unbeaten amateur once more entered for the Diamonds, where he knew he would encounter Cox in earnest, and no longer in play. (Casamajor was by no means in good health, and the grave closed over him in the following August.)

In the race in question Cox darted away with the lead. Casamajor had hitherto led all opponents in real racing, and *amour propre* seemed to prompt him to bid for the lead against the new flyer ; he quickened and quickened his stroke, till his long swing back vanished, and his boat danced up and down, but he could not hold Cox. Brickwood was last, rowing his own style, and sculling longest of the three. After passing the Farm gate, Casamajor suddenly changed his style, and went back to his old swing. Maybe, Cox had already begun to come to the end of his tether ; but, be that as it may, from the instant that Casamajor re-adopted his old swing back, he held Cox. (It did not look as if the pace was really falling off, for both the leaders were still drawing away from Brickwood.) In another minute Casamajor began to draw up to the leader, still swinging back as before. Then he went ahead, and all was over. Brickwood in the end rowed down Cox, and came in a good second. Casamajor at that time edited the 'Field' aquatics. His own description therein of himself in the race seems to imply that he realised how he had at first thrown away his speed by bidding for the lead, and that he purposely, and not unconsciously, changed his style about the end of the first minute and a half of the race. His description of his own sculling at that juncture (modestly penned) was 'now rowing longer and with all his power.' This was quite true—he was not using his full power until he relapsed to his old style. These illustrations of two of the best scullers ever seen bidding for impossible leads, and then realising their mistakes in time, may be taken to heart by all modern and future aspirants to sculling honour.

SCULLING RACE, WITH PILOTS IN EIGHT-OARS.

Another reason why scullers like a lead is that it saves them from being 'washed' by a leader, and, conversely, enables them to 'wash an opponent.' In old days of boat-racing under the old code, lead was of importance, to save water being taken. Under new rules of boat-racing (which figure elsewhere in this volume), water can only be taken at peril. There is not, therefore, so much importance in lead as of old. As to 'wash,' if a man can sit a sculling boat, he does not care much for wash. Anyhow, he can, if in his own water, and if his adversary crosses him, steer exactly in his leader's wake; the wash then spreads like a swallow's tail on either side of the sternmost man, and does not affect him. His opponent must get out of his way, if not overtaken, so he need not disturb himself; and if the leader insists on steering to right or left simply to direct the wash, he loses more ground by this meandering than even the pursuer will lose by the slight perturbations of a sculling boat's wash for a few strokes. It is good practice for any sculler to take his boat now and then in the wake of another sculler, and try to 'bump' him. It will teach him how to sit his boat under such circumstances, and he will be surprised before long to find out how little he cares for being washed by another sculler.

A sculler, when practising over a course, especially when water is smooth, may with advantage time himself from day to day at various points of the course. He will thus find out what his best pace is, and will ascertain whether his speed materially falls off towards the end, if he forces extra pace at the start or halfway or so on. He must be careful to judge *proportionately* of times and distances, and not positively; for streams may vary, and so may wind.

On the tideway in sculling matches, it is usual for pilots to conduct scullers. The pilot sits in the bow of an eight. The sculler may rely on the pilot to signal to him whether he is in the required direction; but when he once knows that his boat points right, he should note where her stern points, just as if he were steering upon his own resources, and should endeavour so to regulate his hands that his stern keeps straight, as shown by some distant landmark which he selects. This straight line he should then maintain to the best of his ability, bringing his stern-post back to it, if it deflects, until his pilot again signals to him to change his course, for rounding some curve or for clearing some obstacle. The pilot cannot inform his charge of each small inaccuracy which leads eventually to deflection from the correct line; this the sculler must provide against on his own account. It is only when the course has to be changed, or when the sculler has palpably gone out of his course, that the signals of the pilot come into play. Some scullers seem to make up their minds to leave everything to their pilots; the result is that their boats are never in a straight line ; first they go astray to one side, and then, when signalled back, they take a stroll to the other side. Such scullers naturally handicap themselves greatly by thus losing ground through these tortuous wanderings. The simplest method of signalling by pilot is to hold a white handkerchief. In the right or left hand it means 'pull right or left,' respectively. When down, it means 'boat straight and keep it so.' If the pilot gets far astern, or if dangers are ahead which are beyond pilotage, taking off the hat means 'look out for yourself.'

When wind is abeam, a pilot cutter can materially aid a sculler by bringing its bow close on his windward quarter, thereby sheltering his stern from the action of the wind. Races such as that of Messrs. Lowndes and Payne for the Wingfield Sculls in 1880, when Mr. Payne did not row his opponent down until the last mile had well begun, should remind all scullers that a race is never lost till it is won, and that, however beaten you may feel, it is possible that your opponent feels even worse, and that he may show it in the next few strokes.

PUMPED OUT.

CHAPTER XI.

BOAT-BUILDING AND DIMENSIONS.

THE 'trim built wherry' of song has been improved off the face of the Thames. Originally it was purely a passenger craft : it contained space for two or more sitters in the stern, and was fitted for two pair of sculls or a pair of oars at option. Larger wherries were also built, 'randan' rig (for a pair of oars with a sculler amidships, or three pairs of sculls at option). Such boats were the passenger craft of the silent highway before steamers destroyed the watermen's trade. When match racing came into vogue, wherries began to be constructed for purely racing purposes ; they had but one seat, for the sculler, and were carried as fine as they could be, at either end, with regard to the surf which they often had to encounter. Their beam on the waterline was reduced to a minimum ; but at the same time it was necessary, for mechanical purposes, that the gunwale, at the points where the rowlocks were placed, should be of sufficient width to enable the sculler to obtain the necessary leverage and elevation of his sculls. The gunwale was accordingly flared out wide at these points, above the waterline. This flared gunwale had nothing to do with the flotation of the boat ; it was in effect nothing more than a wooden outrigger, and it was this which eventually suggested to the brain of old Harry Clasper the idea of constructing an iron outrigger, thereby enabling the beam to be reduced, and at the same time the sculling leverage to be preserved without the encumbrance of the top hamper of these flared gunwales. Such was the old wager wherry, and its later development of the wager outrigger.

We have said that the wherry is obsolete. Modern water-men use, for passenger purposes, a craft called a 'skiff.' She is an improvement on the 'gig,' a vessel which came into vogue on the Thames for amateur pleasure purposes about the year 1830. The 'gig' was originally adopted from naval ideas. She had a flush gunwale, and the rowlocks were placed on the top of it. So soon as the outrigger came in, oarsmen realised the advantage to be gained by applying it to the gig, in a modi-fied form. Half-outrigged gigs became common ; they had a reduced beam, and commanded more speed ; they were used for cruising purposes as well as for racing. Many regattas offered prizes for pair oars with coxswains in outrigged gigs. Theoretically a gig was supposed to be 'clinker' built, i.e. each of her timbers were so attached to each other that the lower edge of each upper timber overlapped the upper edge of the timber below it, the timbers being 'clincked,' hence the name. 'Carvel' (or caravel) build is that in which the timbers lie flush to each other, presenting a smooth surface. This offers less resistance, and before long builders constructed so-called 'gigs' for racing purposes, which were carvel built. From this it was but a step to build racing gigs with but two or even one 'streak' only, i.e. the side of the hull, instead of being constructed of several planks fastened together, was made of one, or at most two planks. The ends of the vessel were open--uncanvassed, and in this respect only was there anything in common with a 'gig' proper. This system of stealing advantages by tricks of build caused gig races to be fruitful sources of squabbles, until regatta committees recognised the importance of laying down conditions as to build when advertising their races.

To return to gigs proper. This craft did not find the same favour fifty years ago with the professional classes that it did with amateurs. The wherry was still adhered to for traffic ; but meantime Thames fishermen, especially those who plied flounder fishery on the upper tideway, used what is called a skiff; a shorter boat, with as much beam as the largest wherry, a bluff bow, and flared rowlocks. She was strongly built, adapted to carry heavy burdens, and, by reason of being shorter, was easier to turn, and handier for short cruises. A similar class of boat, but often rougher and more provincial in construction, was to be found in use at some of the up-river ferries. The wherry, when once under way, had more speed than the skiff, but when long row-boat voyages ceased in consequence of the introduction of steamers, the advantage of the skiff over the wherry was recognised by watermen. Their jobs came down to ferrying, to taking passengers on board vessels lying in the stream, and such like work ; and for these services speed was not so important as handiness in turning.

During the last fifteen years the skiff build has found more favour for pleasure purposes than the gig. The outrigged gig is liable to entanglement of rowlock in locks, and where craft are crowded, as at regattas. (It would be a salutary matter if the Thames Conservancy would peremptorily forbid the presence of any such craft at Henley Regatta.) Inrigged craft glide off each other when gunwales collide, whereas outriggers foul rowlocks of other boats, and cause delay and even accidents. An outrigged gig has two alternative disadvantages, compared to the skiff build ; if she is as narrow at the water-line as the skiff, her flush gunwale reduces the leverage for oar or scull. If, on the other hand, she is built to afford full leverage, this entails more beam on the waterline than in a skiff, the rowlocks of which are raised and flared above the gunwale. Hence it is that the skiff build is gradually super-seding the once universally popular gig.

A dingey is a short craft, originally designed as a sort of tender to a yacht, but adopted for pleasure purposes on the Thames for nearly half a century. It is sometimes built with a flush gunwale like a gig, but more commonly with flared rowlocks like a skiff, thereby affording the required leverage for swells, while at the same time reducing the beam on the waterline.

Besides the above mentioned craft, which are designed to carry at least two oarsmen (or scullers) and a coxswain, modern boat-builders construct what are called sculling dingies and gigs, which are fitted with only one pair of rowlocks, and are intended mainly for occupation by a single sculler, though they will at a pinch carry sitters both in the stern sheets and in the bows. They also build sailing gigs and dingies, which are usually fitted with a 'centreboard,' and are of greater beam than those specially designed for rowing or sculling ; though they can be also propelled by oars or sculls when required, they are less handy for the latter purposes, in consequence of their construction for the double duties of both sailing and oarsmanship. The following are dimen-sions commonly adopted by builders, such as Messrs. Salter of Oxford, for various classes of gigs, dingies, and pleasure skiffs :—

	Length.	Beam.
Gig, pair-oared, inrigged	22 ft.	3 ft. 9 in.
ditto randan	25 ft.	3 ft. 9 in.
Skiffs, pair-oared	25 ft.	4 ft. 0 in.
ditto	23 ft.	4 ft. 6 in.
ditto	20 ft.	5 ft. 0 in.

The variations in beam being in such vessels designed con-versely as regards the lengths, in order to obtain approximate equivalent of displacement—

	Length.	Beam.
Skiffs, randan . . .	26 ft. to 27 ft.	4 ft. 0 in.
ditto . . .	25 ft.	4 ft. 6 in. to 5 ft.

L

Where the beam ranges as high as 5 feet the vessel will carry about four sitters in the stern. The narrower craft carry about two, sitting abreast in the stern.

Dingies (inrigged) range from about 12 feet in length with 4 feet beam to 16 feet in length with about 3 ft. 6 in. beam.

Some dingies are built as short as 9 feet, but they command but little speed, and are useful only as tenders to larger vessels for the purpose of going ashore, &c. Their shortness makes them handy to turn, and compensates in short journeys for their want of speed.

The prices of the various builds enumerated above depend much upon the materials used, whether oak, mahogany, cedar, or pine ; and also upon length of keel, and upon fittings, such as oars, sculls, cushions, stern-rails, &c., masts and sails. Figures vary from about 40*l.* for a best quality randan skiff, all found, to as low as 20*l.* for a gig, and 12*l.* for a dingey, turned out new from the builder's yard.

It is customary to fit all rowing boats such as above described with a hole in the bow seat, and also in the flooring below, in order to carry a lug or sprit sail when required ; but the shallow draught of such vessels as are not fitted with centre-boards causes them to make a good deal of leeway and so disables them from sailing near the wind.

Racing boats are generally built of cedar, sometimes of white pine. The history of the introduction of the various improvements of outriggers, keelless boats, and sliding seats, has been given in other chapters. We propose here simply to give a few samples of dimensions of racing boats.

Various builders have various lines, and no exact fixed scale can be laid down as correct more than another.

Dimensions of a sculling-boat recently used by Bubear in a sculling match for the ' Sportsman Challenge Cup,' built by Jack Clasper.

Length	31 ft. 0 in.
Width	0 ft. 11 in.
Depth, amidships	0 ft. 5¾ in.
,, forward	0 ft. 3½ in.
,, sternpost	0 ft. 2¼ in.

Historical Eight-oars (Keelless).

	Length.	Beam.	Builder.
1. Oxford boat,[1] 1857	54 ft. 0 in.	2 ft. 2½ in.	Mat Taylor.
		(at No. 3's rowlock)	
2. Eton, 1863 .	57 ft. 0 in.	2 ft. 1 in.	Mat Taylor.
	Depth at stern 6 in.		
3. Radley, 1858	56 ft. 0 in.	2 ft. 0¼ in.	Sewell, for King.
	Depth at stern 7¼ in.		
4. Oxford, 1878	57 ft. 0 in.	1 ft. 10 in.	Swaddell & Winship.
	Depth at stern 6 in.		
5. Oxford, 1883	58 ft. 0 in.	1 ft. 10½ in.	J. Clasper.
	Depth at stern 6½ in.		

These boats are selected because each in its turn won some reputation, and also because they exemplify the builds of different constructors.

No. 1 was always highly esteemed by those who rowed in her.

No. 2 carried Eton at Henley Regatta from 1863 to 1870 or 1871.

No 3 was eulogised by Mr. T. Egan in 'Bell's Life,' on the occasion of her *début* in the above-mentioned school match *v.* Eton. She retained a high reputation for several seasons, was once specially borrowed by Corpus (Oxon) during the summer eights, and was said by that crew to be a vast improvement on their own ship.

No 4 carried Oxford from 1878 to 1882 inclusive, losing only the match in 1879, in which year the crew and not the boat were to blame.

No. 5, after one or two trials, was in 1883 found to be faster than No. 4 (which was then getting old !), and in her the Oxonians won a rather unexpected victory ; odds of 3 to 1 being laid against them.

In addition to these builds, the dimensions recorded by the well-known authority 'Argonaut,' in his standard work on 'Boat Racing,' are here given. That writer does not commit himself to saying that they are the *best*, but simply states that they are

[1] The first keelless eight that won a University match.

the 'average dimensions' of modern racing boats. Unfortunately, the writer cannot trace the dimensions of the celebrated 'Chester' boat, Mat Taylor's first keelless *chef-d'œuvre*, but he recollects that her length was only 54 feet ; and her stretchers were built into her and were fixed.

The cost of a racing eight, with all fittings, is about 55*l.* Some builders will build at as low a price as 50*l.*, especially for a crack crew, or for an important race, because the notoriety of the vessel, if successful, naturally acts as an advertisement. A four-oar costs 35*l.* to 40*l.* ; a pair-oar 20*l.* to 25*l.* ; and a sculling boat 12*l.* We have known some builders ask 15*l.* for a sculling boat. On the whole, racing boats are from eight to ten per cent. cheaper nowadays than they were a quarter of a century ago. Although the introduction of sliding seats necessarily adds to the expense of making them, competition seems to have brought down the prices somewhat.

'Argonaut's' Dimensions of Modern Boats.

Particulars	Racing Eight		Racing Fours: With Cox.		Racing Fours: Without Cox.		Pair Oars		Sculling Boats	
	ft.	in.	ft.	in.	ft.	in.	ft.	in.	ft.	in.
Length of boat	58	6	41	0	40	0	34	4	30	0
Breadth (over all)	2	0	1	9	1	8	1	4⅜	1	4[2]
Depth, amidships	1	1½	1	0½	1	0	0	10½	0	8½
" stem	0	8	0	7¼	0	7½	0	4¼	0	3½
" stern	0	7¼	0	6¾	0	6½	0	3¾	0	2¾
Distance from seat to thowl[1]	0	5	0	5	0	5	0	4½	0	4
Height of work from level of slide	0	7¾	0	7¾	0	7¾	0	7½	0	7½
Length of slide	1	4	1	4	1	4	1	5	1	5½
Length of amidship oars	12	6	12	6	12	6	—		—	
Buttoned at	3	6	3	5½	3	5½	—		—	
Length of bow and stroke oars	12	4	12	4	12	4	12	3	—	
Buttoned at	3	4½	3	4½	3	4½	3	4	—	
Length of sculls	—		—		—		—		10	0
Buttoned at	—		—		—		—		2	8
Space between cox.'s thwart and stroke's stretcher (cox.'s thwart 18 inches deep)	1	8	1	8	—		—		—	

The writer thinks, and believes that 'Argonaut' would agree with him, that these recorded average dimensions could

[1] Measured from front edge of slide to plane of thowl.
[2] Breadth on boat, 11½ inches.

be improved upon in divers respects, e.g. as to oars, for sliding seats the length 'inboard' should not be less than 3 ft. 7½ in. to 3 ft. 8 in. ; otherwise, when the oarsman swings back there is not sufficient length of handle to enable his outside hand to finish square to his chest, and with the elbow well past the side. The sliding-seat oar requires to be at least 10 inches longer inboard than the fixed-seat oar, for the above reason ; and in order to counterpoise this extra leverage, it is customary to use blades an inch wider for slides than for fixed seats, viz. 6 inches wide at the greatest breadth, instead of 5 inches as of old.

Again, as to distance of the plane of the thowl perpendicularly from that of the front of the slide when full forward. This should not be less than 6½ inches, in the writer's opinion, even with a 16-inch slide. If the oarsman slides nearer than the above to his work, he does not gain ; for much of his force is thus expended in jamming the oar back against the rowlock, rather than in propelling the boat. He 'feels' extra resistance, and may accordingly delude himself that he is doing more work, if the slides close up ; but in reality he is wasting his powers.

In modern racing boats, the men slide too close to their work ; and if any builder will have the courage to set his men further aft than is the custom (say about 6½ to 7 inches), he will find his ship travel all the faster.

As to shapes of hull : the earliest Mat Taylor boats have never been surpassed, in the writer's opinion, and were much faster than the modern builds. The peculiarity of Mat Taylor's build was that he put his greatest beam well forward, about No. 3's middle or seat. Such boats held more 'way' than more modern craft, which are fullest amidships.

Builders of the present day construct as if the only problem which they had to solve was to force a hole through the water in front of the boat. This is not all that is necessary in order to get a boat to travel well. A racing boat leaves a vacuum behind her, and until that is filled she is sucked back into that vacuum.

A boat built like the half of a split porcupine's quill could enter the water with the least resistance, but would leave it with the greatest ; in fact, she would not travel at all, because her bluff stern would create a sudden vacuum behind her, which would retard her progress. This is a *reductio ad absurdum*, but it shows the effect of having the greatest beam too far aft. The problem to be solved in designing the lines of a boat is so to arrange her entry into the water, that what she displaces in front may with greatest ease flow aft to fill the vacuum aft which she leaves as she progresses. Otherwise she pushes a heavy wave in front of her, and drags another behind her. If anyone will watch the bank as a racing eight passes, noting the level of the water at a rathole, he will see the level of the stream first rise as the boat comes nearly abreast of his point of observation. Then, as she passes, the water will sink, and after she has passed it will rise again higher than before she neared the spot.

The first rise is caused by the boat pushing a wave in front of her : the following depression is caused by the vacuum which she is leaving behind her, and the final rise by the wave which runs behind her to fill her vacuum. Obviously, the less water the vessel moves the easier she travels. If by any designing the wave pushed in front could be induced to run more or less back to the stern, then the second (following) wave would be more or less reduced in bulk, and the labour would be proportionately lighter.

The finer the lines taper aft, the easier the front wave displaced finds its way to the vacuum aft. *Per contra*, the more bluff the midship and stern sections, the greater the difficulty in filling the vacuum aft.

Builders hamper themselves by adhering to a red-tape idea that all oarsmen in a boat should be seated at equal distances from each other. So long as designers adhere to this, they require a good deal of beam aft, if Nos. 6, 7 and stroke are of anything like average size. Of course, there must be a minimum of space for each man to reach out in ; but there is no reason why in some of the seats the space should not exceed this minimum, e.g. to set the first four men at the minimum, and then to place No. 5 an extra inch past No. 4 and so on, with perhaps stroke and 7 $1\frac{1}{2}$ inches further apart than the forward men, would enable the builder to attain a greater longitudinal displacement at the sternmost part of the boat than he would otherwise require to carry his men. In lieu of this gain, he can then reduce his beam and depth aft, and so make his lines taper more to the stern.

Mat Taylor built on this principle. Detractors used to laugh sometimes to see him chalk off his seats, and say, 'A rowlock here—a seat there.' The fact was, Mat Taylor placed his men, man for man, over the section of vessel built to carry them, allowing the minimum distance for reach in all cases, but by no means tying himself down to that distance where in his · opinion the boat required elongating aft. They said he built by rule of thumb ; so, perhaps, he did, but his builds have never been surpassed. Modern eights travel faster than of old, thanks to sliding seats and good oarsmanship, but if some of the old lost lines could be now reproduced, the speedy crews of modern days would be speedier still.

We offer one more illustration to show the effect of having too sudden a termination to a boat aft of her greatest beam, or of a certain amount of beam. Let anyone construct two models of racing boat hulls ; probably he will not succeed in making two of equal speed, but such as they are he can handicap the speedier in his experiment. Let him place the two models to race, each towed by a line carried over a pulley, with a weight at the end of the line. The weights which tow the two models can be adjusted till the two run dead heats.

Then cut off the stern of one of the models, and bulkhead her, say about coxswain's seat, and let them race once more with the forces which previously produced a dead heat. The model with a docked stern will have become the smaller vessel, and will now weigh less. Nevertheless, she will become decidedly slower than she was before, and will be beaten by her late duplicate.

In order to do justice to this experiment, the weights should tow at a pace equivalent to about four miles or more an hour. It will then be seen that this docked model leaves a whirlpool behind her stern, which is retarding her. This experiment of course exaggerates the principle of full afterlines, and their evil, but it may none the less serve to illustrate the importance of a finer run aft from a point further forward than amidships. *En passant,* the boat built by Salter of Oxford for the O.U.B.C. in 1865 may be mentioned ; her dimensions are not to be traced, but she was specially designed to carry the heaviest man (E. F. Henley) at bow. She was certainly never surpassed by any other boat which Salter built. She won in 1865. In 1866 a heavier crew were in training, and the 1865 boat was supposed to be too small. She was not tried at all at Oxford with the crew. A new boat was built, this time to carry E. F. Henley at 5. When the crew reached Putney the writer felt dissatisfied with the movement of the new boat, and persuaded the crew to try the old one, even though she would be rather too small for them. They sent for her, and launched for a trial paddle the Monday before the race ; so soon as they had rowed a dozen strokes in her they stopped, and declared she was the only light boat they had felt that season. They rowed the race in her, and won, and never took the trouble to set foot again in the new and rejected boat.

This victorious boat was then bought by the Oxford Etonians. They won the Grand Challenge of 1866 and 1867 in her, took her to Paris, and there won the eight-oared race at the International Regatta. She was sold and left behind in Paris. The writer suspects that her undeniable speed was mainly owing to the fact that Salter designed some extra displacement at No. 3, in order to carry E. F. Henley at that seat.

'POETRY.'

CHAPTER XII.

TRAINING.

DIET.

THAT 'condition' tells in all contests, whether in brain labours such as chess matches or in athletics, is known to children in the schoolroom.

Training is the *régime* by means of which condition is attained. Its dogmas are of two orders : (1) Those which relate to exercise, (2) those which refer to diet. Diet of itself does not train a man for rowing or any other kind of athletics. What trains is hard work ; proper diet keeps the subject up to that work.

The effect of a course of training is twofold. It develops

those muscles which are in use for the exercise in question, and
it also prepares the internal organs of heart and lungs for the
extra strain which will be put upon them during the contest.
All muscles tend to develop under exercise, and to dwindle
under inaction. The right shoulder and arm of a nail-maker
are often out of all proportion to the left ; the fingers of a
pianist develop activity with practice, or lose it if the instrument
be discontinued.

Training is a thorough science, and it is much better understood in these days than when the writer was in active work ;
and again, the trainers of his day were in their turn far ahead
of those of the early years of amateur oarsmanship. From the
earliest recorded days of athletic contests, there seems to have
been much faith pinned to beefsteaks. When Socrates rebukes
Thrasymachus, in the opening pages of Plato's ' Republic,' he
speaks of beefsteaks as being the chief subject of interest to
Polydamos, who seems to have been a champion of the P.R.
of Athens of those days. The beefsteak retains its prestige to
the present day, but it is not the *ne plus ultra* which it was in
1830.

The earliest amateur crews seem to have rowed in many
instances without undergoing a course of training and of reduction of fat. But when important matches began to be
made, the value of condition was appreciated. Prizefighters
had then practical training longer than any other branch of
athletics, and it was by no means uncommon for watermen,
when matched by their patrons, to be placed under the supervision of some mentor from the P.R. as regards their diet and
exercise. But before long watermen began to take care of
themselves in this respect. Their system of training did not
differ materially from that in vogue with the P.R. It consisted
of hard work in thick clothing, early during the course of preparation, to reduce weight ; and a good deal of pedestrian
exercise formed part of the day's programme ; a material result
of the association of the P.R. system of preparation. The diet
was less varied and liberal than in these days, but abstinence

from fluid to as great an extent as possible was from the outset recognised as all-important for reducing bulk and clearing the wind.

A prizefighter or waterman used to commence his training with a liberal dose of physic. The idea seems to have a stable origin, analogous to the principle of physic balls for a hunter on being taken up from grass. The system was not amiss for men of mature years, who had probably been leading a life of self-indulgence since the time when they had last been in training. But when University crews began to put themselves under the care of professional trainers, those worthies used to treat these half-grown lads as they would some gin-sodden senior of forty, and would physic their insides before they set them to work. They would try to sweat them down to fiddle-strings, and were not happy unless they could show considerable reduction of weight in the scale, even with a lad who had not attained his full growth. Still, though many a young athlete naturally went amiss under this severe handling, there is no doubt that these professional trainers used to turn out their charges in very fine condition, on the average.

No trainer of horses would work a two-year-old on the same system that he would an aged horse ; and the error of these old professional trainers lay in their not realising the difference in age between University men and the ordinary classes of professional athletes. In time University men began to think and to act for themselves in the matter of training. When college eights first began to row against each other, there were only three or four clubs which manned eights ; and these eights now and then were filled up with a waterman or two. (In these days few college crews would take an Oxford waterman at a gift — *quâ* his oarsmanship !) These crews, when they began to adopt training, employed watermen as mentors. Before long there were more eights than watermen, and some crews could not obtain this assistance. The result was, a rule against employing professional tuition within a certain date of the race. This regulation threw University men upon their own resources, and before long they came to the conclusion that good amateur coaching and training was more effective than that of professionals. Mr. F. Menzies, the late Mr. G. Hughes, and the Rev. A. Shadwell, had much to do in converting the O.U.B.C. to these wholesome doctrines. From that time amateurs of all rowing clubs have very much depended on themselves and their *confrères* for tuition in oarsmanship and training.

The usual *régime* of amateur training is now very much to the following effect.

Réveille at 6.30 or 7 A.M.—Generally a brief morning walk ; and if so, the 'tub' is usually postponed until the return from the walk. If it is summer, and there are swimming facilities, a header or two does no harm, but men should not be allowed to strike out hard in swimming, when under hard rowing rules. For some reason, which medical science can better explain, there seems to be a risk of straining the suspensory or some other ligaments, when they are suddenly relaxed in water, and then extended by a jerk. (This refers to arms that have lately been bearing the strain of rowing.) Also, the soakage in water for any length of time tends to relax the whole of the muscular system. Whether tub or swim be the order of the morning, the skin should be well rubbed down with rough towels after the immersion. In old days there used to be a *furore* for running before breakfast. Many young men find their stomachs and appetites upset by hard work on an empty stomach, more especially in sultry weather. The Oxford U.B.C. eight at Henley in 1857 and 1859 used to go for a run up Remenham Hill before breakfast, and this within two or three days of the regatta. Such a system would now be tabooed as unsound.

Breakfast consists of grilled chops or steaks ; cold meat may be allowed if a man prefers it. If possible, it is well to let a roast joint cool *uncut*, to supply cold meat for a crew. The gravy is thus retained in the meat.

Bread should be one day old ; toast is better than bread. Many crews allow butter, but as a rule a man is better without it. It adds a trifle to adipose deposit, and does not do any special service towards strengthening his tissues or purifying his blood.

Some green meat at breakfast is a good thing. Watercress for choice—next best are small salad and lettuce (plain).

Tea is the recognised beverage ; two cups are ample for a man. If he can dispense with sugar it will save him some ounces of fat, if he is at all of a flesh-forming habit of body. A boiled egg is often allowed, to wind up the repast.

GOING TO SCALE.

Luncheon depends, as to its substance, very much upon the time of year and the hours of exercise. If the work can be done in two sections, forenoon and afternoon, all the better. In hot summer weather it may be too sultry to take men out between breakfast and the mid-day meal. Luncheon now usually consists of cold meat, to a reasonable amount, stale bread, green meat, and a glass of ale. In the days when the writer was at Oxford, the rule of the O.U.B.C. was to allow no meat at luncheon (only bread, butter, and watercress). This

was a mistake; young men, daily wast'ng a large amount of
tissue under hard work, had a natural craving for substantial
food to supply the hiatus in the system.   By being docked of it
at luncheon, they gorged all the more at breakfast and dinner,
where there was no limit as to quantity (of solids) to be consumed.   They would have done better had their supply of
animal food been divided into three instead of two daily allow-
ances.   They used to be allowed one slice of cold meat during
their nine days' stay at Putney; it would have been well to
have allowed this all through training.

Dinner consists mainly of roast beef or mutton, or choice
of both.   It is the custom to allow 'luxuries' of some sort
every other day, e.g. fish one day, and a course of roast
poultry (chicken) on another.   'Pudding' is sometimes allowed daily, sometimes it only appears in its turn with 'luxuries.'   It generally consists of stewed fruit, with plain boiled
rice, or else calves'-foot jelly.   A crust, or biscuit, with a little
butter and some watercress or lettuce, make a final course
before the cloth is cleared.

Drink is ale, for a standard; light claret, with water, is
nowadays allowed for choice, and no harm in it.   A pint is the
normal measure; sometimes an extra half-pint may be conceded
on thirsty days.

An orange and biscuit for dessert usually follow.   In the
writer's days every man had two glasses of port wine.   He
thinks this was perhaps more than was required (as regards
alcohol); one glass may suffice, but there may be no reason
against the second wineglass being conceded, with water substituted, if the patient is really dry.   Claret also may take the place
of port after dinner.   Fashions change; in the writer's active
days, claret would have been scorned as un-English for athletes.

Such is the usual nature of training diet; of the exercise
of the day, more anon.   There does not seem to be much
fault to find with the *régime* above sketched; in fact, the proof
of soundness of the diet may be seen in the good condition
usually displayed by those who adopt it.

All the same, the writer, when he has trained crews, has slightly modified the above in a few details. He has allowed (a little) fish or poultry daily, as an extra course, and for the same reason has always endeavoured to have both beef and mutton on the table. He believes that change of dish aids appetite, so long as the varieties of food do not clash in digestion. Men become tired with a monotony of food, however wholesome. Puddings the writer does not think much of, provided that other varieties of dish can be obtained. A certain amount of vegetable food is necessary to blend with the animal food, else boils are likely to break out ; but green vegetables such as are in season are far better than puddings for this purpose. Salad, daily *with the joint*, will do good. It is unusual to see it, that is all. The salad should not be dressed. Lettuce, endive, watercress, smallcress, beetroot, and some minced spring onions to flavour the whole, make a passable dish, which a hungry athlete will much relish. Asparagus, spinach, and French beans may be supplied when obtainable. Green peas are not so good, and broad beans worse. The tops of young nettles, when emerald green, make a capital dish, like spinach, rather more tasty than the latter vegetable. Such nettles can only be picked when they first shoot ; old nettles are as bad as flowered asparagus.

If a crew train in the fruit season, fruit to a small amount will not harm them, as a finale to either breakfast or dinner. But the fruit should be *very* fresh, not bruised nor decomposed ; strawberries, gooseberries, grapes, peaches, nectarines, apricots (say one of the last three, or a dozen of the smaller fruits, for a man's allowance), all are admissible. Not so melons, nor pines—so medical friends assert.

In hot summer weather it is as well to dine about 2 P.M., to row in the cool of the evening, towards 7 P.M., and to sup about 8.30 or 9 P.M. It is a mistake to assume that because a regatta will come off midday, therefore those who train for it should accustom themselves to a burning sun for practice. With all due deference to Herodotus (who avers that the skeleton skulls of quondam combatant Persians and Egyptians could be known apart on the battle-field, because the turban-clad heads of Persians produced soft skulls which crumbled to a kick, while the sun-baked heads of Egyptians were hard as bricks), we do not believe in this sort of acclimatisation. If men have to be trained to row a midnight race, they would be best prepared for it by working at their ordinary daylight hours, not by turning night into day for weeks beforehand. On the same principle it would seem to be a mistake to expose oarsmen in practice to excessive heat to which they have not been accustomed, solely because they are likely eventually to row their race under a similar sun. In really oppressive weather at Henley the writer and his crews used to dine about 2 P.M. as aforesaid, finish supper at 9 or 9.30, and go to bed two hours later. They rose proportionately later next day, taking a good nine hours in bed before they turned out. So far as their records read, those crews do not seem on the whole to have suffered in condition by this system of training.

Many men are parched with thirst at night. The heat of the stomach, rather overladen with food, tends to this. The waste of the system has been abnormal during the day ; the appetite, i.e. instinct to replenish the waste, has also been abnormal, and yet the capacity of the stomach is only normal. Hence the stomach finds it hard work to keep pace with the demands upon it. Next morning these men feel 'coppered,' as if they had drunk too much overnight, and yet it is needless to say they have not in any way exceeded the moderate scale of alcohol already propounded above as being customary.

The best preventive of this tendency to fevered mouths is a cup of 'water gruel,' or even a small slop-basin of it, the last thing before bedtime. It should not contain any milk ; millet seed and oatmeal grits are best for its composition. The con-sumption of this light supper should be _compulsory_, whether it suits palates or not. The effect of it is very striking ; it seems to soothe and promote digestion, and to allay thirst more than three times its amount of water would do. Some few men cannot, or profess to be unable to, stomach this gruel. The writer has had to deal with one or two such in his time. He had his doubts whether their stomach or their whims were to blame ; but in such cases he gave way, and allowed a cup of chocolate instead—*without milk*. (Milk blends badly with meat and wine at the end of a hard day.) Chocolate is rather more fattening than gruel, otherwise it answers the same purpose, of checking any disposition to 'coppers.'

It has been a time-honoured maxim with all trainers, that it is the fluids which lay on fat and which spoil the wind. Accordingly, reduction in the consumption of fluid has always been one of the first principles of training, and it is a sound one so long as it is not carried to excess. It is not at the outset of training that thirst so oppresses the patient, but at the end of the first week and afterwards, especially when temperature rises and days are sultry. Vinegar over greens at dinner tends to allay thirst ; the use of pepper rather promotes it. In time the oarsman begins to accustom himself somewhat to his diminished allowance of fluid, and he learns to economise it during his meals, to wash down his solids.

A coach should be reasonably firm in resisting unnecessary petitions for extra fluid, but he must exercise discretion, and need not be always obdurate. On this subject the writer reproduces his opinion as expressed in 'Oars and Sculls' in 1873 :—

The tendency to 'coppers' in training is no proof of insobriety. The whole system of training is unnatural to the body. It is an excess of nature. Regular exercise and plain food are not in themselves unnatural, but the amount of each taken by the subject in training is what is unnatural. The wear and tear of tissue is more than would go on at ordinary times, and consequently the body requires more commissariat than usual to replenish the system. The stomach has all its work cut out to supply the commissariat, and leave the tendency to indigestion and heat in the stomach. A cup of gruel seldom fails to set this to rights, and a glass of water besides may also be allowed if the coach is satisfied that a complaint of thirst is genuine. There is no greater folly than stinting a man in his liquid. He should not be allowed to blow himself out

M

with drink, taking up the room of good solid food ; but to go to the other extreme, and to spoil his appetite for want of an extra half-pint at dinner, or a glass of water at bedtime, is a relic of barbarism. The appetite is generally greatest about the end of the first week of training. By that time the frame has got sufficiently into trim to stand long spells of work at not too rapid a pace. The stomach has begun to accustom itself to the extra demands put upon it, and as at this time the daily waste and loss of flesh is greater than later on, when there is less flesh to lose, so the natural craving to replenish the waste of the day is greater than at a later period. At this time the thirst is great, and though drinking out of hours should be forbidden, yet the appetite should not, for reasons previously stated, be suffered to grow stale for want of sufficient liquid at meal times in proportion to the solids consumed.

Such views would have been reckoned scandalously heretical twenty-five or more years ago, but the writer feels that he is unorthodox in good company, and is glad to find Mr. E. D. Brickwood, in his treatise on 'Boat-racing,' 1875, laying down his own experiences on the same subject to just the same effect. Mr. Brickwood's remarks on the subject of 'thirst' (as per his index) may be studied with advantage by modern trainers. He says (page 201) :—

As hunger is the warning voice of nature telling us that our bodies are in need of a fresh supply of food, so thirst is the same voice warning us that a fresh supply of liquid is required. Thirst, then, being, like hunger, a natural demand, may safely be gratified, and with water in preference to any other fluid. The prohibition often put upon the use of water or fluid in training may often be carried too far. To limit a man to a pint or two of liquid per day, when his system is throwing off three or four times that quantity through the medium of the ordinary secretions, is as unreasonable as to keep him on half-rations. The general thirst experienced by the whole system, consequent upon great bodily exertion or extreme external heat, has but one means of cure—drink, in the simplest form attainable. Local thirst, usually limited to the mucous linings of the mouth and throat, may be allayed by rinsing the mouth and gargling the throat, sucking the stone of stone fruit, or a pebble, by which to excite the glands in the affected part, or even by dipping the hands into cold water. Fruit is here of very little benefit, as the fluid passes at once to the stomach, and affords no relief to the parts affected; but after rinsing the mouth, small quantities may be swallowed slowly. The field for the selection of food to meet the waste of the body under any con- dition of physical exertions is by no means restricted. All that the exceptional requirements of training call for is to make a judicious selection; but, in recognising this principle, rowing men have formed a dietary composed almost wholly of restrictions the effect of which has been to produce a sameness in diet which has almost been as injurious in some cases as the entire absence of any laws would be in others.

It should be borne in mind that Mr. Brickwood's field as an amateur lay principally in sculling, which entailed solitary train- ing, unlike that of a member of an eight or four. He had therefore to train himself, and to trust to his own judgment when so doing, blending self-denial with discretion. He is, in the above quotation, apparently speaking of the principles under which he governed himself when training. That they were crowned with good success his record as an athlete shows, for he twice won the Diamond Sculls, and also held the Wingfield (amateur championship) in 1861. Such testimony therefore is the more valuable coming from a successful and self-trained sculler.

As regards sleep, the writer lays great stress upon obtaining a good amount of it. Even if a night is sultry, and sleep does not come easily, still the oarsman can gain something by mere physical repose, though his brain may now and then not obtain rest so speedily as he could wish. The adage ascribed to King George III. as to hours of sleep, 'six for a man, seven for a woman, and eight for a fool,' is unsound. He who is credited with having propounded it, showed in his later years that, either his brain had suffered from deficiency of rest, or that it never had been sufficiently brilliant to justify much attention being bestowed on his philosophy. Probably he never did a really hard day's (still less a week's) labour, of either brain or body, in his life. Had he done so, he would have found that not six, nor seven, and often not eight hours, are too much to enable the wasted tissues of brain or body, or both, to recuperate. It is when in a state of repose that the blood, newly made from the latest meal, courses through the system and replenishes what has been wasted during the day. Recruits are never measured for the standard at the end of a day's march, but next day—after a good rest. Cartilage, sinew, muscle, alike waste. The writer used, after racing the Henley course, perhaps thrice in an evening's practice (twice in a four or eight and afterwards in a pair-oar or sculling boat, &c.), to take a good nine hours' sound sleep, and awoke all the better for it. Some men keep on growing to a comparatively late age in life ; such men require more sleep, while thus increasing in size, than others who have earlier attained full bulk and maturity. As a rule, and regardless of what many other trainers may say to the contrary, the writer believes that the majority of men in training may sleep nine hours with advantage.

The period of training varies according to circumstances. A man of twenty-five and upwards, who has been lying by for months, it may be for a year or two, can do with three months of it. The first half should be less severe than the last. He can begin with steady work, to redevelope his muscles, and to reduce his bulk (if he is much over weight) by degrees. The last six weeks should be 'strict' in every sense. He can get into ' hunting ' condition in the first six weeks, and progress to ' racing ' condition in the succeeding six.

University crews train from five to six weeks. The men are young, and have, most of them, been in good exercise some time before strict training begins.

College crews cannot give much more than three weeks to train for the summer bumping races ; tideway crews have been doing a certain amount of work for weeks before they go into strict training for Henley ; this last stage usually lasts about four weeks.

It is often supposed that a man needs less training for a short than for a long course. This is a mistake. The longer he prepares himself, so long as he does not overdo himself, the better he will be. Long and gradual training is better than short and severe reductions. Over a long course, when an untrained man once finds nature fail him, more ground will be lost than over a short course : *cela va sans dire* : but that is no argument against being thoroughly fit for even a half-mile row. The shorter the course, the higher the pressure of pace, and the crew that cracks first for want of condition—loses (*ceteris paribus*).

Athletes of the running path will agree that it is as impor-

SMOKING IS FORBIDDEN.

tant to train a man thoroughly for a quarter-mile race as for a three-mile struggle. Pace kills, and it is condition which enables the athlete to endure the pace.

Smoking is, as every schoolboy knows, forbidden in training. However, *pro formâ*, the fact must be recorded that it is illicit. It spoils the freedom of the lungs, which should be as elastic as possible, in order to enable them to oxygenate properly the extra amount of blood which circulates under violent exertions.

Aperients at the commencement of training used to be *de*

rigueur. Young men of active habits hardly need them. Anyhow, no trainer should attempt to administer them on his own
account ; if he thinks the men need physic at the outset, let
him call in a medical man to prescribe for them.

WORK.

We have said that proper diet keeps an oarsman up to the
work which is necessary to bring him into good condition.   Having detailed the *régime* of diet, and its appurtenances, such as
sleep, we may now deal with the system of work itself.

One item of work we have incidentally dealt with, to wit, the
morning walk ; but it was necessary to handle this detail at that
stage because it had a reference to the morning tub and morning
meal.

The work which is set for a crew should be guided by the
distance of time from the race.   If possible, oarsmen should
have their work lightened somewhat towards the close of training, and it is best to get over the heavy work, which is designed
to reduce weight as well as to clear the wind, at a comparatively
early stage of the training.

There is also another factor to be taken into calculation by
the trainer, and that is whether, at the time when sharp work is
necessary to produce condition, his crew are sufficiently advanced as oarsmen to justify him in setting them to perform
that work at a fast stroke in the boat.   Not all crews require to
be worked upon the same system, irrespective of the question
of stamina and health.

Suppose a crew are backward as oarsmen and also behindhand in condition.   If such a crew are set to row a fast stroke
in order to blow themselves and to accustom their vascular
system to high pressure, their style may be damaged.   If on
the other hand they do no work except rowing at a slow stroke
until within a few days of the race, they will come to the post
short of condition.   Such a crew should be kept at a slow stroke
in the boat, in order to enable them to learn style, for a fortnight
or so ; but meantime the trainer should put them through some

sharp work upon their legs. He should set them to run a mile or so after the day's rowing. This will get off flesh, and will clear the wind, and meantime style can be studied in the boat. Long rows without an easy are a mistake for backward men who are also short of work. When the pupil gets blown at the end of a few minutes he relapses into his old faults, and makes his last state worse than the first. Training not only gets

'RUN A MILE OR TWO.'

off superfluous flesh, but also lays on muscle. The sooner the fat is off the sooner does the muscle lay on. The commissariat feeds the newly developing muscles better if there is no tax upon it to replenish the fat as well. For this reason, apart from the importance of clearing the wind, heavy work should come early in training. When a crew who have been considerably reduced in weight early in their course of training, feed up towards the last, and gain in weight, it is a good sign, and shows that their labours have been judiciously adjusted ; the weight which they pick up at the close of training is new muscle replacing the discarded fat.

In training college eights for summer races there is not scope for training on the above system. The time is too short, some of the men are already half-fit, and have been in work of some sort or other during the spring ; while one or two of them may have been lying idle for a twelvemonth. In such cases a captain must use his own discretion ; he can set his grosser men to do some running while he confines those who are fitter to work only in the ship. As a rule, however, unless men have no surplus flesh to take off, all oarsmen are the better for a little running at the end of the day during the early part of training. It prepares their wind for the time when a quick stroke will be required of them. A crew who have been rowing a slow stroke and who have meantime been improved in condition by running, will take to the quick stroke later on more kindly than a ditto class crew who have done no running, and whose condition has been obtained only by rowing exercise. The latter crew have been rowing all abroad while short of wind, and have thereby not corrected, and probably have contracted, faults. The former crew will have had better opportunities of improving their style, will be more like machinery, and will be less blown when they are at last asked to gallop in the boat.

For the first few days it will be well to row an untrained crew over easy half-miles. A long day's work in the boat will not harm them : on the contrary, it will tend to shake them together ; tired men can row well as to style, but men out of breath cannot row. At the end of a week or so, the men can cover a mile at a hard slow grind without an easy. If there is plenty of time, i.e. some five weeks of training, a good deal of paddling can be done, alternating with hard rowing at a slow stroke. If there are only three weeks to train, and men are gross, much paddling cannot be spared. If again time is short and men have already been in work for other races, and do not want much if any reduction in weight, then a good deal of the day's work may be done at a paddle.

Thirty strokes a minute is plenty for slow rowing. Some strokes, though good to race behind, have a difficulty in rowing slow, especially after having had a spell at a fast stroke. It is important to inculcate upon the stroke that thirty a minute should be his 'walking' pace, and should always be maintained except when he is set to do a course, or a part of one, or to row a start. When once he is told to do something like racing over a distance, he must calculate his stroke to orders, whether thirty-two, -four, -six, -eight, &c. But when the 'gallop' is over, then the normal 'thirty' should resume. It is during the 'off' work, when rowing or paddling to or from a course, that there is most scope for coaching, and faults are best cured at a slow stroke.

In training for a short course, such as Henley and college races, a crew may be taken twice each day backwards and forwards over the distance ; the first time at thirty a minute each way, the second time at the 'set' pace of the day, over the course, relapsing into the usual 'thirty' on the reverse journey. The 'set' stroke depends on the stage of training. A fortnight before the race the crew may begin to cover the course, on the second journey, at about thirty-one a minute. A stroke a day can be added to this, until racing pace is reached. If men seem stale, an off-day should be given at light work. Meantime, each day, attention should be paid to 'starting,' so that all may learn to get hold of the first stroke well together. In order to accustom the men to a quicker stroke and to getting forward faster, a few strokes may be rowed, in each start, at a pace somewhat in advance of the rate of stroke set for the day's grind over the course. A couple such starts as this per diem benefit both crew and coach. The crew begin to feel what a faster stroke will be like, without being called upon to perform it over the whole distance before they are fit to go ; the coach will be able to observe each man's work at the faster stroke. Many a green oarsman looks promising while the stroke is slow, but becomes all abroad when called upon to row fast. It is best to have some insight to these possible failings early in training, else it may be too late to remedy them or to change the man on the eve of battle.

Towards the close of training the crew should do their level best once or twice over the course, to accustom them to being rowed out, and to give them confidence in their recuperative powers ; also to enable the stroke to feel the power of his crew, and to form an opinion as to how much he can ask them to do in the race. The day before the racing begins, work should be light.

In bumping races, if a college has no immediate fear of foes from the rear, it is well not to bring men too fine to the post ; else, though they may do well enough for the first day or two, they may work stale or lose power before the end of the six days of the contest. It is better that a crew should row itself into condition than out of it. In training for long-distance racing, it is customary to make about every alternate day a light one, of about the same work as for college racing. The other days are long-course days of long grinds, to get men together, and to reduce weight. When men have settled to a light boat, and have begun to row courses against time, and especially when they reach Putney water, two long courses in each week are about enough. Many crews do not do even so much as this. As a rule a crew are better for not being taken for more than ten or eleven minutes of hard, uninterrupted racing, within three days of the race. A long course wastes much tissue, and it takes a day or two to feed up what they have wasted. Nevertheless, crews have been known to do long courses within 48 hours of a Putney match, and to win withal : e.g. the Oxonians of 1883, who came racing pace from Barnes to Putney two days before the race, and 'beat record' over that stretch of water.

Strokes and coaches do a crew much harm if they are jealous of 'times' prematurely in practice. Suppose an opponent does a fast time, there is no need to go to the starting point and endeavour to eclipse time. Possibly his rapid time has been accomplished by dint of a prematurely rapid stroke, while the pace of our own boat, with regard to the rate of stroke em-

BUMPING RACE—WAITING FOR THE GUN

ployed, discloses promise of better pace than our opponents, when racing shall arrive in real earnest. Now if we, for jealousy, take our own men at a gallop before they are ripe for it, we run great risk of injuring their style, and of throwing them back instead of improving them. After the day's race, the body should be well washed in tepid water, and rubbed dry with rough towels. It is a good thing for an oarsman to keep a toothbrush in his dressing-room. He will find it a great relief against thirst to wash his mouth out with it when dressing, more especially so if he also uses a little tincture of myrrh.

One 'odd man' is of great service to training, even if he cannot spare time to row in the actual race. Many a man in a crew is the better for a day's, or half a day's, rest now and then. Yet his gain is loss of practice to the rest, unless a stop-gap can be found to keep the machinery going. The berth of ninth man in a University eight often leads to promotion to the full colours in a following season, as U.B.C. records can show.

With college eights there used to be a *furore*, some twenty years ago, for taking them over the long course in a gig eight. These martyrs, half fit, were made to row the regulation long course, from 'first gate' to lasher, or at least to Nuneham railway bridge, at a hard and without an easy. The idea was to 'shake them together.' The latter desideratum could have been attained just as well by taking them to the lasher and back again, but allowing them to be eased once in each mile or so. Many crews that adopted the process met with undoubted success, but we fancy that their success would have been greater had their long row been judiciously broken by rest every five minutes. To behold a half-trained college eight labouring past Nuneham, at the end of some fifteen minutes of toil, jealous to beat the time of some rival crew, used to be a pitiable sight. More crews were marred than made by this fanaticism.

On the morning of a race it is a good thing to send a crew to run sprints of seventy or eighty yards, twice. This clears the wind greatly for the rest of the day, without taking any appreciable strength out of the man. A crew thus 'aired' do not so much feel the severity of a sharp start in the subsequent race, and they gain their second wind much sooner.

The meal before a race should be a light one, comparatively: something that can be digested very easily. Mutton is digested sooner than beef. H. Kelley used to swear by a wing of boiled chicken (without sauce) before a race. The fluid should be kept as low as possible just before a race ; and there should be about three hours between the last meal and the start. A preliminary canter in the boat is advisable ; it tests all oars and stretchers, and warms up the muscles. Even when men are rowing a second or third race in the day, they should not be chary of extending themselves for a few strokes on the way to the post. Muscles stiffen after a second race, and are all the better for being warmed up a trifle before they are again placed on the rack.

Between races a little food may be taken, even if there is only an hour to spare : biscuit soaked in port wine stays the stomach ; and if there is more than an hour cold mutton and stale bread (no butter), to the extent of a couple of sandwiches or more (according to time for digestion), will be of service. Such a meal may be washed down with a little cold tea and brandy. The tea deadens the pain of stiffened muscles ; the brandy helps to keep the pulse up. If young hands are fidgetty and nervous, a little brandy and water may be given them ; or brandy and tea, not exceeding a wine-glass, rather more tea than brandy. The writer used often to pick up his crew thus, and was sometimes laughed at for it in old days. He is relieved to find no less an authority than Mr. E. D. Brickwood, on page 219 of 'Boat-racing,' holding the same view as himself, and commending the same system of 'pick-me-up.'

AILMENTS.

A rowing man seems somehow to be heir to nearly as many ailments as a racehorse. Except that he does not turn 'roarer,' and that there is no such hereditary taint in rowing clubs, he may almost be likened to a Derby favourite.

Boils are one of the most common afflictions. They used to be seen more frequently in the writer's days than now. The modern recognition of the importance of a due proportion of vegetable food blended with the animal food has tended to reduce the proportion of oarsmen annually laid up by this complaint. A man is not carnivorous purely, but omnivorous, like a pig or a bear. If he gorges too much animal food meat, he disorders his blood, and his blood seeks to throw off its humours. If there is a sore anywhere on the frame at the time, the blood will select this as a safety valve, and will raise a fester there. If there is no such existing safety valve, the blood soon broaches a volcano of its own, and has an unpleasant habit of selecting most inconvenient sites for these eruptions. Where there is most wear and tear going on to the cuticle is a likely spot for the volcano to open, and nature in this respect is prone to favour the seat of honour more than any other portions of the frame. Next in fashion, perhaps, comes the neck ; the friction of a comforter when the neck is dripping with perspiration tends often to make the skin of the neck tender and to induce a boil to break out there. A blistered hand is not unlikely to be selected as the scene of outbreak, or a shoulder chafed by a wet jersey.

A crew should be under strict orders to report *all* ailments, if only a blister, *instantly* to the coach. It is better to leave *no* discretion in this matter to the oarsman, even at the risk of troubling the mentor with trifles. If a man is once allowed to decide for himself whether he will report some petty and incipient ailment, he is likely to try to hush it up lest it should militate against his coach's selection of him ; the effect of this is that mischief which might otherwise have been checked in the bud, is allowed to assume dangerous proportions for want of a stitch in time. An oarsman should be impressed that nothing is more likely to militate against his dream of being selected than disobedience to this or any other standing order. The smallest pimple should be shown forthwith to the coach, the slightest hoarseness or tendency to snuffle reported ; any tenderness of joint or sinew instantly made known.

To return to boils. If a boil is observed in the pimple stage, it may be scotched and killed. Painting it with iodine will drive it away, in the writer's experience. 'Stonehenge', advises a wash of nitrate of silver, of fifteen to twenty grains to the ounce, to be painted over the spot. Mr. Brickwood also, while quoting 'Stonehenge' on this point, recommends bathing with bay salt and water.

Anyhow, these external means of repression do not of themselves suffice. They only bung up the volcano ; the best step is to cure the blood, otherwise it will break out somewhere else. The writer's favourite remedy is a dose of syrup of iodide of iron; one teaspoonful in a wineglass of water, just before or after a meal, is about the best thing. A second dose of half the amount may be taken twenty-four hours later. This medicine is rather constipating ; a slight aperient, if only a dose of Carlsbad salts before breakfast or a seidlitz powder, may be taken to counteract it in this respect. It is a strong but prompt remedy ; anything is better than to have a member of a crew eventually unable to sit down for a week or so ! An extra glass of port after dinner, *and plenty of green food*, will help to rectify the disordered blood.

Another good internal remedy is brewer's yeast, a tablespoonful twice a day after meals. Watermen swear by this, and Mr. Brickwood personally recommends it.

If care is taken a boil can be thus nipped in the bud (figuratively) ; to do this *literally* is the very worst thing. Some people pinch off the head of a small boil. This only adds fuel to the fire. If a boil has become large, red, and angry before any remedies are applied, it is too late to drive it in, and the next best thing is to coax it out. This is done with strong linseed poultices. A doctor should be called in, and be persuaded to lance it, to the core, and to squeeze it, so soon as he judges it to be well filled with pus.

Raws used to be more common twenty-five years ago than

now : boat cushions had much to do with them. Few oarsmen in these days use cushions. Raws are best anointed with a mixture of oxide of zinc, spermaceti and glycerine, which any chemist can make up, to the consistency of cold cream. It should be buttered on thickly, especially at bed-time.

Blisters should be pricked with a needle (*never* with a *pin*); the water should be squeezed out, and the old skin left on to shield the young skin below.

Festers are only another version of boils. The internal remedies, to rectify the blood, should be the same as for boils. Cuts or wounds of broken skin may be treated like raws if slight ; if deeper, then wrapped in lint, soaked in cold water, and bound with oilskin to keep the lint moist.

Abdominal strains sometimes occur (i.e. of the abdominal muscles of recovery) if a man does a hard day's work before he is fairly fit. A day's rest is the best thing ; an hour's sitting in a hot hip bath, replenishing the heat as the water cools, gives much relief. The strain works off while the oarsman is warm to his work, but recurs with extra pain when he starts cold for the next row. If there is any suspicion of hernia (or 'rupture') work should instantly stop, even ten miles from home ; the patient should row no more, walk gently to a resting-place, and send for a doctor. Once only has the writer known of real hernia in a day's row, and then the results were painfully serious. Inspection of the abdomen will show if there is any hernia.

Diarrhœa is a common complaint. It is best to call in a doctor if the attack does not pass off in half a day. If a man has to go to the post while thus affected, it is a good thing to give him some *raw* arrowroot (three or four table-spoonfuls) in *cold* water. The dose should be well stirred, to make the arrowroot swill down the throat. To put the arrowroot into hot water spoils the effect which is desired.

Many doctors have a tender horror of consenting to any patient rowing, even for a day, so long as he is under their care, though only for a boil which does not affect his action.

Professional instinct prompts them to feel that the speediest possible cure is the chief desideratum, and of course that object is best attained by lying on the shelf. A doctor who will consent to do his best to cure, subject to assenting to his patient's continuing at work so long as actual danger is not thereby incurred, and so long as disablement for the more important race day is not risked, is sometimes, but too rarely, found.

Sprains, colds, coughs, &c., had better be submitted at once to a doctor. A cold on the chest may become much more serious than it appears at first, and should never be trifled with. Slightly sprained wrists weaken, but need not necessarily cripple a man. Mr. W. Hoare, stroke of Oxford boat in 1862, had a sprained wrist at Putney, and rowed half the race with only one hand, as also much of the practice. He was none the worse after Easter, when the tendons had rested and recuperated.

Oarsmen should be careful to wrap up warmly the instant that they cease work. Many a cold has been caught by men sitting in their jerseys—cold wind suddenly checking perspiration after a sharp row—while some chatter is going on about the time which the trial has taken, or why No. So-and-so caught a small crab halfway. A woollen comforter should always be at hand to wrap promptly round the neck and over the chest when exertion ceases, and so soon as men land they should clothe up in warm flannel, until the time comes to strip and work.

Siestas should not be allowed. There is a temptation to doze on a full stomach after a hard day, or even when fresh after a midday meal. No one should be allowed to give way to this ; it only makes men 'slack,' and spoils digestion.

If a man can keep his bedclothes on all night, and keep warm, he will do himself good if he sleeps with an open window, winter or summer. He thereby gets more fresh air, and accordingly has not to tax the respiratory muscles so much, in order to inhale the necessary amount of oxygen. Eight hours' sleep with open windows refresh the frame more than nine hours and upwards in a stuffy bedroom. A roaring fire may obviate an open window, for it forces a constant current of air through the apartment. The writer has slept with windows wide open, winter and summer, since he first matriculated at his University, save once or twice for a night or two when suffering from cold (not contracted by having slept with open windows). If a bed is well tucked up, and the frame well covered, the chest cannot be chilled, and the mouth and nose are none the worse for inhaling cool fresh air, even below freezing-point. This refers to men of sound chests. Men of weak constitution have no business to train or to race.

FOUR-OAR.

CHAPTER XIII.

ROWING CLUBS.

THE formation of a 'club' for the pursuit of any branch of sport gives a local stimulus at once to the game, and lends facilities for the acquisition of merit in the performance. This is peculiarly the case with rowing, and for more than one reason. Theoretically a man might, by unaided scientific study, elaborate for himself the most improved system or principle of oarsmanship. Practically he will do nothing of the sort, and if left to teach himself will develop all sorts of faults of style, which tend to the outlay of a maximum of exertion for a minimum of progress. The tiro in oarsmanship requires instruction from the outset ; the sooner he is taught, the more likely is he to become proficient. If he begins to teach himself, he will certainly acquire faulty action, which will settle to habit. If later on he has recourse to a mentor, the labours of both pupil and tutor will be more arduous than if the pupil were a complete beginner ; the pupil will require first to be *un*taught from his bad style before he is adapted for instruction in good action of limbs and body.

Moreover, all rowing becomes so mechanical that the polished oarsman is almost as unconscious of merit in his style (save from what others may tell him of himself) as the duffer is of his various inelegancies. The very best oarsman is liable insidiously to develop faults in his own style which he himself, or a less scientific performer, would readily notice in another person.

Hence, where men row together in a club, each can be of service to the other, in pointing out faults, of which the performer is unconscious. So that half-a-dozen oarsmen or scullers of equal class, if they will thus mutually assist each other, can attain between them a higher standard than if each had rowed like a hermit. Still more is the standard of oarsmanship raised among juniors when the older hands of a club take them in charge and coach them.

In addition to this system of reciprocal education, a club fosters rivalry, and organises club races ; and, in like manner, a plurality of clubs stimulates competition between clubs, and produces open racing between members of the rival institutions.

College clubs seem to be the oldest on record. Some of them go back as early as the concluding years of George the Third. The rise of British oarsmanship has been traced in a preceding chapter. The oldest 'open' rowing club is the 'Leander.' When it originated seems to be uncertain, but it was considered relatively to be an 'old' club in 1837.

Mr. G. D. Rowe, Hon. Secretary of the Club, has kindly extracted the following memoranda from the Club's history of its records :—

It would seem that the earliest known metropolitan rowing clubs were 'The Star' and 'The Arrow,' which existed at the end of the last century, and expired somewhere about 1820. Out of the ruins sprang the Leander Club, which is still a flourishing institution, and which includes amongst its members most of the great University oarsmen of the last thirty years or so. So far as can be ascertained, the Leander Club did not exist in 1820, but it was in full swing in 1825, and in 1830 was looked upon as a well-known and long-established boat club.

In 1837, 1838, and 1841 Leander rowed races against Cambridge, losing the first and winning the last, whilst in 1838 the race was declared a draw owing to fouling.

In all three the course was from Westminster to Putney.

In 1839 Leander was beaten for the Grand Challenge Cup at Henley by the Oxford Etonians ; but in 1840 the Leander crew won the Cup, whilst in 1841 they came in first, but were disqualified on a foul. In consequence of this Leander did not again compete for the G.C.C. till 1858,[1] as the Club considered the ruling of the Umpire unfair.

Meanwhile, however, in 1843, -4, and -5 Leander won the Challenge Cup at the Thames Regatta, and between 1845 and 1855 Leander won the Presentation Cup at Erith for Four-oars, several times.

Leander, however, was as much a social association as a competing rowing club. Up till 1856 the number of members was limited to twenty-five men, who used to meet at Westminster once or twice a week, and row to Putney or Greenwich, and take dinner together. Sometimes they would go to the Albert Docks, and dine on board a ship, at the expense of one of their members, who was a large shipowner.

After 1856 the number of members was increased to thirty-five, and in 1862 the Club was put on a more modern footing after the example of the London Rowing Club, and no limit was put on the number of members.

The Club quarters were moved to Putney, where a small piece of ground was rented on which a tent was erected for housing boats. This piece of ground was acquired by the London Rowing Club in 1864, and on it was built the present L.R.C. boat-house. Leander, however, were able to get a lease of a piece of land adjoining, and in 1866 built a boat-house, which still exists, though the Club has of late thought of departing from Putney and establishing themselves on one of the upper reaches of the Thames.

The rowing successes of Leander of late years have not been very great, though a Leander crew is always formidable 'on paper' and

---

[1] The Leander entry at Henley, 1858, arose thus. A mixed team of old Blues of *both* colours got up an eight, and qualified by rowing under the Leander flag.

comprises a good selection of 'Varsity oars. Want of practice and of combination usually outweighs individual skill. In 1875 and 1880 the Grand Challenge Cup was won by Leander under the leadership of Goldie and Edwardes-Moss respectively, but since 1880 all attempts to carry off the much-coveted prize have proved futile.

It must have been a curious sight in old days to see a Leander crew rowing in front of the 'Varsity race in their 'cutter' steered by Jim Parish, their waterman coxswain. The crew used to wear the orthodox top-hats on their heads, whilst the coxswain was arrayed in all the glories of 'green plush kneebreeches, silk stockings, " Brummagem " coat, and tall white silk hat.'

The match between Oxford and Leander in 1831 had ended in the defeat of Oxford, and when, six years later, Cambridge challenged Leander, it was thought by the London division to be a rash venture on the part of the Cantabs. But we read in the Brasenose B.C. records that in the opinion of some experts the Leander oarsmanship was observed to have rather fallen off of late, and that there were not wanting good judges who were prepared for the Cantab victory in which the match resulted. This casual remark seems to show that Leander was a club of some years' standing at the time of this match. There seems to have been a 'scullers' club, hailing from Wandsworth, even earlier than this. But if it had a name, the title is lost. There must have been a fair amount of sculling among amateurs prior to 1830, in order to induce Mr. Lewis Wingfield in 1830 to present the silver challenge sculls which still bear his name, and which to this day carry with them the title of Amateur Championship. The University clubs, when once founded, rapidly developed strength ; new college clubs were founded, and eights were manned by colleges and halls which hitherto had not entered for the annual bumping races. But London oarsmanship gradually deteriorated between 1835 and 1855. The cause of this decay is intelligible. The tideway was churned up by steamers, rowing from Westminster was no longer the pleasant sport which it had been, and railway facilities for suburban rowing had hardly developed. Leander made one show at Henley after its foundation and failed to score a win. After that Leander crews absented themselves from the scene until the days of their modern revival. There was a club called the 'St. George's' which put on a good four-oar or two in the 'forties' at Henley ; and after them came a 'Thames' club, which lasted some seasons, and chiefly distinguished itself by winning thrice running the 'Gold Cup' of the old Thames Regatta of the 'forties.' The Thames Club also won the Grand at Henley ; but they died out, and a lot of local small-fry clubs dismembered the rowing talent of the metropolis for the next few years. Of these, the most distinguished were the 'Argonauts,' between 1853 and 1856. They were not numerically strong, but they made up in quality for quantity. They were not enough to man an eight, and the Grand Challenge Cup at Henley was farmed for several seasons by the Universities. The Chester men came and went like a meteor in 1856. Their performances will be found under the description of the first keelless eight. In that year the London Rowing Club was founded, and in 1857, being then a year old, it made its *début* at Henley, and won the Grand Challenge, Mr. Wood in the Oxford crew breaking an oar in the last two hundred yards of the race. The foundation of the London Club did more to raise the standard of amateur rowing than anything in modern times. It created a third great factor in eight-oared rowing, and served to keep the Universities up to the mark. It also encouraged other clubs. Kingston soon followed suit, first with a four and afterwards with an eight. After them the new (modern) Thames Club also made its appearance at Henley, beginning like Kingston with fours before aspiring to eights. In these days Thames are rivals with London for the pick of the rowing talent of the tideway, and each acts as a stimulus to the other. It is no exaggeration to say that at an average Henley Regatta, during the present decade, four or five eights may often be seen, any one of which would, *ceteris paribus* (and sliding seats barred), have been considered a good winner of the Grand Challenge a quarter of a century ago, so great has been the advance in the standard of amateur rowing.

The Leander Club has been a practical reality once more for nearly twenty years ; it has competed periodically for the Grand Challenge and Stewards' Cups, and has twice won the Grand, but its composition is now widely different from what it was in the palmy 'Brilliant' days of fifty years ago. In those times it represented the rowing talent of the metropolitan element ; it filled the same position that the London and Thames Clubs now jointly occupy. In these days it is almost entirely composed of University men, past and present. Having vacated its old functions, it has in turn filled those formerly performed by the 'Subscription Rooms' of the Universities, which in the 'forties' used to hail from Stangate. There is but little junior rowing done or taught in Leander ; most of its recruits are already more or less proficient before they join it. It is not a nursery of oarsmanship, but a colony, to which rowing men from the Universities resort. It is of value in promoting sport and competition, but it does not, from the very nature of its elements, fill the same sort of position that the London and Thames Clubs hold in the rowing world—as nurseries of junior talent on the tideway. On the upper Thames, Kingston holds a position of much the same nature as London and Thames. Twickenham are an old club, but it is only of late years that they have aspired to Grand Challenge form ; they owe this aspiration to a reinforcement from Hertford College, Oxon. Besides these leading clubs there are sundry smaller bodies, which content themselves chiefly with junior rowing. Such are the 'West London' and 'Grove Park,'[1] the 'East Sheen,' and others of this class. Five-and-thirty years ago it was a rarity to see even a scratch amateur eight on the tideway, so much had London rowing gone downhill. In the present day, on a June or July evening, especially on Saturday, half-a-dozen or more may be seen between Wandsworth and Richmond.

Provincial oarsmanship has made considerable advance during the last thirty years. The Chester Club was the first to make

---

[1] Since the above was written, West London and Grove Park Clubs have become extinct.

a great mark, as mentioned elsewhere. The Eastern Counties
are the most behindhand in the science, although they have
good rivers in the Orwell and Yare. Newcastle produces
strong local clubs, and once a champion, Mr. Fawcus, came
from the Tyne. Mr. Wallace, a high-class sculler, also came
south, but without absolute success, some years before Mr.
Fawcus. Durham, what with its school, its University, and its
town, shows plenty of sport on the Wear. Lancashire sent a
fair 'Mersey' four to Henley in 1862, and in 1870 the 'John
o' Gaunt' men from the same river made a decided hit at
Henley, although they failed to win. Bath has produced some
good men before now, chiefly under the tuition of Mr. C.
Herbert, a London oarsman. The Severn has woke up considerably. In 1850 we doubt whether four men could have
been found on the whole river who could sit in an outrigger ;
but during the last fifteen years amateur rowing has made great
advances at Worcester, Bewdley, Bridgnorth, and other towns.
Tewkesbury started a regatta about a quarter of a century ago,
and other towns on the Severn have followed suit. At present
the Severn clubs confine their rowing very much to contests
among themselves, and do not try their luck on the Thames
in the leading regattas. The time may come when they will
acquire sufficient talent to enable them to make a creditable
display against the greater clubs of the Thames. The Trent,
though one of the finest of our English rivers, does very little
for oarsmanship. Some very second-class rowing is now and
then seen at Nottingham, and also at Burton-on-Trent. The
latter, many years ago, sent a pair-oar to Henley Regatta ; but,
so far as we can recall, the men, or one of them, was a Cantab
(Mr. Nadin), and we may surmise that he owed his oarsmanship
to the Cam rather than to the Trent. One curious feature in
provincial rowing is, and has been, the absence of any professional talent. The Tyne alone has really rivalled the Thames
in respect of producing leading professionals. A good four
once or twice came from Glasgow to the Thames Regatta about
sixteen years ago, and now and then a fair second-class sculler
(such as Strong, of Barrow-in-Furness) has appeared from the

provinces, but in other respects great apathy seems to prevail as regards professional oarsmanship on all our rivers except Thames and Tyne. The later decadence of professional talent òn these once famous rivers will be treated in another chapter.

Mr. Brickwood, in his book on 'Boat-racing,' gives some admirable suggestions for the formation of rowing clubs, which should be read by all who aspire to found such institutions. For the benefit of those who may hereafter take the lead in establishing new boat clubs, or in remodelling old ones, he propounds a 'draft' code of general rules ; it would be presumptuous to attempt to improve upon them, and we take the liberty of giving them *in extenso*, as sketched by this eminent authority.

DRAFT RULES.

1. This club shall be called the —— Rowing (or Boat) Club ; and the colours shall be ——.

2. The object of this club shall be the encouragement of rowing on the river —— amongst gentlemen amateurs.

3. Any gentleman desirous of becoming a member shall cause a notice in writing, containing his name, occupation, and address, together with the names of his proposer and seconder (both of whom must be members of the club, and personally acquainted with him, and one of whom must be present at the ballot), to be forwarded to the secretary fourteen days prior to the general meeting at which the candidate shall be balloted for ; one black ball in five shall exclude. In the case of neither the proposer nor seconder being able to attend the ballot for a new member, the committee may institute such inquiries as they may deem requisite, and on the receipt of satisfactory replies in writing from both proposer and seconder such attendance may be waived, and the election may proceed in the usual manner.

4. The annual subscription shall be ——, due and payable on February 1 in each year.

5. Subscriptions becoming due on February 1 shall be paid by April 1, and subscriptions becoming due after February 1 be paid within two months ; or, in default, the names of the members whose subscriptions are in arrears may be placed conspicuously in the club-room, with a notice that they are not entitled to the benefits of the club.

6. The name of any member whose subscriptions shall be in

arrear twelve months shall be posted in the club-room as a defaulter, and published in the circular next issued.

7. The proposer of any candidate shall (upon his election) be responsible to the club for the entrance-fee and first annual subscription of such candidate.

8. Members wishing to resign shall tender their resignation in writing to the secretary before February 1, otherwise they will be liable for the year's subscription ; the receipt of such resignation shall be acknowledged by the secretary.

9. The officers of the club shall consist of a president, vice-president, captain, and secretary, to be elected by ballot at the first general meeting in February in each year; the same to be *ex-officio* members of the committee.

10. The captain shall be at liberty, from time to time, to appoint a member of the club to act as his deputy, such appointment to be notified in the club-room.

11. The general management of the club shall be entrusted to a committee of —— members, and —— shall form a quorum ; such committee to be chosen by ballot at the first general meeting in February in each year.

12. A general meeting shall be held in every month, in the club-room, during the rowing season, and at such time and place during the winter as may be selected by the committee.

13. A notice containing the names of candidates for election at the general meeting shall be sent to every member of the club.

14. Any member who shall wilfully or by gross negligence damage any property belonging the club shall immediately have the same repaired at his own expense. The question of the damage being or not being accidental shall be decided by the committee from such evidence as they may be able to obtain.

15. A general meeting shall have power to expel any member from the club who has made himself generally obnoxious ; but no ballot shall be taken until fourteen days' notice shall have been given ; one black ball to three white to expel such member. This rule shall not be enforced except in extraordinary cases, and until the member complained of shall have been requested by the committee to resign.

16. No crew shall contend for any public prize, under the name of the club, without the sanction of the committee. All races for money are strictly prohibited.

17. The committee shall have the management of all club matches.

18. The rules and by laws of the club shall be printed, and posted in the club-room, and the copy sent to every member ; and any member who shall wilfully persist in the infraction of any such rules or by-laws shall be liable to be expelled.

19. Any member wishing to propose any alteration in the rules of the club shall give notice in writing to the secretary, two weeks prior to the question being discussed, when, if the notice be seconded, a ballot shall be taken, and to carry the proposed alteration the majority in favour must be two to one.

20. The committee shall have power to make, alter, and repeal by-laws.

By-Laws.

1. The boats of the club shall be for the general use of the members on all days during the season (Sundays excepted), subject to the following by-laws.

2. That no visitor be permitted to row in a club boat to the exclusion of a member of the club.

3. That the club day be —— in each week during the season, and the hour of meeting ——.

4. That on club days members be selected by the captain (or in his absence by his deputy) to form crews ; the members present at the hour of meeting to have priority of claim. Should the decision of the captain or his deputy be considered unsatisfactory by the majority of members present, the matter in dispute shall be settled by lot.

5. All boats shall be returned to the boathouse by ten o'clock at night, except on club days, when club boats taken out before the usual hour must be returned half an hour before the time fixed for meeting. Any expense incurred by the club through an infringement of this by-law shall be paid by the member offending.

6. Any dispute as regards rowing in any particular boat or boats shall be settled by lot, this provision having reference more particularly to club days.

7. In the event of there being more members present than can be accommodated in the club boats, it shall be at the discretion of the captain or his deputy, or of such members of the committee as may be present, to hire extra boats at the expense of the club.

8. The committee shall from time to time appoint one of their number to superintend the management of the boathouse, and to make all necessary arrangements for keeping the boats of the club in a thorough state of repair and cleanliness.

9. All crews sent by the club to contend at a public regatta shall be formed by the captain and two other experienced members to be named by the committee, such crews when formed to be subject to the approval of the committee.

10. In the event of a crew being chosen to contend in any public race or match, such crew shall be provided by the club with a boat for their exclusive use during their time of training, and shall have their entrance-fees paid by the club.

11. The expense of conveying boats to public regattas at which crews of the club contend shall be paid by the crews, but the committee shall have power to repay the whole or any part of such expenses out of the club funds.

12. The committee, on the occasion of a club race or other special event, shall appoint a member of the club to take charge of and conduct all arrangements connected with the same.

13. The member pulling the stroke-oar in any club boat shall have command of the crew.

14. Upon the arrival of a crew at the place appointed for stopping, the captain of the boat shall (if required) fix the time for returning ; and, if any member be absent at the appointed time, the crew shall be at liberty to hire a substitute at the expense of the absentee.

15. Every member, on landing from a club boat, shall be bound to assist in housing such boat, and in doing so shall follow the direction of the captain or other officer.

16. Any member using a private boat without the consent of its owner shall thereby render himself liable to a vote of censure, and, if need be, expulsion.

Clubs are often but ephemeral. Some leading spirit founds one, and, when his influence vanishes with himself, the club wanes ; perhaps it pales before a rival, perhaps it amalgamates with another. From various causes many minor clubs have risen and set on the Thames within the writer's memory during the last two decades ; others which were in full swing when he was at school or college have ceased to exist. In the summer of 1886 this question of extinction of small clubs became a subject of correspondence in the aquatic columns of the 'Field.' Subsequently the writer of this chapter discussed the question in the following leading article, published in the 'Field' on July 17,

1886, and now reproduced by the courtesy of the proprietors.· It is given *in extenso* for the sake of the history and reminiscences embodied in it.

The Extinction of Small Rowing Clubs.

We published a fortnight ago a letter of complaint on this subject from a correspondent who signed himself 'Senior Oarsman.' We quite admit the fact that the tendency of the great rowing clubs of the Thames has been to absorb the numerous petty clubs which at one time abounded on the tideway, but we entirely fail to agree with his view that this consummation is to be deprecated, either in the interests of oarsmanship or of regattas. Our own opinion is, that four or five strong clubs raise the standard of rowing and the prestige of regattas to a far greater extent than if these same societies were split up into a dozen or more minor associations. We can remember when there were a large number of petty clubs of that description, many of them hailing from Putney. The ground-floor doors of the annexe to the 'Star and Garter' at Putney still commemorate the names of some of them, though the clubs have been extinct for ages. 'Nautilus' and 'Star' are among the titles which are still painted on the doors. Prior to the founding of the London Rowing Club in 1856, the rowing talent of the Thames was split up into many such small sections. None of them, save the 'Argonauts,' were fit to man one decent four between them. The L.R.C. consolidated these small societies for the time being; but there are always to be found oarsmen who prefer to pose as leaders of small-fry clubs rather than play second or third fiddle in first-class clubs. Hence, no sooner had the L.R.C. consolidated one batch of small clubs than others sprang into existence. At the date of the founding of the Metropolitan Regatta in 1866 there were once more a host of these minor societies on the Thames, and one of the causes of weakness in the executive of that regatta arose from the recognition of these small clubs by the L.R.C. as factors to be consulted in its organisation. These petty clubs had no chance of winning the open prizes, but they were keen to distinguish themselves and have a hand in the gathering, and accordingly the 'metropolitan' eights and pairs for local second-raters had to be established, in order to induce the small clubs to join the undertaking. The result of this policy was, that before long the L.R.C. provided by far the larger proportion of the funds for the regatta, and yet had to defer to the majority of votes of the small clubs in the matter of executive. At that date Kingston was the only other club (except those of the U.B.C's.) which was up to Grand Challenge form, like the L.R.C. Since that date there has been an expansion of other strong clubs, and, as a necessary corollary, a gradual decay of minor ones. Thames has grown to be a worthy rival of London, and has done much to raise the standard of oarsmanship. Leander has been revived, and Twickenham, which at one time (in the sixties) was quite a small local club, now comes out also in Grand Challenge form. This club have not yet actually landed the great prize, but they have more than once been good enough to win it, had they been fortunate enough to draw the best station. Besides these clubs, there has been the Molesey Club, which in 1875 and 1876 was capable of making the best crews gallop at Henley, and won the Senior fours at sundry minor Thames regattas later in the season. Its later absence from Henley is due to the retirement from active oarsmanship of Mr. H. Chinnery and others, whose personal energies alone sufficed to combat the difficulty of distance from London. Meantime, clubs like the Ariel, Corsair West London, Ino, and others have become 'fine by degrees and beautifully less,' until they expired of inanition. There are, and always will be, sundry ambitious second-class oarsmen who regret the extinction of societies of this sort, and who recall with regret the pot-hunting for junior prizes which sometimes fell in their way. But when we recollect that clubs of this stamp were conspicuously absent from the winning roll, and usually even from the competition in senior races in minor Thames regattas, we fail to see wherein rowing science suffers by their absorption. Junior oarsmen obtain far better instruction in the ranks of the crack clubs than they could hope to find in the small-fry institutions, and they have found this out. When men have matriculated as oarsmen in weak clubs, they constantly contract insidious faults of style, the result of being put to race in light boats before they have mastered the first principles of oarsmanship. If such men subsequently aspire to join the better clubs, they have a worse chance of attaining a seat in a first or even a second crew than if they had joined the big club at the outset, and had been carefully taught in tubs till they were fairly proficient. They have to be 'untaught' from a bad style before they can be moulded in a good one. The Thames cup eights at Henley are of a higher order now than they were seven or eight years ago, and we are inclined to ascribe this fact to the 'absorption' system, which not only strengthens the large clubs, but also provides better instruction for the rising generation than was the case when talent was more split up. Oarsmen of good standard who are really desirous of distinguishing themselves, and are not too proud to serve in the ranks of a big club after having held office in a smaller one, freely gravitate from minor to leading clubs. The juniors of their clubs follow their leaders, and so the minor clubs become gradually depleted.

We do not consider that regatta entries are practically injured by the development of the large clubs at the expense of the smaller ones. We have already said that these small clubs are of little or no use for senior races, whereas their ingredients, consolidated in larger bodies, create one or two more strong clubs which are good enough to produce competent senior crews, and so swell senior entries. We admit that to some extent junior entries may fall off in numbers, in consequence of the breaking up of petty clubs ; but, even allowing this, we hold that the quality of junior entries increases in proportion as those juniors hail from a good club endowed with scientific coaching. Clubs whose powers are limited to the production of junior crews do not contribute much to the standard of oarsmanship, and at the same time they divert material which in good hands might attain a good standard. The many petty clubs of fifteen or twenty years ago used to labour, each by itself, through a whole season to produce just one junior crew ; and this possibly won a race at last, on a sort of tontine principle, through the gradual victories of former opponents in junior races, which on each occasion removed a rival from the field of the future. The modern strong and first-class clubs turn out one junior crew after another in the season ; so that batch after batch of juniors are thus taken in hand, and competently coached during the season. Besides regatta rowing, there are club contests, and these are to be found in even greater abundance and variety under the management of the leading clubs, and afford more scope for rising oarsmen, than ever was the case in the expiring and expired minor clubs. We gave publicity to our correspondent's complaint, as a matter of fair play in a subject that might be of interest to many ; but, all things considered, we come to the conclusion that his deductions break down in every respect, and that rowing and regattas alike benefit rather than lose by consolidation of material in the first-class clubs of the day.

EARLY AMATEURS.

CHAPTER XIV.

THE AMATEUR, HIS HISTORY AND DESCRIPTION.

THE old theory of an amateur was that he was a 'gentleman,' and that the two were simply convertible terms. The amateur of old might make rowing his sport, so long as he did not actually make it his ostensible means of livelihood. The Leander oarsmen who matched themselves against University crews between 1830 and 1840 did not consider that they lost caste by rowing for a stake.

In 1831 Oxford and Leander rowed at Henley for 200*l.* a side, with watermen steering them. Much later than this it was not considered improper for two 'gentlemen' to row a match (or race one) for a mutual *stake* (not a bet). Until 1861, when the conditions of the Wingfield Sculls were remodelled at a meeting of ex-champions and old competitors, it had been the custom for all entries for that prize to pay a fee of 5*l.*, and the winner swept the pool ! No one dreamed of suggesting that this was in any way derogatory to the status of an amateur.

But as rowing became more popular, and more widely adopted as a pastime, it began to be felt that it was invidious to leave the question 'Is he an amateur?' to the local opinion of the regatta committee, before whom such a question might be raised. Oarsmen came to the conclusion that some written definition of the qualification was necessary ; some hard and fast rule, prospective, if not retrospective. Till then, various executives had adopted various opinions as to what constituted an amateur. One year, about 1871, the Henley executive declined to recognise one of the local crews engaged in the ' Town Cup' as 'amateurs ;' and on this ground refused to allow them to start for the Wyfold Cup. It was not alleged that any of this crew had ever laboured as a mechanic, or rowed for money. The allegation of the Henley executive was that this crew were not 'gentlemen amateurs,' and as such they declined to admit them. A few days later another regatta executive freely admitted this same crew, and none of the recognised amateur clubs opposed to them raised any objection to the local crew's status.

This variety of opinion led to consultation among certain old amateurs whose ideas were universally respected, and as a result, on April 10, 1878, a meeting was held at Putney, at which there were present—

FRANCIS PLAYFORD, L.R.C., *Chairman.*
T. EDMUND HOCKIN, Secretary, C.U.B.C.
T. C. EDWARDES-MOSS, President, O.U.B.C.
F. S. GULSTON, Captain, London R.C.
HENRY P. MARRIOTT, for Secretary, O.U.B C.
C. GURDON, President, C.U.B.C.
JAMES HASTIE, Captain, Thames R.C.
M. G. FARRER, Captain, Leander B.C.
C. D. HEATLEY, Captain, Kingston R.C.
ROBERT W. RISLEY, O.U.B.C.
FRANK WILLAN, O.U.B.C.

O

J. G. CHAMBERS, C.U.B.C.
EDWARD H. FARRIE, C.U.B.C.
JNO. IRELAND, L.R.C.
H. H. PLAYFORD, Vice-President, L.R.C.
E. D. BRICKWOOD, L.R.C., *Secretary*.

These gentlemen drew up and passed the following :—

Definition of an Amateur.

An amateur oarsman or sculler must be an officer of her Majesty's Army, or Navy, or Civil Service, a member of the Liberal Professions, or of the Universities or Public Schools, or of any established boat or rowing club not containing mechanics or professionals ; and must not have competed in any competition for either a stake, or money, or entrance-fee, or with or against a professional for any prize ; nor ever taught, pursued, or assisted in the pursuit of athletic exercises of any kind as a means of livelihood, nor have ever been employed in or about boats, or in manual labour ; nor be a mechanic, artisan, or labourer.

In the following year the Henley executive drew up a definition of their own, much to the same effect, but slightly different in phraseology (this was on April 8, 1879). It read thus :—

No person shall be considered as an amateur oarsman or sculler—

1. Who has ever competed in any open competition for a stake, money, or entrance-fee.

2. Who has competed with or against a professional for any prize.

3. Who has ever taught, pursued, or assisted in the practice of athletic exercise of any kind as a means of gaining a livelihood.

4. Who has been employed in or about boats for money or wages.

5. Who is or has been, by trade or employment for wages, a mechanic, artisan, or labourer.

This definition, with a further slight verbal alteration, will be found still embodied in the rules of Henley regatta, which are given at p. 48. This new definition was adopted by the 'Amateur Rowing Association.'

This latter body arose in 1879. The original object of its constitution was to found a general club which could comprise all the best amateur talent of Britain, and from which, in the event of any foreign or colonial crew, composed of the full force of its own country, coming to these shores, could be put forward to represent the honour of the mother country ; so that the individual clubs of Britain should never hereafter be in danger of being attacked separately, with forces divided, by the concentrated resources of some foreign or colonial country. The association was first called the 'Metropolitan Rowing Association,' but eventually it took its present name. The rules of this association are here given *in extenso*, and sufficiently explain the *raison d'être*.

RULES OF THE AMATEUR ROWING ASSOCIATION, LATE
METROPOLITAN ROWING ASSOCIATION.

Committee.

The President of the Oxford University Boat Club
The President of the Cambridge University Boat Club.
The Captain of the Dublin University Boat Club.
The Captain of the Dublin University Rowing Club.
The Captain of the Leander Boat Club.
The Captain of the London Rowing Club.
The Captain of the Kingston Rowing Club.
The Captain of the Thames Rowing Club.

Ex officio.

JAMES CATTY, T.R.C.	F. S. GULSTON, L.R.C.
H. J. CHINNERY, L.R.C.	JAMES HASTIE, T.R.C.
F. FENNER, L.R.C.	Rev. R. W. RISLEY, O.U.B.C.
J. H. D. GOLDIE, C.U.B.C.	S. LE BLANC SMITH, L.R.C.

Hon. Secretary.
S. LE BLANC SMITH, Esq.

Head Quarters, pro tem.
LONDON ROWING CLUB, PUTNEY.

1. That this Club be called ' The Amateur Rowing Association.'
2. That the object of the Association be to associate members of existing amateur rowing clubs for the purpose of forming

representative British crews to compete against Foreign and Colonial representative crews, in the event of such entering at any regattas in the United Kingdom, or challenging this country.

3. That the government and management of the Association be vested in a committee of fifteen members (of whom five shall be a quorum), with power to add to their number, who, except the *ex-officio* members, shall retire annually, and be eligible for re-election.

4. That the Presidents of the Oxford University Boat Club and Cambridge University Boat Club, the Captains of the Dublin University Boat Club, Dublin University Rowing Club, Leander Boat Club, London Rowing Club, Kingston Rowing Club, and Thames Rowing Club, for the time being be *ex-officio* members of the committee.

5. That no one be eligible as a member of the Association unless he be a member of a recognised Amateur Rowing Club.

6. That candidates for election must be proposed and seconded by two members of the committee, and unanimously elected by the committee.

7. That, when members of different clubs are selected to form a crew, they must, for the time being, place themselves exclusively at the disposal of the Association.

8. That general meetings of the members be summoned by the Honorary Secretary at such times as not less than five of the committee think fit, and that committee meetings be held once, at least, in every three months, and as much oftener as a quorum shall, from time to time, decide.

This Amateur Rowing Association began modestly, and without any assumption, to dictate to the rowing world. It was content to take the patriotic part of guarding national amateur prestige in aquatics. But all leading clubs so fully recognised the value of the new association, that pressure was often put upon it to make a *coup d'état*, and to take the sceptre of amateur rowing and the control of amateur regattas, a position analogous to that held respectively by the 'Jockey Club' on the turf, the 'Grand National Hunt Committee' in steeple-chasing, and the 'Amateur Athletic Association' on the running path. To some extent the Association have followed the course urged upon them, and last season (1886) they propounded a

code of regatta rules, which will doubtless be adopted by all
regattas that desire to entice first-class amateur competitions on
their waters. These rules read thus :—

AMATEUR ROWING ASSOCIATION.
Established 1879.

(Hon. Sec., S. LE BLANC SMITH, Esq., Coombeside, Sydenham, S.E.)

Cambridge University Boat Club—Cambridge.
Kingston Rowing Club—Surbiton.
Leander Club—Putney.
London Rowing Club—Putney.
Oxford University Boat Club—Oxford.
Reading Rowing Club—Reading.
Royal Chester Rowing Club—Chester.
Thames Rowing Club—Putney.
Twickenham Rowing Club—Twickenham.
West London Rowing Club—Putney.
Marlow Boat Club—Marlow.
Henley Rowing Club—Henley.

Rules for Amateur Regattas.

1. The committee shall state on their programmes, and all
other official notices and advertisements, that their regatta is held
under the Rules of the A.R.A.

2. No 'value' prize (*i.e.* a cheque on a tradesman) shall be
offered for competition, nor shall a prize and money be offered as
alternatives.

3. Entries shall close at least three clear days before the date
of the regatta.

4. No assumed name shall be given to the secretary unless
accompanied by the real name of the competitor.

5. No one shall be allowed to enter twice for the same race.

6. The secretary of the regatta shall not be permitted to divulge
any entry, nor to report the state of the entrance list, until such
list be closed.

7. The committee shall investigate any questionable entry
irrespective of protest.

8. The committee shall have absolute power to refuse or return

any entry up to the time of starting, without being bound to assign a reason.

9. The captain or secretary of each club or crew entered shall, at least three clear days before the day of the regatta, deliver to the secretary of the regatta a list containing the names of the actual crew appointed to compete, to which list the names of not more than four other members for an eight-oar and two for a four-oar may be added as substitutes ; provided that no person may be substituted for another who has already rowed a heat.

10. The secretary of the regatta, after receiving the list of the crews entered, and of the substitutes, shall, if required, furnish a copy of the same with the names, real and assumed, to the captain or secretary of each club, or in the case of pairs or scullers to each competitor entered.

11. The committee shall appoint one or more umpires, to act under the Laws of Boat Racing.

12. The committee shall appoint one or more judges, whose decision as to the order in which the boats pass the post shall be final.

13. Objections to the qualification of a competitor should be made in writing to the secretary of the regatta at the earliest moment practicable. No protest shall be entertained unless lodged before the prizes are distributed.

14. Every competitor must wear complete clothing from the shoulders to the knees—including a sleeved jersey.

15. In the event of there being but one crew or competitor entered for any prize, or if more than one enter and all withdraw but one, the sole competitor must row over the course to become entitled to such prize.

16. Boats shall be held to have completed the course when their bows reach the winning post.

17. The whole course must be completed by a competitor before he can be held to have won a trial or final heat.

18. In the event of a dead heat any competitor refusing to row again, as may be directed by the committee, shall be adjudged to have lost.

19. A junior oarsman is one (A) who has never won any race at a regatta other than a school race, a race in which the construction of the boats was restricted, or a race limited to numbers of one club ; (B) who has never been a competitor in any International or Inter-University match.

A junior sculler is one (A) who has never won any sculling race at a regatta other than a race in which the construction of the boats was restricted, or a race limited to members of one club ; (B) who has never competed for the Diamond Sculls at Henley, or for the Amateur Championship of any country.

N.B.—The qualification shall in every case relate to the day of the regatta.

20. All questions not specially provided for shall be decided by the committee.

With these safeguards, and with the guidance of this leading Association, it is to be hoped that the status of amateurs in England will be preserved at that high standard which alone can properly demarcate the amateur from the professional.

Foreign crews which seek to compete at our regattas are often of a very dubious character as regards amateurship. The imposture of Lee, the Yankee professional, at Henley regatta in 1878, was not discovered until too late ; and his case has been by no means an isolated one. The Henley executive now impose certain conditions upon foreign countries, which enable our own authorities to make timely inquiries as to the real status of proposed visitors. These conditions will be found under No. 4 of the 'General Rules' of Henley (p. 49).

WINDSOR.

CHAPTER XV.

ROWING AT ETON COLLEGE.

THE River Thames flows so near the College of Eton that it necessarily affords an attraction to the boys at least equal to the playing fields, and has always been frequented for bathing and rowing as well as other aquatic pursuits. All such amusements have been styled from time immemorial 'Wet bobbing,' as distinguished from cricket, which is 'Dry bobbing:' the boys who boat are called 'Wet bobs' and the cricketers 'Dry bobs.' In the good old times, by which we mean the times told of by old men of our early acquaintance, extending to the end of the last and beginning of this century, the river was used by the boys for some other delightful though unlawful sports. Fishing was in those times more attractive to them than it has been in recent years, and many boys who did not join the boats would go out gudgeon, pike, or trout fishing with persistent zeal. Old gentlemen have told us of getting up in the early morning in the summer half, breaking out through the windows of their dame's or tutor's houses, and getting on the river to fish before the early school. Shooting was also practised on the river both at such times and during the legitimate play hours. The watermen took care of guns for sporting boys, and went with them in pursuit of water-hens, kingfishers, swallows, or any bird that might be found about the eyots, in the willow beds, or up the backwaters of Clewer or Cuckoo Weir. Of course these sports were interdicted; but the use of the river for any purpose whatever was so far forbidden that masters must be shirked in going to or coming from it, and the river itself was out of bounds. The sixth form also had to be shirked in old times, and could have any lower boy punished for being out of bounds; but it must have been a sixth-form boy of no sporting propensities himself who could have given 100 lines to a lower boy caught shooting in the Clewer stream. Was it more or was it less praiseworthy of one of the tutors who caught the same lad with his gun, and only remonstrated with him because it might be dangerous, and not because he was breaking the rules of the school?

No one but an Etonian could possibly understand the anomalous condition of things which made the river out of bounds, though no boy was really prevented from going on it unless he was caught on the way by a master and actually sent back. The fact was that, when on the river, the boy was safe from interference. Once only did a headmaster attempt to stop an eight which he heard was to row up to Surly; this was Dr. Keate, and he was so finely hoaxed that he never even made a second attempt. Hearing that an eight was to go out on a certain day, he threatened to expel anyone who should take part in the expedition, and then went for a walk along the towpath to waylay them. There issued from the Brocas a crew of watermen dressed like the Eton eight, and wearing masks over their faces. Crowds of people followed to see what would happen. Keate caught them between the Hopes and shouted, 'Foolish boys, I know you all. Lord ——, I know you. A ——, you had better come ashore. Come here or you will all be expelled.' The boat however pursued its course, several of the masters followed on horseback, and the ruse was not discovered until the crew disembarked and took off their masks with a loud 'Hurrah!' Keate was furious, and vowed that there should be no Easter holidays unless the boys who had been hooting him behind hedges gave themselves up, and some twenty victims were accordingly swished.

As a matter of fact the river was permitted from March 1 till Easter holidays for long boats, and from Easter till Midsummer for boats of all kinds. In going to or from the river a boy had to shirk a master by getting into a shop out of his sight. . The masters avoided going along the river when rowing was practised; they ignored, or pretended to ignore, the procession of boats on June 4 and Election Saturday, and winked at the Fireworks and the boys being late for lock-up on those days. On June 4, 1822, Dr. Keate sent for the captain of the boats and said to him, 'The boys are often very noisy on this evening and late for lock-up. You know I know nothing! But I hear you are in a position of authority. I hope you will not be late to-night, and do your best to prevent disorder. Lock-up time will be twenty minutes later than usual: it is your customary privilege.'

On March 1, 1860, the captain of the boats went boldly up to Dr. Goodford and requested that the 'boats' (or boys who belonged to the eight-oared boats) might be allowed to go to the Brocas without shirking, and somewhat to his surprise the Doctor gave his consent. In the following half shirking was abolished in Eton for all the school.

There is however one important condition on which a boy may boat : he must 'pass' in swimming. When the authorities ignored the boating, boys who could not swim daily risked their lives, and casualties sometimes occurred. It was in 1840

OFF THE BROCAS

that C. F. Montagu was drowned near Windsor Bridge, and
such an effect had this calamity, that the masters thenceforth
ordained that boating should be formally recognised, and
that no boy should be allowed to get into a boat until he had
passed an examination in swimming. One or two masters
were appointed river masters. Bathing-places were made at
Athens, Upper Hope, and Cuckoo Weir, and the eighth and
sixth form were allowed to bathe in Boveney Weir. No boy
might bathe at any place but Cuckoo Weir until he had passed.
Watermen were engaged to teach swimming, and be ready with
their punts at bathing-places and elsewhere to watch the boys
on the river, to prevent accidents and report unlawful acts.
Bathing is permitted as soon after the Easter holidays as
weather is warm enough, and two days a week the river masters
attend at Cuckoo Weir for 'Passing.' This examination (so
much pleasanter than any other) is conducted as follows : a
number of boys whom the waterman thinks proficient enough
appear undressed in a punt. A pole is stuck up in the water
(which is out of depth at the place) about thirty yards off ; the
master stands on a high place called Acropolis, and as he calls
the name, each in turn takes a header and swims round the
pole once or twice. He must not only be able to take a header
and swim the distance, but must also swim in approved form so
as to be capable of swimming in his clothes. Since 'passing'
was established there has been only one boy drowned, though
many are swamped under all kinds of circumstances. A boy
who has not passed belongs to the class called 'non nant.'

The Thames at Eton has changed somewhat from what it
was in the 'old times.' Boveney and Bray Locks were made
in 1839, and before that the river was much more rapid, and
there was no sandbank at Lower Hope. At the weir below
Windsor Bridge the fall of water was not so great as it is now,
and many a boy used to amuse himself in the dangerous adventure of shooting the weir in a skiff or funny.

Although boating was formally recognised by the masters in
1840, it is a fact that the first race honoured by the presence of

a headmaster was the Sculling Sweepstakes in 1847, when Dr. Hawtrey was rowed in a boat to see the racing by two under-masters, the Rev. H. Dupuis and Mr. Evans.

From time immemorial there was a ten-oar and several eight and six-oared boats, with regular crews, captains and steerers. In the early state of things a waterman always rowed stroke and drilled or coached the crew, and this practice was continued with some of the eights till 1828, and after that the captain of each crew rowed the stroke oar. The crews had to subscribe for the waterman's pay, his beer, and clothes. The best remembered watermen were Jack Hall, 'Paddle' Brads, Piper, Jack Haverley, Tom Cannon and Fish. There were upper boats manned by sixth and fifth form boys, and lower boats originally with six oars for lower boys. A lower boy could not get into the upper boats however well he might row. From more recent times no lower boy can get into the 'boats' at all, but must content himself with his own lock-up skiff, gig, or outrigger. We should explain here that a lock-up means a boat which a boy, for himself or jointly with a friend, hires for the summer half and keeps exclusively. The boat-builders also allow other boats (not lock-ups) to be used indiscriminately on payment of a less sum, which are called 'chance boats.' Boys in the 'boats' generally also have a lock-up or outrigger of their own, or jointly with others.

The ten-oar was always called the 'Monarch,' and is the head boat in all processions. The captain of the boats rows stroke of the 'Monarch,' and until 1830 the second captain rowed nine. After that date the second captain became captain of the second boat. The boats themselves bore certain names. In the early lists (none exist earlier than 1824) the 'Britannia' was the second boat, and in that year there were five upper boats, 'Hibernia,' 'Etonian,' and 'Nelson' being the other three. And the lower boats with six oars were the 'Defiance,' 'Rivals,' and 'Victory.' The following year there were only three upper boats, which has remained the custom till this day, except in 1832, when there was a fourth upper boat called the

'Adelaide.' The 'Victory' has always been the second boat
since 1834. And the favourite names of other boats whose places
have changed in different years are the 'Rivals,' 'Prince of Wales,'
'Trafalgar,' 'Prince George, 'Thetis,' and 'Dreadnought.' There
has never been any difficulty in getting crews for the one ten-
oar and seven eight-oared boats, and in fact the names put
down usually have exceeded the number of vacancies. In
1869 an additional boat was put on in consequence of the
collegers being allowed to join, and in 1877 the 'Alexandra ' was
added to the list owing to the increased number of entries. Before 1869 the collegers had fours and sometimes an eight to
themselves, but did not join the procession of the boats ; and as
they did not belong to the oppidan 'boats' they could not row in
the eight of the school.[1] But they rowed some successful matches
against University men on several occasions. There was never
any racing between collegers and oppidans, and the collegers
could only race between themselves. Before 1840 they kept
their boats at a wharf by the playing fields and had a bathing
place there. They used to row down to Datchet and Bells of
Ouseley, but from that time were forbidden to go below bridge
and were put on the same recognised footing as oppidans.

As soon as the boys return to school after the Christmas holidays a large card is placed at Saunders' shop, on which those fifth
and sixth form who wish to join and are not then in the boats in-
scribe their names. There is some excitement for a time while
the captain of the boats appoints the captain to each boat, which
he does usually in the order of ' choices ' (a term which is explained hereafter) of the previous year ; but sometimes it is
thought best to put a high 'choice' or two in the 'Victory ' and
appoint as captain of some of the lower boats some good fellow
who is not likely to get into the eight of the school, in order
that when the eight is practising these boats should have the
advantage of their captains to take them out. The captain of
the lower boats ranks higher than the captain of the third upper

[1] In 1864, however, Marsden, a colleger, rowed in the eight, though
collegers were still excluded from the boats.

boat. The crew of the 'Monarch' (ten-oar) is then selected by the captain of the boats, and he places a high choice as 'nine,' that position being considered about the fifth highest place. His crew is chosen not of the best oars, for they are always placed in the 'Victory' or second boat, but usually of boys high up in the school, and sometimes a good cricketer or two gets a place in the Easter half and leaves it afterwards. The captain of the cricket eleven is almost always formally asked to take an oar in the ten. The second captain then makes up his crew, then the captain of the third upper, and so on. Each captain has to submit his list to the captain of the boats, who advises him on his selection. The steerers are chosen in the same order, and the best steerer (who is also to have the honour of steering the eight of the school) always steers the ten. The crews are always selected on what is known of their merits as good oars, and there is never any preference given to favouritism or rank. When the lists are all made out they are printed and published in the 'Boating Calendar.'

Boating begins on March 1 'after twelve,' unless the weather is excessively bad, or the river unusually high, when it has to be stopped for a few days. It ends practically at the summer holidays. The half from after the summer holidays till Christmas is devoted to football and fives. Before the Easter holidays the long boats only are allowed, but towards the end of that half some fours are allowed by special permission of the river master. We remember a four going out in this half without permission and an attempt being made to row up to Maidenhead when lock-up was at 6.30, but it was swamped in Bray Lock and the crew had to walk or run home ; on their way they met the river master, and he gave them all 200 lines to write out, though the day being very cold he might have thought them sufficiently punished by the ducking they had got.

The first day opens with a procession of all the boats to Surly Hall ; each crew dressed in flannel shirt and straw hats of different colours, and the name of the boat on the hatband The last boat starts first, then the others in inverse order to their

places, and after rowing a short way they 'easy all' and await
the ten-oar, which pursues an uninterrupted course to Boveney
Lock, followed by the others in their proper order. All go
into the lock together, and then on to Surly Hall, where they
land, play games, and perhaps drink a glass of beer. 'Oars' are
called by the captain after about twenty minutes or half an hour,
and all go back in the same processional order. Before locks
were built there was always a sort of race from Rushes to Surly,
each boat trying to catch and bump the one before it, and the fun
was to try and get the rudders off and have a regular jostle.
After 12 there is not time to get further than Surly, but on a
half-holiday after 4 several of the boats get to Monkey Island,
and occasionally when lock-up was at 6.30 there was time for
an eight to row to Maidenhead. The distance from Windsor
Bridge to Rushes is 1 mile 6 furlongs, to Boveney Lock 2 miles
1¾ furlong, to Surly (about) 3 miles, to Monkey 4 miles 3
furlongs, to Bray Lock 5 miles, to Maidenhead 6 miles.

The usual practice is for the eights to go out occasionally
with the captain steering and coaching them, and for long rows
to Surly or Monkey. In the summer half there is so much
practising for races that the upper boats seldom get a row with
their proper crews. The boys who 'wet bob' and are not in
the boats row in skiffs, gigs, or outriggers to the bathing-places
and to Surly, or paddle about from Brocas to Lower Hope.
Canoes, punting, and sailing are not allowed. On June 4
(and formerly on Election Saturday) there is a procession in the
evening, and the crews wear striped cotton shirts, straw hats
lettered, and sailors' jackets. The steerers are dressed as
admirals, captains or midshipmen of the Royal Navy, and have
a large bouquet of flowers ; we need not further describe the
well-known scene. On the three Check nights of old days the
upper boats went to Surly in the evening to partake of ducks
and green peas, and were joined by the lower boats as they
came home all dressed in 4th June costume.

The captain of the boats is the acknowledged 'swell' of
the school. He has unlimited power over the boats, managing

and controlling all affairs connected with them ; as treasurer and secretary he keeps the accounts, and writes a journal of the races and events. No one disputes his authority. No money can be levied without the authority of the headmaster. The changes effected in 1861 in abolishing Check nights and Oppidan dinner were ordered and carried out by him without the least idea that anyone might have objected. He was always asked to play *ex officio* in the collegers' and oppidans' football match if he was anything of a good football player, and in the cricket match whether he could play cricket or not. He still manages the foot races of the school. It has happened four times that a boy has been captain two years, and his power in his second year is if possible greater than ever.

The eight of the school are the best rowers, whether captains or not, and are alone entitled to wear white flannel trousers and the light blue coats. Now that the race at Henley is an institution they are selected for that event. Before the Radley race of 1858 there was no regular race, and if a casual crew came down to row it was generally without the challenge being given long beforehand, so that no training could take place. The last race of the season was upper eights, the captain and second captain tossing up for first choice and choosing alternately ; the first eight choices were generally the eight, and paper lists were given out afterwards of these choices which ruled the position of the boys who stayed on for the next year.

The earliest school event we hear of was a race against a Christ Church four in 1819, which was won by the Eton four.

An attempt was made in 1820 to have a match against Westminster ; the challenge from them was accepted, and an eight chosen, but the authorities forbade it. The first race between the two schools was rowed on July 27, 1829, from Putney Bridge to Hammersmith and back, and was won easily by Eton, and Westminster were beaten at Maidenhead in 1831, at Staines in 1836, and at Putney in 1843 and 1847. Eton were beaten by Westminster at Datchet in 1837, and at Putney in 1842, 1845, and 1846. From 1847 till 1858 there were races only against scratch crews, and Oxford or Cambridge colleges. In 1858 a match, which was thought a grand event at the time, was rowed on the Henley course against Radley and won by Eton. In 1860, 1861, 1862, and 1864 the Westminster race was revived and was rowed from Putney Bridge to Chiswick Eyot, and Eton was so easily the winner that it has not been thought worth while to continue this match.

In 1860 Mr. Warre came to Eton as an assistant master, and at the request of the captain of the boats assisted him to arrange the Westminster race, and engaged to coach the eight. It was with his assistance that Dr. Goodford was persuaded to allow the eight to go to Henley Regatta in 1861, and the tacit understanding was made that if the authorities would allow this, and also the boating bill by which two long boats might escape six o'clock absence and have time to row to Cliefden, the boats would give up Oppidan dinner and Check nights. Mr. Warre, with the greatest kindness and with unremitting zeal and energy, first coached the eight for the Westminster races, and then continued coaching for the Henley Regatta evening after evening during their training every year for twenty-four years, until he was appointed headmaster. The Rev. S. A. Donaldson has since undertaken the coaching. University men at first disliked the appearance of Eton at Henley. Old oarsmen thought it would ruin the regatta, as men would hate to be beaten by boys. Masters predicted that the coaching by a master would spoil the boys, but time has dissipated these objections, and the Regatta has flourished better than ever.

It will be seen that Eton has on several occasions beaten trained college and other crews without winning the plate, and we may fairly say that her place on the river is about equal to that of the best colleges. After all, the boys are boys of seventeen and eighteen, and if they are not as strong or heavy as men a year or two older, they have the advantage of practically always being in training, are easily got together, and are living a regular and active life.

P

RESULTS OF HENLEY REGATTA.

Year	Race	Eton was beaten by	Eton beat	Average Weight of Eton crew
				st. lb.
1861	Ladies' Plate .	Trinity College, Oxford	Radley . . .	9 12
1862	Ladies' Plate .	University College, Oxford	Radley . . .	10 7¾
1863	Ladies' Plate .	University College, Oxford	Trinity Hall, Cambridge ; Brasenose, Oxford ; Radley	10 7½
1864	Ladies' Plate . (winners)	. . .	Trinity Hall, Cambridge ; Radley	10 6¾
1865	Grand Challenge	London R. C. ; Third Trinity, Cambridge	. . . .	10 4½
	Ladies' Plate .	Third Trinity, Cambridge (by a foul)	Radley . . .	—
1866	Grand Challenge	Oxford Etonians ; London R.C.	. . . .	—
	Ladies' Plate . (winners)	. . .	First Trinity or Black Prince, Cambridge ; Radley	10 9½
1867	Grand Challenge	(scratched)	Kingston R.C.	10 7
	Ladies' Plate . (winners)	. . .	Radley	
1868	Grand Challenge	London R.C.	University College, Oxford ; Kingston R.C.	10 8
	Ladies' Plate . (winners)	. . .	University College, Oxford ; Pembroke College, Cambridge	—
1869	Grand Challenge	Oxford Etonians	. . .	10 10¾
	Ladies' Plate . (winners)	. . .	Lady Margaret, Cambridge	—
1870	Grand Challenge	London R.C.	. . .	—
	Ladies' Plate . (winners)	. . .	Dublin Trinity College	10 9⅞
1871	Grand Challenge	Oxford Etonians ; London R.C.	Dublin Trinity College Oscillators	—
	Ladies' Plate .	Pembroke College, Cambridge	. . . .	—
1872	Ladies' Plate .	Jesus College, Cambridge	. . . .	10 6
1873	Grand Challenge	London R.C.	Balliol College, Oxford	10 9½
	Ladies' Plate .	Dublin Trinity College	. . .	—

Year	Race	Eton was beaten by	Eton beat	Average Weight of Eton crew
1874	Grand Challenge	London R.C.	First Trinity, Cambridge; B.N.C., Oxford; Thames R.C.	st. lb. 10 7¾
	Ladies' Plate .	First Trinity Cambridge	Radley . . .	—
1875	Ladies' Plate .	Dublin Trinity College	. . . .	10 5¼
1876	Ladies' Plate .	Caius College, Cambridge	. . . .	10 3¼
1877	Ladies' Plate .	Jesus College, Cambridge	Cheltenham . .	—
1878	Ladies' Plate .	Jesus College, Cambridge	Cheltenham . .	10 5¼
1879	Ladies' Plate .	Lady Margaret, Cambridge .	Hertford College, Oxford	11 0
1880	Ladies' Plate .	Trinity Hall, Cambridge	Exeter College, Oxford; Caius College, Cambridge	11 7½
1881	Grand Challenge	Leander R.C.	. . .	11 1⅝
	Ladies' Plate .	First Trinity, Cambridge	. . .	—
1882	Ladies' Plate . (winners)	. . .	Trinity Hall, Cambridge; Radley	11 10¼
1883	Ladies' Plate .	Christ Church, Oxford .	Radley . . .	11 0
1884	Ladies' Plate . (winners)	. . .	Caius College, Cambridge; Radley	11 5¼
1885	Ladies' Plate . (winners)	. . .	Oriel College, Oxford ; Corpus College, Oxford	11 5¼
1886	Ladies' Plate .	Pembroke College, Cambridge	Radley ; Bedford	10 12¼
1887	Ladies' Plate .	Trinity Hall, Cambridge	Hertford College, Oxford	11 1¾

The eight are permitted during training below bridge at
Datchet. Of the races at the school in old times, upper sixes
was the great event. It was rowed from Brocas up to Surly
and back before the lock was made, and in after times round
Rushes. All races were rowed round a turning point, and
there was more or less bumping. There were no rules of
racing then, and bumping or jostling, knocking off a rudder,
and foul play of any kind was part of the fun ; the only object
was to get in first anyhow. There was a match in 1817

P 2

between a four of Mr. Carter's house and four watermen which
caused great excitement, and was unexpectedly won by the boys.
Two sides of college, and dames and tutors, were annual events,
but were done away with in 1870. Tutors had won thirteen, and
dames the same number of races. There used to be an annual
punting race, but punting was forbidden after 1851. One of
the masters used to give a prize for tub-sculling, in which about
100 or more started and afforded great amusement. This was
before outrigged sculling and pair-oared boats were much used,
and since they became fashionable there have been junior pairs
and junior sculling. House fours as a regular institution was
begun in 1857, when the Challenge cup was procured by means
of a school subscription. In 1876 trial eights were first rowed,
and the race took place in the Easter half. There are challenge
prizes for the house fours and for the sculling and pulling, as
the pair-oar outrigger race is called. The number of races had
to be curtailed owing to the time taken to train the eight for
Henley. The four and eight-oared races start from Rushes, and
are rowed down stream ; total distance 1 mile 6 furlongs. The
pulling and sculling races start from Brocas and go round a
ryepack at Rushes and back, a distance of 3 miles 4 furlongs.
The winning point is always Windsor Bridge. The Brocas is
the name given to the field between the railway and the boathouses, and is so called from the family of Brocas, who used
to own the property. The times vary so much with the state
of the river that little comparison can be made between
the merits of individual oarsmen or scullers. It takes about
$7\frac{1}{2}$ minutes for an eight to row down from Rushes with a
fair stream, and about 8 minutes 20 seconds for a four. A
good sculler can get round Rushes and back in about 20 to 21
minutes. Pair-oared rowing without coxswains was introduced
in 1863, and a good pair now wins in 19 to 20 minutes. Fours
still continue to carry coxswains.

The boats themselves that are used are very different now
from what they were forty years ago. Up to 1839 they were still
built of oak (a very heavy wood), and measured fifty-two feet in

length and were painted all over. The first outriggers used in the University boat race in 1846 were built in streaks, and it was not until 1857 that both University crews rowed in the present sort of boats with smooth skins made of mahogany without keels and with round loomed oars. The first time an outrigger was used at Eton was in 1852, and until 1860 the 'Victory' was the only one in regular use : all the other eights and fours were built with streaks and had rowlocks in the gunwale, with a half-outrigger for stroke and bow. The ten-oar had half-outriggers in that year, but soon afterwards all the eights became fully outrigged. Sliding seats were first used about 1874. The builders were Mr. Searle, Tolliday, and Goodman. Perkins, better known for many years by the sobriquet of 'Sambo,' has now become owner of Mr. Searle's premises.

In the old-fashioned boats rowing was to a certain extent done in an old-fashioned style. The boats went steadily along without any spring to the first touch of the oars in the water. The stroke was rapid forward, but became a slow drag from the first dash of the oar into the water till recovered. Now the boat leaps to the catch, whereas when the first note was sounded by a University oarsman to 'catch the beginning,' the Eton boy in the old heavy boat found it impossible to respond. But Eton boys knew what was meant by Mr. Warre when they got the celebrated Mat Taylor boat in 1860, and soon learned the new style. The stroke became quicker, the recovery sharp, and every nerve was strained to cover the blade of the oar at the first touch in the water when the whole pull had to be made. From the time when the watermen used to coach and row, no regular coaching had been done by anyone but the captains. A neat and traditional style was handed down with all the essential points of good oarsmanship. But the art of propelling the Mat Taylor, and boats afterwards used of the same sort of type, was taught by Mr. Warre.

We have alluded to the doubts at first in the minds of old Etonians about the eight going to Henley, and the great changes effected at that time. No one now will say that it was anything

but unmixed good for the school. The convivial entertainments
of Check nights and Oppidan dinners had already become institutions of a past age. Drinking and smoking had died out, and
all that was wanted to stir the boys from lounging about in
their skiffs under willow bushes and back streams was the excitement of a great annual race and the effort to qualify for a
place in the eight. There have almost always been Eton men
in the University crews, and since 1861 there have sometimes
been as many as five in one crew, and certainly as many, if not
more, in every ' Varsity ' race. Eton has always had its full share
of the Presidentships. Third Trinity, Cambridge, has never
ceased to hold its own in a high position on the Cam, and we
have never heard a word of any deterioration, and much the
other way, of the moral effect on the boys of being coached
during their training. The special advantage of having the
river as a recreation place in addition to the playing fields puts
Eton to the front in athletics among our public schools ; and
the use of varieties of boats from early life, under all sorts of
difficulties, on a rapid stream, and having to keep his proper
side to avoid other craft, makes the ' Wet bob ' a first class
waterman. *Floreat Etona.*

CAPTAINS OF THE BOATS AND NOTABLE EVENTS.

Year	Captain of the Boats	Notable Events
1812	G. Simson	—
1814	R. Wyatt .	—
1815	T. Hill .	—
1816	Bridgeman Simpson .	—
1816	M. Bligh .	.—
1817	J. O. Secher	—
1818	J. H. Tuckfield	—
1819	R. Tuckfield	—
1820	Lord Dunlo	—
1821	M. Ashley	—
1822	J. A. Kinglake .	—
1823	P. J. Nugent	—
1824	W. Carew	—-
1825	A. Leith .	—
1825	M. Clifford	—
1826	T. Staniforth .	—

Year	Captain of the Boats	Notable Events
1827	T. H. Taunton.	—
1828	T. Edwardes-Moss	—
1829	Lord Alford	Beat Westminster
1830	G. H. Ackers	—
1831	C. M. Roupell.	Beat Westminster; beaten by Leander
1832	E. Moore.	—
1833	G. Arkwright	—
1834	J. Quicke.	—
1835	E. Stanley	—
1836	E. Fellowes	Beat Westminster
1837	W. J. Garnett	Beaten by Westminster
1838	P. J. Croft	—
1839	W. C. Rayer	—
1840	W. R. Harris-Arundell	Beat Old Etonians, and an Oxford Etonian Club
1841	W. R. Harris-Arundell	Beat Cambridge Subscription Room
1842	F. J. Richards.	Beaten by Westminster
1843	F. E. Tuke	Beat Westminster
1844	W. W. Codrington	—
1845	H. A. F. Luttrell	Beaten by Westminster
1846	G. F. Luttrell.	Beaten by Westminster
1847	C. H. Miller	Beat Westminster; beaten by Thames in Putney Regatta
1848	H. H. Tremayne	—
1849	R. B. H. Blundell	—
1850	G. M. Robertson	Beat scratch Cambridge crew; beaten by Oxford
1851	J. B. H. Blundell	—
1852	C. H. R. Trefusis	Beaten by an Oxford crew
1853	J. J. Harding	—
1854	J. C. Moore	Beat a scratch Oxford crew
1855	R. L. Lloyd	Beaten by a Cambridge crew and by Balliol
1856	G. S. F. Lane-Fox	Beat an Oxford and Cambridge mixed crew by a foul, and beaten by an Oxford eight
1857	T. Baring.	Beaten by an Oxford eight
1858	Mr. Lawless[1]	Beat Radley at Henley
1859	C. A. Wynne.	—
1860	R. H. Blake Humfrey[2]	Beat Westminster
1861	R. H. Blake Humfrey	Beat Westminster and Radley; beaten by Trinity College, Cambridge
1862	C. B. Lawes	Beat Westminster and Radley; beaten by University College at Henley
1863	W. R. Griffiths.	Beat Trinity Hall, Brasenose, and Radley; beaten by University College at Henley

[1] Now Lord Cloncurry.   [2] Changed his name to Mason.

Year	Captain of the Boats	Notable Events
1864	S. C. Cockran . .	Beat Trinity Hall, Cambridge, and Radley, and won Ladies' Plate at Henley
1865	J. Mossop . .	—
1866	E. Hall . . .	Won Ladies' Plate against Black Prince, Cambridge
1867	W. D. Benson . .	Won Ladies' Plate against Radley
1868	J. M'Clintock-Bunbury	Won Ladies' Plate against University College and Pembroke, Oxford
1869	T. Edwardes-Moss .	Won Ladies' Plate against Lady Margaret, Cambridge
1870	F. A. Currey . .	Won Ladies' Plate against Dublin Trinity College
1871	F. C. Ricardo . .	Won heats of Grand Challenge and of Ladies' Plate
1872	E. R. S. Bloxsome .	—
1873	T. Edwardes-Moss .	Won first heat of Grand Challenge against Balliol
1874	T. Edwardes-Moss .	Won second heat of Grand Challenge against First Trinity, Cambridge, and B.N.C., Oxford
1875	A. J. Mulholland .	Beaten by Dublin in Ladies' Plate
1876	G. Cunard . .	Beaten by Caius College, Cambridge, in Ladies' Plate
1876	S. Sandbach . .	—
1877	M. F. G. Wilson .	Beat Cheltenham, but beaten by Jesus College for Ladies' Plate
1878	G. Grenville-Grey .	Won second heat against Cheltenham ; beaten by Jesus College in final for Ladies' Plate
1879	L. R. West . .	Won second heat against Hertford College ; beaten by Lady Margaret in final for Ladies' Plate
1880	G. C. Bourne . .	Won first heat, beaten by Trinity Hall, Cambridge, in final for Ladies' Plate
1881	G. C. Bourne . .	—
1882	F. E. Churchill .	Won Ladies' Plate, after interval of twelve years
1883	H. S. Close . .	Won first heat Ladies' Plate ; lost with broken stretcher in final
1884	H. McLean . .	Won Ladies' Plate
1885	C. Barclay . .	Won Ladies' Plate
1886	C. T. Barclay . .	Beaten by Pembroke College in final for Ladies' Plate
1887	Lord Ampthill . .	Beaten by Second Trinity Hall in final for Ladies' Plate
1888	Lord Ampthill . .	—

CHAPTER XVI.

WATERMEN AND PROFESSIONALS.

THE London waterman is the oldest type of professional oars-manship. He was called into existence for the purpose of loco-motion, and race-rowing was a very secondary consideration with him in the first instance. Just as in the present day credentials of respectability are required by the Commissioners of Police of drivers of cabs and omnibuses (and none may ply for hire in these capacities within the metropolis unless duly licensed), so in olden days great stress was laid on the due quali-fication of watermen. An aspirant was and is required to serve seven years' apprenticeship before he can be 'free' of the river, and until he is 'free' of it he may not ply for hire upon it under heavy penalties for so doing. This regulation is in the interests of public safety. If apprentices exhibit special talent for rowing they can win what are called 'coats and badges,' given by certain corporate bodies, and by so doing they can take up their 'freedom' without paying fees for the privilege. We believe that no such restrictions exist on our other British rivers. The rule survives on the Thames because in olden times the Thames was a highway for passenger traffic in 'wherries.' In those times, where a passenger would now go to a thorough-fare or call a cab, he would have gone to the nearest 'stairs' and have hailed a wherry. London had not then grown to its present dimensions, and the Thames lay conveniently as a high-way between Westminster, the City, and the docks.

Amateurs began to take up rowing early in the present century as a sport ; and these contests seem to have fostered the idea of match-making among watermen. The title of a Champion of the Thames seems first to have been held by one R. Campbell, who beat C. Williams, another waterman, in a match on September 9, 1831, and also beat R. Coombes in a match the date of which is doubtful, but it was in heavy boats. Campbell was a powerful and heavy man, while Coombes weighed less that ten stone. Coombes turned the tables on Campbell a few years later (in 1846), and for some years Coombes was held to be invincible. In those times London watermen could, at scratch, man an eight to hold or even beat the best trained crew of amateurs. The original waterman's wherry was a vehicle of conveyance ; it was of much greater size than would be required to carry one man alone in a sheer contest for speed, but so soon as 'racing' came into vogue among watermen, lighter craft were built for matches, and were called 'wager' boats. The hull of the wherry was constructed as narrow as possible, and the sides flared out just at the greatest beam, so as to allow of sufficient width to carry the rowlocks with the requisite leverage for the sculls. This detail has already been treated in Chapter XI. under the head of 'boat building.'

Coombes had been beaten by Campbell in old-fashioned wherries, such as could be used for the business of conveying passengers. When he in turn defeated Campbell both men used 'wager boats.' The time came when years told on Coombes, and he had to yield to his own pupil Cole. Coombes was not convinced by his defeat, and made another match, but Cole this time won with greater ease. They rowed in 'outriggers' on these occasions. Cole in turn succumbed to Messenger of Teddington in 1855, and two years later Harry Kelley, the best waterman the Thames ever produced, either as an oarsman or as a judge of rowing, beat Messenger. Up to this time London watermen had been considered invincible at sculling. Harry Clasper had produced four-oar crews from the Tyne to oppose Coombes and his four, but no Tyne sculler had dared to lay claim to the Championship. However, in 1859 Robert Chambers was matched with Kelley, and to the horror of the Thames

THAMES WATERMAN—CIRC. 1825

men their favourite was beaten, and with considerable ease.
The Tyne man was the bigger, and had a very long sweep with
his sculls ; on that day he showed to great advantage, the more
so because Kelley was not sculling up to his best form. Defeated men can always suggest excuses for failure, and Kelley,
for years after that race, averred that he had not been beaten
on his merits; he had been kept waiting a long time at the post,
and was cold and stiff at the start. In those days, whether in
University matches or in public sculling races, the lead was a
matter of special importance. In the first place the old code
of rules were in force, which enabled a leading sculler to take
his opponent's water, to wash him, to retain the captured course,
and to compel his adversary to row round him in order to pass
him. Secondly, and even more important, was the action of
the crowds of steamers which followed such races. The Thames
Conservancy had no control over them, and they would lie
half-way up Putney Reach waiting for a race, and then steam
alongside of or even ahead of the sternmost competitor. Their
paddles drew away the water from him, and caused him literally
to row uphill. Under such circumstances even the champion
of the day would have found it next to impossible to overhaul
even an apprentice sculler, if the latter were in clear water ahead
of the steamer fleet and the former were a few lengths behind
in the 'draw' of the paddles.

All this was well known, and could be seen any day in an
important Thames race (the hollowness of the Oxford wins
of 1861 and 1862 against Cambridge was undoubtedly owing
to the treatment which the Cantabs experienced from the
steamers when once the lead had become decisive). Kelley
argued to his friends that all that could be said of the race was
that he could not go as fast that day as Chambers for the first
mile, and that after this point, whether or not he could have
rowed down his opponent was an open question, for the
steamers never gave him a chance of fair play. However, for
a long time Kelley could not find backers for a new match.
Meantime, Tom White and Everson in turn tried their luck

against Chambers and were hopelessly beaten. In 1863 Green the Australian came to England to make a match with Chambers. Green was a square, powerful man, about Kelley's height, but a stone heavier. He sculled upright in body, and with too much arm work for staying power, and did not make enough use of his body, especially as to swing back at the end of the stroke. He sculled a fast stroke, and so long as his arms lasted went a tremendous pace. Kelley and he fraternised, and practised together. When the match came off against Chambers, Green went right away for a mile, and then maintained his lead of three or more clear lengths for another half-mile. Chambers sculled rather below his form at first, wildly, as if flurried at being so easily led, but off Craven he settled down to his old long sweep, and held Green. The end came suddenly ; off the Soap Works Green collapsed, clean rowed out, and Chambers finished at his leisure. This match did Kelley good with his friends, for they knew that he could always in private practice go by Green after a mile or so had been sculled, quite as easily as Chambers eventually had done. Proposals were broached for a match between the cracks of the Thames and Tyne, and although the Tyne party pressed to have the race on the Tyne, they gave way at last, and the venue was the Thames. The stakes were 200*l.* a side, as usual in Champion matches, and there was also a staked ' bet ' of 300*l.* to 200*l.* on Chambers. (The race was on August 8, 1865.) The Tyne man was a strong favourite at the start, but Kelley got away with the lead, and was never again caught, winning cleverly by four lengths, and sculling in form such as was never seen before or after, on old-fashioned fixed seats. Just at this time there was a speedy Tyne sculler called Cooper ; he lately had sculled a mile match with Chambers on the Tyne, and Chambers had won by *one yard* only, in a surf which was all in favour of the bigger man (Chambers). A week or two after the aforesaid Champion race, Kelley, Cooper, and Chambers met for a 300*l.* sweepstake (specially got up for these three men, over the two-mile tidal course of the ' Eau Brink Cut ' at King's Lynn). Both Kelley and Chambers had been indulging a little after their Champion's training. Cooper, who had been lately beaten by Chambers in the Thames Regatta, for a 50*l.* purse (Hammersmith to Putney), was very fit, and jumped away from both the cracks. Chambers was short of wind, and was never in the race. Kelley stuck to Cooper, and rowed him down half a mile from the finish. Cooper then rowed across Kelley, fouled him, and drove him ashore. Cooper was properly disqualified on the foul. Next year Hammill the American came over to scull Kelley, and the races took place on the Tyne. One race was end on end, and the other round a stake boat. Kelley won each race with utter ease. Hammill's style was an exaggeration of Green's, all arm work, and a stroke up to 55 a minute at the start. About this time J. Sadler was rising to fame. He had been a chimney-sweep, and afterwards was 'Jack in the water' to Simmonds' yard at Putney. He, unfortunately for himself, exposed much of his merits when rowing for the Thames Regatta Sculls in 1865, and instead of making a profitable series of matches up the scale, beginning with third-rate opponents, he had to make his first great match with T. Hoare, who was reputed second only to Kelley on the Thames. Sadler beat Hoare easily, and was at the close of 1866 matched to scull Chambers for the Championship, Kelley having 'retired' from the title (Kelley and Sadler were allies at the time, and Sadler was Kelley's pupil). In the match Sadler went well and fast at Hammersmith, and then tired, fouled Chambers, and lost the race.

In the following year Kelley and Chambers were once more matched. Kelley came out of his retirement in consequence of some wrangling which had arisen out of the previous defeat of his pupil Sadler by Chambers. The new match took place on the Tyne, on a rough day and with a bad tide, on May 6. Kelley won and with some ease. It was evident that Chambers was no longer the man that he had been. He never again sculled for the Championship, but he took part in the Paris International Regatta in July of the same year. Very soon after this his lungs showed extensive disease, and he gradually sank of decline.

En passant we may say of Chambers that, apart from grand physique and science as an oarsman, he displayed qualities throughout his career which would stamp him as a model for champions of the present day. He was always courteous, never puffed up with success, never overbearing, and yet at the same time always fondly confident in his own powers and stamina. A more honourable man never sat in a boat. The writer recalls a little incident as characteristic of Chambers. Just before the 1865 match against Kelley, he accosted Chambers at Putney and asked him if he wished to sell his boat after the match. (It was a common practice for Tyne scullers to do this, to save the cost of conveyance back to the Tyne.) Chambers replied, he would sell her. The writer asked if he might try her after the race. 'Hoot mon,' said Chambers, 'try her noo, if ye like.' Now the writer was known to be an ally of Kelley (who usually accompanied him when training on the tideway for sculling races). In these days we much doubt whether any championship candidate would allow a third person—whether amateur or professional—known to be in sympathy with his opponent, to set foot in his racing craft on the eve of a match. Nothing would be easier than to have an 'accident' with her ; and all scullers know that to have to adopt a strange boat on the day of a match would be a most serious drawback. That Chambers never for a moment harboured such suspicion of his rivals shows that he judged them by his own faultless standard of fair play.

Not that we suggest for an instant that amateurs of this or of former days were ever suspected of being prone to foul play, but none the less do we believe that in these days few scullers in such a position as Chambers would have made the gratuitous offer which he did upon the occasion referred to.

In the autumn of 1867, Kelley and his pupil, J. Sadler, fell out ; the result was a Champion match between them. On the first essay Kelley came in first after having been led, and having fairly tired Sadler out. But a foul had occurred when Kelley was giving Sadler the go-by, and the referee was unable to decide which was in the wrong. He accordingly ordered them to row again next day. The articles of the match provided for a start by 'mutual consent,' and somehow Sadler did not 'consent' at any moment when Kelley was ready. Strong opinions were expressed by several persons who watched the affair from the steamers, and eventually the referee ordered Kelley to row over the course. The stakes were awarded to Kelley by the referee, but Sadler brought an action against the stakeholder, M. J. Smith, then proprietor of the 'Sportsman' newspaper. The case became a *cause célèbre.* The Court decided that the referee had acted *ultra vires* in awarding the stakes to Kelley, inasmuch as he had not first taken the trouble to observe for himself Sadler's manœuvres at the starting post. He had formed his opinion from hearsay and separate statements. Eventually both parties withdrew their stakes.

In the year 1868 a new sculler of extraordinary merit came suddenly to the fore. The late Mr. J. G. Chambers, C.U.B.C., had got up a revived edition of the old Thames professional regattas, and with a liberal amount of added money. The sculls race brought out all the best men of the day, and among them Kelley; the distance was the full metropolitan course. Renforth, a Tyne sculler, electrified all by the ease with which he won. He was a heavier man than Kelley; he had a rather cramped finish at the chest, but a tremendous reach and grip forward. He slid on the seat to a considerable extent, especially when spurting.

Kelley was rather over weight at the time, and excuses were made for him on this score. As a matter of prestige he had to defend his title to the championship in a match, and he met Renforth on November 17. He made a better fight on that day than in the regatta sculls, but the youth and strength of Renforth were too much for the old champion. Renforth remained in undisputed possession until his death, which took place under very tragic circumstances during a four-oared match between an English and Canadian crew in Canada. The Englishmen were well ahead, when Renforth, rowing stroke, faltered, fainted, and died shortly after reaching shore. Some

attributed his death to poison, some to epilepsy. The matter
remains a mystery.

Sadler was now tacitly acknowledged to be the best sculler
left in the kingdom (Kelley having retired). But Sadler could
not claim the title of champion without winning it in a match.
At last, in 1874, a mediocre Tyne sculler named Bagnall was
brought out to row him for the title, and Sadler won easily
enough.[1] Next year R. W. Boyd was the hope of the Tyne.
He had a bad style for staying. He was all slide and no body
swing ; his body at the end of the stroke was unsupported by
any leg work. So long as the piston action of his legs continued he went fast, but when the legs began to tire he stopped
as if shot. His bad style was the result of his having taken to
a slide before he had mastered the first principles of rowing
upon a fixed seat, or had learned how to swing his body from
the hips. Sadler, on the other hand, had been rowing for years
on fixed seats before he ever saw a sliding seat ; the veteran
did not discard his old body swing when he took to the slide,
but simply added slide to swing, whereas Boyd substituted slide
for swing. The difference in style between the two was most
marked when they showed in the race. Boyd had youth and
strength on his side. Sadler was getting old and stale, his hair
was grey, and he was not nearly so good as when he had rowed
Kelley in 1867 (save that the slide added mechanically to his
powers for speed). Boyd darted away with a long lead ; before
a mile had been crossed his piston action began to flag and
his boat to go slower. Sadler plodded on, and when once up
to him left him as if standing still, led easily through Hammersmith Bridge, and won hands down. Boyd never seemed to
profit by this lesson. He stuck to his bad style so long as he
was on the water, else he might have made a good sculler.

In 1876 Australia once more challenged England. Sadler
was the holder of the championship, and Trickett was the crack
of Australia. The Australian was a younger and bigger man
than Sadler ; he slid well, but he bent his arms much too early

[1] This was the first champion race rowed on sliding seats.

in the stroke. This would tend to tire them prematurely, and if the pace could be kept up, Trickett would soon have realised the effects of this salient fault of his. But Sadler was older, staler, and more grizzled than ever. He made a poor fight against Trickett, and a few weeks later in the Thames Regatta Sculls he came in nowhere, finishing even behind old 'Jock' Anderson, who never had been more than a third-rate sculler. Enough was then seen to show that our best sculler, as to style, was hopelessly old and stale, and that our new men, even if faster than he, had no style to make them worthy to uphold the old country's honours on the water. Trickett returned to Australia without trying conclusions with any other of our scullers for the championship. He made a match with Lumsden, a Tyne man, but the latter forfeited. If at the moment it had been known that the Sadler of 1876 was some ten lengths in the mile inferior to the Sadler of 1875, it is likely that Lumsden would have gone to the post, and that some other British sculler would also have endeavoured, while there was time, to arrange a match with the Australian.

The title of Champion of the World had now left England. Sadler retired, and there was still an opening for candidature for his abandoned title. As regards the now purely local honours of the representatives of Britain in sculling, Mr. Charles Bush, a well-known supporter of professional sculling, had found a coal-heaver, by name Higgins, who had shown good form in a Thames regatta, and was looked upon as the rising man of the Thames. There was also a rising sculler of the name of Blackman, who had won the Thames Regatta Sculls. Higgins was matched for champion honours against Boyd, and the match came off on May 20, 1877. The wind blew a gale from S.W., and Boyd had the windward station. In such a cross wind station alone sufficed to decide the race, and Boyd won easily. The two met again on October 8 of the same year, and Higgins proved himself the better stayer of the two. He had a better idea of sliding than Boyd, and used his legs better and swung farther back. Boyd stuck to his piston action, and

Q

was rowed out in six minutes. They met a third time on the following January 11, this time on the Tyne, and once more Higgins won, after a foul. He was plainly the better man of the two for any distance beyond a mile.

In the succeeding summer a Durham pitman, one W. Elliott, came out as a Championship candidate. He was short and thick-set, and was decidedly clumsy at his first essay. He met Higgins, and was beaten easily. He improved rapidly and came out again the following September. The proprietors of the 'Sportsman' had established a challenge cup, to be won by three successive victories, under certain conditions. Higgins, Boyd, and Elliott competed for it, and Elliott beat them both. The final heat was on September 17. In the following year, 1879, Elliott and Higgins met on the Tyne, on February 21, and once more Elliott held his own. He remained the representative of British professional sculling until the arrival of Edward Hanlan in this country.

Hanlan first attracted notice at the Philadelphia regatta of 1876. Mr. R. H. Labat, of the Dublin University, London, and Thames Rowing Clubs, took part in that regatta, and entered into conversation with Hanlan. He, as one of the L.R.C. men, lent Hanlan a pair of sculls for the occasion, and with them Hanlan won the Open Professional Sculling Prize. He beat among others one Luke, who had beaten Higgins in a trial heat. Higgins was at the moment suffering from exertions in a four-oared race earlier in the day, so that his defeat did not occasion much surprise ; but Mr. Labat on his return to England told the writer of this chapter that in his opinion Hanlan was far and away the best sculler he had ever seen, and that even if Higgins had been fresh and fit, Hanlan would have been too good for him. At that date Hanlan had not made his great reputation, but the soundness of Mr. Labat's estimate of his powers was fully verified subsequently.

In 1879 Hanlan, having beaten the best American scullers, came to England to row for the 'Sportsman' Challenge Cup. He commenced his career in England by beating a second-rate northern sculler, in a sort of trial match ; but this was only a feeler before trying conclusions with Elliott. The two met on the Tyne on June 16, and Elliott was simply 'never in it.' Hanlan led him, played with him, and beat him as he liked.

It did not require any very deep knowledge of oarsmanship to enable a spectator to observe the vast difference which existed between his style and that of such men as Boyd or Elliott. Hanlan used his slide concurrently with swing, carrying his body well back, with straight arms long past the perpendicular, before he attempted to row the stroke in by bending the arms. His superiority was manifest, and yet our British (professional) scullers seemed wedded to this vicious trick of premature slide and no swing, and doggedly declined to recognise the maxim

Fas est et ab hoste doceri.

At that rate the two best British scullers were, in the writer's opinion, two amateurs—viz., Mr. Frank Playford, holder of the Wingfield Sculls, and Mr. T. C. Edwardes-Moss, twice winner of the Diamonds at Henley. Either of these gentlemen could have made a terrible example of the best British professionals, could amateur etiquette have admitted a match between the two classes. The only time that these gentlemen met, Mr. Playford proved the winner, over the Wingfield course. A sort of line as to relative merit between amateur and professional talent is gained by recalling Mr. Edwardes-Moss's victory for the Diamond Sculls in 1878. In that year he met an American, Lee, then self-styled an amateur, but who now openly practises as a professional, and who is quite in the first flight of that class in America. He could probably beat any English professional of to-day, or at least make a close fight with our best man. When the two met at Henley Mr. Edwardes-Moss was by no means in trim to uphold the honour of British sculling. He had gone through three commemoration balls at Oxford about ten days before the regatta. He had only an old sculling boat, somewhat screwed and limp. He had lent her freely to Eton and Windsor friends during the preceding summer, not anticipating

that he would need her to race in again ; but when the regatta
drew nigh he could find no boat to suit him, and had to make
shift with the old boat. In the race he had to give Lee the
inside, or Berks station ; and all who have known Henley
Regatta are well aware of the advantage of that side ; it gives
dead water for some hundreds of yards below Poplar Point, and
still further gains on rounding the point. Three lengths would
fairly represent the minimum of the handicap between the two
stations on a smooth day, such as that of the race. The two
scullers raced round the point, Lee leading slightly ; but the
Oxonian caught him and just headed him on the post. Lee
stopped one stroke too soon, whether from exhaustion or error
is uncertain, but the performance plainly stamped the English
amateur as his superior, half trained and badly boated as he
was. Over a champion course, in a match, Lee would in his
Henley form have been a score or more lengths behind the
Oxonian.

Enough can be guessed from these calculations to show that
there would have been a most interesting race, to say the least,
if it could have been arranged for a trial of power between Mr.
Playford and Hanlan. The latter sculler used to admit, so we
always understood, that the London Rowing Club sculler was
the only man he had seen whom he did not feel confident of
being able to beat.

Hanlan's style, good though it undoubtedly was, appeared
to even greater advantage when seen alongside of the miserable
form of our professionals. Hanlan was a well-made man, of
middle height, and a thoroughly scientific sculler. He was the
best exponent of sliding-seat sculling among professionals, only
a long way so ; but we, who can recall Kelley and Chambers in
their best days, must hold to the opinion that the two latter
were, *ceteris paribus*, as good professors of fixed-seat sculling as
ever was Hanlan of the art on a slide. Had sliding seats been
in vogue in 1860, and the next half-dozen years, we believe that
Kelley and Chambers would have proved themselves capable of
doing much the same that Hanlan did in his own generation.

We have seen Kelley scull on a sliding seat. He was fat and short of wind, and never attempted to make a study of the leg-work of sliding ; but, being simply an amateur at it, his style was a model for all our young school to copy. Like all old fixed-seat oarsmen who have attained merit ·in the old school, he stuck to his traditional body swing, and added the slide to it, as it were instinctively. There could hardly be a greater con-trast of action than to see scullers like Boyd or Blackman kicking backwards and forwards, with piston action and helpless bodies doubled up at the finish, and to observe, paddling within sight of these, old stagers like Biffen and Kelley in a double-sculling boat fitted with slides. It was easy to see that until the new generation of British professionals could be taught first prin-ciples of rowing on a fixed seat, there was small chance of their ever acquiring the proper use of the slide as exemplified by Hanlan.

To return to Hanlan's performances. The Championship of the ' World ' still rested in Trickett, who had further main-tained his title (since he had beaten Sadler), by defeating Rush on the Paramatta, Sydney, on June 30, 1877. Rush had once been the Australian champion ; Trickett had beaten him before tackling Sadler, and this was a new attempt by Rush to regain his lost honours. Technically, Trickett could have claimed to defend his title in his own country ; but plenty of money was forthcoming to recoup him for expenses of travel, and he assented to meet Hanlan on the Thames for the nominal trophy of the ' Sportsman ' Challenge Cup, but really for the wider honour of champion of the world. The match came off on November 16, 1880, and Trickett was defeated with even greater ease than Elliott on the Tyne.

Just about this date a sculling regatta, open to the world, was organised on the Thames. It was got up purely for com-mercial purposes by a company called the ' Hop Bitters,' who required to advertise their wares. Nevertheless, it produced good sport. Hanlan did not compete in it. It came off only two days after his match with Trickett. Our British scullers took part in it, and with most humiliating results. Not one of them could gain a place in the final heat, for which four prizes were awarded to the four winners of trial heats. The four winners of the contest were one and all either colonials or Americans, and the winner was one Elias Laycock, also a Sydney man, and undoubtedly a better sculler than Trickett, although the latter was the nominal champion of Australia at the time. Laycock sculled in good style, so far as leg-work and finish of the stroke ; his body action was not cramped, but he had not so long a swing as should, if possible, be displayed by a man of his size. He scaled rather above twelve stone. Wallace Ross, who finished second to him, after leading him some distance, had been the favourite, and had been reputed as only a trifle inferior to Hanlan. The forward reach and first part of Ross's stroke was as good as could be wished, but he had a cramped, tiring, and ugly finish with his arms and shoulders. When Laycock succeeded in beating him a furore was created ; Laycock's staying powers were unmistakable, and many who saw him fancied that his stamina would enable him to give Hanlan trouble before the end of four miles. Laycock himself was not endued with so high an opinion of his own merits ; but he was too game a man to shirk a contest when it was proposed to him, and the result was that he was soon matched to scull Hanlan.

The match came off on the following February 14, 1881, over the Thames course. Laycock stuck to his work all the way, but was never in it for speed. Hanlan led from start to finish, and won easily. A year later Hanlan was back in England to row Boyd on the Tyne. Boyd's friends fondly fancied that he had developed some improvement, but it was a delusion. Never was an oarsman more wedded to vicious style and wanton waste of strength than the pet of the Tyne. The race came off on April 3, 1882, and was, of course, an easy paddle for Hanlan. The knowledge that Hanlan was going to be again on English waters, brought about a return match between him and Trickett. This was rowed on the Thames on May 1 following, and once more the Canadian won easily.

No one in Britain thought fit to challenge Hanlan again, after the decisive manner in which he had disposed of all his opponents ; but in his own country he twice defended his title, in 1883. On May 31 in that year he rowed J. L..Kennedy, a comparatively new man, in Massachusetts, and beat him ; and on the following July 18 he once more met his old opponent, Wallace Ross, on the St. Lawrence, and beat him, though after a closer race than heretofore.

In England about this time sculling had sunk even lower among professionals than in the days when Boyd and Elliott were the professors of the science. These men had retired ; there were sundry second and third class competitors for champion honours, among them one Largan, who had been to Australia to scull a match or two, and one Perkins, and one Bubear. The latter at first was inferior to Perkins, and was a man of delicate health and somewhat difficult to train. He often disappointed his backers by going amiss just before a match was due, but he took rather more pains with his style than other British scullers had done of late, and eventually he succeeded in surpassing them, and in becoming the representative (such as it was) of British professional oarsmanship.

We should mention that in 1881 the brothers Messrs. Walter and Harry Chinnery most generously made an expensive attempt to raise the lost standard of British sculling, by giving 1000*l.* in prizes for a series of years, to be sculled for. These two gentlemen were well-known leading amateur athletes in their day. The elder had been a champion amateur long-distance runner ; the younger had won the amateur boxing championship, and had rowed a good oar at Henley regattas and elsewhere. It may be invidious to look a gift horse in the mouth, but we feel that this generous subsidy of the Messrs. Chinnery was practically wasted for want of being fettered with a certain condition. That condition should have been, that the competitions for the Chinnery prizes should be on fixed seats. One reason why professional racing has fallen off of late so much, compared to amateur performances, may be found in the fact that amateurs are taught, and are willing to be taught, from first principles : whereas our professionals nowadays are little better than self-taught. Rowing and sculling require scientific instruction more than ever on slides. In old days the main business of a professional oarsman was to carry passengers in his boat ; the calling produced a large following, and out of these some few were good oarsmen and took to boat-racing as well as to mere plying for hire. Here there was a natural nursery for professional racing oarsmen. The disuse of the wherry for locomotion destroyed this nursery ; we have already shown that our later professionals are as a rule neither London watermen nor Tyne keelmen. They are a medley lot by trade ; a chimney-sweep, a collier, a coal-heaver, a miner, a cabman, &c., all swell the ranks. Such men as these take to the water simply for what they can make out of it, by racing on it. Their one ambition is to race, and to run before they can decently walk. Hence they do not go through the school of fixed-seat rowing before they graduate on sliders, and they have no instructors, nor will they listen to advice.

Amateurs, on the other hand, belong as a rule to clubs ; and all clubs of any prestige coach their juniors carefully, and lay down rules for their improvement. Two very usual club rules are, that juniors shall not begin by racing in keelless crank boats, but in steady 'tub'-built craft. No such control exists over junior professionals ; if a bricklayer's apprentice takes to the water in spare hours, and begins to fancy himself as an oarsman, he will probably find friends who will back him for a small stake against some brother hobbledehoy. Each of these aspirants will thus endeavour to use the speediest boat and appliances that he can obtain. Unfortunately it so happens that sliding seats give so much extra power that even bad sliding à *la* Boyd produces more pace than good fixed-seat rowing. The result of this is, that, however little a tiro may know of rowing, he will, in a day or two, get more pace on a slide than if he adhered to a fixed seat. So the two cripples race each other on slides, before they have acquired the barest rudiments of swing, and as a natural result they can never be expected hereafter to progress beyond mediocrity.

Now, if there were prizes offered for rising professionals, subject to the condition that sliding seats should not be used, these tiros would have some chance of being induced to study the art of using the body for swing, and of mastering this all-important feature in oarsmanship, before they ventured to fly so high as to race upon slides.

Twenty and more years ago there was a class of match-making on the Thames which is now obsolete. This was to row in what were called 'old-fashioned' wager boats, i.e. the lightest form of wherry which used to be built before H. Clasper established outriggers. The keelless boat requires a sharp catch up at the beginning to get the best pace out of it, and it also requires more 'sitting' to keep it on an even keel. (If it is not on an even keel, the hands do not grip the water evenly, and power thereby is wasted.) It was because this fact used to be realised in those days better than now, that so many rough scullers were matched in 'old-fashioned' boats, rather than in 'best and best' boats, as the fastest built craft were usually styled in the articles of matches. It would do good if this quondam practice of matching duffers on even terms in steady old-fashioned craft could be re-introduced on the Thames.

Another incident has tended greatly to the deterioration of professional rowing, and this is the lapse of professional regattas. Certain gentlemen connected with the University and the leading Thames boat clubs used formerly to get up an annual summer regatta for the benefit of professional oarsmen. In the 'forties' a somewhat similar regatta had also existed for a time, but it had consisted of amateur competitions as well as of professional. This earlier regatta faded away when its chief trophy, the 'Gold Cup' for amateur eight oars, was won thrice in succession by, and became the property of, the 'Thames Club.' (That Thames Club is now extinct, and must not be confounded with the well-known 'Thames *Rowing* Club' of the present day.) Some of the members of the Thames crew that won this 'Gold Cup' in the forties are still to be found, the most notable of them being Messrs. Frank Playford, senr. (amateur champion in 1849) ; and Rhodes Cobb, the president of the Kingston Rowing Club. (The sons of each of these old athletes have similarly made their mark in aquatics of the present generation.) Owing to the action of the chairman of a steamboat company and other gentlemen who had other interests than those of boating to serve, these regattas have lapsed.

To resume—as to Thames regattas. The Thames Sub- scription Club, between 1861 and 1866, got up a Thames regatta, which annually produced fine sport between Thames and Tyne men, and once or twice good Glasgow crews joined in the competition. In 1866 the amateur element was intro- duced as a mixture. This was the last year of the series.

Meantime the late Mr. H. H. Playford had for three years laboured to form a sort of 'nursery' regatta for professionals. It was styled the 'Sons of the Thames' regatta, and it had the effect of bringing out several good men, such as the Biffens, Wise, Tagg, &c., who afterwards distinguished themselves in the greater regattas on the Thames, which were open to the world. Never was professional rowing at higher flood than just at this date, thanks to the gentleman referred to.

In 1867 there was no regatta ; but in 1868 a new series was founded. The late Messrs. J. G. Chambers, George Morrison, Allan Morrison, Rev. R. W. Risley, the Playfords, Brickwood and other prominent amateurs, gave money and labour to aid the scheme, and it flourished right well for nine seasons. It produced, like the preceding series, fine rowing, and many a subsequent sculling or four-oar match arose out of the regatta contests. So far these regattas had been promoted solely for sport, and in pure unselfishness. In 1876 a steamboat company originated the idea of a Thames regatta, and advertised a scheme. Subscriptions were obtained from several of the City sources which had formerly subscribed to the *bonâ fide* Thames regatta, and thus the funds of the old-established meeting were sapped. The latter came off all the same that year. there thus being two

Thames regattas for one season. But there were not funds to carry on two such meetings, and the amateur promoters of the old established regatta retired next year in favour of the speculative promoters. The speculative regatta lived just one year more, and then its promoters gave up, and left our British professionals with no regatta at all to encourage them.

And this was just at a time when our champion honours had been wrested from us, and when we needed more than ever some disinterested assistance, in order to revive and encourage the falling fortunes of professional oarsmanship ! It was too late to revive the old regatta ; the hand of Death was busy among the old amateurs who had founded the second series, and the four or five gentlemen whose names headed the list of promoters (*supra*) have passed rapidly away, from one cause or another, in the prime of life. Whether hereafter any combination of later amateurs will once more come to the rescue, as did the late Messrs. Chambers, H. Playford, the Morrisons, and Risley, remains to be seen. If they do so, we hope they will found something, at first, more on the lines of the Playford series of 'Sons of the Thames' regatta, to bring out new blood ; and that they will insist upon *no slides* being used in any race of the meeting, for at least two seasons. Slides are not allowed in the public schools fours (lately rowed for at Henley, and now competed for at Marlow), nor in Oxford torpids, nor in Cambridge lower division races. Nor do the leading amateur tideway clubs allow their juniors to race on them in club matches. If we are to educate a new generation of professional talent, we must do so on the same general principle that we teach our junior amateurs in rowing clubs.

Since the date of Hanlan's invasion of Britain, British scullers have not been in the hunt for champion competitions. Such champion racing as has taken place has been confined to Canadians, Americans, or Australians. In 1884, May 22, Laycock was once more brought out to row Hanlan on the Nepean river, New South Wales, and Hanlan again held his own. Meantime an emigrant (in childhood) from Chertsey, one

William Beach, had been rapidly improving his style in New South Wales. He took hints from his conquerors until, when he was about forty, a time when most scullers are past their prime, he could beat all comers in his own colony. Hanlan was persuaded to visit Australia to row him, and the first match between them came off August 16, 1884, on the Paramatta. To the surprise of all, Beach went as fast as Hanlan, and outstayed him. Excuses were made for this reverse to one who had been reckoned invincible : Hanlan had been unfairly washed by a steamer, and some fancied he had held Beach too cheap, and was not fully trained. Another match was made for March 28, 1885. Meantime Beach easily beat, on February 28 of that year, another colonial challenger, T. Clifford. In his return match with Hanlan he fairly tired the Canadian out. Beach scales a trifle over twelve stone, and proves the truth of the old saying that a good big one is better than a good little one.

In December of 1885 Hanlan beat Neil Matterson, a young and rising Australian candidate for the championship.

In the summer of 1886, a large amount was subscribed for a series of sculling prizes on the Thames. Beach was in England, training for a match against Gaudaur of St. Louis, U.S., who had lately beaten the best American scullers. Gaudaur did not row in this regatta of scullers, but Beach did.

The trial heats of this regatta were rowed in stretches of about three miles each, following the tide over different parts of the tideway. In the first heat Neil Matterson beat Ross. In the second, Teemer, U.S., beat Perkins, a London sculler. Bubear rowed over for the third heat, and the fourth was won by Beach beating Lee, U.S. (once a pseudo amateur and an unsuccessful competitor for the Diamond Sculls of Henley !) Next day Beach beat Bubear, and Teemer beat Matterson. The final heat took place over the regulation course of Putney to Mortlake. Beach won as he liked, on a tide that was not first class, in 22 min. 16 secs. The racing occupied August 31, and September 1 and 2.

On September 18, Beach met Gaudaur for the champion ship over the Putney course. Beach was, as the race showed, a little 'off;' apparently he had been indulging; for to look at Gaudaur few would have expected him to make such a close fit of the race as he did. The stakes were 500*l.* a side. The tide was a good one, and the water was smooth beyond Hammersmith. Beach led, and seemed to have the race safe off Chiswick. Then he began to lose ground, Gaudaur came up to him, and Beach stopped, apparently rowed out. Possibly he had 'stitch,' as the sequel shows. Gaudaur got just in front of Beach, and could not get away. Beach stopped again, and still Gaudaur could do little better than paddle. Half way up Horse Reach Beach seemed to recover, and once more came up with his man. He led by a few feet at Barnes Bridge, and after that drew steadily away, winning by three lengths in the exceptionally good time of 22 min. 30 secs. or 22 min. 29 secs.

A week later Beach did a much finer performance, for time. He rowed Wallace Ross for the championship, over the usual course, and beat him in a common paddle, without being extended, and with wind foul, on a *neap* tide, in 23 min. 5 secs. The pace of this tide, let alone foul wind, must have been about a minute to a minute and a quarter (if not more) slower than the tide on which Beach and Gaudaur had sculled some days before. Those who know the effect of tides on pace, will admit that this last performance, all things considered, is Beach's best, and is also the best ever accomplished by any sculler over the Thames tideway course. Had Beach been on a spring tide that day, and been doing his best, he would probably have done a good deal faster than 21 min. 30 secs. over our champion course. All factors considered, we believe that the present champion sculler is the fastest that the world has yet produced, better than even Hanlan at his best. To compare him with the best old fixed-seat champions would be invidious to all parties. Each in his day made the best of the mechanical appliances at his disposal, and was A1 in style for their use.

A FOUL.

CHAPTER XVII.

LAWS OF BOAT-RACING (THEIR HISTORY, AND RULES OF
THE ROAD).

LAWS of boat-racing, until 1872, were variously read by various
executives. One rule was common to all, and yet differently
interpreted by many an umpire or referee. It was that which
related to a boat's course.

The old rule was, that a boat which could take a clear lead
of an opponent, and which could cross the proper track of
that opponent with such clear lead, became entitled to the
'water' so taken. The boat astern had then to change its
course, and to take its leader's vacated course. If thereafter

they fouled, through the leader returning to the vacated water, the leader lost ; if through the sternmost boat catching the leader in the 'captured' water, then the pursuer lost. Also, under the old code, a foul, however slight, lost a race, if one boat was in its right and the other in its wrong course at the time. If both were in the wrong, the foul did not count.

This code led to many a wrangle over fouls. It also opened the door to sharp practice—e.g. a leader might cross an opponent, by dint of pure speed ; and then, being in his 'right' water, by dint of having crossed with a 'clear lead,' the leader might 'accidentally' shut off speed, before the boat behind had time to change its course. This forced on a foul, and the leader could then claim his pound of flesh, and the race. An umpire had no discretion in the matter.

In 1872 a meeting of leading amateurs drew up a new code. This code was put in force at the Thames watermen's regattas, governed by amateurs. In time Henley adopted them, as did all leading regattas. Watermen for some time had a liking for the old code and its facilities for 'win, tie, or wrangle' in a match, but as time passed on the new code gained ground, and gradually the old one became obsolete. The late Mr. John Graham Chambers, C.U.B.C., was the leading spirit in this reform.

The revised code is now part of the creed of the Amateur Rowing Association, of which mention has already been made. These rules are now appended. The Henley executive publish a similar code, but differently numbered. Rule 15 is more of a *regatta* rule. It is usually waived in sculling matches, and in the Wingfield Sculls for the amateur championship its operation is, by order of the parliament of old champions, suspended.

THE LAWS OF BOAT-RACING AS APPROVED BY THE
AMATEUR ROWING ASSOCIATION.

1. The starter, on being satisfied that the competitors are ready, shall give the signal to start.

2. If the starter considers the start false, he shall at once recall

the boats to their stations, and any boat refusing to start again shall be disqualified.

3. Any boat not at its post at the time specified shall be liable to be disqualified by the umpire.

4. The umpire may act as starter as he thinks fit; when he does not so act, the starter shall be subject to the control of the umpire.

5. Each boat shall keep its own water throughout the race, and any boat departing from its own water will do so at its peril.

6. A boat's own water is its straight course, paralleled with those of the other competing boats, from the station assigned to it at starting to the finish.

7. The umpire shall be sole judge of a boat's own water and proper course during the race.

8. No fouling whatever shall be allowed; the boat committing a foul shall be disqualified.

9. It shall be considered a foul when, after the race has commenced, any competitor by his oar, boat, or person comes in contact with the oar, boat, or person of another competitor, unless in the opinion of the umpire such contact is so slight as not to influence the race.

10. The umpire may, during the race, caution any competitor when in danger of committing a foul.

11. The umpire, when appealed to, shall decide all questions as to a foul.

12. A claim of foul must be made to the judge or the umpire by the competitor himself before getting out of his boat.

13. In case of a foul the umpire shall have the power—

(*a*) To place the boats—except the boat committing the foul, which is disqualified—in the order in which they come in;

(*b*) To order the boats engaged in the race, other than the boat committing the foul, to row over again on the same or another day;

(*c*) To re-start the qualified boats from the place where the foul was committed.

14. Every boat shall abide by its accidents.

15. No boat shall be allowed to accompany a competitor for the purpose of directing his course or affording him other assistance. The boat receiving such direction or assistance shall be disqualified at the discretion of the umpire.

16. The jurisdiction of the umpire extends over the race, and all matters connected with it, from the time the race is specified to

start until its final termination, and his decision in all cases shall be final and without appeal.

17. Any competitor refusing to abide by the decision or to follow the directions of the umpire shall be disqualified.

18. The umpire, if he thinks proper, may reserve his decision, provided that in every case such decision be given on the day of the race.

The 'rule of the road' on the river is not settled quite as hard and fast as on land, or in marine navigation ; but certain general principles are recognised by all rowing men of experience, for the sake of mutual safety. The following draft of the recognised principles referred to is set forth by the editor of the 'Rowing Almanack,' and other authorities, to whom rowing men are much indebted for the publication.

In case of any 'running-down' action, arising out of a collision between pleasure-boats on the Thames, it would probably go hardly with the occupants of a boat which had brought about an accident by disregard of these 'rules of the road.'

'The Rule of the Road' on the River.

The following are the generally recognised rules adopted by the leading rowing clubs :—

1. A row-boat going against the stream or tide should take the shore or bank—which bank is immaterial—and should keep inside all boats meeting it.

2. A row-boat going with stream or tide should take a course in mid-river, and should keep outside all boats meeting it.

3. A row-boat overtaking another boat proceeding in the same direction should keep clear of the boat it overtakes, which should maintain its course.

4. A row-boat meeting another end-on in still or open waters, or lakes, should keep to the right as in walking, leaving the boat passed on the port or left side.

5. A row-boat with a coxswain should give way to a boat without a coxswain, subject to the foregoing rules, in so far as they apply.

6. A boat towing with stream or tide should give way to a boat towing against it, and if it becomes necessary to unship or drop a

R

tow-line, the former should give way to the latter ; but when a barge towing is passed by a pleasure-boat towing, the latter should give way and go outside, as a small boat is the easier of the two to manage, in addition to which the river is the barge's highway.

7. A row-boat must give way to a sailing-boat.

8. When a row-boat and a steamer pass each other, their actions should, as a rule, be governed by the same principle as on two row-boats passing ; but in shallow waters the greater draughts of the steam-vessel should be remembered, and the row-boat give way to her.

CLIEFDEN

'THE TEMPLE OF FAME.'

WINNERS OF THE WINGFIELD SCULLS.

Time	Winner	m. s.	Losers
1830	J. H. Bayford . .	—	Lewis, Wood, Horneman, Revel, A. Bayford, C. Duke, Hume
1831	C. Lewis . .	—	Bayford
1832	A. A. Julius . .	—	Lewis
1833	aC. Lewis. . .	—	Julius
1834	A. A. Julius . .	—	rowed over
1835	A. A. Julius . .	—	rowed over
1836	H. Wood . .	—	Patrick Colquhoun
1837	P. Colquhoun . .	—	Wood, Jones
1838	aH. Wood . .	—	Colquhoun, C. Pollock, H. Chapman
1839	aH. Chapman . .	—	Pollock, Crockford
1840	T. L. Jenkins . .	—	Crockford, Wallace, A. Earnshaw
1841	aT. L. Jenkins . .	—	Chapman
1842	H. Chapman . .	—	Wallace
1843	H. Chapman . .	—	Wallace, Kennedy, A. Earnshaw
1844	T. B. Bumpstead .	—	Chapman, Hon. G. Denman, Romayne
1845	aH. Chapman . .	—	Bumpstead
1846	aW. Russell . .	—	Walmsley, Fellows, Dodd
1847	J. R. L. Walmsley .	—	H. Murray, C. Harrington
1848	aJ. R. L. Walmsley .	—	rowed over
1849	abF. Playford . .	—	T. R. Bone
1850	T. R. Bone . .	—	rowed over
1851	aT. R. Bone . .	—	rowed over
1852	E. G. Peacock .	—	rowed over
1853	aJ. Paine . . .	—	A. Rippingall, J. Nottidge, H. C. Smith

(a) Resigned.
(b) The course before this race was from Westminster to Putney, but for the first time it took place from Putney to Kew.

WINNERS OF THE WINGFIELD SCULLS—*continued.*

Time	Winner	m. s.	Losers
1854	H. H. Playford	—	rowed over
1855	A. A. Casamajor	—	H. H. Playford
1856	A. A. Casamajor	—	rowed over
1857	A. A. Casamajor	—	rowed over
1858	A. A. Casamajor	—	rowed over
1859	A. A. Casamajor	—	rowed over
1860	aA. A. Casamajor	—	rowed over
1861	bE. D. Brickwood	29 0	G. R. Cox, A. O. Lloyd
1862	aW. B. Woodgate	27 0	E. D. Brickwood, G. R. Cox
1863	aJ. E. Parker	25 0	E. B. Michell, J. Wallace
1864	W. B. Woodgate	25 35	W. P. Cecil, G. Ryan
1865	aC. B. Lawes	27 4	{ W.B.Woodgate,E.B. Michell, W. P. Cecil, T. Lindsay
1866	aE. B. Michell	27 26	{ W. B. Woodgate, J. G. Chambers
1867	W. B. Woodgate	—	rowed over
1868	aW. Stout	26 52	{ E. B. Michell, W. B. Woodgate
1869	A. de L. Long	—	rowed over
1870	A. de L. Long	—	{ J. Ross, A. C. Yarborough, W. Chillingworth
1871	W. Fawcus	26 13	A. de L. Long
1872	C. C. Knollys	28 30	W. Fawcus
1873	A. C. Dicker	25 40	{ C. C. Knollys, N. H. Eyre, F. S. Gulston
1874	A. C. Dicker	25 45	{ W. H. Eyre, W. Fawcus, W. Chillingworth
1875	F. L. Playford	27 6	A. C. Dicker
1876	F. L. Playford	24 46	{ A. C. Dicker, A. V. Frere, R. H. Labat
1877	F. L. Playford	24 20	{ T. C. Edwardes-Moss, A. H. Grove, J. H. Bucknill
1878	F. L. Playford	24 13	Alexander Payne
1879	aF. L. Playford	25 51	J. Lowndes
1880	Alex. Payne	24 8	J. Lowndes, C. G. White
1881	J. Lowndes	25 13	W. R. Grove
1882	A. Payne	27 40	W. R. Grove
1883	J. Lowndes	—	rowed over
1884	W. S. Unwin	24 12	{ C. J. S. Batt, E. F. Green, W. Hawkes, R. H. Smith
1885	W. S. Unwin	—	F. J. Pitman, C. W. Hughes
1886	aF. J. Pitman	24 12	{ W. H. Cumming, A. M. Cowper-Smith
1887	G. Nickalls	—	J. C. Gardner.

(*a*) Resigned.
(*b*) The course was altered again this year to the present one, from Putney to Mortlake.

WINNERS AT HENLEY REGATTA.

GRAND CHALLENGE CUP.

		m. s.			m. s.
1839	Cambridge, Trin. Coll.	8 30	1863	Oxford University .	7 45
1840	Leander Club . .	9 15	1864	Kingston R.C. . .	7 43
1841 *a*	London, Camb. Rooms	—	1865	Kingston R.C. . .	7 21
1842	London, Camb. Rooms	8 30	1866	Oxford, Etonian Club	8 22
1843 *b*	Oxford University .	9 0	1867	Oxford, Etonian Club	7 54
1844	Oxford, Etonian Club	8 25	1868	London R.C. . .	7 20
1845	Cambridge University	8 30	1869	Oxford, Etonian Club	7 28
1846	London, Thames Club	8 15	1870 *d*	Oxford, Etonian Club	7 17
1847	Oxford University .	8 0	1871	Oxford, Etonian Club	7 55
1848	Oxford University .	9 11	1872	London R.C. . .	8 38
1849 *a*	Oxford, Wadham Coll.	8 0	1873	London R.C. . .	7 52
1850	Oxford University .	r.o.	1874	London R.C. . .	7 42
1851 *c*	Oxford University .	7 45	1875	Leander R.C. . .	7 19
1852	Oxford University .	—	1876	Thames R.C. . .	7 27
1853	Oxford University .	8 3	1877 *e*	London R.C. . .	8 16½
1854	Cambridge, Trin. Coll.	8 15	1878	Thames R.C. . .	7 41
1855	Cambridge University	8 32	1879	Camb., Jesus Coll. .	8 39
1856	Royal Chester R.C. .	—	1880	Leander B.C. . .	7 3
1857	London R.C. . .	7 55	1881	London R.C. . .	7 24
1858	Cambridge University	7 43	1882	Oxford, Exeter Coll.	8 11
1859	London R.C. . .	7 45	1883	London R.C. . .	7 51
1860	Cambridge, First Trin.	8 45	1884	London R.C. . .	7 27
1861	Cambridge, First Trin.	8 10	1885	Camb. Jesus Coll. .	7 22
1862	London R.C. . .	8 5	1886	Camb., Trin. Hall .	6 53½

1887 Camb., Trin. Hall, 6 56.

(*a*) Won on a foul.   (*b*) The winners only rowed seven oars in the final heat.
(*c*) Cambridge carried away a rowlock soon after starting.
(*d*) The fastest on record for the final.
(*e*) In the preliminary heat London did the course in 7 min. 12 secs.—the fastest time on record after that date.

STEWARDS' CUP.

		m. s.			m. s.
1841 *a*	First class fours for medals. Won by Oxford Aquatic Club . . .	10 5	1842	Oxford Club, London	9 16
			1843	London, St. George's Club . . .	10 15
			1844	Oxford University .	9 16

(*a*) The prize which is now known as the Stewards' Challenge Cup was not instituted until the following year.

		m. s.			m. s.
1845	Oxford University .	8 25	1865	Camb., Third Trin.	8 8
1846	Oxford University .	—	1866	Oxford, Univ. Coll.	9 20
1847 *b* Oxford C.C C. .		r.o.	1867	Oxford University .	8 45
1848	Oxford C.C.C. .	r.o.	1868	London R.C. . .	—
1849	London, Leander		1869	London R.C. . .	8 36
	Club . . .	r.o.	1870 *c* Oxon., Etonian Club		8 5
1850	Oxford University .	r.o.	1871	London R.C. . .	—
1851	Cambridge Univ. .	8 54	1872	London R.C. . .	9 21
1852	Oxford University .	—	1873 *d* London R.C. . .		8 25
1853	Oxford University .	8 57	1874	London R.C. . .	9 0
1854	Oxon, Pembroke		1875 *e* London R.C. . .		7 56
	Club . . .	9 54	1876 *f* London R.C. . .		—
1855	Royal Chester R.C.	—	1877	London R.C. . .	9 7
1856	Argonaut Club .	—	1878	London R.C. . .	8 37
1857	London R.C. . .	8 25	1879	Camb., Jesus Coll. .	9 37
1858	London R.C. . .	r.o.	1880	Thames R.C. . .	7 58
1859	Camb., Third Trin.	8 25	1881	Oxford, Hert. Coll. .	8 15
1860	Camb., First Trin. .	9 26	1882	Oxford, Hert. Coll. .	—
1861	Camb., First Trin. .	9 35	1883	Thames R.C. . .	—
1862	Oxon., Brasenose		1884	Kingston R.C. .	—
	Coll. . . .	8 40	1885	Camb., Trin, Hall .	7 53
1863	Oxford, Univ. Coll.	8 24	1886	Thames R.C. . .	7 39
1864	London R.C. . .	—	1887	Camb., Trin. Hall. .	7 53

(*b*) Worcester College, Oxford, were also entered, but withdrawn.
(*c*) Fastest time on record with coxswains.   (*d*) Coxswains abolished.
(*e*) Fastest time on record.   (*f*) Won on a foul.

PAIR-OARS.

	Won by	m. s.		Won by	m. s.
1845 *a*	Arnold and Mann,		1850 *c*	Chitty and Hornby,	
	Cambridge . .	—		Oxford . . .	r.o.
1846	Milman and Haggard,		1851	Chitty and Guess .	—
	Christ Church .	—	1852 *d*	Barker and Nind .	r.o.
1847 *b*	Falls and Coulthard,		1853	Barbee and Godson,	
	London . .	—		Cambridge . .	10 0
1848 *b*	Thompson and John-		1854	Cadogan and Short,	
	son, Oxford . .	—		Oxford . .	9 5
1849	Peacock and Rayford	—			

(*a*) The first pair-oared race rowed at Henley, which was then called the Silver Wherries till 1850.
(*b*) Won on a foul.
(*c*) The race was rowed this year for the first time as the Silver Goblets.
(*d*) Short and Irving, of Oxford, withdrew in the final.

	Won by	m.	s.		Won by	m.	s.
1855	Nottidge and Casa-major, London	—		1874	Gulston and Long, London R.C.	10	3
1856	Nottidge and Casa-major, London	—		1875	*b* Herbert and Chilling-worth	—	
1857	Warren and Lons-dale, Oxford	—		1876	S. Le B. Smith and F. S. Gulston	8	35
1858	Playford and Casa-major, London	—		1877	W. H. Eyre and J. Hastie	10	30
1859	Warre and Arkell, Oxford	9	0	1878	W. A. Ellison and T. C. Edwardes-Moss	9	14
1860	Casamajor and Wood-bridge, London	11	50	1879	F. S. Gulston and R. H. Labat, Lon-don R.C.	11	6
1861	Woodgate & Champ-neys, Oxford	—		1880	E. H. Eyre and J. Hastie, Thames R.C.	8	45
1862	Woodgate & Champ-neys, Oxford	8	45				
1863	Woodgate and Shep-herd, Oxford	r.o.		1881	W. H. Eyre and J. Hastie, Thames R.C.	9	4
1864	Selwyn and Kinglake, Cambridge	9	29	1882	D. E. Brown and J. Lowndes, Hertford Coll., Oxford	—	
1865	May and Fenner, London R.C.	9	7	1883	G. Q. Roberts and D. E. Brown, Twickenham R.C.	9	22
1866	Woodgate and Cor-rie, Kingston R.C.	9	15				
1867	Corrie and Brown, Eton and Radley	8	49	1884	J. Lowndes and D. E. Brown, Twick-enham R.C	9	1
1868	Crofts and Wood-gate, Oxford	—		1885	H. McLean and D. H. McLean, Etoni-ans, Oxford	—	
1869	Long and Stout, Lon-don R.C.	9	25				
1870	Corrie and Hall, Kingston R.C.	—		1886	F. E. Churchill and A. D. Muttlebury, Third Trin., Cam-bridge.	8	40
1871	Gulston and Long, London R.C.	—					
1872	Long and Gulston, London R.C.	—		1887	C. T. Barclay and A. D. Muttlebury	8	45
1873	Knollys and Trower, Kingston R.C.	9	22				

(*b*) Won on a foul.

DIAMOND SCULLS.

	m. s.			m. s.
1844 *a* Bumpstead, Scullers' Club, London	10 32	1867	W. C. Crofts, Oxford	10 2
1845 Wallace, Leander Club	11 30	1868	W. Stout, London R.C.	—
1846 Sir Frederick Moon, Magdalen, Oxford	—	1869	W. C. Crofts, Kingston	8 57
1847 Maule, Trinity Coll., Cambridge	10 45	1870	J. B. Close, Camb.	9 43
1848 Bagshawe, Camb.	—	1871	W. Fawcus, Tynemouth R.C.	10 9
1849 Bone, Meteor Club, London	—	1872	C. C. Knollys, Oxford	10 48
1850 Bone, Meteor Club, London	—	1873	A. C. Dicker, Camb.	9 13
1851 Edwards, London	—	1874	A. C. Dicker, Camb.	10 47
1852 Macnaghten, Camb.	—	1875	A. C. Dicker, Camb.	9 15
1853 Rippingall, Camb.	10 2	1876	F. L. Playford, London R.C.	9 28
1854 *b* Playford, Wandle College	—	1877	T. C. Edwardes-Moss, Oxford	10 20
1855 Casamajor, Argonauts	9 27	1878	T. C. Edwardes-Moss, Oxford	9 37½
1856 Casamajor, Argonauts	—	1879	J. Lowndes, Oxford	12 30
1857 Casamajor, Argonauts	—	1880	J. Lowndes, Derby	9 10
1858 Casamajor, Argonauts	r.o.	1881	J. Lowndes, Derby	9 28
1859 E. D. Brickwood, London	10 0	1882	J. Lowndes, Derby	11 43
1860 H. H. Playford, London	12 8	1883	J. Lowndes, Thames R.C.	10 2
1861 Casamajor, Argonauts	10 4	1884	W. S. Unwin, Magdalen	9 44
1862 *c* E. D. Brickwood	9 40	1885	W. S. Unwin, Magdalen	9 22
1863 C. B. Lawes, Camb.	9 43	1886	F. J. Pitman, Third Trinity, Cambridge	9 5
1864 W. B. Woodgate	10 10	1887	J. C. Gardner, Cambridge	8 51
1865 E. B. Michell, Oxford	9 5			
1866 E. B. Michell, Oxford	—			

(*a*) After two fouls the race was given in favour of Wallace.
(*b*) At Newenham a foul took place, and the race was awarded to Playford.
(*c*) After a dead heat, which was rowed in 10 minutes 22 seconds.

LADIES' CHALLENGE PLATE FOR EIGHT-OARS.

Established 1845.

	m. s.			m. s.
1845 London, St. George's Club	8 25	1846	Camb., First Trin.	—
		1847	Oxford, Brasenose	9 0

		m. s.			m. s.
1848	Oxon., Christ Church	—	1868	Eton College B.C. .	7 25
1849	Oxon., Wadham Coll.	—	1869	Eton College B.C. .	7 56
1850	Oxon., Lincoln Coll.	r.o.	1870	Eton College B.C. .	7 47
1851	Oxford, Brasenose .	8 10	1871	Oxford, Pembroke	
1852	Oxford, Pembroke			College. . .	7 56
	College . .	—	1872	Camb., Jesus Coll. .	8 39
1853	Camb., First Trin. .	8 15	1873	Camb., Jesus Coll. .	7 54
1854	Camb., First Trin. .	7 55	1874	Camb., First Trin. .	8 9
1855	Oxford, Balliol Coll.	7 58	1875	Dublin, Trin. Coll. .	7 28
1856	Royal Chester R.C.	—	1876	Camb., Jesus Coll. .	7 31
1857	Oxford, Exeter Coll.	7 57	1877	Camb., Jesus Coll. .	8 22
1858	Oxford, Balliol Coll.	7 51	1878	Camb., Jesus Coll. .	8 52
1859	Camb., First Trin. .	7 55	1879	Cambridge, Lady	
1860	Camb., First Trin. .	r.o.		Margaret B.C. .	8 52
1861	Cambridge, First		1880	Camb., Trin. Hall .	7 26
	Trinity (r.o.) .	8 17	1881	Camb., First Trin. .	7 51
1862	Oxford, Univ. Coll.	8 17	1882	Eton College B.C. .	8 37
1863	Oxford, Univ. Coll.	7 23	1883	Oxon., Christ Church	7 50
1864	Eton College B.C. .	7 56	1884	Eton College B.C. .	7 37
1865	Camb., Third Trin.	7 38	1885	Eton College B.C. .	7 21
1866	Eton College B.C. .	8 16	1886	Camb., Pembroke	
1867	Eton College B.C. .	7 56		College . .	7 17

1887   Trinity Hall, Cambridge (2nd crew)   7 10

VISITORS' CHALLENGE CUP FOR FOUR-OARS.
Established 1847.

		m. s.			m. s.
1847	Oxon., Christ Church	9 0	1860	Camb., First Trin. .	—
1848	Oxon., Christ Church	—	1861	Camb., First Trin. .	8 5
1849	Oxon., Christ Church	—	1862	Oxford, Brasenose	
1850	Oxon., Christ Church	—		College . .	8 40
1851	Oxon., Christ Church	9 0	1863	Oxford, Brasenose	
1852	London, Argonauts			College . .	—
	Club . . .	—	1864	Oxford, Univ. Coll.	—
1853	London, Argonauts		1865	Camb., Third Trin. .	—
	Club . . .	—	1866	Oxford, Univ. Coll.	8 49
1854	Camb., St. John's .	8 48	1867	Oxford, Univ. Coll.	—
1855	Camb., St. John's .	—	1868	Oxford, Univ. Coll.	8 15
1856	Camb., St. John's .	—	1869	Oxford, Univ. Coll.	9 7
1857	Oxford, Pembroke		1870	Dublin, Trin. Coll. .	8 37
	College . .	8 40	1871	Camb., First Trin. .	9 8
1858	Camb., First Trin. .	—	1872	Oxford, Pembroke	
1859	Camb., Third Trin.	—		College . . .	9 28

		m. s.			m. s.
1873	Dublin, Trin. Coll. .	—	1880	Camb., Third Trin.	8 16
1874	Dublin, Trin. Coll. .	8 50	1881	Camb., First Trin. .	8 22
1875	Oxford, Univ. Coll.	8 20	1882	Oxford, Brasenose	
1876	Oxford, Univ. Coll.	8 5		College . .	9 23
1877	Camb., Jesus Coll. .	9 7	1883	Oxon., Christ Church	—
1878	U.S.A, Columbia		1884	Camb., Third Trin. .	8 39
	College . .	8 42	1885	Camb., Trin. Hall .	7 41
1879	Cambridge, Lady		1886	Cambridge, First	
	Margaret B.C. .	9 21		Trinity B.C. .	8 20½

1887 Trinity Hall, Cambridge 8 8

WYFOLD CHALLENGE CUP FOR FOUR-OARS.
Established 1856.

		m. s.			m. s.
1856	London, Argonauts		1870	Thames R.C. .	8 34
	Club . .	—	1871	Thames R.C. .	—
1857	Oxford, Pembroke .		1872	Thames R.C. .	10 8
	College . .	8 30	1873	Kingstown Harbour	
1858	Camb., First Trin.	—		B.C. . . .	8 37
1859	Camb., First Trin.	8 21	1874	Newcastle A.R.C. .	8 58
1860	London R.C. .	10 8	1875	Thames R.C. .	8 10
1861	Oxford, Brasenose		1876	West London R.C.	8 56
	College . .	—	1877	Kingston R.C. .	—
1862	London R.C. .	9 20	1878	Kingston R.C. .	8 44
1863	Kingston R.C. .	8 50	1879	London R.C. .	9 56
1864	Kingston R.C. .	—	1880	London R.C. .	8 4
1865	Kingston R.C. .	8 23	1881	Dublin Univ. R.C. .	8 8
1866	Kingston R.C. .	—	1882	Camb., Jesus Coll.	8 58
1867	Kingston R.C. .	—	1883	Kingston R.C. .	8 51
1868	Kingston R.C. .	8 32	1884	Thames R.C. .	8 58
1869	Surbiton, Oscillators		1885	Kingston R.C. .	—
	B.C. . . .	8 58	1886	Thames R.C. .	8 4

1887 Pembroke College, Cambridge 7 50

THAMES CHALLENGE CUP FOR EIGHT-OARS. .
Established 1868.

		m. s.			m. s.
1868	Oxford, Pembroke		1870	Surbiton, Oscillators	
	College . .	7 46		B.C. . . .	—
1869	Surbiton, Oscillators		1871	London, Ino R.C. .	8 3
	B.C. . . .	—	1872	Thames R.C. . .	8 42

		m. s.			m. s.
1873	Thames R.C. .	. 8 2	1880	London R.C. .	. 7 43
1874	Thames R.C. .	. 8 19	1881	Twickenham R.C. .	7 50
1875	London R.C. .	. 7 33	1882	Royal Chester R.C.	—
1876	West London R.C. .	7 37	1883	London R.C. .	. 8 5
1877	London R.C. .	8 29	1884	Twickenham R.C. .	7 48
1878	London R.C. .	. 7 55	1885	London R.C. .	. 7 36
1879	Twickenham R.C. .	8 55	1886	London R.C. .	. —

1887   Trinity Hall, Cambridge (2nd crew)   7   20

PUBLIC SCHOOLS' CHALLENGE CUP FOR FOURS.

Established 1879.

		m. s.			m. s'
1879	Cheltenham College B.C. .	. . 11 6	1882	Magdalen College B.C. .	. . —
1880	Bedford Grammar School B.C.	. 8 42	1883	Hereford School B.C.	—
			1884	Derby School B.C.	—
1881	Bedford Grammar School B.C.	. 8 22	1885	Bedford Model School B.C.[1]	. —

TOWN CHALLENGE CUP.

1839	Wave B.C.		1864	Henley B.C.
1840	Dreadnought Cutter Club		1865	Henley B.C.
1841	Dreadnought Cutter Club		1866	Eton Excelsior B.C.
1842	Dreadnought Club		1867	Eton Excelsior B.C.
1843	Albion Club		1868	Henley R.C.
1844	Aquatic Club		1869	Eton Excelsior B.C.
1845	Aquatic Club		1870	Eton Excelsior B.C.
1846	Dreadnought Cutter Club		1871	Reading R.C.
1847	Dreadnought Cutter Club		1872	Marlow R.C.
1848	Dreadnought Cutter Club		1873	Henley R.C.
1849	Albion Club		1874	Marlow R.C.
1850	Albion Club		1875	Marlow R.C.
1854	Wargrave Club		1876	Marlow R.C.
1855	Henley B.C.		1877	Marlow R.C.
1856	Henley B.C.		1878	Henley R.C.
1857	Henley B.C.		1879	Greenwood Lodge B.C.
1858	Henley B.C.		1880	Reading R.C.
1859	Henley B.C.		1881	Reading R.C.
1860	Dreadnought Cutter Club		1882	Reading R.C.
1862	Oxford, Staff B.C.		1883	Marlow R.C.[2]
1863	Henley B.C.			

[1] Transferred to Marlow Regatta in 1886.   [2] Ditto in 1884.

OXFORD AND CAMBRIDGE BOAT RACE.

WINNERS since 1828.

Year	Place	Winner	Time	Won by
			m. s.	
1829	Hambledon Lock to Henley Bridge	Oxford	14 30	easy
1836	Westminster to Putney .	Cambridge	36 0	1 m.
1839	Westminster to Putney .	Cambridge	31 0	1 m. 45 s.
1840	Westminster to Putney .	Cambridge	29 30	¾ length
1841	Westminster to Putney .	Cambridge	32 30	1 m. 4 s.
1842	Westminster to Putney .	Oxford	30 45	13 s.
1845	Putney to Mortlake . .	Cambridge	23 30	30 s.
1846	*a*Mortlake (Church) to Putney	Cambridge	21 5	2 lengths
1849	Putney to Mortlake (Ship) .	Cambridge	22 0	4 lengths
1849	Putney to Mortlake . .	Oxford	—	foul
1852	Putney to Mortlake . .	Oxford	21 56	27 s.
1854	Putney to Mortlake . .	Oxford	25 29	11 strokes
1856	*b*Barker's rails to Putney .	Cambridge	25 50	½ length
1857	*c*Putney to Mortlake . .	Oxford	22 55	35 s.
1858	Putney to Mortlake . .	Cambridge	21 23	22 s.
1859	Putney to Mortlake . .	Oxford	24 40	C. sank
1860	Putney to Mortlake . .	Cambridge	26 5	1 length
1861	Putney to Mortlake . .	Oxford	23 28	43 s.
1862	Putney to Mortlake . .	Oxford	24 41	30 s.
1863	*b*Barker's rails to Putney .	Oxford	23 6	43 s.
1864	Putney to Mortlake . .	Oxford	22 15	26 s.
1865	Putney to Mortlake . .	Oxford	21 24	4 s.
1866	Putney to Mortlake . .	Oxford	25 14	15 s.
1867	Putney to Mortlake . .	Oxford	22 30	½ length
1868	Putney to Mortlake . .	Oxford	20 37	6 lengths
1869	Putney to Mortlake . .	Oxford	20 6½	3 lengths
1870	Putney to Mortlake . .	Cambridge	21 30½	2 lengths
1871	Putney to Mortlake . .	Cambridge	23 9½	1 length
1872	Putney to Mortlake . .	Cambridge	21 14	2 lengths
1873	*d*Putney to Mortlake . .	Cambridge	19 36	3 lengths
1874	Putney to Mortlake . .	Cambridge	22 35	3½ lengths
1875	Putney to Mortlake . .	Oxford	22 2	29 s.
1876	Putney to Mortlake . .	Cambridge	20 19	5 lengths
1877	*e*Putney to Mortlake . .	Dead heat	24 6½	dead heat
1878	Putney to Mortlake . .	Oxford	22 15	40 s.

(*a*) This was the first race rowed in outrigged eights.

(*b*) These races were rowed from Barker's rails to Putney, about 1,200 yards more than the usual course. Barker's rails are still marked by a brick pedestal under Middlesex shore.

(*c*) This was the first race rowed in keelless boats.

(*d*) Sliding seats first used in these races.

(*e*) This is the only dead heat ever rowed in this race. Bow in Oxford boat broke his oar.

Year	Place	Winner	Time	Won by
1879	Putney to Mortlake . .	Cambridge	21 18	3½ lengths
1880	Putney to Mortlake . .	Oxford	21 23	4 lengths
1881	Putney to Mortlake . .	Oxford	21 52	3½ lengths
1882	Putney to Mortlake . .	Oxford	20 12	20 s.
1883	Putney to Mortlake . .	Oxford	22 18	2⅗ lengths
1884	Putney to Mortlake . .	Cambridge	21 39	3 lengths
1885	Putney to Mortlake . .	Oxford	21 36	5 lengths
1886	Putney to Mortlake . .	Cambridge	22 20	⅘ length
1887	Putney to Mortlake . .	Cambridge	20 52	2¼ lengths
1888	Putney to Mortlake . .	Cambridge	20 48	5 lengths

UNIVERSITY MEETINGS AT HENLEY,

FOR THE GRAND CHALLENGE CUP.

Year	Winner	Time (m. s.)	Won by
1845	Cambridge	8 30	2 lengths
1847	Oxford	8 4	2 lengths
1851	aOxford	7 45	6 lengths
1853	Oxford	8 3	6 inches
1855	Cambridge	8 32	2½ lengths

(*a*) Cambridge broke a rowlock off Remenham farm.

Also at the Thames Regatta, June 22, 1844, Oxford beat Cambridge for the Gold Cup.

UNIVERSITY OARSMEN.

The following lists show what oarsmen in eights or fours repre-sented their respective Universities from year to year, whether in matches or at regattas. Those whose names appear as having thus represented their University are recognised as 'old Blues.' In some cases crews are given which are not strictly University crews, e.g. the 'Cambridge Subscription Rooms,' 'Oxford Aquatic Club,' &c. These crews sometimes took the place of U.B.C. crews, and though all these members may not be strictly 'Blues,' the performances are recorded, in order to give as far as possible a continuous history.

UNIVERSITY OARSMEN.

1829.

Hambledon Lock to Henley, Wednesday, June 10, 1829, 7.56 p.m.

OXFORD, 1.　　　　　　　　　　　st. lbs.

1. Carter, J., St. John's . . . . —
2. Arbuthnot, J. E., Balliol . . . . —
3. Bates, J. E., Christ Church . . . .—
4. Wordsworth, Charles, Christ Church 11 10
5. Toogood, J. J., Balliol 14 10
6. Garnier, T. F., Worcester . . . . —
7. Moore, G. B., Christ Church 12 4
Staniforth, T., Christ Church (stroke) 12 0
Fremantle, W. R., Christ Church (cox.) . . . . . —

CAMBRIDGE, 2.　　　　　　　　　　st. lbs.

1. Holdsworth, A. B. E., First Trinity 10 7
2. Bayford, A. F., Trinity Hall . . . : . . . 10 8
3. Warren, C., Second Trinity 10 10
4. Merivale, C., Lady Margaret 11 0
5. Entwisle, T., Trinity 11 4
6. Thompson, W. T., Jesus 11 13
7. Selwyn, G. A., Lady Margaret 11 13
Snow, W., Lady Margaret (stroke) 11 4
Heath, B. R., First Trinity (cox.) 9 4

Average 11 1¾

1831.

Leander Match v. Oxford, Henley Course, June 12.

LEANDER, 1.　　　　　　　　OXFORD, 2.

1. Horniman　　　　　　　1. Carter
2. Revell　　　　　　　　2. Waterford (Marquis of)
3. Weedon　　　　　　　3. Marsh
4. Cannon　　　　　　　4. Peard
5. Lewis　　　　　　　　5. Pelham
6. T. Bayford　　　　　　6. Barnes
7. Capt. Shaw　　　　　　7. Lloyd
Bishop (stroke)　　　　　Copplestone (stroke)
Noulton, waterman (cox.)　　G. West, waterman (cox.)

1836.

Westminster to Putney, June 17, 1836, 4.20 p.m.

CAMBRIDGE, 1.

	st.	lbs.
1. Solly, W. H., First Trinity	11	0
2. Green, F. S., Caius	11	2
3. Stanley, E. S., Jesus	11	4
4. Hartley, P., Trinity Hall	12	0
5. Jones, W. M., Caius	12	0
6. Keane. J. H., First Trinity	12	0
7. Upcher, A. W., Second Trinity	12	0
Granville, A. K. B., C.C.C. (stroke)	11	7
Egan, T. S., Caius (cox.)	9	0
Average	11	8⅝

OXFORD, 2.

	st.	lbs.
1. Carter, G., St. John's	10	0
2. Stephens, E., Exeter	10	7
3. Baillie, W., Christ Church	11	7
4. Harris, T., Magdalen	12	4
5. Isham, J. V., Christ Church	12	0
6. Pennefather, J., Balliol	12	10
7. Thompson, W. S., Jesus	13	0
Moysey, F. L., Christ Church (stroke)	10	6
Davies, E. W. L., Jesus (cox.)	10	3
Average	11	7¾

1837.

First Leander Match (C.U.B.C), Westminster to Putney, June 9, 1837.

CAMBRIDGE, 1.

	st.	lbs.
1. Nicholson, W. N., First Trinity	11	0
2. Green, F. S., Caius	11	2
3. Budd, R. H., Lady Margaret	12	0
4. Keane, J. H., First Trinity	12	0
5. Brett, W. B., Caius	12	0
6. Penrose, C. T., First Trinity	12	0
7. Fletcher, R., Lady Margaret	11	10
Granville, A. K. B., Corpus (stroke)	11	7
Moulton, W. (cox.)	—	
Average	11	9⅝

LEANDER, 2.

1. Shepheard	6. Dalgleish
2. Layton	7. Lewis
3. Wood	Horneman (stroke)
4. Lloyd	James Parish (cox.)
5. Sherrard	

1838.

Second Leander Match (C.U.B.C.)

CAMBRIDGE, I.	LEANDER, 2.
1. Shadwell, A. H., Lady Margaret.	1. Shepheard
2. Smyth, W. W., Second Trinity.	2. Sherrard
3. Gough, Walter R., First Trinity.	3. Lloyd
4. Yatman, W. H., Caius.	4. Layton
5. Penrose, C. T., First Trinity.	5. Wood
6. Paris, A., Corpus.	6. Dalgleish
7. Brett, W. B., Caius.	7. Bishop
Stanley, E., Jesus (stroke).	Lewis (stroke)
Moulton, W. (cox.)	Parish (cox.)

(A foul.)

1839.

Westminster to Putney, April 3, 1839, 4.47 p.m.

CAMBRIDGE, I.	st.	lbs.
1. Shadwell, Alfred H., Lady Margaret	10	7
2. Smyth, W. W., Second Trinity	11	0
3. Abercrombie, J., Caius	10	7
4. Paris, A., Corpus	—	
5. Penrose, C. T., First Trinity	12	0
6. Yatman, W. H., Caius	—	
7. Brett, W. B., Caius	12	0
Stanley, E. S., Jesus (stroke)	—	
Egan, T. S., Caius (cox.)	9	0

OXFORD, 2.	st.	lbs.
1. Lee, S., Queen's	10	4
2. Compton, J., Merton	11	5
3. Maberly, S. F., Christ Church	11	4
4. Garnett, W. J., Christ Church	12	10
5. Walls, R. G., Brasenose	13	0
6. Hobhouse, R., Balliol	12	0
7. Powys, P. L., Balliol	12	0
Bewicke, C., University (stroke)	11	5
Ffooks, W. W., Exeter (cox.)	10	2
Average	11	10½

1840.

Westminster to Putney, Wednesday, April 15, 1840, 1.30 p.m.

CAMBRIDGE, 1.

		st.	lbs.
1. Shadwell, A. H., Lady Margaret.		10	7
2. Massey, W., First Trinity		11	0
3. Taylor, S. B., First Trinity		11	7
4. Ridley, J. M., Jesus		12	8
5. Uppleby, G. C., Magdalene		11	12
6. Penrose, F. C., Magdalene		12	1
7. Jones, H., Magdalene		11	9
Viales, C. M., Third Trinity (stroke)		11	6
Egan, T. S., Caius, (cox.)		9	0
Average		11	8

OXFORD, 2.

		st.	lbs.
1. Mountain, J. G., Merton		11	0
2. Pocock, J. J. I., Merton		11	2
3. Maberly, S. E., Christ Church		11	4
4. Rogers, W., Balliol		12	10
5. Walls, R. G., Brasenose		12	7
6. Royds, E., Brasenose		12	4
7. Meynell, G., Brasenose		11	10
Somers Cocks, J. J. T., Brasenose (stroke)		11	3
Garnett, W. B., Brasenose (cox.)		9	7
Average		11	10½

1841.

Westminster to Putney, Wednesday, April 14, 1841, 6.10 p.m.

CAMBRIDGE, 1.

		st.	lbs.
1. Croker, W. R., Caius		9	12
2. Denman, Hon. L. W., Magdalene		10	12
3. Ritchie, A. M., First Trinity		11	10
4. Ridley, J. M., Jesus		12	7
5. Cobbold, R. H., Peterhouse		12	4
6. Penrose, F. C., Magdalene		12	0
7. Denman, Hon. G., First Trinity		10	7
Viales, C. M., Third Trinity (stroke)		11	7
Croker, J. M., Caius (cox.)		10	8
Average		11	5⅜

OXFORD, 2.

		st.	lbs.
1. Bethell, R., Exeter		10	6
2. Richards, E. V., Christ Church		11	2
3. Mountain, J. G., Merton		10	9
4. Royds, E., Brasenose		11	13
5. Hodgson, H. W., Balliol		11	10
6. Lea, W., Brasenose		11	7
7. Meynell, G., Brasenose		11	11
Somers Cocks, J. J. T., Brasenose (stroke)		11	4
Wollaston, C. B., Exeter (cox.)		9	2
Average		11	4⅜

S

1841.

Grand Challenge Cup, Henley, 1841.

CAMBRIDGE SUBSCRIPTION ROOMS, 1.

		st. lbs.
1. Denman, Hon. G., First Trinity		10 8
2. Shadwell, A. H., Lady Margaret		10 9
3. Cross, W. A., First Trinity		10 6
4. Anson, T. A., Jesus		12 8
5. Yatman, W. H., Caius		10 10
6. Jones, W. M., Caius		11 10
7. Viales, C. M., Third Trinity		11 9
Brett, W. B., Caius (stroke)		11 10
Egan, T. S., Caius (cox.)		9 6

LEANDER, 2.

		st. lbs.
1. Shepheard		10 2
2. Layton		10 11
3. Julius, W.		11 6
4. Romayne		11 8
5. Jenkins		12 3
6. Wallace		11 7
7. Wood		10 12
Dalgleish (stroke)		11 2
Gibson, H. (cox.)		11 0

1842.

Westminster to Putney, Saturday, June 11, 1842.

OXFORD, 1.

		st. lbs.
1. M'Dougall, F. T., Magdalen Hall		9 8
2. Menzies, Sir R., University		11 3
3. Breedon, E. A., Trinity		12 4
4. Brewster, W. B., St. John's		12 10
5. Bourne, G. D., Oriel		13 12
6. Cox, J. C., Trinity		10 8
7. Hughes, G. E., Oriel		11 6
Menzies, F. N., University (stroke)		10 12
Shadwell, A. T. W., Balliol (cox.)		10 4
Average		11 9¾

CAMBRIDGE, 2.

		st. lbs.
1. Tower, E., Lady Margaret		10 2
2. Denman, Hon. L. W., Magdalene		10 11
3. Watson, W., Jesus		10 13
4. Penrose, F. C., Magdalene		11 10
5. Cobbold, R. H., Peterhouse		12 6
6. Royds, J., Christ's		11 7
7. Denman, Hon. G., First Trinity		10 9
Ridley, J. M., Jesus (stroke)		12 0
Pollock, A. B., First Trinity (cox.)		9 7
Average		11 3¾

1842.

Grand Challenge Cup, Henley, 1842.

CAMBRIDGE SUBSCRIPTION ROOMS, 1.   st. lbs.

1. Yatman, W. H., Caius		10 10
2. Shadwell, A., John's		10 9
3. Appleby, G. C., Magdalene		11 2
4. Lonsdale, J. G., First Trinity		12 4
5. Ritchie, A. M., First Trinity		12 0
6. Jones, W. M., Caius		11 10
7. Selwyn, C. J., Second Trinity		11 12
Beresford, J., Peter's (stroke)		10 10
Egan, T. S., Caius (cox.)		9 2
Average		11 5½

CAMBRIDGE UNIVERSITY BOATING CLUB, 2.   st. lbs.

1. Tower, E., John's		10 2
2. Denman, Hon. L. W., Magdalene		10 11
3. Watson, W., Jesus		10 13
4. Viales, C. M., Third Trinity		11 9
5. Cobbold, R. H., Peter's		12 6
6. Royds, J., Christ's		11 7
7. Denman, Hon. G., First Trinity		10 9
Ridley, J. M., Jesus (stroke)		12 0
Pollock, J. C., Third Trinity (cox.)		10 2
Average		11 3⅝

1843.

Grand Challenge Cup, Henley, 1843.

OXFORD, THE 'SEVEN OAR,' 1.   st. lbs.

1. Menzies, Sir R., University		11 3
2. Royds, E., Brasenose		12 0
3. Brewster, W. B., St. John's		13 0
4. Bourne, G. D., Oriel		13 12
5. Cox, J. C., Trinity		11 12
6. Lowndes, R., Christ Church		11 2
7. Hughes, G. E., Oriel		11 11
Shadwell, A. T. W., Balliol (cox.)		10 8
Menzies, F. (stroke), *æger*		—
Average		12 1⁴⁄₇

CAMBRIDGE SUBSCRIPTION ROOMS, 2.   st. lbs.

1. Yatman, W. H., Caius		10 12
2. Shadwell, A. H., Lady Margaret		11 0
3. Mann, G., Caius		12 0
4. Ridley, J. M., Jesus		12 6
5. Cobbold, R. H., Peterhouse		12 5
6. Jones, W. M., Caius		11 12
7. Denman, Hon. L. W., Magdalene		10 11
Viales, C. M., Third Trinity (stroke)		11 13
Egan, T. S., Caius (cox.)		9 6
Average		11 9

1843.

Gold Cup, Thames Regatta.

OXFORD, 1.

Crew same as 'Seven oar' *supra*, except W. Chetwynd-Stapylton, Merton, 10 st. 6 lbs. at bow.

1844.

Gold Cup, Thames Regatta. Chiswick Eyot to Putney Bridge.

OXFORD, 1.	st.	lbs.
1. Chetwynd-Stapylton, W., Merton	10	8
2. Spottiswoode, W., Balliol	10	6
3. Milman, W. H., Christ Church	11	0
4. Morgan, H., Christ Church	12	11
5. Buckle, W., Oriel	13	12
6. Dry, W. J., Wadham	11	5
7. Wilson, F. M., Christ Church	12	8
Tuke, F. E., Brasenose (stroke)	11	9
Shadwell, A. T. W., Balliol (cox.)	10	8
Average	11	1⅞

CAMBRIDGE, 2.	st.	lbs.
1. Raven, J., Magdalene	8	13
2. Venables, H., Jesus	10	2
3. Mann, G., Caius	10	7
4. Cloves, W. P., First Trinity	11	11
5. Brookes, T. W., First Trinity	11	9
6. Richardson, J., First Trinity	11	12
7. Nicholson, W. W., First Trinity	10	3
Arnold, F. M., Caius (stroke)	11	11
Egan, T. S., Caius (cox.)	10	0
Average	10	12

LEANDER, 3.	st.	lbs.
1. Soanes	9	3
2. Peacock	10	0
3. Lee	12	0
4. Hodding	11	6
5. Julius	12	0
6. Bumpstead	12	0
7. Jefferies	9	4
Dalgleish (stroke)	10	6
Shepheard (cox.)	10	0
Average	10	11½

1844.

Grand Challenge Cup, Henley.

OXFORD, I.   st. lbs.

1. Chetwynd-Stapylton, W., Merton 10 8
2. Spottiswoode, W., Balliol 10 6
3. Chetwynd-Stapylton, H. E., University 10 10
4. Spankie, J., Merton 11 4
5. Wilson, F. M., Christ Church 12 8
6. Tuke, F. E., Brasenose 11 9
7. Ccnant, J. W., St. John's 12 7
    Morgan, H., Christ Church (stroke) 12 7
    Shadwell, A. T. W., Balliol (cox.) 10 0

            Average 11 7⅜

1844.

The Stewards' Cup, Henley. *(Final Heat.)*

OXFORD, I.	ST. GEORGE'S CLUB, LONDON, 2.
	st. lbs.
1. Chetwynd-Stapylton, W., Merton	1. Wadham . . . 9 10
2. Dry, W. J., Wadham	2. M'Kay 10 11
3. Wilson, F. M., Christ Church	3. Ross 11 4
Tuke, F. E., Brasenose (stroke)	Smith (stroke) . . 10 4
Lewis, G. B., Oriel (cox.)	Johnson, A. (cox.) . 7 11

1845.

Putney to Mortlake, Saturday, March 15, 1845, 6.1 p.m.

CAMBRIDGE, I.   st. lbs.

1. Mann, G., Caius 10 7
2. Harkness, W., Lady Margaret 10 0
3. Lockhart, W. S., Christ's 11 3
4. Cloves, W. P., First Trinity 12 0
5. Arnold, F. M., Caius 12 0
6. Harkness, R., Lady Margaret 11 0
7. Richardson, J., First Trinity 12 0
    Hill, C. G., Second Trinity (stroke) 10 11
    Munster, H., First Trinity (cox.) 9 2

            Average 11 2⅝

OXFORD, 2.   st. lbs.

1. Haggard, M., Christ Church 10 3
2. Chetwynd-Stapylton, W., Merton 10 12
3. Milman, W. H., Christ Church 11 0
4. Lewis, H., Pembroke 11 7
5. Buckle, W., Oriel 13 12
6. Royds, F. C., Brasenose 11 5
7. Wilson, F. M., Christ Church 12 3
    Tuke, F. E., Brasenose (stroke) 12 2
    Richards, F. J., Merton (cox.) 10 10

            Average 11 9

1845.

Grand Challenge Cup, Henley.

	CAMBRIDGE, 1.	st.	lbs.
1.	Mann, G., Caius	10	8
2.	Harkness, W., Lady Margaret	10	1
3.	Lockhart, W. S., Christ's	11	3
4.	Cloves, W. P., First Trinity	12	1
5.	Hopkins, F. L., First Trinity	12	7
6.	Potts, H. J., Second Trinity	11	9
7.	Arnold, F. M., Caius	12	2
	Hill, C. G., Second Trinity (stroke)	10	12
	Munster, H., Second Trinity (cox.)	9	2
	Average	11	5¼

	OXFORD 2.	st.	lbs.
1.	Chetwynd-Stapylton, W., Merton	10	6
2.	Spottiswoode, W., Balliol	10	11
3.	Milman, W. H., Christ Church	10	12
4.	Buckle, W., Oriel	13	7
5.	Breedon, E. A., Trinity	11	10
6.	Penfold, E. H., St. John's	11	10
7.	Conant, J. W., St. John's	11	13
	Wilson, F. M., Christ Church (stroke)	12	11
	Shadwell, A. T. W., Balliol (cox.)	10	4
	Average	11	10

1845.

The Stewards' Cup, Henley. (*Final Heat.*)

	OXFORD, 1.	st.	lbs.
1.	Chetwynd-Stapylton, W., Merton	10	6
2.	Milman, W. H., Christ Church	10	10
3.	Conant, J. W., St. John's	11	3
	Wilson, F. M., Christ Church (stroke)	12	1
	Lewis, G. B., Oriel (cox.)	—	

	ST. GEORGE'S CLUB, LONDON, 2.	st.	lbs.
1.	Wadham	10	0
2.	Ross	11	0
3.	Coulthard	11	11
	Smith (stroke)	10	12
	Johnson, A., (cox.)	8	4

1845.
Gold Cup, Thames Regatta.

CAMBRIDGE LONDON ROOMS, 1.

1. Rippingall, C., Lady Margaret
2. Shadwell, A. H., Lady Margaret
3. Lockhart, W. S., Christ's
4. Cloves, W. P., First Trinity
5. Wilder, E., Magdalen
6. Hopkins, F. L., First Trinity
7. Arnold, F. M., Caius
   Hill, C. G., Second Trinity (stroke)
   Egan, T. S., Caius (cox.)

OXFORD AQUATIC CLUB, 2.

1. Chetwynd-Stapylton, W., Merton
2. Milman, W. H., Christ Church
3. Meynell, G., Brasenose
4. Buckle, W., Oriel
5. Breedon, E. A., Trinity
6. Hughes, G. E., Oriel
7. Conant, J. W., St. John's
   Wilson, F. M., Christ Church (stroke)
   Richards, F. J., Merton (cox.)

1846.
Mortlake to Putney, April 3, 1846, 11.10 a.m.

CAMBRIDGE, 1.

					st.	lbs.
1. Murdoch, G. F., Lady Margaret	.	.	.	.	10	2
2. Holroyd, G. F., First Trinity	.	.	.	.	11	1
3. Clissold, S. T., Third Trinity	.	.	.	.	12	0
4. Cloves, W. P., First Trinity	.	.	.	.	12	12
5. Wilder, E., Magdalene	.	.	.	.	12	2
6. Harkness, R., Lady Margaret	.	.	.	.	11	6
7. Wolstenholme, E. P., First Trinity	.	.	.	.	11	1
Hill, C. G., Second Trinity (stroke)	.	.	.	.	11	1
Lloyd, T. B., Lady Margaret (cox.)	.	.	.	.	9	8
Average	.	.	.	.	11	8¾

OXFORD, 2.

					st.	lbs.
1. Polehampton, H. S., Pembroke	.	.	.	.	10	9
2. Burton, E. C., Christ Church	.	.	.	.	11	0
3. Heygate, W. U., Merton	.	.	.	.	11	8
4. Penfold, E. H., St. John's	.	.	.	.	11	8
5. Conant, J. W., St. John's	.	.	.	.	12	4
6. Royds, F. C., Brasenose	.	.	.	.	11	9
7. Chetwynd-Stapylton, W., Merton	.	.	.	.	10	12
Milman, W. H., Christ Church (stroke)	.	.	.	.	11	0
Soanes, C. J., St. John's (cox.)	.	.	.	.	9	13
Average	.	.	.	.	11	4½

1846.

The Stewards' Cup, Henley. (*Final Heat.*)

O.U.B.C., 1.

			st.	lbs.
1.	Chetwynd Stapylton, W., Merton	. .	10	6
2.	Wilson, F. M., Christ Church	. . .	12	1
3.	Conant, J. W., St. John's	. . .	11	13
	Milman, W. H., Christ Church (stroke)	.	10	10
	Haggard, M., Christ Church (cox.)	. .	—	
	Average	. .	11	4

GUY'S CLUB, LONDON, 2.

1. Forster
2. Gruggen
3. Ferguson
   Cooper (stroke)
   Roland (cox.)

1847.

Grand Challenge Cup, Henley.

OXFORD, 1.

			st.	lbs.
1.	Moon, E. G., Magdalen	. . . . .	10	4
2.	Haggard, M., Christ Church	. . . .	10	8
3.	Oldham, J., Brasenose	. . . . .	11	7
4.	Royds, F. C., Brasenose	. . . .	11	10
5.	Griffiths, E. G. C., Worcester	. . .	12	6
6.	King, W., Oriel	. . . . .	11	0
7.	Winter, G. R., Brasenose	. . . .	11	3
	Burton, E. C., Christ Church (stroke)	. . .	11	0
	Soanes, C. J., St. John's (cox.)	. . .	9	10
	Average	. . .	11	3

CAMBRIDGE, 2.

			st.	lbs.
1.	Maule, W., First Trinity	. . . . .	9	12
2.	Gisborne, T. M., Lady Margaret	. . .	10	10
3.	Wolstenholme, E. P., First Trinity	. . .	10	10
4.	Garfit, A., First Trinity	. . . .	12	8
5.	Nicholson, C. A., First Trinity	. . .	13	5
6.	Harkness, R., Lady Margaret	. . . .	11	4
7.	Vincent, S., First Trinity	. . . .	10	10
	Jackson, F. C., Lady Margaret (stroke)	. . .	11	0
	Murdoch, G. F., Lady Margaret (cox.)	. .	10	3
	Average	. .	11	$3\frac{7}{8}$

1848.

Grand Challenge Cup, Henley. (*First Heat.*)

OXFORD, I.	st.	lbs.
1. Rich, W. G., Christ Church	10	11
2. Haggard, M., Christ Church	10	4
3. Sykes, E., Worcester	11	0
4. Royds, F. C., Brasenose	11	4
5. Winter, G. R., Brasenose	11	6
6. Mansfield, A., Christ Church	10	10
7. Milman, W. H., Christ Church	11	0
Burton, E. C., Christ Church (stroke)	11	0
Soanes, C. J., St. John's (cox.)	9	13
Average	10	11⅞

THAMES CLUB, LONDON, 2.	st.	lbs.
1. Bruce	10	6
2. Thompson	10	8
3. Blake	10	12
4. Playford	11	4
5. Robinson	12	0
6. Wallace	12	8
7. Chapman	11	3'
Walmsley (stroke)	10	6
Field (cox.)	9	7

1849

Putney to Mortlake, Thursday, March 29, 5.49 *p.m.* (*First Race.*)

CAMBRIDGE, I.	st.	lbs.
1. Proby, H., Second Trinity	9	13
2. Jones, W. J. H., Second Trinity	10	13
3. De Rutzen, A., Third Trinity	11	8
4. Holden, C. J., Third Trinity	11	8
5. Bagshawe, W. L. G., Third Trinity	11	10
6. Waddington, W. H., Second Trinity	11	10
7. Hodgson, W. C., First Trinity	11	2
Wray, J. C., Second Trinity (stroke)	10	12
Booth, G., First Trinity (cox.)	10	7
Average	11	2½

OXFORD, 2.	st.	lbs.
1. Wauchope, D., Wadham	10	4
2. Chitty, J. W., Balliol	11	2
3. Tremayne, H. H., Christ Church	11	5
4. Burton, E. C., Christ Church	11	0
5. Steward, C. H., Oriel	12	0
6. Mansfield, A., Christ Church	11	8
7. Sykes, E., Worcester	11	0
Rich, W. G., Christ Church (stroke)	10	0
Soanes, C. J., St. John's (eox.)	10	8
Average	11	0⅝

1849

Putney to Mortlake, Saturday, December 15, 2.44 *p.m.* (*Second Race.*)

OXFORD, 1.		st. lbs.
1.	Hornby, J. J., Brasenose	11 8
2.	Houghton, W., Brasenose	11 2
3.	Wodehouse, J., Exeter	11 9
4.	Chitty, J. W., Balliol	11 9
5.	Aitken, J., Exeter	12 1
6.	Steward, C. H., Oriel	12 2
7.	Sykes, E., Worcester	11 2
	Rich, W. G., Christ Church (stroke)	10 2
	Cotton, R. W., Christ Church (cox.)	9 0
	Average	11 5⅞

CAMBRIDGE, 2.		st. lbs.
1.	Baldry, A., First Trinity	10 10
2.	Pellew, H. E., Third Trinity	11 9
3.	De Rutzen, A., Third Trinity	11 8
4.	Holden, C. J., Third Trinity	11 11
5.	Bagshawe, W. L. G., Third Trinity	12 0
6.	Miller, H. J., Third Trinity	12 0
7.	Hodgson, W. C., First Trinity	11 3
	Wray, J. C., Clare (stroke)	11 0
	Booth, G., First Trinity (cox.)	10 8
	Average	11 5¾

1850.

Grand Challenge Cup, Henley.

O.U.B.C. (*Walked over.*)		st. lbs.
1.	Cheales, H. J., Exeter	10 11
2.	Houghton, W., Brasenose	11 2
3.	Hornby, J. J., Brasenose	11 8
4.	Aitken, J., Exeter	12 1
5.	Steward, C. H., Oriel	12 2
6.	Chitty, J. W., Balliol	11 9
7.	Sykes, E., Worcester	10 2
	Rich, W. G., Christ Church (stroke)	11 2
	Cotton, R. W., Christ Church (cox.)	9 0
	Average	11 4⅝

1850.

The Stewards' Cup, Henley.

O.U.B.C. (*Walked over.*)		st. lbs.
1.	Hornby, J. J., Brasenose	11 8
2.	Aitken, J., Exeter	12 1
3.	Steward, C. H., Oriel	12 2
	Chitty, J. W., Balliol (stroke)	11 9
	Rich, W. G., Christ Church (cox.)	11 2
	Average	11 12¼

1851.

Grand Challenge Cup, Henley. (*Final Heat.*)

OXFORD, 1.   st. lbs.

		st.	lbs.
1. Rich, W. G., Christ Church	. .	10	0
2. Nixon, W., Worcester .	. .	11	4
3. Hornby, J. J., Brasenose . .	. .	11	0
4. Houghton, W., Brasenose . .	. .	11	10
5. Aitken, J., Exeter . . .	. .	11	12
6. Greenall, R., Brasenose . .	. .	11	2
7. Sykes, E., Worcester . . .	. .	11	4
Chitty, J. W., Balliol (stroke) .	. .	11	3
Burton, E. C., Christ Church (cox.)	. .	11	0
Average .	. .	11	4¾

CAMBRIDGE, 2.   st. lbs.

		st.	lbs.
1. Page, A. S., Lady Margaret . . .	.	10	1
2. Longmore, W. S., Sydney	.	10	4
3. Formby, R., First Trinity	.	11	11
4. Cowie, H., First Trinity	.	11	12
5. Brandt, H., First Trinity	.	11	5
6. Holden, C. J., Third Trinity . .	.	11	11
7. Tuckey, H. E., Lady Margaret . . .	.	10	13
Johnson, F. W., Third Trinity (stroke) . .	.	10	11
Crosse, C. H., Caius (cox.)	.	9	1
Average .	.	11	1½

The Stewards' Cup, Henley. (*Final Heat.*)

C.U.B.C., 1.   st. lbs.

		st.	lbs.
1. Page, A. S., Lady Margaret	.	10	1
2. Longmore, W. S., Sydney	.	10	4
3. Tuckey, H. E., Lady Margaret	.	10	13
Johnson, F. W., Third Trinity (stroke)	.	10	11
Crosse, C. H., Caius (cox.)	.	9	1

BRASENOSE COLLEGE, OXON, 2.

    1. Mescott
    2. Errington
    3. Hornby
       Greenall (stroke)
       Balguy (cox.)

1852.

Putney to Mortlake, Saturday, April 3, 1.4 p.m.

OXFORD, I.		st.	lbs.
1. Prescot, K., Brasenose	.	10	0
2. Greenall, R., Brasenose	.	10	12
3. Nind, P. H., Christ Church	.	11	2
4. Buller, R. J., Balliol	.	12	4
5. Denne, H., University	.	12	8
6. Houghton, W., Brasenose	.	11	8
7. Meade-King, W. O., Pembroke	.	11	11
Chitty, J. W., Balliol (stroke)	.	11	7
Cotton, R. W., Christ Church (cox.)	.	9	2
Average	.	11	6½

CAMBRIDGE, 2.		st.	lbs.
1. Macnaghten, E., First Trinity	.	11	0
2. Brandt, H., First Trinity	.	11	5
3. Tuckey, H. E., Lady Margaret	.	11	3
4. Foord, H. B., First Trinity	.	12	6
5. Hawley, E., Sidney	.	12	4
6. Longmore, W. S., Sidney	.	11	4
7. Norris, W. A., Third Trinity	.	11	9
Johnson, F. W., Third Trinity (stroke)	.	11	8
Crosse, C. H., Caius (cox.)	.	9	7
Average	.	11	8½

1852.

The Stewards' Cup, Henley. (*Final Heat.*)

OXFORD, I.

1. Greenall, R., Brasenose
2. Barker, H. R., Christ Church
3. Nind, P. H., Christ Church
   Meade-King, W. O., Pembroke (stroke)
   Balguy, F. St. J., Brasenose (cox.)

ARGONAUTS, LONDON, 2.

1. Pryor
2. Payne
3. L. Payne
   H. H. Playford (stroke)
   Burchett (cox.)

1853.

Grand Challenge Cup, Henley.

	OXFORD, 1.	st.	lbs.
1.	Short, W. F., New	10	8
2.	Moore, P. H., Brasenose	9	12
3.	King, W., Merton	11	11
4.	Buller, R. J., Balliol	12	0
5.	Denne, R. H., University	12	10
6.	Nind, P. H., Christ Church	10	12
7.	Prescot, K., Merton	10	3
	Meade-King, W. O., Pembroke (stroke)	11	7
	Marshall, T. H., Exeter (cox.)	10	1
	Average	11	4⅜

	CAMBRIDGE, 2.	st.	lbs.
1.	Forster, G. B., Lady Margaret	10	10
2.	Stephenson, S. V., Caius	10	8
3.	Bramwell, A., First Trinity	10	12
4.	Hawley, E., Sidney	12	1
5.	Courage, E., First Trinity	12	12
6.	Tomkinson, H. R., First Trinity	10	9
7.	Blake, H., Corpus	10	11
	Macnaghten, E., First Trinity (stroke)	10	6
	Freshfield, E., First Trinity (cox.)	8	6
	Average	11	1⅞

1854.

Putney to Mortlake, April 8, 10.40 a.m.

	OXFORD, 1.	st.	lbs.
1.	Short, W. F., New	10	3
2.	Hooke, A., Worcester	11	0
3.	Pinckney, W., Exeter	11	2
4.	Blundell, T., Christ Church	11	8
5.	Hooper, T. A., Pembroke	11	5
6.	Nind, P. H., Christ Church	10	13
7.	Mellish, G. L., Pembroke	11	2
	Meade-King, W. O., Pembroke (stroke)	11	8
	Marshall, T. H., Exeter (cox.)	10	3
	Average	11	1¾

	CAMBRIDGE, 2.	st.	lbs.
1.	Galton, R. C., First Trinity	9	11
2.	Nairne, S., Emmanuel	10	2
3.	Davis, J. C., Third Trinity	11	1
4.	Agnew, S., First Trinity	10	12
5.	Courage, E., First Trinity	12	0
6.	Johnson, H F., Third Trinity	10	13
7.	Blake, H., Corpus	11	1
	Wright, J., Lady Margaret (stroke)	10	2
	Smith, C. T., Caius (cox.)	9	12
	Average	10	10¼

1855.

Grand Challenge Cup, Henley. (*Final Heat.*)

CAMBRIDGE, 1.

		st.	lbs.
1. Pearson, P. P., Lady Margaret		11	0
2. Graham, E. C., First Trinity		11	3
3. Schreiber, H. W., Trinity Hall		11	3
4. Fairrie, E. H., Trinity Hall		11	12
5. Williams, H., Lady Margaret		11	8
6. Johnson, H. F., Third Trinity		11	6
7. Blake, H., Corpus		11	11
Jones, H. R. M., Third Trinity (stroke)		10	2
Wingfield, W., First Trinity (cox.)		8	6
Average		11	5⅛

OXFORD, 2.

		st.	lbs.
1. Short, W. F., New		10	9
2. Codrington, J. E., Brasenose		10	9
3. Everett, C. H., Balliol		11	2
4. Denne, R. H., University		12	6
5. Craster, T. H. University		12	7
6. Nind, P. H., Christ Church		11	8
7. Pinckney, W., Exeter		11	2
Hooke, A., Worcester (stroke)		10	6
Marshall, T. H., Exeter (cox.)		10	8
Average		11	4⅞

1856.

Mortlake to Putney, Saturday, March 15, 10.45 *a.m.*

CAMBRIDGE, 1.

		st.	lbs.
1. King-Salter, J. P., Trinity Hall		9	13
2. Alderson, F. C., Third Trinity		11	3
3. Lewis-Lloyd, R., Third Trinity		11	12
4. Fairrie, E. H., Trinity Hall		12	10
5. Williams, H., Lady Margaret		12	8
6. M'Cormick, J., Lady Margaret		13	0
7. Snow, H., Lady Margaret		11	8
Jones, H. R. M., Third Trinity (stroke)		10	7
Wingfield, W., First Trinity (cox.)		9	0
Average		11	9⅞

OXFORD, 2.

		st.	lbs.
1. Gurdon, P., University		10	8
2. Stocken, W. F., Exeter		10	1
3. Salmon, R. T., Exeter		10	10
4. Rocke, A. B., Christ Church		12	8
5. Townsend, R. N., Pembroke		12	8
6. Lonsdale, A. P., Balliol		11	4
7. Bennett, G., New		10	10
Thorley, J. T., Wadham (stroke)		9	12
Elers, F. W., Trinity (cox.)		9	2
Average		11	0¹¹⁄₁₈

1857.

Putney to Mortlake, Saturday, April 4, 11.10 *a.m.*

OXFORD, 1.		st. lbs.
1. Risley, R. W., Exeter		11 3
2. Gurdon, P., University		10 0
3. Arkell, J., Pembroke		10 10
4. Martin, R., Corpus		12 1
5. Wood, W. H., University		11 13
6. Warre, E., Balliol		13 3
7. Lonsdale, A. P., Balliol		12 0
Thorley, J. T. Wadham (stroke)		10 1
Elers, F. W., Trinity (cox.)		9 2
Average		11 9½

CAMBRIDGE, 2.		st. lbs.
1. Holme, A. P., Second Trinity		11 8
2. Benn, A., Emmanuel		11 5
3. Holley, W. H., Trinity Hall		11 8
4. Smith, A. L., First Trinity		11 3
5. Serjeantson, J. J., First Trinity		12 4
6. Lewis-Lloyd, R., Magdalene		11 11
7. Pearson, P. P., Lady Margaret		11 2
Snow, H., Lady Margaret (stroke)		11 8
Wharton, R., Magdalene (cox.)		9 2
Average		11 8

1858.

Putney to Mortlake, Saturday, March 27, 1 *p.m.*

CAMBRIDGE, 1.		st. lbs.
1. Lubbock, H. H., Caius		11 4
2. Smith, A. L., First Trinity		11 4
3. Havart, W. J., Lady Margaret		11 4
4. Darroch, D., First Trinity		12 1
5. Williams, H., Lady Margaret		12 4
6. Lewis-Lloyd, R., Magdalene		11 13
7. Fairbairn, A. H., Second Trinity		11 12
Hall, J., Magdalene (stroke)		10 7
Wharton, R., Magdalene (cox.)		9 2
Average		11 7⅞

OXFORD, 2.		st. lbs.
1. Risley, R. W., Exeter		11 8
2. Arkell, J., Pembroke		11 3
3. Lane, C. G., Christ Church		11 10
4. Austin, W. G. G., Magdalen		12 7
5. Lane, E., Balliol		11 10
6. Wood, W. H., University		12 0
7. Warre, E., Balliol		13 2
Thorley, J. T., Wadham (stroke)		10 3
Walpole, H. S., Balliol (cox.,		9 5
Average		11 10⅝

1858.

Grand Challenge Cup, Henley. (*Final Heat.*)

CAMBRIDGE, 1.		st. lbs.
1. Paley, G. A., Lady Margaret	. . .	11 2
2. Smith, A. L., First Trinity .	. . .	11 4
3. Havart, W. J., Lady Margaret .	. .	11 6
4. Darrock, D., First Trinity .	. .	12 2
5. Fairbairn, A. H., Second Trinity	. .	11 13
6. Lewis-Lloyd, R., Magdalene .	. .	11 13
7. Royds, N., First Trinity .	. .	10 4
Hall, J., Magdalene (stroke) .	. .	10 5
Morland, F. T., First Trinity (cox.) . .	. .	8 12

L.R.C., 2.		st. lbs.
1. Leeds-Paine, F. . . .	. .	10 3
2. Walter, F. . . .	. .	10 0
3. Schlotel, C. . .	. .	10 11
4. Ditton, E. G. . .	. .	10 10
5. Farrar, W. . .	. .	12 2
6. Paine, J. . .	. .	12 5
7. Casamajor, A. . .	. .	11 0
Playford, H. H. (stroke) .	. .	10 4
Weston, H. (cox.) .	. .	6 0
Average . . .	.	10 13¼

1859.

Putney to Mortlake, Friday, April 15, 11 a.m.

OXFORD, 1.		st. lbs.
1. Baxter, H. F., Brasenose .	. .	10 12
2. Clarke, R. F., St. John's .	. .	11 13
3. Lane, C. G., Christ Church .	.	11 9
4. Lawless, Hon. V., Balliol .	.	12 3
5. Morrison, G., Balliol .	.	13 1
6. Risley, R. W., Exeter .	.	11 2
7. Thomas, G. G. T., Balliol .	.	12 0
Arkell, J., Pembroke (stroke) .	.	10 12
Robarts, A. J., Christ Church (cox.) .		9 1
Average	.	11 8¾

CAMBRIDGE, 2.		st. lbs.
1. Royds, N., First Trinity .	.	10 6
2. Chaytor, A. J., Jesus .	.	10 13
3. Smith, A. L., First Trinity .	.	11 11
4. Darroch, D., First Trinity .	.	12 4
5. Williams, H., Lady Margaret .	.	12 6
6. Lewis-Lloyd, R., Magdalene .		11 9
7. Paley, G. A., Lady Margaret .	.	11 7
Hall, J., Magdalene (stroke) .	.	10 2
Morland, J. T., First Trinity (cox.) . .		9 0
Average . . .	.	11 5½

1859.

Grand Challenge Cup, Henley. (*First Heat.*)

	LONDON, 1.		st. lbs.
1.	Dunnage, G.	9	5
2.	Foster C.	10	0
3.	Potter, F.	10	4
4.	Dunnage, W.	11	7
5.	Farrar, W.	12	4
6.	Paine, T.	12	10
7.	Casamajor, A. A. . . .	10	9
	Playford, H. H. (stroke) . .	10	3
	Weston, H. cox.) . . .	6	4
	Average .	10	12

	OXFORD, 2.		st. lbs.
1.	Strong, C. T., University	10	11
2.	Baxter, H. F., Brasenose	11	3
3.	Lane, E., Balliol	12	1
4.	Warre, E., Balliol	12	10
5.	Morrison, G., Balliol	13	5
6.	Arkell, J., Pembroke	11	2
7.	Lane, C. G., Christ Church	11	12
	Risley, R. W., Exeter (stroke) . . .	11	1
	Robarts, A. J., Christ Church (cox.) . . .	9	1
	Average .	11	10⅞

Final Heat.

LONDON, 1. (as before.)

	CAMBRIDGE, 2.		st. lbs.
1.	Heathcote, S., First Trinity . . .	9	7
2.	Chaytor, H. J., Jesus . . .	11	2
3.	Ingham, J. P., Third Trinity . .	10	12
4.	Lewis-Lloyd, R., Magdalene . .	11	10
5.	Holley, W. H., Trinity Hall . .	12	0
6.	Collings, H. H., Third Trinity . .	10	12
7.	Royds, N., First Trinity . . .	10	4
	Hall, J., Magdalene (stroke) . .	10	5
	Morland, J. T., First Trinity (cox.). .	8	13
	Average . .	10	11¾

T

1860.

Putney to Mortlake, Saturday, March 31, 8.15 *a.m.*

CAMBRIDGE, 1.

	st. lbs.
1. Heathcote, S., First Trinity	10 3
2. Chaytor, H. J., Jesus	11 4
3. Ingles, D., First Trinity	10 13
4. Blake, J. S., Corpus	12 9
5. Coventry, M., Trinity Hall	12 8
6. Cherry, B. N., Clare	12 1
7. Fairbairn, A. H., Second Trinity	11 10
Hall, J., Magdalene (stroke)	10 4
Morland, J. T., First Trinity (cox.)	9 0
Average	11 6¼

OXFORD, 2.

	st. lbs.
1. Macqueen, J. N., University	11 7
2. Norsworthy, G., Magdalen	11 0
3. Halsey, T. F., Christ Church	11 11
4. Young, J., Corpus	12 8
5. Morrison, G., Balliol	12 13
6. Baxter, H. F., Brasenose	11 7
7. Strong, C. T., University	11 2
Risley, R. W., Exeter (stroke)	11 8
Robarts, A. J., Christ Church (cox.) . . .	9 9
Average . . .	11 10½

1861.

Putney to Mortlake, Saturday, March 23, 11 *a.m.*

OXFORD, 1.

	st. lbs.
1. Champneys, W., Brasenose	10 11
2. Merriman, E. B., Exeter	10 1
3. Medlicott, H. E., Wadham	12 4
4. Robertson, W., Wadham	11 3
5. Morrison, G., Balliol	12 8
6. Poole, A. R., Trinity	12 3
7. Hopkins, H. G., Corpus	10 8
Hoare, W. M., Exeter (stroke)	10 10
Ridsdale, S. O. B., Wadham (cox.)	9 0
Average	11 4¼

CAMBRIDGE, 2.

	st. lbs.
1. Richards, G. H., First Trinity	10 4
2. Chaytor, H. J., Jesus	11 3
3. Tarleton, W. H., St. John's	11 0
4. Blake, J. S., Corpus	12 10
5. Coventry, M., Trinity Hall	13 3
6. Collings, H. H., Third Trinity	10 11
7. Fitzgerald, R. U. P., Trinity Hall . . .	11 2
Hall, J., Magdalene (stroke)	10 6
Gaskell, T. K., Third Trinity (cox.) . . .	8 3
Average	11 4⅞

1862.

Putney to Mortlake, Saturday, April 12, 8 p.m.

	OXFORD, 1.	st.	lbs.
1.	Woodgate, W. B., Brasenose	11	6
2.	Wynne, O. S., Christ Church	11	3
3.	Jacobson, W. B. R., Christ Church	12	4
4.	Burton, R. E. L., Christ Church.	12	5
5.	Morrison, A., Balliol	12	8½
6.	Poole, A. R., Trinity	12	5
7.	Carr, C. R., Wadham.	11	2½
	Hoare, W. M., Exeter (stroke)	11	1
	Hopwood, F. E., Christ Church (cox.)	7	3
	Average	11	11⅜

	CAMBRIDGE, 2.	st.	lbs.
1.	Gorst, P. F., Lady Margaret	10	4
2.	Chambers, J. G., Third Trinity	11	8
3.	Sanderson, E., Corpus	10	10
4.	Smyly, W. C., First Trinity	11	5
5.	Fitzgerald, R. U. P., Trinity Hall	11	3
6.	Collings, H. H., Third Trinity	11	2
7.	Buchanan, J. G., First Trinity	10	12
	Richards, G. H., First Trinity (stroke)	10	5
	Archer, F. H., Corpus (cox.)	5	2
	Average	10	13½

1863.

Mortlake to Putney, Saturday, March 28, 10.25 a.m.

	OXFORD, 1.	st.	lbs.
1.	Shepherd, R., Brasenose	11	0½
2.	Kelly, F. H., University	11	5½
3.	Jacobson, W. B. R., Christ Church	12	4
4.	Woodgate, W. B., Brasenose	11	11
5.	Morrison, A., Balliol	12	4
6.	Awdry, W., Balliol	11	4
7.	Carr, C. R., Wadham.	11	3½
	Hoare, W. M., Exeter (stroke)	11	7½
	Hopwood, F. E., Christ Church (cox.)	8	4½
	Average	11	8½

	CAMBRIDGE, 2.	st.	lbs.
1.	Hawkshaw, J. C., Third Trinity	11	0
2.	Smyly, W. C., First Trinity	11	4
3.	Morgan, R. H., Emmanuel.	11	3
4.	Wilson, J. B., Pembroke	11	10
5.	La Mothe, C. H., St. John's	12	3
6.	Kinglake, R. A., Third Trinity	12	0
7.	Chambers, J. G., Third Trinity	11	6
	Stanning, J., First Trinity (stroke)	10	6
	Archer, F. H., Corpus (cox.)	5	9½
	Average	11	5¾

1864.

Putney to Mortlake, Saturday, March 19, 11.30 *a.m.*

OXFORD, 1. st. lbs.

1. Roberts, C. P., Trinity 10 9
2. Awdry, W., Balliol 11 4½
3. Kelly, F. H., University 11 9
4. Parson, J. C., Trinity 12 9
5. Jacobson, W. B. R., Christ Church 12 3½
6. Seymour, A. E., University 11 1
7. Brown, M. M., Trinity 11 0
   Pocklington, D., Brasenose (stroke) 11 4
   Tottenham, C. R. W., Christ Church (cox.) . . . 7 3

Average 11 7½

CAMBRIDGE, 2. st. lbs.

1. Hawkshaw, J. C., Third Trinity 11 3
2. Pigott, E. V., Corpus 11 9
3. Watson, H. S., Pembroke 12 4
4. Hawkins, W. W., Lady Margaret 12 0
5. Kinglake, R. A., Third Trinity 12 4
6. Borthwick, G., First Trinity 12 1
7. Steavenson, D. F., Trinity Hall 12 1
   Selwyn, J. R., Third Trinity (stroke) . . . 11 0
   Archer, F. H., Corpus (cox.) 6 6

Average 11 11½

1865.

Putney to Mortlake, Saturday, April 8, 1.3 *p.m.*

OXFORD, 1. st. lbs.

1. Raikes, R. T., Merton 11 0
2. Senhouse, H. P., Christ Church 11 1
3. Henley, E. F., Oriel 12 13
4. Coventry, G. G., Pembroke 11 12
5. Morrison, A., Balliol 12 6
6. Wood, T., Pembroke 12 2
7. Schneider, H., Trinity 11 10
   Brown, M. M., Trinity (stroke) 11 4
   Tottenham, C. R. W., Christ Church (cox.) . . . 7 13

Average 11 11½

CAMBRIDGE, 2. st. lbs.

1. Watney, H., Lady Margaret 11 1
2. Beebee, M. H. L., Lady Margaret 10 12
3. Pigott, E. V., Corpus 11 12
4. Kinglake, R. A., Third Trinity 12 8
5. Steavenson, D. F., Trinity Hall 12 4
6. Borthwick, G., First Trinity 11 13
7. Griffiths, W. R., Third Trinity 11 8
   Lawes, C. B., Third Trinity (stroke) . . . 11 7
   Archer, F. H., Corpus (cox.) 7 3

Average 11 9

1866.

Putney to Mortlake, Saturday, March 24, 7.48 a.m.

OXFORD, 1.		st. lbs.
1. Raikes, R. T., Merton	. . . . .	11 0
2. Crowder, F., Brasenose	. . . .	11 11
3. Freeman, W. L., Merton	. . . . .	12 7
4. Willan, F., Exeter	. . . . . .	12 2
5. Henley, E. F., Oriel	. . . . .	13 0
6. Wood, W. W., University	. . . . .	12 4
7. Senhouse, H. P., Christ Church	. . . .	11 3
Brown, M. M., Trinity (stroke)	. . . .	11 5
Tottenham, C. R. W., Christ Church (cox.)	.	7 13
Average	. . . .	11 12¾

CAMBRIDGE, 2.		st. lbs.
1. Still, J., Caius	. . . . . .	11 6
2. Selwyn, J. R., Third Trinity	. . .	11 6
3. Bourke, J. U., First Trinity	. . .	12 3
4. Fortescue, H. J., Magdalene	. . .	12 2½
5. Steavenson, D. F., Trinity Hall	. .	12 5
6. Kinglake, R. A., Third Trinity	. . .	12 9
7. Watney, H., Lady Margaret	. .	10 12
Griffiths, W. R., Third Trinity (stroke)	.	11 9
Forbes, A., Lady Margaret (cox.)	. .	8 0
Average	. . .	11 11

1867.

Putney to Mortlake, Saturday, April 13, 8.50 a.m.

OXFORD, 1.		st. lbs.
1. Bowman, W. P., University	. . .	10 11
2. Fish, J. H., Worcester	. . . .	12 1
3. Carter, E. S., Worcester	. . .	11 12
4. Wood, W. W., University	. . .	12 6
5. Tinné, J. C., University	. . .	13 4
6. Crowder, F., Brasenose	. . . .	11 11
7. Willan, F., Exeter	. . . .	12 3
Marsden, R. G., Merton (stroke)	. .	11 11
Tottenham, C. R. W., Christ Church (cox.)	.	8 8
Average	. . . .	12 0⅛

CAMBRIDGE, 2.		st. lbs.
1. Anderson, W. H., First Trinity	. . . . . .	11 0
2. Collard, J. M., Lady Margaret	. . . . .	11 4
3. Bourke, J. U., First Trinity	. . . . .	12 9
4. Gordon, Hon. J. H., First Trinity	. . . .	12 3
5. Cunningham, F. E., King's	. . . . .	12 12
6. Still, J., Caius	. . . .	11 12
7. Watney, H., Lady Margaret	. . . .	11 0
Griffiths, W. R., Third Trinity (stroke)	. . .	12 0
Forbes, A., Lady Margaret (cox.)	. . . .	8 2
Average	. . . . . .	11 12

1868.

Putney to Mortlake, Saturday, April 4, 12 noon.

	OXFORD, 1.	st. lbs.
1.	Benson, W. D., Balliol	10 13
2.	Yarborough, A. C., Lincoln	11 8
3.	Ross of Bladensburgh, R., Exeter	11 8
4.	Marsden, R. G., Merton	11 13
5.	Tinné, J. C., University	13 7
6.	Willan, F., Exeter	12 5
7.	Carter, E. S., Worcester	11 8
	Darbishire, S. D., Balliol (stroke)	11 3
	Tottenham, C. R. W., Christ Church (cox.)	8 7
	Average	11 12

	CAMBRIDGE, 2.	st. lbs.
1.	Anderson, W. H., First Trinity	11 2
2.	Nichols, J. P., Third Trinity	11 3
3.	Wood, J. G., Emmanuel	12 6
4.	Lowe, W. H., Christ's	12 4
5.	Nadin, H. T., Pembroke	12 11
6.	MacMichael, W. F., Downing	12 2
7.	Still, J., Caius	12 1
	Pinckney, W. J., First Trinity (stroke)	10 10
	Warner, T. D., Trinity Hall (cox.)	8 4
	Average	11 11

1869.

Putney to Mortlake, Wednesday, March 17, 3.58 p.m.

	OXFORD, 1.	st. lbs.
1.	Woodhouse, S. H., University	10 13
2.	Tahourdin, R., St. John's	11 11
3.	Baker, T. S., Queen's	12 8
4.	Willan, F., Exeter	12 2½
5.	Tinné, J. C., University	13 10
6.	Yarborough, A. C., Lincoln	11 11
7.	Benson, W. D., Balliol	11 7
	Darbishire, S. D., Balliol (stroke)	11 9
	Neilson, D. A., St. John's (cox.)	7 10
	Average	12 0¼

	CAMBRIDGE, 2.	st. lbs.
1.	Rushton, J. A., Emmanuel	11 5
2.	Ridley, J. H., Jesus	11 10
3.	Dale, J. W., Lady Margaret	11 12
4.	Young, F. J., Christ's	12 4
5.	MacMichael, W. F., Downing	12 4
6.	Anderson, W. H., First Trinity	11 4
7.	Still, J., Caius	12 1
	Goldie, J. H. D., Lady Margaret (stroke)	12 1
	Gordon, H. E., First Trinity (cox.)	7 8
	Average	11 12⅜

1869.

Putney to Mortlake, August 27.

OXFORD, 1.		st. lbs.
1. Willan, F., Exeter	. . . . . .	11 10
2. Yarborough, A. C., Lincoln	. . . . . .	12 2
3. Tinné, J. C., University	. . . . . .	13 8
Darbishire, S. D., Balliol (stroke)	. . . . .	11 6
Hall, J. H., Corpus (cox.)	. . . . . .	7 2

HARVARD, 2.		st. lbs.
1. Fay, J. S., Boston	. . . .	11 1
2. Lyman, F. O., Hawaiian Islands.	. .	11 1
3. Simmonds, W. H., Concord	. .	12 2
Loring, A. P., Boston (stroke)	. .	11 0
Burnham, A., Chicago (cox.)	. .	7 10

1870.

Putney to Mortlake, Wednesday, April 6, 5.14 p.m.

CAMBRIDGE, 1.		st. lbs.
1. Randolph, E. S. L., Third Trinity	. . . . . .	10 11½
2. Ridley, J. H., Jesus	. . . . . .	11 9½
3. Dale, J. W., Lady Margaret	. . . . . .	12 2½
4. Spencer, E. A. A., Second Trinity	. . . . . .	12 4½
5. Lowe, W. H., Christ's	. . . . . .	12 7½
6. Phelps, E. S., Sidney	. . . . . .	12 1½
7. Strachan, J. F., Trinity Hall	. . . . . .	11 13
Goldie, J. H. D., Lady Margaret (stroke)	. . . . .	12 0
Gordon, H. E., First Trinity (cox.)	. . . . .	7 12
Average	. .	11 13

OXFORD, 2.		st. lbs.
1. Mirehouse, R. W. B., University	. . . . .	11 0
2. Lewis, A. G. P., University	. . . . .	11 2½
3. Baker, T. S., Queen's	. . . . . .	12 9
4. Edwardes Moss, J. E., Balliol	. . . . .	13 0
5. Payne, F. E. H., St. John's	. . . . .	12 10
6. Woodhouse, S. H., University	. . . . .	11 4
7. Benson, W. D., Balliol	. . . . .	11 13
Darbishire, S. D., Balliol (stroke)	. . . . .	11 11
Hall, F. H., Corpus (cox.)	. . . . .	7 7
Average	. .	11 13

1871.

Putney to Mortlake, Saturday, April 1, 10.8 a.m.

CAMBRIDGE, 1.   st. lbs.

1. Follett, J. S., Third Trinity 11 6½
2. Close, John B., First Trinity 11 8
3. Lomax, H., First Trinity 12 2
4. Spencer, E. A. A., Second Trinity 12 9
5. Lowe, W. H., Christ's 12 10
6. Phelps, E. L., Sidney 12 1
7. Randolph, E. S. L., Third Trinity 11 10
   Goldie, J. H. D., Lady Margaret (stroke) 12 6½
   Gordon, H. E., First Trinity (cox.) 7 13

   Average 12 2

OXFORD, 2.   st. lbs.

1. Woodhouse, S. H., University 11 6½
2. Giles, E., Christ Church 11 13½
3. Baker, T. S., Queen's 13 3½
4. Malan, E. C., Worcester 13 1
5. Edwardes-Moss, J. E., Balliol 12 8½
6. Payne, F. E. H., St. John's 12 9½
7. Bunbury, J. M'C., Brasenose 11 8
   Lesley, R., Pembroke (stroke) 11 10½
   Hall, F. H., Corpus (cox.) 7 10½

   Average 12 4

1872.

Putney to Mortlake, Saturday, March 23, 1.35 p.m.

CAMBRIDGE, 1.   st. lbs.

1. Close, James B., First Trinity 11 3
2. Benson, C. W., Third Trinity 11 4
3. Robinson, G. M., Christ's 11 12
4. Spencer, E. A. A., Second Trinity 12 8½
5. Read, C. S., First Trinity 12 8
6. Close, John B., First Trinity 11 10
7. Randolph, E. S. L., First Trinity 11 11
   Goldie, J. H. D., Lady Margaret (stroke) . . . 12 5
   Roberts, C. H., Jesus (cox.) 6 6½

   Average 11 12

OXFORD, 2.   st. lbs.

1. Ornsby, J. A., Lincoln 11 0½
2. Knollys, C. C., Magdalen 10 12
3. Payne, F. E. H., St. John's 12 11
4. Nicholson, A. W., Magdalen 12 2½
5. Malan, E. C., Worcester 13 3
6. Mitchison, R. S., Pembroke 12 4½
7. Lesley, R., Pembroke 11 13
   Houblon, J. H. A., Christ Church (stroke) . . . 10 5
   Hall, F. H., Corpus (cox.) 8 0

   Average 11 11⅛

1873.

Putney to Mortlake, Saturday March 29, 2.32 p.m.

CAMBRIDGE, 1.				st. lbs.
1. Close, James B., First Trinity	.	.	. . .	11 3
2. Hoskyns, E., Jesus	.	.	. . .	11 2
3. Peabody, J. E., First Trinity			. . .	11 7
4. Lecky-Brown, W. C., Jesus			. . .	12 1½
5. Turnbull, T. S., Trinity Hall			. . .	12 12
6. Read, C. S., First Trinity	.		. . .	12 13
7. Benson, C. W., Third Trinity			. . .	11 5½
Rhodes, H. E., Jesus (stroke)			. . .	11 1½
Candy, C. H., Caius (cox.) .			. . .	7 5
Average . .			. .	11 10

OXFORD, 2.			st. lbs.
1. Knollys, C. C., Magdalen	.	.	. 10 11
2. Little, J. B., Christ Church .	.	.	. 10 11
3. Farrer, M. G., Brasenose	.	.	. 11 13½
4. Nicholson, A. W., Magdalen	.		. 12 5
5. Michison, R. S., Pembroke			. 12 2
6. Sherwood, W. E., Christ Church			. 11 1
7. Ornsby, J. A., Lincoln	.	.	. 11 3
Dowding, F. T., St. John's (stroke)	.		. 11 0
Frewer, G. E., St. John's (cox.) .	.		. 7 10
Average . .			. 11 5

1874.

Putney to Mortlake, Saturday, March 28, 11.14 a.m.

CAMBRIDGE, 1.				st. lbs.
1. Hibbert, J. P., Lady Margaret	.	.	.	. 11 1½
2. Armytage, G. F., Jesus	.	.	.	. 11 8
3. Close, James B., First Trinity	.	.	.	. 11 0½
4. Escourt, A. S., Trinity Hall	.	.	.	. 11 10½
5. Lecky-Brown, W. C., Jesus	.	.	.	. 12 5
6. Aylmer, J. A., First Trinity .	.	.	.	. 12 11
7. Read, C. S., First Trinity	.	.	.	. 12 11½
Rhodes, H. E., Jesus (stroke)	.	.	.	. 11 7
Candy, C. H., Caius (cox.) .	.	.	.	. 7 5
Average	.	. .	.	. 11 10¾

OXFORD, 2.				st. lbs.
1. Benson, H. W., Brasenose .	.	.	.	. 11 0
2. Sinclair, J. S., Oriel	.	.	.	. 11 5½
3. Sherwood, W. E., Christ Church	.		.	. 11 8
4. Harding, A. R., Merton	.	.		. 11 1½
5. Williams, J., Lincoln .	.	.		. 13 0½
6. Nicholson, A. W., Magdalen	.		.	. 12 10
7. Stayner, H. J., St. John's	.	.		. 11 10½
Way, J. P., Brasenose (stroke) .	.		.	. 10 9
Lambert, W. F. A., Wadham (cox.) .		.		. 7 2
Average	.	. . . .		. 11 9½

1875.

Putney to Mortlake, Saturday, March 20, 1.13 *p.m.*

OXFORD, 1.

		st. lbs
1. Courtney, H. M'D., Pembroke.		11 0
2. Marriott, H. P., Brasenose		11 12
3. Banks, J. E., University		11 11
4. Mitchison, A. M., Pembroke		12 12
5. Stayner, H. J., St. John's		12 2½
6. Boustead, J. M., University		12 4
7. Edwardes Moss, T. C., Brasenose		12 5
Way, J. P., Brasenose (stroke)		10 11
Hopwood, E. O., Christ Church (cox.)		8 3½
Average		11 12

CAMBRIDGE, 2.

		st. lbs.
1. Hibbert, J. P., Lady Margaret		11 3
2. Close, W. B., First Trinity		11 10
3. Dicker, G. C., First Trinity		11 8
4. Michell, W. G., First Trinity		11 11
5. Phillips, C. A., Jesus		12 4½
6. Aylmer, J. A., First Trinity		12 12
7. Benson, C. W., Third Trinity		11 3
Rhodes, H. E., Jesus (stroke)		11 7
Davis, G. L., Clare (cox.)		6 10
Average		11 11

1876.

Putney to Mortlake, Saturday, April 8, 2.2 *p.m.*

CAMBRIDGE, 1.

		st. lbs.
1. Brancker, P. W., Jesus		11 3½
2. Lewis, T. W., Caius		11 8
3. Close, W. B., First Trinity		11 8
4. Gurdon, C., Jesus		12 9¾
5. Pike, G. L., Caius		12 9
6. Hockin, T. E., Jesus		12 8
7. Rhodes, H. E., Jesus		11 13
Shafto, C. D., Jesus (stroke)		11 9½
Davis, G. L., Clare (cox.)		6 13
Average		11 13

OXFORD, 2.

		st. lbs.
1. Courtney, H. M'D., Pembroke		11 1¾
2. Mercer, F. R., Corpus		11 6
3. Hobart, W. H., Exeter		11 11
4. Mitchison, A. M., Pembroke		13 0
5. Boustead, J. M., University		12 5¾
6. Stayner, H. J., St. John's		12 2½
7. Marriott, H. P., Brasenose		11 9¾
Edwardes-Moss, T. C., Brasenose (stroke)		12 3½
Craven, W. D., Worcester (cox.)		7 6½
Average		11 13

1877.

Putney to Mortlake, Saturday, March 24, 8.27 *a.m.* (*Dead Heat.*)

OXFORD. †	st. lbs.
1. Cowles, D. J., St. John's	11 3½
2. Boustead, J. M., University	12 9
3. Pelham, H., Magdalen	12 7¼
4. Grenfell, W. H., Balliol	12 10
5. Stayner, H. J., St. John's	12 5½
6. Mulholland, A. J., Balliol	12 7¼
7. Edwardes-Moss, T. C., Brasenose	12 2
Marriott, H. P., Brasenose (stroke)	12 0½
Beaumont, F. M., New (cox)	7 0
Average	12 3

CAMBRIDGE. †	st. lbs.
1. Hoskyns, B. G., Jesus	10 11½
2. Lewis, T. W., Caius	11 10
3. Fenn, J. C., First Trinity	11 6
4. Close, W. B., First Trinity	11 12
5. Pike, L. G., Caius	12 8
6. Gurdon, C., Jesus	12 13½
7. Hockin, T. S., Jesus	12 11½
Shafto, C. D., Jesus (stroke)	12 1½
Davis, G. L., Clare (cox.)	7 6
Average	11 13

1878.

Putney to Mortlake, Saturday, April 13, 10.15 *a.m.*

OXFORD, 1.	st. lbs.
1. Ellison, W. A., University	10 13½
2. Cowles, D. J., St. John's	11 6
3. Southwell, H. B., Pembroke	12 8
4. Grenfell, W. H., Balliol	12 11
5. Pelham, H., Magdalen	12 9½
6. Burgess, G. F., Keble	13 3½
7. Edwardes-Moss, T. C., Brasenose	12 3
Marriott, H. P., Brasenose (stroke)	12 2½
Beaumont, F. M., New (cox.)	7 5
Average	12 3

CAMBRIDGE, 2.	st. lbs.
1. Jones, L. I. R., Jesus	10 9
2. Watson-Taylor, J. A., Magdalene	11 9¾
3. Barker, T. W., First Trinity	12 6
4. Spurrell, R. J., Trinity Hall	11 13½
5. Pike, L. G., Caius	12 8½
6. Gurdon, C., Jesus	12 10¼
7. Hockin, T. E., Jesus	12 4½
Prest, E. H., Jesus (stroke)	10 12¾
Davis, G. L., Clare (cox.)	7 5½
Average	11 12

1879.

Putney to Mortlake, Saturday, April 5, 12.45 p.m.

CAMBRIDGE, 1.	st.	lbs.
1. Prest, E. H., Jesus	11	2
2. Sandford, H., Lady Margaret	11	6¾
3. Bird, A. H. S., First Trinity	11	8
4. Gurdon, C., Jesus	13	0½
5. Hockin, T. E., Jesus	12	4¼
6. Fairbairn, C., Jesus	12	7½
7. Routledge, T., Emmanuel	12	7¾
Davis, R. D., First Trinity (stroke)	12	4¾
Davis, G. L., Clare (cox.)	7	7
Average	12	1

OXFORD, 2.	st.	lbs.
1. Wharton, J. H. T., Magdalen	11	3½
2. Robinson, H. M., New	11	2½
3. Disney, H. W., Hertford	12	7
4. Southwell, H. B., Pembroke	12	9
5. Cosby-Burrowes, T., Trinity	12	9
6. Rowe, G. D., University	11	13
7. Hobart, W. H., Exeter	11	12
Marriott, H. P., Brasenose (stroke)	12	2½
Beaumont, F. M., New (cox.)	7	5
Average	11	13

1880.

Putney to Mortlake, Monday, March 22, 10.40 a.m.

OXFORD, 1.	st.	lbs.
1. Poole, R. H. J., Brasenose	10	6
2. Brown, D. E., Hertford	12	6
3. Hargreaves, F. M., Keble	12	2
4. Southwell, H. B., Pembroke	13	0
5. Kindersley, R. S., Exeter	12	6
6. Rowe, G. D., University	12	3
7. Wharton, J. H. T., Magdalen	11	11
West, L. R., Christ Church (stroke)	11	1
Hunt, C. W., Corpus (cox.)	7	5
Average	11	13¾

CAMBRIDGE, 2.	st.	lbs.
1. Prest, E. H., Jesus	10	12
2. Sandford, H., Lady Margaret	11	5½
3. Barton, W., Lady Margaret	11	3½
4. Warlow, W. M., Queens'	12	0
5. Armytage, N. C., Jesus	12	2½
6. Davis, R. D., First Trinity	12	8½
7. Prior, R. D., Queens'	11	13
Baillie, W. W., Jesus (stroke)	11	2½
Clarke, B. S., Lady Margaret (cox.)	7	0
Average	11	7

1881.

Putney to Mortlake, Friday, April 8, 8.34 *a.m.*

OXFORD, 1.	st. lbs.
1. Poole, R. H. J., Brasenose	10 11
2. Pinckney, R. A., Exeter	11 3
3. Paterson, A. R., Trinity	12 7
4. Buck, E., Hertford	11 11
5. Kindersley, R. S., Exeter	13 3
6. Brown, D. E., Hertford	12 7
7. Wharton, J. H. T., Magdalen	11 10
West, L. R., Christ Church (stroke)	11 0½
Lyon, E. H., Hertford (cox.)	7 0
Average	11 10

CAMBRIDGE, 2.	st. lbs.
1. Gridley, R. G., Third Trinity	10 7
2. Sandford, H., Lady Margaret	11 10½
3. Watson-Taylor, J. A., Magdalene	12 3½
4. Atkin, P. W., Jesus	11 13
5. Lambert, E., Pembroke	12 0
6. Hutchinson, A. M., Jesus	11 13
7. Moore, C. W., Christ's	11 9
Brooksbank, E. C., Trinity Hall (stroke)	11 8
Woodhouse, H., Trinity Hall (cox.)	7 2
Average	11 9¾

1882.

Putney to Mortlake, Saturday, April 1, 1.2 *p.m.*

OXFORD, 1.	st. lbs.
1. Bourne, G. C., New	10 13
2. De Haviland, R. S., Corpus	11 1
3. Fort, G. S., Hertford	12 3½
4. Paterson, A. R., Trinity	12 12
5. Kindersley, R. S., Exeter	13 4½
6. Buck, E., Hertford	12 0
7. Brown, D. E., Hertford	12 6
Higgins, A. H., Magdalen (stroke)	9 6½
Lyon, E. H., Hertford (cox.)	7 12
Average	11 11⅛

CAMBRIDGE, 2.	st. lbs.
1. Jones, Ll. R., Jesus	11 1
2. Hutchinson, M., Jesus	12 1½
3. Fellowes, J. C., First Trinity	12 7
4. Atkin, P. W., Jesus	12 11½
5. Lambert, E., Pembroke	11 12
6. Fairbairn, S., Jesus	13 0
7. Moore, C. W., Christ's	11 7
Smith, S. P., First Trinity (stroke	11 1
Hunt, P. L., Cavendish (cox.)	7 5
Average	11 12⅝

1883.

Putney to Mortlake, Thursday, March 15, 5.39 p.m.

OXFORD, 1.	st. lbs.
1. Bourne, G. C., New	10 11½
2. De Haviland, R. S., Corpus	11 4
3. Fort, G. S., Hertford	12 0
4. Puxley, E. L., Brasenose	12 6½
5. Maclean, D. H., New	13 2½
6. Paterson, A. R., New Inn Hall	13 1
7. Roberts, G. Q., Hertford	11 1
West, L. R., New Inn Hall (stroke)	11. 0
Lyon, E. H., Hertford (cox.)	8 1
Average	11 12

CAMBRIDGE, 2.	st. lbs.
1. Gridley, R. G., Third Trinity	10 7
2. Fox, F. W., First Trinity	12 2
3. Moore, C. W., Christ's	11 13
4. Atkin, P. W., Jesus	12 1
5. Churchill, F. E., Third Trinity	13 4
6. Swann, S., Trinity Hall	12 12
7. Fairbairn, S., Jesus	13 4
Meyrick, F. C., Trinity Hall	11 7
Hunt, P. L., Cavendish (cox.)	8 1
Average	12 2¾

1884.

Putney to Mortlake, Monday, April 7, 12.54 p.m.

CAMBRIDGE, 1.	st. lbs.
1. Gridley, R. C., Third Trinity	10 6
2. Eyre, G. H., Corpus	11 3½
3. Straker, F., Jesus	12 2
4. Swann, S., Trinity Hall	13 3
5. Churchill, F. E., Third Trinity	13 2½
6. Haig, E. W., Third Trinity	11 6¾
7. Moore, C. W., Christ's	11 12½
Pitman, F. J., Third Trinity (stroke)	11 11½
Biscoe, C. E. T., Jesus (cox.)	8 2
Average	11 13

OXFORD, 2.	st. lbs.
1. Shortt, A. G., Christ Church	11 2
2. Stock, L., Exeter	11 0
3. Carter, C. R., Corpus	12 10
4. Taylor, P. W., Lincoln	13 1
5. McLean, D. H., New	12 11½
6. Paterson, A. R., Trinity	13 4
7. Blandy, W. C., Exeter	10 13.
Curry, W. D. B., Exeter (stroke)	10 4
Humphreys, F. J., Brasenose (cox.)	7 4
Average	11 12¹¹⁄₁₈

1885.

Putney to Mortlake, Saturday, March 28, 12.26 p.m.

OXFORD, 1.	st.	lbs.
1. Unwin, W. S., Magdalen	10	10½
2. Clemons, J. S., Corpus	11	9
3. Taylor, P. W., Lincoln	13	6½
4. Carter, C. R., Corpus	13	2
5. McLean, H., New	12	12
6. Wethered, F. O., Christ Church	12	6
7. McLean, D. H., New	13	1½
Girdlestone, H., Magdalen (stroke)	12	7
Humphreys, F. J., Brasenose (cox.)	8	2
Average	12	6¹³⁄₁₆

CAMBRIDGE, 2.	st.	lbs.
1. Symonds, N. P., Lady Margaret	10	8
2. Hardacre, W. R., Trinity Hall	10	8
3. Perrott, W. H. W., First Trinity	12	2½
4. Swann, S., Trinity Hall	13	3½
5. Churchill, F. E., Third Trinity	13	2½
6. Haigh, E. W., Third Trinity	11	8
7. Coke, R. H., Trinity Hall	12	4
Pitman, F. J., Third Trinity (stroke)	11	11½
Wilson, G., Third Trinity (cox.)	7	11
Average	11	13

1886.

Putney to Mortlake, Saturday, April 3, 1.38 p.m.

CAMBRIDGE, 1.	st.	lbs.
1. Bristowe, C. J., Trinity Hall	10	8½
2. Symonds, N. P., Lady Margaret	10	10
3. Walmsley, J., Trinity Hall	12	1
4. Flower, A. D., Clare	12	8½
5. Fairbairn, S., Jesus	13	9
6. Muttlebury, S. D., Third Trinity	13	3
7. Barclay, C., Third Trinity	11	3
Pitman, F. J., Third Trinity (stroke)	11	10½
Baker, G. H., Queen's (cox.)	6	9
Average	11	13¹¹⁄₁₆

OXFORD, 2.	st.	lbs.
1. Unwin, W. S., Magdalen	10	11
2. Bryne, L. S. R., Trinity	11	11½
3. Robertson, W. St. L., Wadham	11	7½
4. Carter, C. R., Corpus	13	0½
5. McLean, H., New	12	12
6. Wethered, F. O., Christ Church	12	6
7. McLean, D., New	13	0
Girdlestone, H., Magdalen (stroke)	12	9½
Maynard, W. E., Exeter (cox.)	7	12
Average	12	3¹³⁄₁₆

1887.

Putney to Mortlake, March 26. (*Time,* 20 *min.* 52 *sec.*)

CAMBRIDGE, 1.	st.	lbs.
1. McKenna, R., Trinity Hall.	10	7
2. Barclay, F., Third Trinity .	11	1
3. Landale, P., Third Trinity .	12	0½
4. Oxford, J. R., King's .	13	0
5. Fairbairn, S., Jesus .	13	5½
6. Muttlebury, S. D., Third Trinity.	13	6½
7. Barclay, C., Third Trinity .	11	8
Bristowe, C. J., Trinity Hall (stroke) .	10	7½
Baker, G. H., Queen's (cox.) .	7	1

OXFORD,[1] 2.	st.	lbs.
1. Holland, W. F. C., Brasenose .	10	7
2. Nickalls, G., Magdalen .	12	1
3. Williams, L. G., Corpus .	12	5
4. Parker, H. R., Brasenose .	13	3
5. McLean, H., New .	12	8½
6. Wethered, F. O., Christ Church .	12	5
7. McLean, D. H., New .	12	9
Titherington, A. F., Queen's (stroke) .	12	2
Clarke, H. F., Exeter (cox.) .	7	9

[1] Oxford broke an oar (No. 7) at Barnes Bridge.

1888.

Putney to Mortlake, March 24. (*Time,* 20 *min.* 48 *sec.*)

CAMBRIDGE, 1.	st.	lbs.
1. Symonds-Tayler, R. H., Trinity Hall.	10	7
2. Hannen, L., Trinity Hall .	11	3
3. Orde, R. H. P., First Trinity .	11	7
4. Bell, C. B. P., Trinity Hall.	12	13½
5. Muttlebury, S. D., Third Trinity .	13	7
6. Landale, P., Trinity Hall .	12	4
7. Maugham, F. H., Trinity Hall .	11	5
Gardner, J. C., Emmanuel (stroke)	11	7
Roxburgh, J. R., Trinity Hall (cox.) .	8	2

OXFORD, 2.	st.	lbs.
1. Holland, W. F. C., Brasenose .	11	0
2. Parker, A. P., Magdalen .	11	11
3. Bradford, W. E., Christ Church .	11	9
4. Fothergill, S. R., New .	12	10
5. Cross, H., Hertford .	13	0½
6. Parker, H. R., Brasenose .	13	5
7. Nickalls, G., Magdalen .	12	4
Frere, L., Brasenose (stroke)	10	0½
Stewart, A., New (cox.) .	7	13½

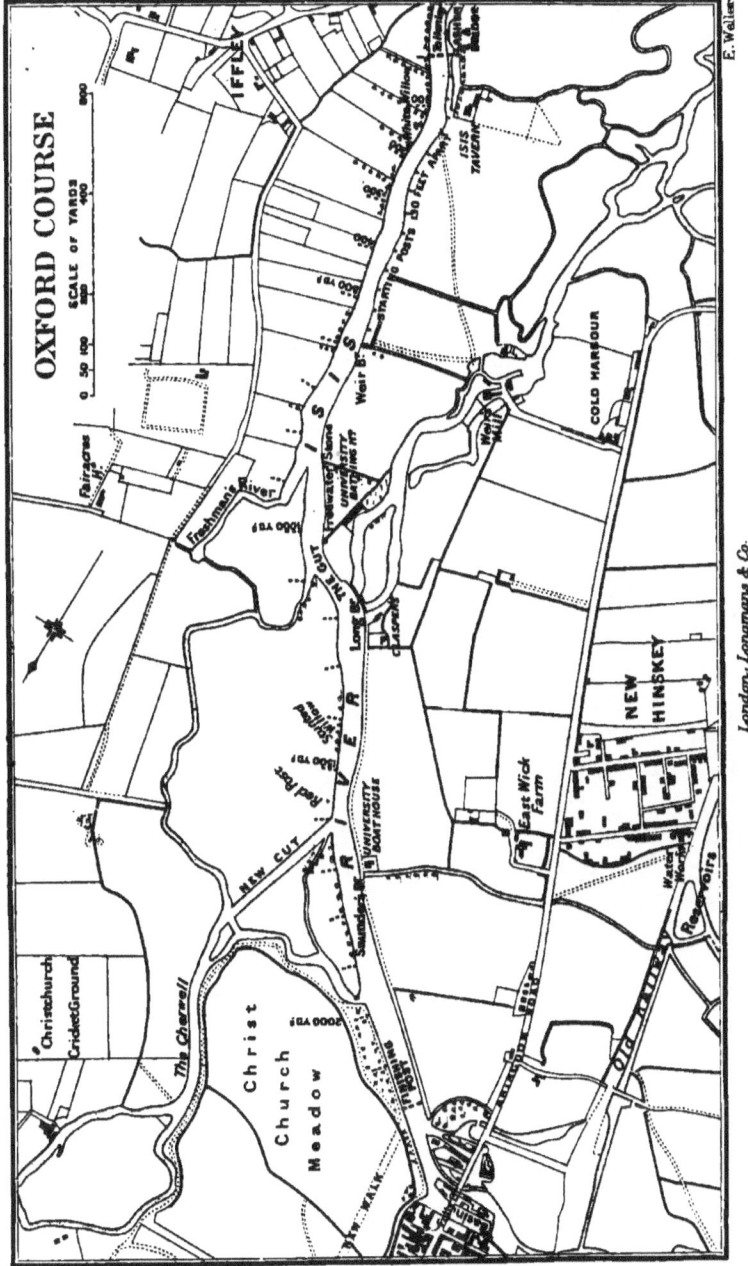

O.U.B.C.: COLLEGE AND CLUB RACES.

OXFORD UNIVERSITY COLLEGE EIGHTS: HEAD OF THE RIVER.

1815	Brasenose (?)	1854	Brasenose
1822	Christ Church	1855	Balliol
1823	No races	1856	Wadham
1824	Exeter	1857	Exeter
1825	Christ Church	1858	Exeter
1826	Christ Church	1859	Balliol
1827	Brasenose	1860	Balliol
1828	{ Balliol / Christ Church later on	1861	Trinity
		1862	Trinity
1829	Christ Church	1863	Trinity
1830	No races	1864	Trinity
1831	} No records	1865	Brasenose
1832		1866	Brasenose
1833	Queen's	1867	Brasenose
1834	Christ Church	1868	Corpus
1835	Christ Church	1869	University
1836	Christ Church	1870	University
1837	Queen's	1871	University
1838	Exeter	1872	Pembroke
1839	Brasenose [1]	1873	Balliol
1840	Brasenose	1874	University
1841	University	1875	University
1842	Oriel	1876	Brasenose
1843	University	1877	University
1844	Christ Church	1878	University
1845	Brasenose	1879	Balliol
1846	Brasenose	1880	Magdalen
1847	Christ Church	1881	Hertford
1848	Christ Church	1882	Exeter
1849	Christ Church	1883	Exeter
1850	Wadham	1884	Exeter
1851	Balliol	1885	Corpus
1852	Brasenose	1886	Magdalen
1853	Brasenose	1887	New College

[1] O.U B C. founded.

U

WINNERS OF THE UNIVERSITY PAIR-OARS.

1839 R. Menzies, F. W. Menzies, R. S. Fox (cox.), University.
1840 O. B. Barttelot, Corpus Christi ; E. Royds, Brasenose ; T. Evett (cox.), Corpus Christi.
1841 II. E. C. Stapylton, W. Bolland, J. H. Griffiths (cox.), University.
1842 W. Wilberforce, G. E. Hughes, G. B. Lewis (cox.), Oriel.
1843 M. Haggard, W. H. Milman, F. J. Prout (cox.), Christ Church.
1844 M. Haggard, W. H. Milman, F. J. Prout (cox.), Christ Church.
1845 M. Haggard, W. H. Milman, C. J. Fuller (cox.), Christ Church.
1846 A. Milman, E. C. Burton, H. Ingram (cox.), Christ Church.
1847 W. G. Rich, A. Milman, Christ Church.
1848 T. II. Michel, C. H. Steward, Oriel.
1849 E. M. Clissold, Exeter ; J. W. Chitty, Balliol.
1850 J. C. Bengough, Oriel ; J. W. Chitty, Balliol.
1851 R. Greenall, R. Prescot, Brasenose.
1852 W. F. Short, W. L. Rogers, New.
1853 C. Cadogan, Christ Church ; W. F. Short, New.
1854 C. Cadogan, Christ Church ; W. F. Short, New.
1855 A. F. Lonsdale, E. Warre, Balliol.
1856 E. Warre, A. F. Lonsdale, Balliol..
1857 P. W. Phillips, J. Arkell, Pemberton.
1858 T. B. Shaw-Hellier, Brasenose ; F. Ho'comb, Wadham.
1859 B. de B. Russell, R. F. Clarke, St. John's.
1860 W. B. Woodgate, H. F. Baxter, Brasenose.
1861 W. Champneys, W. B. Woodgate, Brasenose.
1862 R. Shepherd, W. B. Woodgate, Brasenose.
1863 C. P. Roberts, M. Brown, Trinity.
1864 C. P. Roberts, M. Brown, Trinity.
1865 R. T. Raikes, Merton ; M. Brown, Trinity.
1866 G. II. Swinney, G. II. Morrell, Merton.
1867 W. C. Crofts, F. Crowder, Brasenose.
1868 A. V. Jones, Exeter ; W. C. Crofts, Brasenose.
1869 F. Pownall, A. V. Jones, Exeter.
1870 J. Mair St. Alb, C. J. Vesey, St. John's.
1871 J. W. M'C. Bunbury, Brasenose ; A. G. P. Lewis, University.
1872 H. J. Preston, A. S. Daniel, University.
1873 W. Farrer, Balliol ; M. Farrer, Brasenose.
1874 M. Farrer, H. Benson, Brasenose.
1875 II. J. Preston, University ; Edwardes-Moss, Brasenose.
1876 H. M. Marriott, T. C. Edwardes-Moss, Brasenose.
1877 D. J. Cowles, W. L. Giles, St. John's.

1878   T. C. Edwardes-Moss, Brasenose ; W. A. Ellison, University.
1879   C. R. L. Fletcher, F. P. Bulley, Magdalen.
1880   E. Staniland, Magdalen ; L. R. West, Christ Church.
1881   C. Lowry, R. de Haviland, Corpus.
1882   G. C. Bourne, New ; C. H. Sharpe, Hertford.
1883   A. G. Shortt, A. B. Shaw, Christ Church.
1884   W. S. Unwin, Magdalen ; J. Reade, Brasenose.
1885   H. McLean, D. H. McLean, New.
1886   H. McLean, D. H. McLean, New.
1887   M. E. Bradford, F. W. Douglas, Christ Church.

WINNERS OF THE OXFORD UNIVERSITY SCULLS,

Originally presented by Members of Christ Church.

1841	T. T. Peocock, Merton	1865	J. Rickaby, Brasenose
1842	H. Morgan, Christ Church	1866	W. L. Freeman, Merton
1843	Sir F. E. Scott, Christ Church	1867	W. C. Crofts, Brasenose
		1868	W. C. Crofts, Brasenose
1844	Sir F. E. Scott, Christ Church	1869	A. C. Yarborough, Lincoln
		1870	A. C. Yarborough, Lincoln
1845	J. W. Conant, St. John's	1871	J. W. McC. Bunbury, Brasenose
1846	E. S. Moon, Magdalen		
1847	E. C. Burton, Christ Church	1872	C. C. Knollys, Magdalen
1848	D. Wauchope, Wadham	1873	J. B. Little, Christ Church
1849	T. Erskine Clarke, Wadham	1874	A. Michell, Oriel
1850	T. Erskine Clarke, Wadham	1875	L. C. Cholmeley, Magdalen
1851	W. Heaven, Trinity	1876	D. J. Cowles, St. John's
1852	H. M. Irving, Balliol	1877	T. C. Edwardes - Moss, Brasenose
1853	W. F. Short, New		
1854	W. F. Short, New	1878	J. Lowndes, Hertford
1855	E. Warre, Balliol	1879	J. Lowndes, Hertford
1856	E. Warre, Balliol	1880	H. S. Chesshire, Worcester
1857	R. W. Risley, Exeter	1881	H. S. Chesshire, Worcester
1858	R. W. Risley, Exeter	1882	G. Q. Roberts, Hertford
1859	H. F. Baxter, Brasenose	1883	A. E. Staniland, Magdalen
1860	T. R. Finch, Wadham	1884	W. S. Unwin, Magdalen
1861	W. B. Woodgate, Brasenose	1885	W. S. Unwin, Magdalen
1862	W. B. Woodgate, Brasenose	1886	F. O. Wethered, Christ Church
1863	J. E. Parker, University		
1864	E. B. Michell, Magdalen	1887	G. Nicholls, Magdalen

U 2

WINNERS OF THE UNIVERSITY FOUR-OARS.

1840	Brasenose		1864	University
1841	University		1865	University
1842	University		1866	University
1843	Oriel		1867	University
1844	University		1868	University
1845	Christ Church		1869	Balliol
1846	Christ Church		1870	Balliol
1847	Christ Church		1871	Christ Church
1848	Oriel		1872	Balliol
1849	Brasenose		1873	University
1850	Brasenose		1874	Brasenose
1851	Christ Church		1875	University
1852	Trinity		1876	Brasenose
1853	Trinity		1877	Brasenose
1854	Exeter		1878	Magdalen
1855	Exeter		1879	Hertford
1856	Balliol		1880	Magdalen
1857	Pembroke		1881	Hertford
1858	Balliol		1882	Hertford
1859	University		1883	Corpus
1860	Brasenose		1884	Magdalen
1861	Trinity		1885	Magdalen
1862	University		1886	Magdalen
1863	Trinity		1887	Brasenose

C.U.B.C. : COLLEGE AND CLUB RACES.

CAMBRIDGE UNIVERSITY BOAT CLUB: HEAD OF THE RIVER.

1827	Trinity		1832	First Trinity
1828	St. John's		1833	Lent, First Trinity May, Christ's
1829	St. John's			
1830	Lent, St. John's May, Trinity		1834	Lent, First Trinity May, Third Trinity
1831	Lent, St. John's May, First Trinity		1835	Lent, Third Trinity May, Second Trinity

1836 { Lent, First Trinity
       { May, Corpus
1837 Lady Margaret
1838 Lady Margaret
1839 First Trinity
1840 Caius
1841 Caius
1842 Peterhouse
1843 First Trinity
1844 Caius
1845 First Trinity
1846 First Trinity
1847 First Trinity
1848 Third Trinity
1849 { Lent, Third Trinity
       { May, Second Trinity
1850 First Trinity
1851 { Lent, Lady Margaret
       { May, First Trinity
1852 First Trinity
1853 First Trinity
1854 { Lent, First Trinity
       { May, Lady Margaret
1855 Lady Margaret
1856 Lady Margaret
1857 Lady Margaret
1858 { Lent, Lady Margaret
       { May, First Trinity
1859 { Lent, Trinity Hall
       { May, Third Trinity

1860 First Trinity
1861 First Trinity
1862 Trinity Hall
1863 Third Trinity
1864 Trinity Hall
1865 Third Trinity
1866 First Trinity
1867 First Trinity
1868 First Trinity
1869 First Trinity
1870 First Trinity
1871 First Trinity
1872 Lady Margaret
1873 First Trinity
1874 First Trinity
1875 Jesus
1876 Jesus
1877 Jesus
1878 Jesus
1879 Jesus
1880 Jesus
1881 Jesus
1882 Jesus
1883 Jesus
1884 Jesus
1885 Jesus
1886 Trinity Hall
1887 Trinity Hall

WINNERS OF THE UNIVERSITY PAIR-OARS.

1844 T. W. Brooks and W. P. Cloves, First Trinity.
1845 S. Vincent and E. P. Wolstenholme, First Trinity.
1846 T. M. Hoare and T. M. Gisborne, St. John's.
1847 S. Vincent and W. Maule, First Trinity.
1848 A. B. Dickson and W. L. G. Bagshawe, Third Trinity.
1849 A. Baldry, First Trinity, and W. L. G. Bagshawe, Third Trinity.
1850 J. B. Cane and C. Hudson, St. John's.
1851 E. Macnaghten, First Trinity, and F. W. Johnson, Third Trinity.
1852 W. S. Langmore and E. Hawley, Sidney.
1853 R. Gordon and J. G. Barlee, Christ's.

1854   R. C. Galton, First Trinity, and H. Blake, Corpus.
1855   H. Blake, Corpus, and J. Wright, St. John's.
1856   R. Gordon and P. H. Wormald, Christ's.
1857   R. E. Thompson and N. Royds, First Trinity.
1858   R. Beaumont and F. W. Holland, Third Trinity.
1859   D. Ingles, First Trinity, and J. P. Ingham, Third Trinity.
1860   R. P. Fitzgerald, Trinity Hall, and J. P. Ingham, Third Trinity.
1861   A. D. A. Burney and A. M. Channell, First Trinity.
1862   J. G. Chambers, Third Trinity, and R. Neave, Trinity Hall.
1863   R. A. Kinglake and J. R. Selwyn, Third Trinity.
1864   R. A. Kinglake and W. R. Griffiths, Third Trinity.
1865   J. R. Selwyn and W. R. Griffiths, Third Trinity.
1866   W. R. Griffiths, Third Trinity, and J. U. Bourke, First Trinity.
1867   E. Hopkinson and H. Herbert, Christ's.
1868   C. Pitt-Taylor and J. Blake-Humphrey, Third Trinity.
1869   L. P. Muirhead and E. Phelps, Sidney.
1870   John B. Close and G. L. Rives, First Trinity.
1871   James B. Close and John B. Close, First Trinity.
1872   H. E. Rhodes and E. Hoskyns, Jesus.
1873   P. J. Hibbert and E. Sawyer, Lady Margaret.
1874   G. F. Armytage and C. D. Shafto, Jesus.
1875   W. B. Close and G. C. Dicker, First Trinity.
1876   T. E. Hockin and C. Gurdon, Jesus.
1877   J. G. Pinder and C. O. L. Riley, Caius.
1878   A. H. Prior and H. Sanford, Lady Margaret.
1879   J. A. Watson-Taylor, Magdalene, and T. E. Hockin, Jesus.
1880   L. R. Jones and E. Priest, Jesus.
1881   J. F. Keiser and S. P. Smith, First Trinity.
1882   W. K. Hardacre and F. C. Meyrick, Trinity Hall.
1883   C. J. Bristowe and F. C. Meyrick, Trinity Hall.
1884   P. S. Propert and S. Swann, Trinity Hall.
1885   R. H. Coke and S. Swann, Trinity Hall.
1886   S. D. Muttlebury and C. Barclay, Third Trinity.
1887   S. D. Muttlebury and C. T. Barclay, Third Trinity.

WINNERS OF THE UNIVERSITY FOUR-OARS.

1849	First Trinity	1856	Lady Margaret
1850	Lady Margaret	1857	Magdalene
1851	Third Trinity	1858	Third Trinity
1852	First Trinity	1859	Third Trinity
1853	Lady Margaret	1860	First Trinity
1854	Third Trinity	1861	First Trinity and Trinity
1855	Trinity Hall		Hall rowed a dead-heat

1862	Third Trinity	1875	Jesus
1863	Lady Margaret	1876	Jesus
1864	Lady Margaret	1877	Jesus
1865	Third Trinity	1878	Lady Margaret
1866	First Trinity	1879	Lady Margaret
1867	Emmanuel	1880	Jesus
1868	Sidney	1881	Jesus
1869	Sidney	1882	Third Trinity
1870	First Trinity	1883	Third Trinity
1871	First Trinity	1884	Third Trinity
1872	First Trinity	1885	Third Trinity
1873	Jesus	1886	Trinity Hall
1874	First Trinity and Jesus rowed a dead-heat.	1887	Trinity Hall

WINNERS OF THE CAMBRIDGE UNIVERSITY SCULLS

(COLQUHOUN CHALLENGE SCULLS).

Presented in 1837 *by P. Colquhoun, Esq., to the Lady Margaret Boat Club, and by that Club in* 1842 *to the competition of the C.U.B.C.*

1837	Berney, Lady Margaret	1857	Busk, First Trinity
1838	Antrobus, Lady Margaret	1858	Ingles, First Trinity
1839	Vincent, Lady Margaret	1859	Faley, Lady Margaret
1840	Shadwell, Lady Margaret	1860	Channell, First Trinity
1841	Shadwell (no challenger)	1861	J. C. Hawkshaw, Third Trinity
1842	Denman, First Trinity		
1843	Thompson, Peterhouse	1862	C. B. Lawes, Third Trinity
1844	Miles, Third Trinity	1863	J. G. Chambers, Third Trin.
1845	Cloves, First Trinity	1864	G. D. Redpath, First Trinity
1846	Maule, First Trinity	1865	H. Watney, Lady Margaret
1847	Bagshawe, Third Trinity	1866	G. Shann, First Trinity
1848	Bagot, Second Trinity	1867	G. H. Wright, First Trinity
1849	Miller, Third Trinity	1868	E. Phelps, Sidney, and F. E. Marshall, First Trinity
1850	Cowle and Hudson [1]		
1851	Macnaghten, First Trinity	1869	No race; postponed to 1870
1852	Courage, First Trinity	1870	J. B. Close, First Trinity
1853	Galton, First Trinity	1870	J. H. D. Goldie, Lady Mar.
1854	Wright, Lady Margaret	1871	C. W. Benson, Third Trinity
1855	Salter, Trinity Hall	1872	James B. Close, First Trinity
1856	Beaumont, Third Trinity	1873	A. C. Dicker, Lady Margaret

[1] Dead heat and division.

1874	W. B. Close, First Trinity	1881	J. C. Fellowes, First Trinity
1875	S. A. Saunders, Second Trinity	1882	F. W. Fox, First Trinity
		1883	S. Swann, Trinity Hall
1876	J. C. Fenn, First Trinity	1884	F. J. Pitman, Third Trinity
1877	T. W. Barker, First Trinity	1885	J. M. Cowper-Smith, First Trinity
1878	H. Sandford, Lady Margaret		
1879	Prior, Lady Margaret	1886	J. C. Gardner, Emmanuel
1880	J. Keiser, First Trinity	1887	C. B. P. Bell, Trinity Hall

PROFESSIONAL WINNERS OF REGATTAS AND CHAMPIONSHIPS.

WINNERS OF THE AQUATIC CHAMPIONSHIP.

Date	Winner	Loser	Course	Time
				m. s.
1831, Sept. 9	C. Campbell	C. Williams	W. to P.	—
1838, Nov. 1	C. Campbell	R. Coombes	W. to P.	—
1846, Aug. 19	R. Coombes	C. Campbell	P. to M.	25 15
1847, Sept. 2?	R. Coombes	R. Newell	P. to M.	23 46
1851, May 7	R. Coombes	T. Mackinnery	P. to M.	25 .5
1852, May 24	T. Cole	R. Coombes	P. to M.	25 15
1852, Oct. 14	T. Cole	R. Coombes	P. to M.	23 35
1854, Nov. 20	J. A. Messenger	T. Cole	P. to M.	24 30
1857, May 12	H. Kelley	J. A. Messenger	P. to M.	24 30
1859, Sept. 29	R. Chambers	H. Kelley	P. to M.	25 25
1860, Sept. 18	R. Chambers	T. White	P. to M.	23 15
1863, April 14	R. Chambers	G. W. Everson	P. to M.	25 27
1863, June 16	R. Chambers	R. A. W. Green	P. to M.	25 25
1865, Aug. 8	H. Kelley	R. Chambers	P. to M.	23 25
a 1866, July 4	H. Kelley	Hammill	Tyne	33 29
b 1866, July 5	H. Kelley	Hammill	Tyne	—
1866, Nov. 22	R. Chambers	J. H. Sadler	P. to M.	25 4
1867, May 6	H. Kelley	R. Chambers	Tyne	31 41
1868, Nov. 17	J. Renforth	H. Kelley	P. to M.	23 15
1874, April 16	J. H. Sadler	R. Bagnall	P. to M.	24 15
1875, Nov. 15	T. H. Sadler	R. W. Boyd	P. to M.	29 2
c 1876, June 27	E. Trickett	J. Sadler	P. to M.	24 35
1876,	A match was made between Trickett and Lumsden, but the latter forfeited.			
1876, June 29	A match was made between Sadler and Higgins for the Championship, subject to the former beating Trickett, but after being defeated Sadler forfeited.			

(*a*) This was virtually a row over for Kelley, and no time was taken.
(*b*) Won on a foul.
(*c*) The first occasion of the Championship being taken from England.

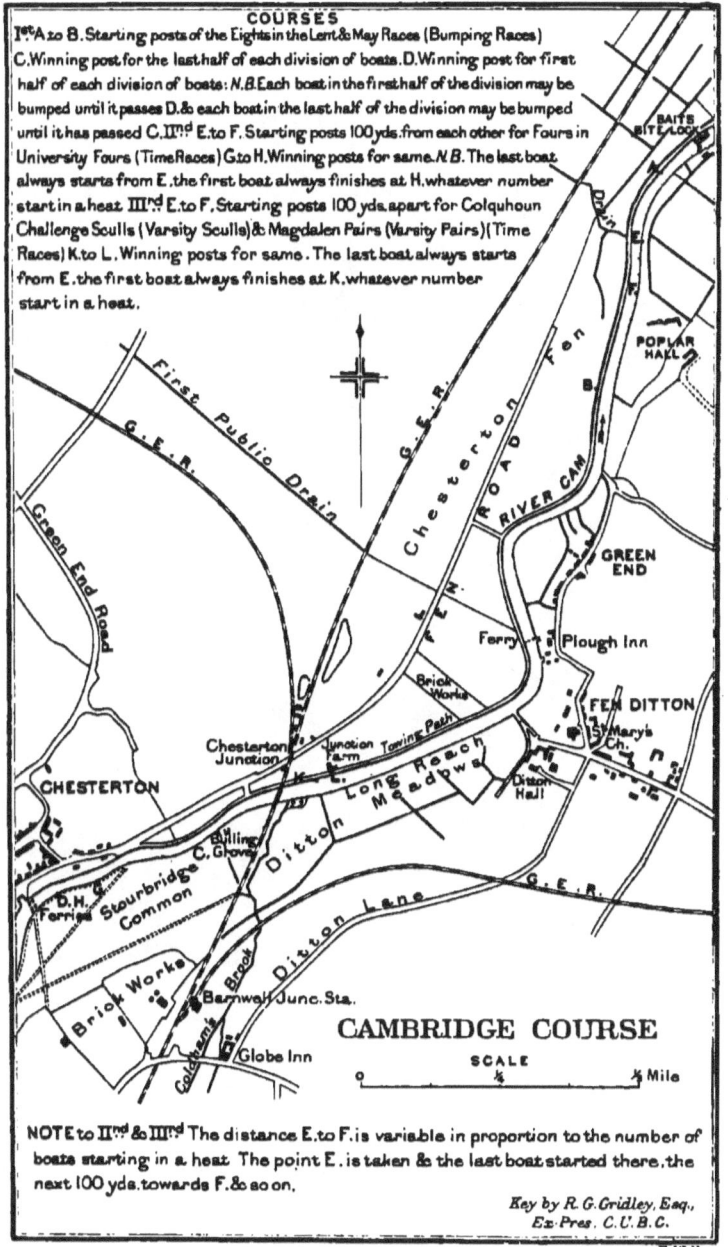

COURSES

Ist A to B. Starting posts of the Eights in the Lent & May Races (Bumping Races)
C. Winning post for the last half of each division of boats. D. Winning post for first
half of each division of boats: N.B. Each boat in the first half of the division may be
bumped until it passes D. & each boat in the last half of the division may be bumped
until it has passed C. IInd E. to F. Starting posts 100 yds. from each other for Fours in
University Fours (Time Races) G. to H. Winning posts for same. N.B. The last boat
always starts from E., the first boat always finishes at H. whatever number
start in a heat IIIrd E. to F. Starting posts 100 yds. apart for Colquhoun
Challenge Sculls (Varsity Sculls) & Magdalen Pairs (Varsity Pairs) (Time
Races) K. to L. Winning posts for same. The last boat always starts
from E. the first boat always finishes at K. whatever number
start in a heat.

CAMBRIDGE COURSE

SCALE

0 _____ ½ _____ ½ Mile

NOTE to IInd & IIIrd The distance E. to F. is variable in proportion to the number of
boats starting in a heat. The point E. is taken & the last boat started there, the
next 100 yds. towards F. & so on.

Key by R. G. Gridley, Esq.,
Ex-Pres. C. U. B. C.

E. Weller

London. Longmans & Co.

WINNERS OF THE AQUATIC CHAMPIONSHIP—*continued.*

Date	Winner	Loser	Course	Time
				m. s.
1877, May 28	R. W. Boyd	J. Higgins	P. to M.	29 0
1877, June 30	Trickett beat Michael Rush for the Championship of the World, on the Paramatta River, New South Wales.			
1877, Oct. 8	J. Higgins	R. W. Boyd	P. to M.	24 10
1878, Jan. 14	J. Higgins	R. W. Boyd	Tyne	Foul
1878, June 3	J. Higgins	W. Elliott	P. to M.	24 38
1878, Sept. 17	*d* W. Elliott beat R. W. Boyd in final heat of race for the 'Sportsman's' Challenge Cup, Putney to Mortlake.			24 20
1879, Feb. 21	W. Elliott	J. Higgins	Tyne	22 1
1879, June 16	E. Hanlan	W. Elliott	Tyne	21 1
1880, Nov. 16	E. Hanlan	E. Trickett	Thames	26 12
1881, Feb. 14	E. Hanlan	E. C. Laycock	P. to M.	25 41
1882, April 3	E. Hanlan	R. W. Boyd	Tyne	21 25
1882, May 1	E. Hanlan	E. Trickett	P. to M.	28 0
1884, May 22	E. Hanlan	E. C. Laycock	Nepean Riv., N.S.W.	—
1884, Aug. 16	W. Beach	E. Hanlan	Paramatta Riv., N.S.W	—
1885, Feb. 28	W. Beach	C. Clifford	Paramatta Riv., N.S.W	26 0
1885, Mch. 28	W. Beach	E. Hanlan	Paramatta Riv., N.S.W.	22 51
1885, Dec. 18	W. Beach	N. Matterson	Paramatta Riv., N.S.W.	24 11¼
1886, Sept. 18	W. Beach	J. Gaudaur	P. to M.	22 29
1886, Sept. 25	W. Beach	Wallace Ross	P. to M.	23 5

(*d*) Boyd passed the post first, but the race was awarded to Elliott on the foul

THAMES NATIONAL REGATTA

FOR WATERMEN.

CHAMPION FOURS (*Winners*).

1854 *Elswick Crew*. —Winship, Cook, Davidson, Bruce, Oliver (cox.,
1855 *Shakspeare Crew*.—Wood, Carrol, Ault, Taylor, Malony (cox.)
1856 *North and South Crew*.—H. Clasper, W. Pocock, R. Chambers,
         T. Mackinney, G. Driver (cox.)
1857 *Newcastle Crew*.—J. H. Clasper, A. Maddeson, R. Chambers,
         H. Clasper, Short (cox.)
1858 *Pride of the Thames Crew*.—G. Francis, S. Salter, T. White,
         G. Hammerton, J. Driver (cox.)
1859 *Newcastle Crew*.—J. H. Clasper, R. Chambers, E. Winship,
         H. Clasper, R. Clasper (cox.)
1860 *London Crew*.—T. Pocock, J. Wise, T. White, H. Kelley, W.
         Peters (cox.)
1861 *Kilmorey Crew*.—G. Hammerton, J. W. Tagg, E. Winship,
         R. Chambers, R. Clasper (cox.)
1862 *Newcastle Crew*.—J. H. Clasper, R. Chambers, E. Winship, H.
         Clasper, R. Clasper (cox.)
1863 *Thames Crew*.—H. Harris, T. G. Tagg, J. W. Tagg, G. Hammer-
         ton, R. W. Hanna (cox.)
1864 *Pride of the Thames Crew*.—T. Hoare, H. Kelley, J. W. Tagg,
         G. Hammerton, R. Hammerton (cox.)
1865 *Sons of the Thames Crew*.—F. Kilsby, R. Cook, G. Cannon,
         J. Sadler, S. Peters (cox.)
1866 *Pride of the Thames Crew*.—T. Hoare, J. Pedgrift, J. Sadler,
         G. Hammerton, J. Hill (cox.)

SCULLS.

1854	H. Kelley, Fulham	1861	H. Kelley, Fulham
1855	R. Chambers, Newcastle	1862	R. Cooper, Redheugh
1856	H. Kelley, Fulham	1863	R. A. W. Green, Australia
1857	R. Chambers, Newcastle	1864	H. Kelley, Putney
1858	R. Chambers, Newcastle	1865	R. Chambers, Newcastle
1859	J. Wise, Kew	1866	R. Cooper, Redheugh
1860	G. Hammerton, Teddington		

PAIR-OARS (*Winners*).

1854 Pocock and Clasper	1862 Winship and Chambers
1855 Winship and Bruce, Elswick	1863 Green and Kelley, Australia
1856 Winship and Bruce	and Putney
1857 Hammerton and Francis,	1864 Kilsby and Cook, London
Teddington	and Oxford
1858 Hammerton and Francis	1865 Kilsby and Cook, London
1860 Winship and Chambers,	and Oxford
Newcastle	1866 G. Hammerton and J. Sad-
1861 Winship and Chambers	ler, Surbiton

APPRENTICES' SCULLS : COAT AND BADGE (*Winners*).

1856 G. Hammerton, Teddington	1862 J. W. Tagg, Moulsey
1857 S. Salter, Wandsworth	1863 R. Cook, Oxford
1858 E. Bell, Richmond	1864 T. Wise, Hammersmith
1859 W. Hemmings, Richmond	1865 J. Callas, Richmond
1860 E. Eagers, Chelsea.	1866 W. Sadler, Putney
1861 T. Hoare, Hammersmith	

THAMES NATIONAL REGATTA (*Second Series*).

FOURS.

1868 *Newcastle Crew.*—J. Taylor, M. Scott, A. Thompson, R. Chambers (Wallsend) (stroke), T. French (cox.)

1869 *Surbiton Crew.*—J. Sadler, J. Pedgrift, W. Messenger, G. Hammerton (stroke), R. Hammerton (cox.)

1870 *Newcastle Crew.*— R. Hepplewhite, J. Percy, J. Bright, R. Chambers (stroke), F. M'Lean (cox.)

1871 *Glasgow Crew.*—J. Moody, T. Smillie, J. Calderhead, W. Calderhead (stroke), J. M. Green (cox.)

1872 *Hammersmith Crew.*—H. Thomas, T. Green, J. Anderson, W. Biffen, jun. (stroke), G. Martin (cox.)

1873 *Hammersmith Crew.*—T. Green, H. Thomas, J. Anderson, W. Biffen (stroke), H. Goldsmith (cox.)

1874 *Hammersmith Crew.*—T. Green, H. Thomas, J. Anderson, W. Biffen (stroke), G. Holder (cox.)

1875　*Newcastle Crew.*—R. Hepplewhite, W. Nicholson, R. Bagnall, R. W. Boyd (stroke), J. Cox (cox.)

1876　*Thames Crew.*—W. F. Spencer, H. Thomas, J. Higgins, T. Green (stroke), J. Holder (cox.)

PAIRS.

1868　J. Taylor and M. Scott, Newcastle
1869　J. Taylor and T. Winship, Newcastle
1870　G. Carr and T. Matfin, Newcastle
1871　W. Biffen, jun. and G. Hammerton
1872　J. Taylor and T. Winship, Newcastle
1873　R. Bagnall and J. Taylor, Newcastle
1874　W. Biffen and H. Thomas
1875　R. Bagnall and R. W. Boyd, Newcastle
1876　T. Green and H. Thomas, Thames

SCULLS.

1868　J. Renforth, Newcastle
1869　J. Renforth, Newcastle
1870　J. H. Sadler, Surbiton
1871 *a*J. Anderson, Hammersmith
1872 *b*J. Anderson, Hammersmith

1873 *b*A. Hogarth, Sunderland
1874 *b*R. W. Boyd, Newcastle
1875 *b*T. Blackman, London
1876　T. Blackman, Dulwich

APPRENTICES' SCULLS: COAT AND BADGE.

1868　W. Biffen, Jun., Hammersmith
1869　J. Griffiths, Wandsworth
1870　W. Messenger, Teddington
1871　T. Green, Hammersmith

1872　H. Messum, Richmond
1873　J. Phillips, Putney
1874　W. Phillips, Putney
1875　J. Tarryer, Rotherhithe
1876　H. Clasper, Oxford

(*a*) Limited to men who have never sculled for a stake of 50*l*.
(*b*) For men who have never sculled for a stake of 100*l*.

THAMES INTERNATIONAL REGATTA.

CHAMPION SCULLS.

1876 R. W. Boyd,   1877 T. Blackman,
          1878 W. Elliott.

CHAMPION FOURS.

1876 *a* Tyne crew,   1877 Thames crew,
          1878 Tyne crew.

CHAMPION PAIRS.

1876 R. W. Boyd and W. Lumsden.
1877 J. Higgins and H. Thomas.
1878 R. W. Boyd and W. Lumsden.

(*a*) After a foul, the Tyne men won on the second day.

· ROYAL THAMES REGATTA,

Established 1843.

WATERMEN'S PRIZES.

1843 No race for professionals.
1844 FOURS.—*London four*, T. Coombes, Phelps, Newell, and R.
          Coombes beat H. Clasper's crew for 100*l.* prize.
          SCULLS.—H. Clasper won in the first 'outrigged' sculling boat.
1845 FOURS.—H. Clasper, R. Clasper, W. Clasper, and Hawtor beat
          Coombes's four.
1846 FOURS.—T. Coombes, Newell, Phelps, and R. Coombes won.
1847 No race.
1848 Clasper's crew won (Coombes in the boat).
1849 Clasper's crew won fours. (This was the last year of the regatta.)

BRITISH REGATTA IN PARIS, 1867

(EXHIBITION YEAR).

CHAMPION FOURS.

1867 *Albion Crew, Newcastle.*—J. Taylor, M. Scott, A. Thompson, R. Chambers (St. Anthony's) (st.), T. Richardson (cox.)

PAIR-OARS.

R. Cook and H. Kelley, Oxford and London.

SCULLS.

H. Kelley, Putney.

WORLD'S REGATTA ON THE THAMES.

1880 On November 18 a sculling regatta organised by an American firm, 'The Hop Bitters' Co., was commenced on the Thames. It lasted three days, and prizes amounting to 1,000*l.* were given and won as under :—

1. Elias C. Laycock, Sydney, N.S.W. . . . . £ 500
2. Wallace Ross, St. John's, New Brunswick . . 300
3. George Hosmer, Boston, U.S.A. 140
4. Warren Smith, Halifax, Nova Scotia . . . 60

WINNERS OF DOGGETT'S COAT AND BADGE.

1791	T. Easton, Old Swan	1825	G. Staples, Battle Bridge
1792	J. Kettleby, Westminster	1826	J. Foett, Bankside
1793	A. Haley, Horselydown	1827	J. Foss, Fountain Stair
1794	J. Franklin, Putney	1828	R. Mallett, Lambeth
1795	W. Parry, Hungerford	1829	S. Stubbs, Old Barge House
1796	J. Thompson, Wapping Old Stairs	1830	W. Butler, Vauxhall
		1831	R. Oliver, Deptford
1797	J. Hill, Bankside	1832	R. Waight, Bankside
1798	T. Williams, Ratcliff Cross	1833	G. Maynard, Lambeth
1799	J. Dixon, Paddington Street	1834	W. Tomlinson, Whitehall
1800	J. Burgoyne, Blackfriars	1835	W. Dyson, Kidney Stairs
1801	J. Curtis, Queenhithe	1836	J. Morris, Horselydown
1802	W. Burns, Limehouse	1837	T. Harrison, Bankside
1803	J. Fowler, Hungerford	1838	S. Bridge, Kidney Stairs
1804	C. Gingle, Temple	1839	T. Goodrum, Vauxhall Stairs
1805	T. Johnson, Vauxhall	1840	W. Hawkins, Kidney Stairs
1806	J. Godwin, Ratcliff Cross	1841	R. Moore, Surrey Canal
1807	J. Evans, Mill Stairs	1842	J. Liddey, Wandsworth
1808	G. Newell, Battle Bridge	1843	J. Fry, Kidney Stairs
1809	F. Jury, Hermitage	1844	F. Lett, Lambeth
1810	J. Smart, Strand	1845	J. Cobb, Greenwich
1811	W. Thornton, Hungerford	1846	J. Wing, Pimlico
1812	R. May, Westminster	1847	W. Ellis, Westminster
1813	R. Farson, Bankside	1848	J. Ash, Rotherhithe
1814	R. Harris, Bankside	1849	T. Cole, jun., Chelsea
1815	J. Scott, Bankside	1850	W. Campbell, Winchester
1816	T. Senham, Blackfriars	1851	G. Wigget, Somer's Quay
1817	J. Robson, Wapping Old Stairs	1852	C. Constable, Lambeth
		1853	J. Finnis, Tower
1818	W. Nicholls, Greenwich	1854	D. Hemmings, Bankside
1819	W. Emery, Hungerford	1855	H. White, Mill Stairs
1820	J. Hartley, Strand	1856	G. W. Everson, Greenwich
1821	T. Cole, sen., Chelsea	1857	T. White, Mill Stairs
1822	W. Noulton, Lambeth	1858	C. J. Turner, Rotherhithe
1823	G. Butcher, Hungerford	1859	C. Farrow, jun., Mill Stairs
1824	G. Fogo, Battle Bridge	1860	H. J. M. Phelps, Fulham

1861	S. Short, Bermondsey	1874	R. W. Burwood, Wapping
1862	J. Messenger, Cherry Garden Stairs	1875	W. Phelps, Putney
		1876	C. T. Bullman, Shadwell Dock
1863	T. Young, Rotherhithe		
1864	D. Coombes, Horselydown	1877	J. Tarryer, Rotherhithe
1865	J. W. Wood, Mill Stairs	1878	T. E. Taylor, Hermitage Stairs
1866	A. Iles, Kew		
1867	H. M. Maxwell, Custom House	1879	Henry Cordery, Putney
		1880	W. G. Cobb, Putney
1868	A. Egalton, Blackwall	1881	G. Claridge, Richmond
1869	G. Wright, Bermondsey	1882	H. A. Audsley, Waterloo
1870	R. Harding, Blackwall	1883	J. Lloyd, Chelsea
1871	T. J. Mackinney, Richmond	1884	C. Phelps, Putney
1872	T. G. Green, Hammersmith	1885	J. Mackinney, Richmond
1873	H. Messum, Richmond	1886	H. Cole, Deptford

1887   W. G. East

RIVERS AND COURSES.

RIVER LEA.

	Distance from	
	LIMEHOUSE	HERTFORD
	m. f.	m. f.
Hertford	27 7	0 0
Hertford Lock	27 2	0 5
Ware Lock	25 7	2 0
Ware	25 2	2 5
Hard Mead Lock	24 3	3 4
Amwell Lock	23 4	4 3
Stanstead Lock	22 7	5 0
Rye House, Hoddesdon	21 4	6 3
Feildep Weir Lock	21 2	6 5
Dobbs's Weir Lock	20 3	7 4
Carthagena Lock	19 6	8 1
Broxbourne Lock	19 1	8 6
Aqueduct Lock	17 5	10 2
Cheshunt Mill	16 7	11 1
Waltham Common Lock	15 7	12 0
Waltham Abbey Lock	14 7	13 0
Romney Marsh Lock	14 3	13 4
Enfield Lock	13 1	14 6
Ponder's End Lock	11 2	16 5

	Distance from			
	LIMEHOUSE		HERTFORD	
	m.	f.	m.	f.
Pickett's Lock	10	2	17	5
Edmonton Lock	9	2	18	5
Stone Bridge Lock	8	2	19	5
Tottenham Lock	7	3	20	4
Tottenham Railway Bridge	6	7	21	0
Lea Bridge	5	0	22	7
Homerton Lock	4	2	23	5
Duckett's Canal Junction	3	1	24	6
Old Ford Lock	2	6	25	1
Bow Railway Bridge	2	3	25	4
Bow Bridge	2	1	25	6
Bromley Lock	1	4	26	3
Britannia Lock	0	1	27	6
Limehouse Cut Entrance	0	0	27	7

LENGTH OF RACING COURSES.

Barnes Regatta Course	$1\frac{1}{2}$ mile
Barrow, Walney Channel	2 miles 600 yards
Bedford Regatta	$\frac{3}{4}$ mile
Blyth, Flanker to Cowper Gut	2 miles
Bristol, from Hotwells to Bristol	$1\frac{1}{2}$ mile
Boston, River Witham	$2\frac{1}{2}$ miles
Cambridge	$1\frac{1}{3}$ mile
Chester	$1\frac{1}{4}$ mile
Clydesdale	$1\frac{1}{2}$ mile
Cork	2 miles
Derby	1 mile
Dublin	$2\frac{1}{4}$ miles
Durham	1 mile 300 yards
Ely, Littleport to Adelaide Bridge	$2\frac{1}{3}$ miles
Exeter	$2\frac{1}{2}$ miles
Halton Water	$1\frac{3}{4}$ mile
Henley-on-Thames	1 mile $2\frac{1}{2}$ furlongs
Huntington	$1\frac{3}{4}$ mile
,, for time races	3 miles
Hollingworth Lake	3 miles
Hereford	1 mile 536 yards
Ipswich	1 mile 700 yards
King's Lynn, Champion Course	2 miles
,, Prince of Wales's Course	$1\frac{1}{4}$ mile

x

Kingston-on-Thames, Seething Wells to Kingston
    Bridge . . . . $1\frac{1}{4}$ mile
Lincoln, sculling and pair-oared . . . . $\frac{3}{4}$ mile
  ,,   four-oared . . . . $1\frac{1}{2}$ miles
London Bridge to Old Swan, Chelsea . . . 4 miles 3 furlongs
Manchester . . . . 2 miles
Moulsey (down stream) . . . . . . $1\frac{1}{4}$ mile
Newark, Devonmouth to Magnus Boathouse . . 1 mile
Oxford, Iffley to the Barges . . . . . $1\frac{1}{8}$ mile
  ,,   Abingdon Lasher to Nuneham Cottage . $1\frac{1}{2}$ mile
Putney to Barnes Bridge . . . . . . 3 miles 6 furlongs
  ,, to Chiswick . . . . . . 2 miles 4 furlongs
  ,, to Hammersmith . . . . . . 1 mile 6 furlongs
  ,, to Mortlake . . . . . . 4 miles 3 furlongs
Richmond, Sion House to Richmond Bridge . . 1 mile 7 furlongs
  ,,   Cross Deep, Twickenham, to Richmond
    Railway Bridge . . . . . . 1 mile 5 furlongs
Stockton-on-Tees, Portrack Course . . . . 4 miles
      ,,   ,,   ,, above bridges . $1\frac{1}{2}$ mile
Stourport . . . . $1\frac{1}{4}$ mile
Sunderland, North Hylton to Spa Well . . . 1 mile
Tyne, High Level Bridge to Waterson's Gates . . 1 mile
  ,,   ,,   ,, Meadow's House . . $1\frac{3}{4}$ mile
  ,,   ,,   ,, Armstrong's Crane . 2 miles
  ,,   ,,   ,, West Point of Paradise
           Quay . . . $2\frac{1}{2}$ miles
  ,,   ,,   ,, Scotswood Suspension
           Bridge . . . 3 miles 713 yards
  ,,   ,,   ,, Lemington Point . . $4\frac{1}{2}$ miles
Tewkesbury . . . . 2 miles
Walton-on-Thames (up stream) . . . . . 1 mile
Warwick . . . . $1\frac{1}{3}$ mile
Worcester . . . . 1 mile

DISTANCES OF WEIRS ETC. OXFORD TO LECHLADE.

	Distance from			
	OXFORD BRIDGE		LECHLADE BRIDGE	
	m.	f.	m.	f.
Oxford Bridge	0	0	36	0
Godstow Lock	3	3	33	0
King's Weir	4	4	31	4
Ensham Bridge	7	5	28	3

	Distance from	
	Oxford Bridge	Lechlade Bridge
	m. f.	m. f.
Pinkhill Lock	10 0	26 0
Skinner's Weir	11 0	25 0
Badlock Ferry	12 4	23 4
Ridge's Weir	16 0	20 0
Newbridge	17 2	18 6
Shifford Weir	19 0	17 0
Dexford Weir	20 0	16 0
Tenfoot Weir Bridge	22 0	14 0
Kent or Tadpole Bridge	23 5	12 3
Bushey Weir	24 5	11 3
Old Nan's Weir	26 1	9 7
Old Man's or Harper's Weir	26 7	9 1
Radcot Bridge	28 3	7 5
Eaton or Hart's Upper Weir	31 3	4 5
Buscot Lock	33 3	2 5
St. John's Bridge	35 2	0 6
Lechlade Bridge	36 0	0 0

TABLES OF DISTANCES OF LOCKS ETC. ON THE THAMES.

	Distance from	
	Oxford Folly Bridge	London Bridge
	m. f.	m. f.
Oxford Folly Bridge (stone) and Lock	0 0	110 $1\frac{1}{2}$
Iffley Lock	1 1	109 $0\frac{1}{2}$
Rose Island	1 $7\frac{1}{2}$	108 $1\frac{3}{4}$
Sandford Lock	2 $5\frac{3}{4}$	107 $3\frac{1}{2}$
Abingdon Lock	7 $0\frac{1}{2}$	103 1
Abingdon Bridge (stone)	7 3	102 $5\frac{1}{2}$
Culham Lock	9 $5\frac{1}{2}$	100 4
Clifton Lock	12 $2\frac{1}{2}$	97 6
Clifton Hampden Bridge (brick)	12 $6\frac{1}{4}$	97 $2\frac{1}{2}$
Day's Lock	15 $3\frac{1}{4}$	94 $6\frac{1}{2}$
Shillingford Bridge (stone)	17 $7\frac{1}{2}$	92 1
Benson Lock	19 $0\frac{1}{2}$	91 1
Wallingford Bridge (stone)	20 $2\frac{3}{4}$	89 $6\frac{1}{2}$
Wallingford Lock	20 $6\frac{3}{4}$	81 7
Little Stocke Ferry	23 $0\frac{3}{4}$	87 $0\frac{1}{2}$
Moulsford Ferry	24 $3\frac{1}{2}$	85 $5\frac{3}{4}$

X 2

	Distance from Oxford Folly Bridge		Distance from London Bridge	
	m.	f.	m.	f.
Cleeve Lock	25	5½	84	3¾
Goring Lock	26	3	83	6¼
Basildon Railway Bridge	27	5	82	4¼
Whitchurch Lock	30	3	79	6¼
Pangbourne Bridge	30	4½	79	4¾
Maple Durham Lock	32	5½	77	3¾
Caversham Bridge (iron)	36	0¼	74	0½
Caversham Lock	36	6	73	3¼
Sonning Lock	39	3	70	6¼
Sonning Bridge (brick)	39	5¼	70	4
Shiplake Lock	42	0¼	68	1
Wargrave Railway Bridge	42	2½	67	7¾
Wargrave Ferry	42	4½	67	4¾
Marsh Lock	44	5	65	4¼
Henley Bridge (stone)	45	4	64	5½
Regatta Island (from this to Henley Bridge is the usual Regatta course)	46	7½	63	1¾
Hambledon Lock	47	6½	62	2¾
Medmenham Abbey and Ferry	49	6½	60	2¾
Hurley Lock	51	2	58	7¼
Temple Lock	51	7½	58	1¾
Marlow Suspension Bridge (iron)	53	3½	56	5¾
Marlow Lock	53	5	56	4¼
Cookham Railway Bridge (wooden)	56	0¼	54	1
Cookham Bridge (iron)	57	2	52	7¼
Cookham Lock	57	5	52	4¼
Boulter's Lock	60	0¾	50	0½
Maidenhead Bridge (stone)	60	6½	49	2¾
Maidenhead Railway Bridge (brick)	60	0¼	49	1
Bray	61	6½	48	2¾
Bray Lock	62	0½	48	0¾
Monkey Island	62	0¼	47	3
Queen's Island	63	2¼	46	7
Boveney Lock	64	7½	45	1¾
Windsor Railway Bridge (iron)	66	6¼	43	3
Windsor Bridge (iron)	67	1¼	43	0
Windsor Lock	67	4¾	42	4½
South-Western Railway Bridge (iron)	67	7	42	2¼
Victoria Bridge (iron)	68	3	41	6¼
Datchet	68	7½	41	1¾

	Distance from Oxford Folly Bridge		Distance from London Bridge	
	m.	f.	m.	f.
Albert Bridge (iron)	69	6	40	3¼
Old Windsor Lock	70	4½	39	4¾
Magna Charta Island	71	7½	38	1¾
Bell Weir Lock	73	3¾	36	5½
Staines Bridge (stone)	74	3½	35	5¾
Staines Railway Bridge (iron)	74	6¼	35	3
Penton Hook Lock	76	1½	33	7¾
Laleham Ferry	76	7¼	33	2
Chertsey Lock	77	7¾	32	1½
Chertsey Bridge (stone)	78	0¾	32	0½
Shepperton Lock	79	6	30	3¼
Shepperton	80	4	29	5¼
Halliford	81	0¾	29	0½
Walton Bridge (iron)	81	7½	28	1¾
Sunbury Lock	83	4¾	26	4½
Hampton Ferry	85	5¾	24	3½
Moulsey Lock	86	4¾	23	4½
Hampton Court Bridge (iron)	86	5¾	23	3½
Thames Ditton Ferry	87	4¾	22	4½
Messenger's Island	88	5¾	21	3½
Kingston Bridge (stone)	89	5¼	20	4
Kingston Railway Bridge (iron)	89	6¼	20	3
Teddington Lock	91	2¼	18	7
Twickenham Ferry	92	5½	17	3¾
Richmond Bridge (stone)	94	0¼	16	0¾
Richmond Railway Bridge (iron)	94	3½	15	5¾
Isleworth (Railhead) Ferry	94	7½	15	1¾
Isleworth	95	2½	14	6¼
Brentford Ferry	96	4½	13	4¾
Kew Bridge (stone)	97	1	13	0¼
Strand-on-the-Green Railway Bridge (iron) about	97	5	12	4¼
Barnes Railway Bridge (iron)	99	0¾	11	0½
Hammersmith South Bridge (iron)	100	7¾	9	1½
Putney Bridge (wooden)	102	5¾	7	3½
Battersea Railway Bridge	104	4¼	5	5
Battersea Bridge (wooden)	105	1¼	5	0
Chelsea Suspension Bridge (iron)	106	1¼	4	0
Vauxhall Bridge (iron)	107	1½	2	7¾
Lambeth Suspension Bridge (iron)	107	6	2	3¼
Westminster Bridge (iron)	108	1½	1	7¾

		Distance from			
		OXFORD FOLLY BRIDGE		LONDON BRIDGE	
		m.	f.	m.	f.
Charing Cross Railway Bridge (iron) . . .		108	4½	1	4¾
Waterloo Bridge (stone)		108	6⅓	1	2¾
Blackfriars Bridge (iron)		109	3	0	6¼
Southwark Bridge (iron)		109	6¾	0	2½
Cannon Street Railway Bridge (iron) . . .		110	0	0	1¼
London Bridge (stone)		110	1¼	0	0

ON THE RIVER MEDWAY.

	Distance from			
	SHEERNESS		TONBRIDGE	
	m.	f.	m.	f.
Tonbridge	46	4	0	0
Tonbridge Lock	46	2	0	2
Giles's Lock	45	5	0	7
Eldridge's Lock	44	4	2	0
Porter's Lock	43	5	2	7
East Lock	42	0	4	4
Nook Weare Lock	41	3	5	1
New Lock	40	4	6	0
Sluice Weare Lock	40	0	6	4
Brandbridge's Lock	39	3	7	1
South-Eastern Railway Bridge . . .	39	0	7	4
Stoneham Lock	38	6	7	6
Yalding Village	37	6	8	6
Hampstead Lock	37	3	9	1
Wateringbury Bridge	35	4	11	0
Yeston Lock	34	2	12	2
Yeston Bridge	34	1	12	3
East Farleigh Lock	32	0	14	0
East Farleigh Bridge	32	0	14	4
Maidstone Lock	29	7	16	5
Maidstone Bridge	29	6	16	6
Gibraltar Lock	27	6	18	6
Aylesford Bridge	25	6	20	6
Snodland Ferry	20	4	26	0
Lower Halling Ferry	18	4	28	0
Rochester Bridge	14	0	32	4
Rochester Railway Bridge	14	0	32	4
Chatham	12	4	34	0

		Distance from			
		SHEERNESS		TONBRIDGE	
		. m.	f.	m	f.
Chatham Dockyard	. .	. . . 12	0	34	4
Upnor Castle	. . .	. . . 11	0	35	4
Gillingham	. . .	. . . 8	4	38	0
River Swale	. . .	. . . 2	0	44	4
Sheerness .	. . .	. . . 0	0	46	4

ON THE RIVER WEY.

		Distance from			
		THAMES LOCK		GODALMING	
		m	f.	m.	f.
Godalming .	. .	 20	1	0	0
Catshail Lock	. .	. . . 19	3	0	0
Unsted Lock	. .	. . . 18	3	1	6
Broadford Bridge	.	. . . 17	5	2	6
Shalford Railway Bridge	.	. . . 17	0	3	0
St. Catherine's Lock .	.	. . . 16	5	3	4
St. Catherine's Ferry .	.	. . . 16	3	3	6
Guildford Lock .	.	. . . 15	5	4	4
Guildford Bridge	.	. . . 15	4	4	5
Stoke Lock	. .	. . . 12	4	7	5
Bower's Lock	. .	. . ·. 11	5	6	4
Trigg's Lock	. .	. . . 9	5	10	0
Scud Heath	. .	. . . 9	1	11	5
Worsfold's Gates .	.	. . . 8	7	11	2
Paper Court Lock	.	. . . 7	3	12	6
Newark Lock	. .	. . . 6	1	14	0
Pirford Lock	. .	. . . 5	2	14	0
South-Western Railway Bridge	.	. . . 3	0	17	1
New Haw Lock .	.	. . . 2	4	17	0
Cox's Lock	. .	. . . 1	5	18	4
Weybridge Lock .	.	. . . 1	0	19	1
Thames Junction Lock	.	. . . 0	0	20	1

APPENDIX.

———•◦•———

THE EARLY HISTORY OF BOAT RACING AT THE UNIVERSITIES.[1]

THE history of early college boat racing is not strictly that of the University boat race itself, but it is closely wound up with it, and it was, moreover, the origin of that aquatic rivalry between the two Universities which led to the first match of 1829.

Oxford had inaugurated eight-oared rowing ; that introduced inter-college bumping races. Cambridge followed suit and established similar races, and hence arose the constant study of aquatics which produced the first match. For these reasons, we think that the history here given will be read with interest by all University oarsmen, the more so because it, to the best of our knowledge, has never before appeared in print. No official record of their early races has been preserved ; the oldest boating record in Oxford is the Brasenose Club Book, dating 1837. That of the O.U.B.C. commences with its establishment, 1839. The 'Charts' of the boat races from 1837, published by Messrs. Spiers & Sons, and which were not invented till after the year 1850, obtain the retrospective racing, prior to the time when they first appeared, from the MS. records of the B.N.C. book, the contents of which were communicated to the publishers by the late Rev. T. Codrington. But prior to 1837 all is blank. For the lost history here unearthed we are indebted to the reminiscences and diaries of oarsmen of those days still in the land of the living.

Oxford started college boat racing before Cambridge. It does not seem quite clear as to when bumping races actually com-

[1] Reprinted from *Land and Water* of December 17, 1881.

menced. Two or three colleges had boat clubs and manned eight oars, and at first it seems to have been the practice for out-college men to join the club and crew of colleges to which they did not belong.

The eight oars seem to have been in the habit of going down to Sandford or Nuneham to dine, and of rowing home in company. From Iffley to Oxford they were inclined to race to see who could be home first. They could not race abreast, so they rowed in Indian file, and those behind jealously tried to overtake the leaders. Hence began the idea of starting in a fixed order out of Iffley Lock, of racing in procession, and of an overtaken boat giving place to its victor on the next night of procession.

In 1822, at all events, there were bumping races. Christ Church seems to have been head. There was a disputed bump between B.N.C. and Jesus, and some violence seems to have occurred, B.N.C. trying to haul down the Jesus flag, and the Jesus men defending their colours. The dispute was finally closed by Post of B.N.C. saying, 'These cries of "Jesus" and "B.N.C." remind me of the old saying :—

> Different people are of different opinions;
> Some like leeks, some like onions.'

(The oars of Jesus were decorated with leeks.) The quarrel was made up, and the crews went together to Nuneham in their racing boats. Unfortunately Musgrave, one of the party, fell overboard and was drowned during the festivities. In 1823 there were no eight-oared races, the sad accident of the year before having cast a gloom over the pursuit. But several boats were manned. Christ Church refused to put on a boat in consequence of Stephen Davis, the boat-builder, rowing in the B.N.C. eight, and Isaac King (who eventually took Davis's business) in the Jesus boat. Some strong feeling was displayed on this point. When the B.N.C. boat came up the river, the Christ Church men used to run alongside of it for many nights shouting, ' No hired watermen.' After this year no watermen rowed in the college crews. Exeter had a boat afloat that year, built by Hall of Oxford. She was called the ' Buccleuch ' in honour of the Duke of that ilk.

Among the Exeter men was one Moresby, who was a relative of a naval captain of that name, and through his advice Exeter ordered an eight-oar of Little, of Plymouth. She was finished in time to be put on in 1824, and became famous as the 'Exeter white boat.' Stephen Davis was sent with a carriage constructed for the purpose, to meet the boat at Portsmouth, whither she was brought by sea. As this boat was built of deal, a raft was provided to receive her—the first use of a raft for this purpose at Oxford. The oars sent with the boat were such as are used at sea, and made of ash. They were discarded in favour of ordinary oars, such as those already in use for fresh-water rowing. She was found to be too high out of the water, so Isaac King cut her down one streak. The boat, as depicted in Turner's water-colour drawing of her, was taken when she was afloat and unmanned ; her crew were painted in her afterwards ; consequently she rides too high out of the water. The boats on the river in 1824 were, at the beginning of the season, Christ Church 1, B.N.C. 2, Exeter 3. Exeter bumped B.N.C. under the willows on the first night ; the next night of racing Christ Church took off, and Exeter became head by the other's default. The races were renewed another day, and B.N.C. bumped Christ Church. This was the *last* year in which the boats started out for Iffley Lock. The racing has hitherto been conducted on this principle ; the start between the boats were just so much as the dexterity of the stroke could obtain. He, the stroke, stood on the bow thwart, and ran down the row of thwarts ; pushing the boat along with his shoulder against the lock gates, he reached his own thwart, by which time the impetus had shot the boat clear of the lock, he dropped on to his own seat, and began to row. The oarsmen had their oars 'tossed' meantime. The boat next in order then followed the same process, and so on. The boats lay in *échelon* while waiting for the start. Bulteel, who was stroke of B.N.C. in the disputed race of 1822 (above mentioned), and who afterwards was elected Fellow of Exeter in 1823, was especially skilful at this. The Exeter crew of 1824 were : Wareing, Dick, Parr, Dowglass, J. C. Clutterbuck, Cole, R. Pocklington (father of D. Pocklington, stroke of Oxford in 1864), Bulteel (stroke), S. Pocklington (cox.) The Rev. J. C. Clutterbuck, now rector of Long Wittenham, near Abingdon, is well known as a conservator of the Thames, to whom the Universities and rowing men are much indebted for the clauses in the Conservancy Acts which give that body powers to clear the river for boat racing. The names of the other two crews of 1824 have not come fully to posterity, but among B.N.C. are Meredith, North and Karle (stroke) ; and in the Christ Church crew were Hussey, Baring and Smyth (stroke).

In 1825 the boats started in line along the bank, each having its umpire to regulate the distance between it and its neighbours (one length). The boats at starting were Exeter, Christ Church Worcester, Balliol (in this order). Exeter had discarded their old love, and had got a 'black boat,' larger than the old 'white boat,' but not so fast, according to later experiments. However, they elected to row in her at first, and Christ Church bumped them, also Worcester on a subsequent night. Later on Exeter rebumped Worcester, and at the close of the racing the order was : Christ Church, Exeter, Worcester, Balliol. Smyth was again strcke of Christ Church, and R. Pocklington stroke of Exeter, in which Messrs. Clutterbuck, Parr, Dowglass, Cole, and Wareing rowed again, with Messrs. Harndon and Day as recruits.

The term 'Torpid' seems to have arisen about this date, and to have been applied to the 'second' boats of colleges, such as Christ Church, who launched a second boat in 1826. Later on the 'Torpids' took to racing among themselves as a separate class, and under distinct qualifications.

In 1826 the following rules were drawn up for the boat-racing, and we give them verbatim :—

Rule 186.—Resolved (1) That racing do commence on Monday, May 1.

(2) That the days for racing be Monday and Friday in each week, and that if any boat does not come out on those days its flag do go to the bottom.

(3) That no out-college crews be allowed to row in any boat except in cases of illness or other unavoidable absence, and then that the cause of such absence be signified to the strokes of the other boats.

(4) That the boats below the one that bumps stop racing, and those above continue it.

(5) That there be a distance of fifty feet between each boat at starting.

(6) That the boats start by pistol shot.

(7) That umpires be appointed by each college to see each boat in its proper position before starting, and to decide any accidental dispute.

H. Saunders, Ch. Ch.	Henry Towers, Ch. Ch.
H. Moresby, Ex. Coll.	T. North, B. N. Coll.
E. A. Hughes, Jes. Coll.	H. Roberts, Ball. Coll.

Of the details of the racing, all that we can gather is that Christ Church finished head.

In 1827 rules were again drawn up and signed at a meeting of strokes; the new code being much the same as its predecessor, but with one or two small alterations. There was no U.B.C. in existence, and therefore no fixed code, but only such as was agreed on from year to year.

Rules for Boat-racing, 1827.

(1) That the racing do begin on May 29.

(2) That the days of racing be Tuesday and Friday in each week, and that if any boat does not come out on those days its flag do go to the bottom.

(3) That no out-college man be allowed to row in any boat.

(4) That no boat be allowed to race with less than eight oars.

(5) That the boats below the one that bumps stop racing, those above continue it.

(6) That there be a distance of fifty feet between each boat at starting.

(7) That the boats start by pistol shot.

(8) That umpires be appointed by each college to see each boat in its proper place at starting, and to settle any accidental dispute.

The rules of the racing signed by :—

C. H. Page, Ch. Ch.	F. C. Chaytor
R. T. Congreve, B.N.C.	Geo. D. Hill, Trin. Coll.
A. C. Budge, Ex. Coll.	David Reid
R. Pennefather, Ball. Coll.	T. Fox

During these races Christ Church lost their pride of place. Balliol seems to have first displaced them, and they in turn fell victims to B.N.C. who remained head. The exact details of the racing and full list of boats in this are unfortunately wanting.

The racing of 1828 began as usual. No MS. copy of the rules has come to our hands for this year, but they are believed to be a reproduction of those of 1827.

The racing resulted thus :—

June 1.—Order of starting B.N.C., Balliol, University, Christ Church, Trinity, Oriel.

B.N.C. and Balliol remained in *statu quo*; Christ Church claimed a bump against University which the latter disputed.

Oriel bumped Trinity.   The disputed race between University and
Christ Church was renewed on June 3, and the Christ Church men
put wet paint on their bows so as to make sure of leaving their
mark if they should touch their opponents.   They effected their
bump.   The other boats do not seem to have raced on June 3.

The next race was on June 4 between B.N.C., Balliol, Christ
Church, University, Trinity, and Oriel.   Balliol bumped B.N.C.,
and the other boats therefore ceased rowing according to the rules.

The third race was on June 7.   Balliol, B.N.C., Christ Church,
University, Trinity, and Oriel, started in this order : Balliol kept
ahead ; Christ Church bumped B.N.C., and the two between them
had therefore to cease rowing ; Trinity then took off.   On June
10 the races were renewed, but no bump was effected by any boat.

On June 13 there was another race, and Christ Church displaced
Balliol and went head.

The races concluded on June 16, when Christ Church retained
the headship, and B.N.C. rebumped Balliol.

The Christ Church crew of 1828 were :— (bow) Goodenough ;
2, Gwilt ; 3, Lloyd ; 4, Moore ; 5, Hamilton ; 6, Mayne ; 7, Bates ;
(stroke) Staniforth.   Hamilton became Bishop of Salisbury.

In 1829, in consequence of the first match of its kind being
then arranged with Cambridge, and the date being fixed for March
10, there were no bumping races.   Christ Church were accredited
as head of the river, from their having held that position from the
preceding year ; and they were saluted as such.   A scratch race,
however, was improvised on Commemoration afternoon, between
the boats, apparently manned by mixed crews of all colleges.   It
seems to have been a bumping and not a level race, for the record
of the race is ' no bump.'

In 1830 the races were renewed, and the following colleges put
on eights :—Christ Church, B.N.C., Balliol, University, St. John's,
in the order named.

The racing began on June 8, and Balliol bumped B.N.C.

On June 11, another race, and no bump by any boat.

On June 15, St. John's bumped University, the others above
them retaining their places and rowing to the end, as the bump
was astern of them.

On June 18 another race, but no bump.

On June 20 another race, and no bump.

We hope at a later period to supply the hiatus in history between this last mentioned year and 1837, in which year the written

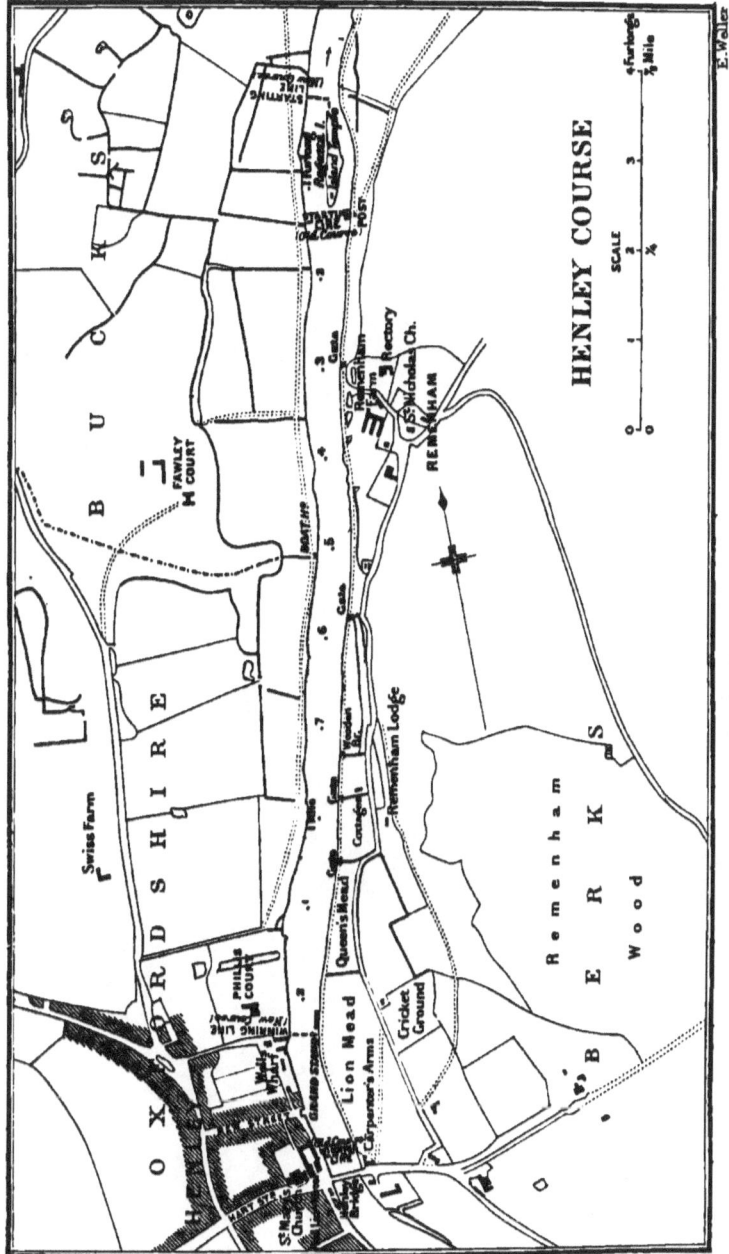

HENLEY COURSE

SCALE

¼ furlongs
½ Mile

London, Longmans & Co.

E.Walker

records of the B.N.C. book commenced, and for which charts of
the races are published. Meanwhile we shall thankfully receive
any information on this subject from the heroes of those days who
may now be alive and hearty.

HENLEY, PAST AND FUTURE.[1]

THE inauguration of a new era in the history of Henley Regatta
naturally tends to make the mind wander into vistas of the past,
perhaps even more than into speculations of the future. There
are oarsmen living who can recollect when Henley Regatta did not
even exist, and yet we are within an appreciable distance (three
years) of the 'jubilee' of the gathering. There are sundry old
Blues of the 1829 match still hale and hearty, and the regatta was
not founded until ten years after that date. *Apropos* of that 1829
match, we have never seen it officially recorded that in the race
Cambridge steered up the Bucks and Oxford in the Berks channel
of the river, where the island divides it. Yet we have heard the
Rev. T. Staniforth, the Oxford stroke, relate the fact. For some
strange reason, the general opinion of *habitués* of the river prior to
that match was that the Bucks channel gave the better course. The
boughs of the island trees obstructed the Berks channel more than
now, and this may explain the delusion. However, the Oxonians
doubted the soundness of local opinion, and tested in practice the
advantages of the two channels by timing themselves through
each. They naturally found the inside course the shorter cut. In
the race they adopted it, while Cambridge, so we hear, took the
outside channel; and the previous lead of Oxford was more than
trebled by the time that the boats came again into the main river.

Times and ideas of rowing have changed much since the first
regatta at Henley opened and closed with contests for the Grand
Challenge Cup, the only prize at its foundation. The 'Town'
Cup seems to have been the next addition, under the name of the
'District Challenge' Cup, in 1840; but it does not figure again
until 1842, and in 1843 takes the name of the Town Cup. There
were first class fours 'for medals' in 1841, but the Stewards' Cup
was not founded till the following year. The 'Diamonds' appeared

[1] From the *Field*, July 5, 1886.

in 1844. 'Pairs' came into existence in 1845, styled 'silver wherries,' and the then winners, Arnold and Mann, of Caius, have ever
been handed down by tradition as something much above the average. The prize became 'silver goblets' in 1850, and the first winners
of them were Justice Sir Joseph Chitty and Dr. Hornby, provost
of Eton. The Ladies' Plate was called the 'New' Cup when it
appeared in 1845. At that time it was open to the world, like the
Grand. Clubs from the Thames won it on sundry occasions. In
1857 it was restricted to schools and colleges as now, copying the
'Visitors' Cup' for fours, founded upon parallel principles in 1847.
The Wyfold Cup dates from 1847, though it does not figure in the
local official calendar of the regatta as a four-oar prize until 1856.
In the latter year it became a four-oar prize, open to all, and the
Argonauts won it and the 'Stewards,' with the same crew. Later
on it obtained its present qualification. As to the forgotten
functions of the 'Wyfold' between 1847 and 1856, we venture to
record them. The cup originally was held by the winner of the
trial heats for the Grand. If the best challenger won the Grand
also, or if the 'holders' did not compete, then the same crew
would take both Grand and Wyfold for the season ; but the Grand
holders were ineligible to row for the Wyfold. This latter anomaly
in time induced the executive to obtain leave from the donor to
alter the destination of the cup and to devote it to fours. Local
races flourished in the forties and fifties. Besides the Town Cup,
there were local sculls, sometimes for a 'silver wherry,' and sometimes for a presentation cup. Local pairs existed from 1858 to
1861 inclusive. The Thames Cup began life in 1868 as a sort of
junior race, but later on obtained its present qualification. There
was a presentation prize for fours without coxswains in 1869, but
the Stewards' Cup was not opened for fours of the modern style
till 1873 ; and the Visitors' and Wyfold were similarly emancipated a year later. The advent and disappearance of the Public
Schools' Cup need no comment.

We well recollect the sensation produced by the first keelless
eight, that of Chester, in 1856. The club came like a meteor, and
won both Grand and Ladies' (the latter being an open race for the
last time in that year). The art of 'watermanship' had not then
reached its present pitch. The Chester men could not sit their
boat in the least ; they flopped their blades along the water on the
recovery in a manner which few junior crews at minor regattas
would now be guilty of; but they rowed well away from their

opponents, who were only college crews. In that year, in consequence of the Chester ship being some dozen feet shorter than the
iron keeled craft of Exeter and Lady Margaret, a question arose as
to how the boats should be adjudicated past the post. The boats
started by *sterns*, therefore Chester would be giving several feet
start if adjudged at the finish by bows. So the stewards ordered
the races to be decided by *sterns* past the post. This edict remained in force, but unknown to the majority of competitors, till
after 1864. In that year the winner of the Diamonds reached the
post several lengths before his opponent, but stopped opposite to
it in a stiff head wind. The loser came up behind him leisurely,
chatted, and shoved the winner past the post by rowlocks locking.
Presently it transpired that the official fiat was 'won by a foot,'
and that the judge did not consider the race over until the winner's
stern was clear of the line ! This discovery caused some inquiry,
and the half-forgotten edict of 1857 was thus repealed ; and races
have since then been adjudged again by bows. Among other
reminiscences, we can recall the old starting 'rypecks,' with bungs
and cords attached ; these bungs had to be held by competitors
till the signal to start ; the ropes often fouled rudder lines, and
were awkward to deal with. In 1862 the system of starting with
sterns held from moored punts, now in vogue, was first adopted.

Such are some of the recollections which evolve themselves at
this date, when we are on the eve of a new era and a new course.
The old 'time' records, which have been gradually improving
and which, to our knowledge, are recorded in the most random
manner in the local calendar, will now have to stand or fall by
themselves. A new course, with less slack water in it, will hardly
bear close comparison with an old one as to time. The old sore-
ness of fluky winds, and ' might have beens,' laid to the discredit of
much-abused Poplar Point, must now find no longer scope. Luck
in station there still will be, inevitably, when wind blows off shore ;
but there now will be no bays to coast, and no Berks corner to
cut. The glories of Henley bridge have been on the wane for some
years past ; we can remember when enterprising rustics ranked
their muck carts speculatively along the north side of the bridge ;
but fashion and the innovation of large moored craft have lost
the bridge much of its old popularity. Besides, the newly planted
aspens along the towpath, which were given to replace the old
time-honoured 'poplars,' shut off the view of the reach from the
bridge. It is no longer possible, telescopically, to time opponents

Y

in practice from the Lion and Angel window, as of old. It is not so much as twenty years ago that steamers were unknown on the reach. The 'Ariel' (the late Mr. Blyth's) was the first of her kind built by Mr. Thornycroft. Till then, row-boats had the reach to themselves. We are old enough to recall the Red Lion flourishing as a coaching inn; then came its breakdown, when 'rail' broke the road,' and it shut up, until Mrs. Williams, the veteran landlady, who erst welcomed, and is still welcomed by, so many retired generations of oarsmen, migrated from the Catherine Wheel in 1858, and re-opened the Lion once more.

The strength of amateur talent is treble what it was twenty-five years ago. After the pristine Leander retired from action, and the St. George's shut up, and the Old Thames Club dispersed, the Universities had Henley almost to themselves as to eights and fours until Chester woke them up in eights in 1856, and the Argonauts four a year or two before produced the nucleus of the talent which in 1857 burst upon the world under the new flag of the L.R.C. They were joined by Kingston in a four in 1859. In 1861 Kingston had their first eight. Thames, in like manner, began modestly with a four, which in due time developed winning Grand eights. We have already spoken of the march of watermanship. A quarter of a century ago the idea of amateurs sitting a keelless eight or four, without rolling rowlocks under, until they had first practised for days or weeks in a steady craft, would have been derided. In these days three or four scratch eights can be manned any day at Putney, capable of sitting a racing ship, and of trying starts with trained University crews. We are not *laudatores temporis acti* as to oarsmanship; sliding seats spoilt form and style at first until they were better understood; but, in our opinion, there are now (*cæteris paribus* as to slides *versus* fixed seats) many more high-class oarsmen than were to be found thirty, or even twenty, years ago. There are more men rowing, and more science, and better coaching than of old. 'Vixere fortes ante Agamemnona;' but we believe that there are on the average some five Agamemnons now afloat for every two in the fifties and early years of the sixties. Nor do we wonder at it with four or five times as many men on the muster rolls of rowing clubs of the present day. As to boat-building, we think that the 'lines' of racing eights have fallen off. We can recall no such capacity for travelling between the strokes as in Mat Taylor's best craft, *e.g.* the Chester boat and the old 'Eton' ship; both of which did duty and beat all comers for many years. While look-

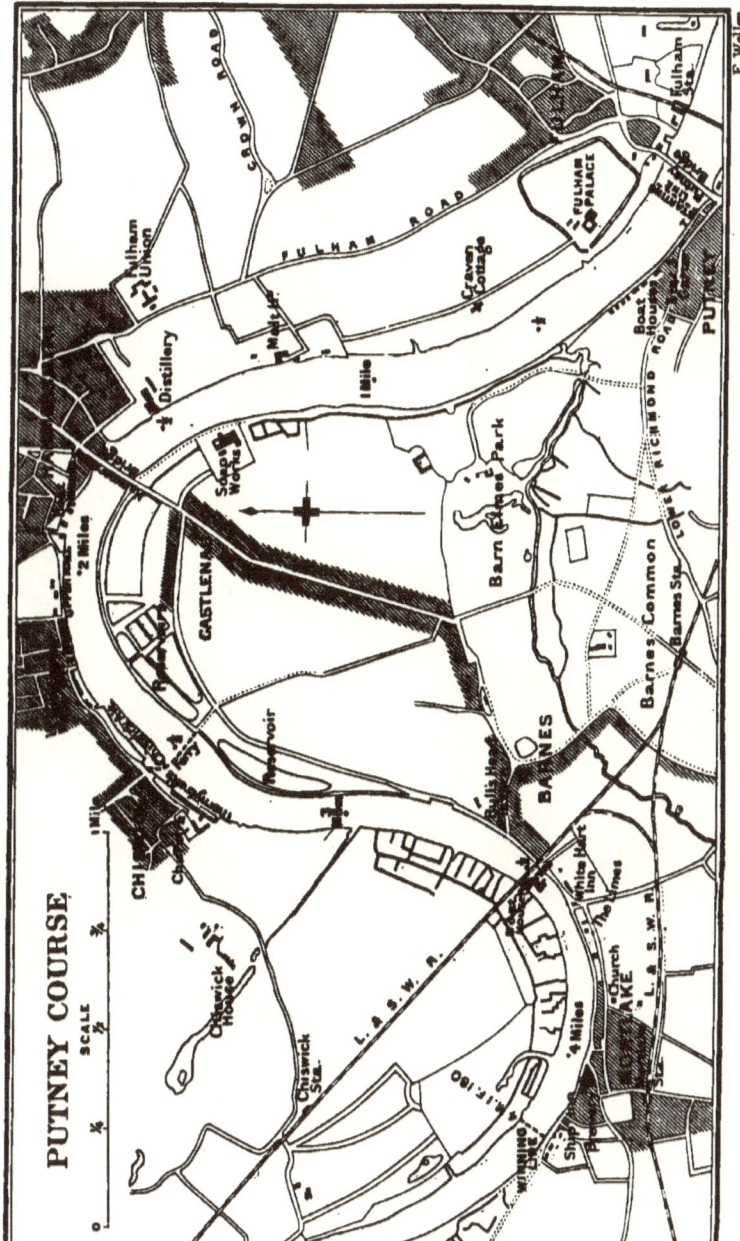

PUTNEY COURSE.

SCALE

London: Longmans & Co.

E. Weller

ing back with interest, we look forward with hope, and believe that the new Henley will maintain, and perhaps improve, its modern enhanced and extended standard of oarsmanship, and that the new course, when fairly tried, will encourage, rather than discourage, competition that looks for fair field and no favour.

THAMES PRESERVATION ACT.

In 1884 a Committee of the House of Commons sat to inquire into the best method of preserving public rights and those of riparians on the Thames. The latter had developed so much pleasure traffic during the last quarter of a century that some 'highway' legislation on the subject became imperative. An Act for regulating steam-launch traffic on the Thames had been passed in 1883. The report of the Committee produced the following Act, which should be read by all who intend to navigate the Thames for pleasure.

Draft by-laws, to carry out the provisions of this Act in detail, have twice been propounded by the Thames Conservancy during 1886, and a third code was drafted early in 1887, but the first two editions provoked so much hostile criticism that the Conservancy withdrew them ; and, up to the date of going to press, the third edition of proposed by-laws, which still seems too objectionable in many details, has not received the sanction of the Board of Trade, which is necessary before the code can become law.

THAMES PRESERVATION ACT, 1885.

48 & 49 VICT. CAP. 76.

An Act for the preservation of the River Thames above Teddington Lock for purposes of public recreation, and for regulating the pleasure traffic thereon. [*August* 14, 1885.]

WHEREAS the River Thames is a navigable highway ; and whereas, by reason of the increase of population in London and other places near the said river, it has come to be largely used as a place of public recreation and resort, and it is expedient that provision should be made for regulating the different kinds of traffic in the said river between the town of Cricklade and Teddington Lock, and upon the banks thereof within the limits aforesaid, and for the keeping of public order and the prevention of nuisances, to the intent that the said river should be preserved as a place of regulated public recreation :

Be it therefore enacted by the Queen's most Excellent Majesty, by and with the advice and consent of the Lords Spiritual and Temporal, and Commons, in this present Parliament assembled, and by the authority of the same, as follows :

PART I.—NAVIGATION.

1. *Public right of navigation.*—It shall be lawful for all persons, whether for pleasure or profit, to go and be, pass and repass, in boats or vessels over or upon any and every part of the River Thames, through which Thames water flows, between the town of Cricklade and Teddington Lock, including all such backwaters, creeks, side-channels, bays and inlets connected therewith as form parts of the said river within the limits aforesaid.

2. *Private artificial cuts not to be deemed parts of the river.*—All private artificial cuts for purposes of drainage or irrigation, and all artificial inlets for moats, boathouses, ponds, or other like private purposes, already made or hereafter to be made, and all channels which by virtue of any conveyance from or agreement with the Conservators, or the Commissioners acting under any of the Acts mentioned in the First Schedule to this Act, or by any lawful title have been enjoyed as private channels for the period of twenty years before the passing of this Act, shall be deemed not to be parts of the said river for the purposes of the last preceding section, or any provisions consequent thereon.

3. *Conservators may exclude the public.*—Notwithstanding anything in the first section contained, it shall be lawful for the Conservators from time to time to exclude the public for a limited period from specified portions of the said river, for purposes connected with the navigation, or with any public work or uses, or for the preservation of public order.

4. *Right of navigation to include anchoring and mooring.*—The right of navigation hereinbefore described shall be deemed to include a right to anchor, moor, or remain stationary for a reasonable time in the ordinary course of pleasure navigation, subject to such restrictions as the Conservators shall from time to time by by-laws determine ; and it shall be the duty of the Conservators to make special regulations for the prevention of annoyance to any occupier of a riparian residence, by reason of the loitering or delay of any house-boat or steam-launch, and for the prevention of the pollution of the river by the sewage of any house-boat or steam-launch. Provided that nothing in this Act, or in any by-law made thereunder, shall be construed to deprive any riparian owner of any legal rights in the soil or bed of the river which he may now possess, or of any legal remedies which he may now possess for prevention of anchoring, mooring, loitering, or delay of any boat or other vessel, or to give any riparian owner any right as against the public, which he did not possess before the passing of this Act, to exclude any person from entering upon or navigating any backwater, creek, channel, bay, inlet, or other water, whether deemed to be part of the River Thames as in this Act defined or not.

Provided also, that the powers given by this clause shall be in addition to, and not to be deemed to be in substitution for, any powers already possessed by the Conservators.

5. *Riparian owner to remove obstructions unless maintained for twenty years.*—Any person obstructing the navigation hereinbefore described, by means of any weir, bridge, piles, dam, chain, barrier, or other impediment, shall be liable to be called upon by the Conservators to remove the same, and his refusal to do so shall be deemed to be a continuing offence within the meaning of this Act, and the obstruction itself shall be deemed to be a nuisance to the navigation unless the same, or substantially the same, has been maintained for the period of twenty years before the commencement of this Act.

6. *Provision against shooting or use of firearms on the river.* -- From and af.er the passing of this Act it shall be unlawful to discharge any firearm, air-gun, gun, or similar instrument over or upon the said river within the limits aforesaid, or the banks or towpaths thereof, or any land acquired by the Conservators under the provisions of this Act, and every person discharging any firearm, air-gun, gun, or similar instrument over or upon the said river limits as aforesaid, or the banks or towpath thereof, or any such land as aforesaid, shall be deemed to have committed an offence under this Act.

PART II.—REGULATION OF PLEASURE-BOATS.

7. *Registration of boats.*—In addition to the rights and duties of the Conservators relating to registration and tolls already created by the Thames Navigation Act, 1870, the Thames Conservancy Act, 1878, and the Thames Act, 1883, or by any other of the Acts in the First Schedule to this Act mentioned, it shall be lawful for the Conservators to direct by by-law that all boats or vessels, with the exception of any such class of boats or vessels as may, together with the reasons of such exception, be specified in any such by-law for pleasure navigation, shall be registered, together with the true names and addresses of the owners thereof respectively, in a General Register to be kept at their chief office in a form by them to be prescribed, and as to all vessels propelled by steam power, and all house-boats, and all rowing or sailing boats plying for hire, and any such other particular class of boats or vessels as by them from time to time by by-law, may be prescribed to issue licences to ply upon any part of the upper navigation, or upon a limited part thereof only, according to regulations in each case by them to be made by by-law in manner hereinafter provided.

8. *Navigating without registration to be an offence.*—From and after the dates by any such by-law to be fixed respectively, it shall be an offence under this Act to use any boat or vessel of the class mentioned in the same by-law, on any part of the river to which such by-law applies, unless such boat or vessel shall have been previously registered or licensed in manner therein provided.

9. *Lists to be kept of private boats and boats for hire.*—In the General Register in the seventh section of this Act mentioned, separate lists shall be kept of boats and vessels used for pleasure navigation by private owners, and of boats and vessels let for hire. The former class of boats or vessels shall be distinguished, according to regulations to be made from time to time by the Conservators, by a registered number, crest, badge, or mark, and the latter class by a registered number ; and the provisions of section eleven and section thirteen of the Thames Act, 1883, as to displaying or concealing the same or number of any steam-launch shall be deemed in all cases to apply to the

said registered numbers, crests, badge, and marks respectively, with such modifications as the Conservators may by such regulations from time to time direct.

10. *Renewal of yearly registration.*—It shall be lawful for the Conservators by by-law to enact as to any or all of the classes of boats or vessels by them from time to time required to be licensed or registered as aforesaid, that such licence or registration shall be renewed at any interval not being less than one year.

11. *Fee for registration.*—It shall be lawful for the Conservators to charge, in respect of boats or vessels registered under this Act, sums not exceeding the sums following ; that is to say, for each registration of a pleasure-boat not being a house-boat, a sum not exceeding two shillings and sixpence, and for each registration of a house-boat a sum not exceeding five pounds ; and if such house-boat shall be more than thirty feet in length, a further sum not exceeding twenty shillings in respect of every complete five feet and the fraction of an incomplete five feet by which such house boat shall exceed thirty feet in length.

Provided always that nothing in this Act shall require a boat or vessel not being a house-boat to be registered oftener than once in three years.

12. *Present registration or licence not to be affected.*—Nothing in this Act shall require any vessel which may under any Act be required to be registered or licensed by the master, wardens, and commonalty of watermen and lightermen of the River Thames to be registered or licensed under this Act.

13. *First registration.*—For the purposes of the last preceding section a fresh registration or licence of any boat or vessel in a class other than that in which the same was first registered or licensed shall be deemed a first registration or licence.

14. *Application of ss. 7, 8, 9, and 14 of The Thames Act, 1883, to all registered boats and vessels.*—The provisions of sections seven, eight, nine, and fourteen of The Thames Act, 1883, as to registered owners of steam-launches, shall apply to the registered owners of all boats or vessels for the time being registered pursuant to the provisions of this Act, and of the by-laws in that behalf from time to time in force, and the same section nine and section fourteen shall be read as if the words ' boat or vessel ' therein were substituted for the word ' steam-launch,' and as if the words ' this Act ' therein referred to the present Act.

15. *Every boat or vessel to be deemed to be in charge of one person.*—Every boat or vessel used for pleasure navigation upon any part of the River Thames within the limits aforesaid shall be deemed to be in charge of one person, who shall be in every case a registered owner, or the person duly appointed or permitted by him to be in charge, or the person hiring such boat or vessel, and, in the absence of any such person, then any person having control or being in command of such boat or vessel.

16. *Person in charge to be responsible for order.*—Every person who for the time being is in charge of any boat or vessel shall be responsible for the preservation of order and decency, and for the observance of the provisions of this Act ; and upon proof that an offence under this Act has been committed by any person on board such boat or vessel, and that the person in charge has

fused to give the name and address of the offender, then the person in charge shall be deemed to have committed an offence under this Act.

PART III.—GENERAL POWERS.

17. *Conservators may accept and hold land for certain purposes.*—In addition to their existing powers to take and hold land, it shall be lawful for the Conservators to accept and hold any land which any person may offer to them for dedication to public uses in connection with the purposes of this Act, upon such terms and conditions as they may see fit, and it shall be lawful for the Corporation of the City of London, or the Metropolitan Board of Works, and for the University of Oxford, or, subject to the provisions of the Municipal Corporations Act, 1882, so far as they are applicable, for the Corporation of the City of Oxford, or any corporation or other person, to give, grant, dedicate, convey, or devise any land or right over land to the extent of their estates and interests respectively, unto the Conservators, for the purpose of enabling the public to use such and or any part thereof as a public highway, or as a place of public resort, or for the purpose of creating bathing-places or camping-grounds or landing-places, or for any other purposes connected with this Act, any of the provisions of the Act passed in the ninth year of the reign of King George the Second, chapter thirty-six, or any other statute or any rule of law to the contrary notwithstanding.

18. *Acquisition by agreement of right of abstracting water from the river.*—Where any company or person is entitled under any Act of Parliament, grant, custom, or otherwise, to any right of abstracting or appropriating water which might otherwise flow or find its way into the river, it shall be lawful for any such person on the one hand and the Conservators or any other person on the other hand, to enter into and carry into effect an agreement or agreements for the conveyance of such right to the Conservators; and every such right may be conveyed to the Conservators by deed, and shall as from the date of such conveyance be absolutely extinguished to the intent that such water shall thereafter be allowed to flow into the river.

And it shall be lawful for any of the companies supplying water within the Metropolis to make contributions out of their capital or revenue in aid of the acquisition and extinguishment of any such right, and for the Conservators to accept such contributions and contributions from any other person or persons and employ them for that purpose.

19. *Alteration and suspension of by-laws.*—It shall be lawful for the Conservators, in addition to all powers of making by-laws already possessed by them under the Acts mentioned in the First Schedule hereto, to make, and from time to time to suspend or alter in the same manner and with the same consent as in the same Acts is provided, all by-laws which they may deem necessary for the purposes mentioned in this Act, or in the Second Schedule hereto.

20. *Continuing offences.*—Any act or default in contravention of any of the said by-laws or of the provisions of this Act, which after due notice is repeated or continued, shall be a continuing offence under this Act.

PART IV.—PROCEDURE.

21. *Penalty for offence against the Act.*—Any person convicted of an offence under this Act shall, where no other penalty is provided by this Act or any of the Acts mentioned in the First Schedule hereto, or by any by-law made there-under respectively, be liable to a penalty not exceeding forty shillings.

22. *Penalty for continuing offence.*—Any person convicted of an offence which is a continuing offence under this Act shall, where no greater penalty has been provided for such offence by any of the Acts mentioned in the First Schedule hereto, be liable to a penalty not exceeding five pounds.

23. *Jurisdiction of certain justices.*—For the purposes of this Act, and of every by-law to be made by the Conservators thereunder, the jurisdiction of all justices of the peace for the counties of Surrey, Berkshire, Wiltshire, Gloucester, Oxford, Buckingham, and Middlesex, and of the magistrates for the city of Oxford, and of every other borough, the police jurisdiction of which extends to any place upon the River Thames within the limits aforesaid, and the jurisdiction, powers, and authority of the Proctors of the University of Oxford and the marshals and officers acting under them, and the power and authority of the Metropolitan Police, and of all police officers and constables acting for any of the said counties or boroughs, shall extend over the whole of the River Thames, and the towpaths, banks, and precincts thereof, within the limits aforesaid.

24. *As to place where offence committed.*—For the purposes of any proceedings in respect of any offence under this Act, or under any of the Acts mentioned in the First Schedule hereto, every such offence shall be deemed to have been committed, and every cause of complaint in respect thereof shall be deemed to have arisen either in the place in which the same actually was committed or arose, or in any place in which the offender or person complained against may be.

25. *Bailiffs and servants of Conservators may be sworn in as police constables.*—It shall be in the power and at the discretion of the Conservators to procure all or any of their water-bailiffs, river-keepers, lock-keepers, or other servants, to be sworn in as police constables for any of the counties or boroughs aforesaid, but they shall not be liable, without the consent of the Conservators, to be called upon to perform the duties of such police constables, except for the purposes of this Act or of the Acts mentioned in the First Schedule hereto.

26. *Proceedings for summary conviction.*—Proceedings in relation to any offence or continuing offence under this Act or any of the Acts mentioned in the First Schedule hereto, or under any by-law already made or hereafter to be made by the Conservators, or for the recovery of any penalty under this Act or any of the said Acts mentioned in the First Schedule hereto, or any by-law made thereunder respectively, may be taken before a court of summary jurisdiction, according to the provisions of the Summary Jurisdiction Acts, and all such penalties, whether recovered summarily or otherwise, shall be paid to the Conservators, and shall form part of their funds.

27. *Moneys paid to the Conservators to be carried to the Conservancy Fund.*

—All moneys recovered or received by the Conservators or their secretary, or other officer under any of the provisions of this Act, shall be carried to the Conservancy Fund, and all moneys arising in respect of the Upper River, as defined by the Acts mentioned in the schedule hereto, shall be credited to the Upper Navigation Fund.

28. *Saving clause.*—Saving always to the Queen's most Excellent Majesty, her heirs and successors, and to all and every other person or persons and body or bodies politic, corporate or collegiate, and his, her, or their heirs, successors, executors, and administrators, all such right, title, estate, and interest, as they or any of them could or ought to have had or enjoyed of, in to or in respect of the river and the banks and towpaths thereof within the limits aforesaid in case this Act had not been passed, excepting so far as relates to the said right of navigation and other rights expressly declared and provided for by this Act.

29. *Definitions.*—In this Act the following terms have the several meanings hereby assigned to them, unless there be something in the subject or context repugnant to such construction (that is to say) :

The terms ' the River Thames ' and ' the said river ' shall for the purposes of this Act mean and include all and every part of the River Thames specified in section one, excepting the cuts, inlets, and channels specified in section two ;

The term 'the Conservators' means the Conservators of the River Thames ;

The term 'due notice' means a notice in writing given by the Conservators or any person duly authorised in writing by them to act in their behalf ;

The words ' consent of the Conservators ' shall mean permission in writing signed by the secretary of the Conservators ;

The term ' by-law ' includes rules, orders, and regulations ;

The term ' person ' includes corporation ;

The term ' land ' includes land of any tenure, and tenements and heredita-ments, corporeal or incorporeal, and houses and other buildings, and also an undivided share in land, and any rights over land whatsoever, whether appendant, appurtenant, or in gross ;

The term ' precincts ' includes any place within a hundred yards of the said river on either side thereof ;

The term ' vessel ' shall include any ship, lighter, barge, launch, house-boat, boat, randan, wherry, skiff, dingey, shallop, punt, canoe, raft, or other craft.

30. *Short title.*—This Act may be cited as ' The Thames Preservation Act, 1885.'

SCHEDULE I.

24 Geo. II. c. 8, 30 Geo. II. c. 21, 11 Geo. III. c. 45, 14 Geo. III. c. 91, 15 Geo. III. c. 11, 17 Geo. III. c. 18, 28 Geo. III. c. 51, 35 Geo. III. c. 106, 50 Geo. III. c. cciv., 52 Geo. III. c. xlvi., 52 Geo. III. c. xlvii., 54 Geo. III. c. ccxxiii., 20 & 21 Vict. c. cxlvii. (the Thames Conservancy Act, 1857), 27 & 28 Vict. c. 113 (the Thames Conservancy Act, 1864), 29 & 30 Vict. c. 89 (the Thames Navigation Act, 1866), 30 & 31 Vict. c. ci. (the Thames Conservancy Act, 1867), 33 & 34 Vict. c. cxlix. (the Thames Navigation Act, 1870), 41 & 42

Vict. c. ccxvi. (the Thames Conservancy Act, 1878), 45 & 47 Vict. c. lxxix. (the Thames Act, 1883).

Schedule II.

Purposes for which By-laws may be made under the Powers and Provisions of this Act.

1. For preventing offences against decency by persons using the River Thames, and the banks and towpaths thereof, or any land acquired by the Conservators under the provisions of this Act.

2. For preventing disorderly conduct, or the use of obscene, scandalous, or abusive language to the annoyance of persons using the said River Thames or the banks or towpaths thereof, or any land acquired by the Conservators under the provisions of this Act.

3. For preventing any nuisance to riparian residents or others by persons using the river.

4. For preventing trespasses upon any riparian dwelling-houses or the curtilages or gardens belonging thereto.

5. For regulating the navigation with a view to the safety and amenity of the said river in relation to the purposes of this Act.

6. For preventing injury to flowering and other plants, shrubs, vegetation, trees, woods and underwoods on or near the said river.

7. For preventing bird-catching, bird-nesting, bird-trapping, and the searching for, taking, or destruction of swans' and other birds' nests, eggs, or the young of any birds or other animals on or about the said river, saving all existing rights of fowling, shooting, hunting, and sporting.

8. For preserving the various notice-boards and other works and things set up by the Conservators or with their consent.

9. For preventing disturbance of the navigation provided for by this Act.

10. For registering and licensing boats or vessels, and for regulating the conditions of such licences, and the letting or hiring of boats, vessels, conveyances, horses or other animals, in connection with the purposes of this Act.

11. For imposing penalties for breaches of by-laws, subject to the provisions of this Act and of the Acts in the First Schedule mentioned.

INDEX.

ABDOMINAL strains, treatment
of, 175
Ailments, 172-176
Amateur, the, anomalous status
of, 193; definition of term, 48,
194; Henley executive definition, 194; foundation of
Amateur Rowing Association,
195; A.R.A. rules, 195; regulations for the conduct of
amateur regattas, 197-199;
conditions imposed on foreign
crews, 199; laws of boat-
racing approved by A.R.A.,
239
Amateur Rowing Association,
195-199, 239, 240
Amateurs, past and present :—
Babcock, J. C., 105; Barnes,
35; Bayford, J., 35, 36;
Birch, R. O., 104; Bishop,
35; Brickwood, E. D., 29,
107, 138, 172, 174, 185, 234;
Brown, M., 86; Brown, W.,
105; Bulteel, 315; Carter,
35; Casamajor, 134, 137,
138; Chambers, J. G., 44,
223, 239; Chinnery, Walter
and Harry, 231; Close, J. B.,
105; Clutterbuck, Rev. J. C.,
315; Cobb, Rhodes, 234;

Copplestone, 35, 36; Cork-
ran, Colonel Seymour, 86;
Cox, J. R., 138; Donaldson,
Rev. S. A., 209; Edwardes-
Moss, T. C., 181, 227; Faw-
cus, 184; Godfrey, 85, 86;
Goldie, J. H. D., 86, 117,
181; Griffiths, W. R., 86;
Gulston, F. S., 87, 88, 105,
107; Henley, E. F., 152;
Herbert, C., 184; Hoare, W.,
86, 176; Hornemann, 35;
Hughes, G., 156; Jacobson,
89; Labat, R. H., 226; Le
Blanc Smith, 195, 197; Les-
ley, R., 86; Lewis, 35; Lloyd,
35; Long, A. de L., 105;
Long, W., 87; Lowndes,
141; Marsh, 35; Marshall,
T. H., 92; Menzies, F., 156;
Montagu, C. F., 203; Morri-
son, Allan, 234, 235; Morri-
son, George, 89, 234, 235;
Mossop, 87; Musgrave, 32,
314; Nadin, 184; Parker, J.
E., 134, 137; Payne, 141;
Peard, 35, 36; Pelham, 34-
46; Percy, 103; Phillips,
R. M., 37; Pitman, 86; Playford, Frank, 134, 227, 234;
Playford, H. H., 234, 235;

AMA

Amateurs :—*continued*
Revell, 35 ; Rhodes, H., 86,
116, 117 ; Risley, Rev. R.
W., 234, 235 ; Rowe, G. D.,
179 ; Shadwell, Rev. A., 92,
156 ; Shaw, Captain, 35, 36 ;
Staniforth, Rev. T., 30, 32,
34, 319; Unwin, W. S., 134 ;
Wallace, 184; Warre, 209,
213 ; Way, 116, 117 ; Weedon, 35 ; West, 86 ; Wood,
182 ; Wynne, 89 ; see under
Temple of Fame, 243-296
Aquatic championship, winners
of the, 296
Authors quoted, see under Books

BATHING, 156
Beach, W., champion of the
world, 236, 237
Biglin-Coulter crew, the, 105
Biremes, 12, 15-17
Blisters, treatment of, 173, 175
Boats, early history of, 3 ; san-
pans, 4, 6, 10; Ulysses' boat,
5 ; dug-outs, 6 ; canoes, 7 ;
cayaks, 8; Madras surf-boats,
9 ; analogy of construction
with that of orders of fishes, 9 ;
Chinese junks, 10 ; Egyptian
boats, 12 ; Phœnician vessels,
13 ; ships of Homer, 13 ; biremes, 15-17, 25 ; triremes,
17, 18, 20-23 ; pace of the
ancient Greek galleys, 24 ;
early Roman vessels, 24 ;
boat-building, 142 ; wherries,
142 ; skiffs, 143, 144 ; gigs,
143, 144 ; 'carvel' build,
143 ; inrig and outrig, 144 ;
dingies, 145 ; dimensions,
145-152 ; prices, 146, 148 ;

BOO

shape, 150, 151 ; position of
seats, 151
Boat-builders:—Archer (of Lambeth), 35 ; Clasper, Jack, 146,
147 ; Goodman, 213 ; Hall
(of Oxford), 314 ; Little (of
Plymouth), 314 ; Perkins
(Sambo), 213 ; Salter, Messrs.,
145, 152 ; Searle, 35, 213 ;
Sewell, 147 ; Swaddell and
Winship, 147 ; Taylor, Mat,
87, 147-149, 151, 213, 322 ;
Thornycroft, 322 ; Tolliday,
213
Boils, treatment of, 173, 174
Books, &c. and authors quoted :
Archéologie Navale, 25 ; Aristophanes, 18 ; 'Argonaut,'
147, 148 ; Bell's Life, 28, 34,
35, 110, 147 ; Boating Calendar, 206 ; Boat Racing, 27,
31, 162, 172, 185 ; Brickwood,
E. D., 27, 31, 32, 95, 103,
104, 162 : Denkmäler (Lepsius's), 10 ; Egan, T., 110,
147 ; Encyclopædia Britannica, 20 ; Field, the, 40, 107,
188, 319 ; Fleet of an Egyptian Queen (Duemichen's),
10 ; Frogs, 18 ; Graser, Dr.,
20 ; Glossaire Nautique, 25 ;
Herodotus, 9 ; Homer, 4, 5,
13 ; Horace, 3 ; Jal, M., 25 ;
Land and Water, 30, 313 ;
Lane, 122 ; Merivale, Dr.,
33 ; Notes on Coaching (Dr.
Warre's), 77 ; Oars and Sculls,
161 ; Old Blues and their
Battles, 34 ; Record of the
University Boat Race, 34 ;
Rowing Almanack, 241 ; Socrates, 154 ; Stonehenge, 174 ;
Staniforth, Rev. T., 30, 32 ;

BOO

Treherne, G. T., 34; Urkunden über das Seewesen das attischen Staates, 20; Warre, Dr., 64, 77; Westminster Water Ledger, 27; Williamson, Dr., 28; Xenophon, 24
Brandy, as a restorative, 172
Building (boat), see under Boats
Bumping races, 33, 313-315, 318
By-laws of boat clubs, 187

CAMBRIDGE University Boat Club, 32, 36, 42; head of the river, 292; pair-oars, 293; four-oars, 294; sculls, 295; races with Oxford, &c., 252-288; college and club races, 292-296; see Temple of Fame
Canoes, 7
Captains, 79; qualifications for, 80; multitude of counsellors, 80; dealing with malcontents, 82-84; enforcement of punctuality, 84; position in boat, 85, 207; former identity of stroke and captain, 86; duties of, 87; recruiting, 87; selection by, of candidates for trial eights, 88; coaching of juniors by, 89; conduct of, on retirement from office, 90; resident in college, 90; lessons of the post, 91; list of captains of Eton boats, 214-216
Championship of the world, 296, 297; see also under Professional racing
Chitty, Sir Joseph, 320
Clothing, Henley rule concerning, 51
Clubs, practical advantages of, 178; Star and Arrow, 179;

CLU

early records of the Leander, 179-181; the Leander's matches with the Universities, 181; the Argonauts, 182; foundation of the London Rowing Club, 182; past and present composition of the Leander, 183; suburban clubs, 183; provincial clubs, 184; draft rules for the formation of, 185; by-laws, 187; extinction of small clubs, 188-191; list of those contending at Henley, 245-73; O. U. B. C. college and club races, 289-292; C. U. B. C. college and club races, 292-296
Clubs:—Argonauts, 189, 269, 320, 322; Ariel, 190; Atalanta (New York), 106; Bath, 184; B. N. C. Oxon, 119, 122, 181, 267; Burton-on-Trent, 184; Cambridge London Rooms, 263; Cambridge Subscription Rooms, 285, 289; Chester, 182, 183; Christ Church, 31, 208; Corsair, 190; C. U. B. C., see under; Dublin, 106, 184; Durham, 184; Grove Park, 183; Guy's Club (London), 264; Ino, 190; John o' Gaunt, 184; Kingston, 43, 79, 87, 106, 109, 182, 183, 190, 210, 234, 322; Lady Margaret, 38, 106; Leander, 33, 34, 79, 117, 179, 180, 183, 190, 192, 211, 254-256, 258, 260, 272; London, 79, 87, 88, 105, 106, 180, 182, 183, 189, 190, 210, 211, 226, 228, 272, 273; Mersey, 184; Molesey, 190; Nautilus, 189;

CLU

Clubs :—*continued*
  Newcastle, 184 ; Nottingham,
  184; Oscillators, 122 ; Oxford
  Aquatic, 263 ; Oxford Radleian, 119 ; Oxford Etonians,
  152, 180, 210 ; O.U.B.C.
  (see under); Pembroke (Oxon),
  106, 109 ; Queen's College,
  Oxford, 31, 38, 85, 86 ; Radley College, 209 ; St. George's,
  182, 261, 262 ; St. John's
  Canadian, 119; Severn, 184 ;
  Star, 189 ; Thames, 42, 79,
  182, 183, 233, 265 ; Thames
  Subscription,   42,   234 ;
  Twickenham, 183, 190 ; University College, 87 ; Wandsworth; 181 ; West London,
  183, 190 ; Westminster, 208,
  209; see also Temple of Fame,
  245-296
Coaching, 66 ; tendency to become ' mechanical,' 66 ; coach
  should be a scientific oarsman,
  67 ; testing rowing apparatus,
  67 ; cause of faults in rowing,
  68 ; ' lateness,' 68 ; over-
  reach of shoulders, 69 ; meeting oar, 70 ; faulty swing, 70 ;
  screwing, 70 ; feather under
  water, 71 ; swing across boat,
  71 ; prematurely bending the
  arms, 71 ; exercise of crew in
  paddling, 72, 73 ; watermanship, good and bad, 74, 75 ;
  firmness in dealing with pupils,
  75 ; selection and arrangement of crew, 76 ; Dr. Warre's
  ' Notes on Coaching,' 77 ;
  consumption of liquid in training, 161
Colds and coughs, treatment of,
  176

ETO

College races, 245-251
Colquhoun Challenge Sculls, 38;
  winners of, 295, 296
Conservators, Thames, powers
  of, 323-327
Course, boat's, 238
Coxswains,   Henley   Regatta
  rules concerning, 51 ; see also
  under Steering

DIAMOND   Challenge   Sculls,
  rules, 48 ; Edwardes-Moss's
  victory, 227 ; winners of, 248
Diarrhœa, treatment of, 175
Diet, 153-163
Dingey, the, 145, 146
Doggett's coat and badge, 26 ;
  list of winners of, 303, 304
Drink, 158
Dublin Trinity College, results
  of matches at Henley Regatta,
  210, 211
Dug-outs, 6

EGYPTIAN boats, 12
Entries, regulations concerning,
  49
Eton, rowing at, 86, 87, 200 ;
  fishing and shooting at, 201 ;
  the river out of bounds, 201 ;
  Dr. Keate and the sham eight,
  201 ; shirking abolished, 202 ;
  swimming   enforced,   202 ;
  river   masters and   bathing
  places, 203 ; ' passing,' 203 ;
  changes in the course of the
  Thames, 203 ; first race under
  official patronage, 204 ; watermen as stroke or coach, 204 :
  upper and lower boats, 204 ;
  names and number of boats,

ETO

204, 205 ; entries for eights, 205 ; captains and 'choices,' 205 ; procession on opening day, 206 ; practice, 207 ; procession on June 4, 207 ; position of captain of boat, 207 ; *v.* Christ Church four, 208 ; *v.* Westminster, 208, 209 ; *v.* Radley, 209 ; lists of results of races at Henley Regatta, 210-211 ; upper sixes, 211 ; four *v.* watermen, 212 ; punting and tub-sculling, 212 ; courses and winning point, 212 ; the Brocas, 212 ; times, 212 ; build of boats, 213 ; style of rowing, 213 ; list of captains of boats and notable events, 214-216

FESTERS, treatment of, 175
' Field,' article on Henley Past and Present, 319-323
Firearms, use of, on river, 325
Foreign crews, regulations concerning, 199
Fouls, 239
Four-oars, 118 ; without coxswain, 119 ; steering apparatus, 119 ; in practice, 122 ; winners of races, 249-251, 292, 294, 298, 299, 301, 302

GIGS, 143, 144
Gold Cup for eights, 42, 260
Goodford, Dr., 202, 209
Grand Challenge Cup, 40 ; rules concerning, 47 ; racing record, 182, 183, 210, 211, 253, 258, 259, 261, 262, 264-268, 270, 272, 273, 319, 320 ; list of winners, 245

LAN

HANLAN, E., Canadian champion, 227, 229-231, 236
Hawtrey, Dr., 204
Henley Regatta, foundation of, 38 ; old and new courses, 40 ; qualification rules for cups, 47 ; general rules, 48 ; definition of an amateur oarsman, 48 ; entries, 49 ; objections to entries, 50 ; course and stations, 50 ; a row over, 50 ; heats, 50 ; clothing, 51 ; coxswains, 51 ; flag, 51 ; umpire and judge, 51 ; prizes, 51 ; committee, 52 ; restrictions on foreign crews, 199 ; Eton eight first at, 209 ; results of Eton racing at, 210 ; advantage of Berks station at, 228 ; Oxford *v.* Cambridge at, 254 ; Leander *v.* Oxford at, 254 ; random recollections of, 319-323 ; see also Temple of Fame, 245-253, 258-262, 264-270, 272, 273
Hornby, Dr., 320
House-boats, 324, 325

JUNKS, Chinese, 10

KEATE, Dr., 201, 202
Kelley, Harry, and his contests, 218, 220, 221, 223

LADIES' Challenge Plate, rules, 47 ; racing record, 210, 211 ; winners of, 248
' Land and Water,' article on Boat-racing at the Universities, 313-319

LAW

Laws of boat-racing, 238 ; boats' course, 238 ; fouls, 239 ; code adopted by Amateur Rowing Association, 239, 240 ; rule of the road on river, 241, 242 Limehouse to Hertford and intermediate distances, 304, 305

MEDWAY (Sheerness to Tonbridge, and intermediate distances), 310
Milk, cautious use of, 161

NAVIGATION of the Thames, regulations for, 324

OXFORD and Cambridge University Boat Race, list of winners since 1828, 252
Oxford to Lechlade and intermediate distances, 306, 307
Oxford to London and intermediate distances of locks, &c., 307-310
Oxford University Boat Club, races of, with C.U.B.C. and other clubs, 32, 36, 42, 89, 252-258, 260-288; college eights (head of the river), 289 ; winners of pair-oars, 290 ; winners of sculls, 291 ; winners of four-oars, 292 ; college and club races, 289-292 ; see Temple of Fame

PADDLING, 72, 73
Pair-oars, the acme of watermanship, 123 ; give-and-take

PRO

action, 124 ; 'jealous' rowing, 124 ; balance and steering, 126 ; the start, 126 ; manipulation of the oars, 126 ; winners of, at Henley, 246, 293
Paramatta, rowing on the, 229, 236
Passing swimmers at Eton, 203
Phœnicians, the, 13
Pleasure-boats, regulation of, 325
Professional races and their winners :—The aquatic championship, 296, 297 ; Thames National Regatta (champion fours), 298 ; sculls, 299; apprentices' sculls (coat and badge), 299 ; T.N.R. (second series), fours, 299 ; pairs, 300 ; sculls, 300; apprentices' sculls (coat and badge), 300 ; Thames International Regatta, champion sculls, fours, and pairs, 301 ; Royal Thames Regatta, watermen's prizes, 301 ; British Regatta in Paris, fours, pairs, and sculls, 302 ; World's Regatta on the Thames, 302 ; winners of Doggett's coat and badge, 303
Professional racing, 217 ; the London waterman, 217 ; first championship of the Thames, 218 ; defeat of Kelley by Chambers, 218 ; Green defeated by Chambers, 220 ; Chambers beaten by Kelley, 220 ; Cooper and Chambers defeated by Kelley, 221 ; Hammill beaten by Kelley, 221 ; Hoare defeated by Sad-

PRO

ler, 221 ; second defeat of
Chambers by Kelley, 221 ;
anecdote of Chambers, 222 ;
Kelley defeats Sadler, 223 ;
Renforth beats Kelley, 223 ;
Sadler defeats Boyd, 224 ;
Trickett defeats Sadler, 225 ;
Boyd beats Higgins, 225 ;
Higgins beats Boyd, 225 ;
Higgins defeats Elliott, 226 ;
Elliott beats Boyd and Hig-
gins, 226 ; Elliott defeated by
Hanlan, 227 ; Trickett beaten
by Hanlan, 229 ; Hanlan's
victories over Laycock and
Boyd, 230 ; he beats Kennedy
and Wallace Ross, 231 ; cause
of deterioration in professional
rowing, 232, 233 ; bad form
with sliding seats, 224, 225,
229, 230, 232, 235 ; lapse of
professional regattas, 233 ;
Beach defeats Hanlan, 236 ;
Gaudaur beaten by Beach,
237 ; Beach paddles away
from Wallace R. ss, 237
Professionals, past and present :
— Anderson, Jock, 225 ; Bagnall, 224 ; Beach, William,
236, 237 ; Biffen, 229, 234 ;
Blackman, 225, 229 ; Boyd,
R. W., 224, 225, 226, 229-
231 ; Bubear, 146, 231, 236 ;
Cannon, Tom, 204 ; Cham-
bers, Robert, 103, 105, 137,
218-222, 228 ; Campbell, 28,
218 ; Clasper, Harry, 124, 143,
218 ; Clasper, Jack, 103, 124 ;
Clifford, T., 236 ; Cole, 29,
218 ; Coombes, R., 218 ;
Cooper, 220, 221 ; Everson,
219 ; Fish, 204 ; Gaudaur,
236, 237 ; Green, 137, 138,

REG

220 ; Elliott, W., 226, 231 ;
Hall, Jack, 204 ; Hammill,
221 ; Hanlan, Edward, 134,
137, 225-230, 235, 236 ;
Haverley, Jack, 204 ; Hoare,
T., 221 ; Kelley, Harry, 138,
172, 218-223, 228 ; Kemp,
29 ; Kennedy, J. L., 231 ;
Largan, 231 ; Laycock, Elias,
230, 231, 235 ; Lee, 199,
227 ; Luke, 226 ; Lumsden,
225 ; Matterson, Neil, 236 ;
Noulton, 36 ; Paddle Brads,
204 ; Perkins, 231, 236 ;
Piper, 204 ; Renforth, 104,
105, 223 ; Ross, Wallace, 230,
231, 237 : Rush, 229 ; Sadler,
J. H., 103, 221-223 ; Strong,
184 ; Tagg, 234 ; Taylor,
105 ; Teemer, 236 ; Trickett,
224, 225, 229, 230 ; West,
George, 33 ; White, Tom,
219 ; Williams, 28 ; Williams,
C., 218 ; Wise, 234 ; see also
296-304
Prizes, rules regarding, 51
Public Schools Challenge Cup
for fours, winners of, 251
Punctuality, 84

RACING courses, length of, 305
Raws, cure of, 174
Regattas, amateur rules govern-
ing, 197-199 ; lapse of profes-
sional, 233 ; see Temple of
Fame
Regattas :—Barnes, 43 ; British
Regatta in Paris, 302 ; Har-
vard, 279 ; Henley, see under ;
International, 44 ; King's
Lynn, 104 ; Metropolitan, 42,
189 ; Molesey, 43 ; National,

REG

Regattas :—*continued*
42 ; Paris International, 119,
152, 221 ; Philadelphia, 226 ;
Reading, 44 ; Royal Thames,
301 ; Sons of the Thames,
234, 235 ; Tewkesbury, 184 ;
Thames, 42, 180, 221, 234,
260, 263 ; Thames International, 301 ; Thames National,
298-300 ; Walton-on-Thames,
43 ; World's Regatta on the
Thames, 302
Registration of boats, 325
Renforth, James, champion, 223
Rivers and courses, 304; distances of locks, &c., on river
Lea from Limehouse to Hertford, 304 ; length of racing
courses, 305 ; distances of
weirs, &c., from Oxford to
Lechlade, 306 ; tables of distances of locks, &c., from
Oxford to London, 307-310 ;
intermediate distances on river
Medway from Sheerness to
Tonbridge, 310 ; intermediate
distances on river Wey from
Thames Lock to Godalming,
311
Rowing, rise of modern, 26 ;
Doggett's prize, 26, 303 ; Westminster ' Water Ledger,' 27 ;
match between randan and
four-oar, 28 ; modest championship stakes, 28 ; Kemp's
match against time, 29 ; foundation of Wingfield Sculls, 29 ;
University training, 30 ; first
University race, 32 ; records
of college racing, 33 ; Oxford
eight steered by professional,
34 ; London and Oxford amateurs, 35 ; adoption of ' light

RYP

blue ' by Cambridge, 37 ;
match between Universities at
Henley, 37, 38 ; foundation
of Henley Regatta, 38 ; pair-
oar races established at Universities, 38 ; Colquhoun sculls
and University sculls, 38 ;
four-oar races, 39 ; regattas,
40 ; Grand Challenge Cup at
Henley, 40, 42 ; the ' seven-
oar episode,' 42 ; Thames
Regatta, 42 ; ' National ' Regatta, 42 ; Metropolitan Regatta, 42 ; Barnes Regatta,
43 ; minor regattas, 43 ; constitution and rules of Henley
Regatta, 45-52 ; first principles of scientific rowing, 53-
56 ; muscular movement and
mental volition, 54, 55 ; instruction in details, 57, 58 ;
stroke, 57 ; set of back, 58,
59 ; swing, 59 ; use of legs
and feet, 59, 60, 62, 64 ; government of oar, 60, 62 ; recovery, 61-63 ; feathering,
63 ; notes on stroke, 64 ;
origin and use of sliding-seats,
102-117 ; four-oared rowing,
118-122 ; pair-oared rowing,
123-126 ; sculling, 127-141 ;
training, 153-177 ; clubs, 178-
191 ; amateurs, 192-199 ;
Eton, 200-216 ; watermen
and professionals, 217-237 ;
laws of racing, 238-242
Rule of the road on river, 241
Rules for boat-racing, 316, 317
Rules for the formation of rowing clubs, 185
Running, 168, 171
Rupture, treatment of, 175
Rypecks, 321

SAN

SANPAN, the, 4, 6
Scientific oarsmanship, art of,
53-65
Sculling, 127 ; management of
sculls, 128, 129, 132, 136 ;
first lessons, 128 ; stretcher,
128 ; rowlocks, 129 ; thowl,
128 ; even action of wrists,
130, 131, 132 ; steering, 131 ;
feathering under water, 131 ;
the swing, 134, 136, 137, 138 ;
steering apparatus, 134 ; slides,
135 ; pace, 137, 138 ; taking
an opponent's water, 139 ;
pilots, 140
Sheerness to Tonbridge, 310
Siestas, 176
Silver Goblets for pair-oars,
rules, 48
Skiffs, 143, 144
Sleep, 163
Sliding seats, their origin, 102-
106 ; use, 107 ; merits and
defects of, 108 ; superiority
over fixed seats, 109 ; practice
at, 112 ; swing, 113 ; recovery,
114 ; remedying faulty work
on, 115 ; introduction at Eton,
213 ; professionals at fault in
use of, 224, 225, 229, 230,
232, 235 ; Hanlan's superiority on, 227, 228
Smoking, 165
' Sportsman ' Challenge Cup,
146, 226, 229
Sprains, treatment of, 176
Steamers at races, 219
Steering, 92 ; early days of the
coxswain, 93 ; the coxswain's
attitude and action, 94 ; handling the rudder-lines, 94 ;
words of command, 94 ; turning, 95 ; ' coaxing with the

TRA

rudder,' 95 ; landmarks, 95,
96 ; characteristics of the
boat, 96 ; four-oars, 119 ; boy
coxswains, 122 ; pair-oars,
125 ; in sculling, 131, 134
Stewards' Cup, rules, 49 ; racing
record, 261, 262, 264, 266,
267, 269, 320 ; winners of,
245
Strains, treatment of, 175
Stroke, notes on the, 64
Surf boats, 9
Swimming at Eton, 202, 203

TEA, 172
Temple of Fame, the, a list of
winners, crews and men, 243-
304
Thames Challenge Cup, rules,
47 ; winners of, 250
Thames Lock to Godalming, 311
Thames Preservation Act, 323 ;
navigation, 324 ; regulation
of pleasure-boats, 325 ; general powers of conservators,
327 ; legislative procedure,
328
Thirst, 160-163
Torpid, the term, 316
Town Challenge Cup, winners
of, 251
Training, 153 ; diet, 154 ; old
training of a prizefighter or
a waterman, 155 ; present
course, 156 ; morning bathing,
156; breakfast, 156; luncheon,
157 ; dinner, 158 ; drink, 158 ;
practice, 160; thirst, 160-163;
consumption of fluids, 161-
163 ; sleep, 163 ; period of
training, 164 ; smoking, 165 ;
aperients, 165 ; work, 166 ;

TRA

running, 168, 171 ; the 'set' stroke, 169 ; starting, 169 ; avoidance of over-fineness of condition, 170 ; use of the tooth-brush, 171 ; value of the 'odd man,' 171 ; the 'long course,' 171 ; meal before and between races, 172 ; ailments, 172-176 ; wraps, 176 ; siestas, 176

Triremes, 17, 18, 20-23

UNIVERSITIES, results of races at Henley Regatta, 210, 211 ; record of inter and club contests, &c., 254-288 ; early history of boat-racing at the, 313 ; Brasenose Club Book, 313 ; bumping races, 314 ; 'no hired watermen,' 314 ; the 'Buccleuch,' 314 ; first use of a raft at Oxford, 315 ; boats and crews in 1824, 315 ; the term 'Torpid,' 316 ; rules drawn up for boat-racing in 1826, 316 ; ditto for 1827, 317 ; results of racing in 1828, 317 ; racing in 1829 and 1830, 318

University oarsmen, lists of,

WYF

with their weights, and races in which they rowed, 243-296

VISITORS' Challenge Cup, winners of, 249

WATER, abstraction of, from river, 327
Waterford, Marquis of, 34, 35
Water-gruel, as a corrective of thirst, 160
Watermanship, as a technical term, explained, 74, 75
Watermen, employed as stroke or coach, 204 ; and see under Professionals
Westminster School, 208, 209
Wey (Thames Lock to Godalming and intermediate distances), 311
Wherries, 142, 218
Wingfield, Mr. Lewis, his institution of the prize which bears his name, 181
Wingfield Sculls, foundation of, 29 ; winners of the, 243, 244
Wraps, 176
Wyfold Challenge Cup, rules, 48 ; conditions held under, 320 ; winners of, 250